John Harris was born in 1
Se_ shall Not Have Then
N__ Hebden and Max _____ ",
j_____list, travel courier, cartoonist and history t_____ng
t_____ond World War he served with two air force____ wo
nav___. After turning to full-time writing, Harris wrote
adventure stories and created a sequence of crime novels
around the quirky fictional character Chief Inspector Pel. A
master of war and crime fiction, his enduring fictions are
versatile and entertaining.

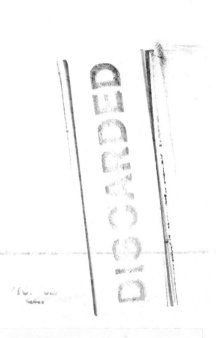

0122909212

JOHN HARRIS

A FUNNY PLACE TO HOLD A WAR

WARWICKSHIRE
COUNTY LIBRARY

CONTROL No.

HOUSE OF STRATUS

Copyright © 1984, 2001 John Harris

All rights reserved. No part of this publication may be reproduced, stored in a retrieval system, or transmitted, in any form, or by any means (electronic, mechanical, photocopying, recording, or otherwise), without the prior permission of the publisher. Any person who does any unauthorised act in relation to this publication may be liable to criminal prosecution and civil claims for damages.

The right of John Harris to be identified as the author of this work has been asserted in accordance with sections 77 and 78 of the Copyright, Designs and Patents Act 1988.

This edition published in 2001 by House of Stratus, an imprint of Stratus Holdings plc, 24c Old Burlington Street, London, W1X 1RL, UK.

www.houseofstratus.com

Typeset, printed and bound by House of Stratus.

A catalogue record for this book is available from the British Library.

ISBN 0-7551-0246-0

This book is sold subject to the condition that it shall not be lent, resold, hired out, or otherwise circulated without the publisher's express prior consent in any form of binding, or cover, other than the original as herein published and without a similar condition being imposed on any subsequent purchaser, or bona fide possessor.

This is a fictional work and all characters are drawn from the author's imagination. Any resemblances or similarities to persons either living or dead are entirely coincidental.

Author's Note

Although this story is fictitious, the struggle against the U-boats from West Africa is not. The author was stationed in Sierra Leone at around the time in question and many of the incidents in the narrative occurred while he was there, many of them involving him. This is mentioned to indicate that the idea is far from unbelievable.

The Germans were always trying to hamper British countermeasures in the Western Desert by their efforts off Freetown where, for the British, there was one large and unchangeable problem: Sierra Leone – indeed every British possession in West Africa – was entirely surrounded by Vichy French territory, and as Captain W S Roskill says in Vol. I of *The War at Sea* '...the possibility of the Germans filtering into the French West African colonies bordering our route to the Cape was alarming...'

The title comes from a comment made there by a famous stage personality in the only professional concert party the author ever saw in six years in uniform.

PART ONE

Stranglehold

'...There is a great need for more surface and air escorts in the area Gambia–Sierra Leone. Convoys for the Middle East via Cape Town from the UK or the USA routed out into the Atlantic via the Azores make their landfall in this area, and Sierra Leone with its good harbour is the only safe place where convoys can put in for supply and watering...'

Commander-in-Chief, South Atlantic,
to Admiralty, 16 Sept 1941

'...There are many local problems in Sierra Leone which could profitably be exploited. The place is a mixture of nationalities – Creoles, tribesmen, Indians, West Indians, Syrians, and Europeans. The Creoles are unpopular with the genuine Africans and the Syrians are unpopular with all. Rice is a constant source of disagreement and the Syrians have been getting a stranglehold on supplies. The anger at this most important of local problems should be used and, because of the long border which is common to French territory, it should not be difficult to plant agents. Trouble in Freetown could well delay the supplying and watering of convoys from England or America for the Middle East...'

Appendix to short appreciation of the
enemy situation–Führer Conference
on Naval Affairs, 9 Sept 1941

With the temperature in the region of a hundred, the heat was stifling. The building stood with all the others that comprised RAF, Jum – the officers' mess, the headquarters block, the sergeants' mess, the dining hall, and all the great elephant-like Nissens that housed the men – on a spit of land that divided into two separate streams a tributary of the Bunce river. The sky above it was brilliant with stars that hung in the sky like globes.

Constructed of timber and roofed with tarred felt, inside the building had been touched out here and there with the pale blue they used on the aircraft to give a fragile semblance of gaiety. At one end was a stage and a proscenium arch made of lengths of salvaged plywood with, in the centre, a crude crest bearing the words *The Jum Jesters*. The curtains, bought cheaply in the native market and run up by local tailors, made it a tawdry imitation of a theatre into which three or four hundred bored men crammed whenever there was a film or a home-made concert to watch. Neither was ever very professional. The projector was old – *Blood and Sand*, with Tyrone Power and Rita Hayworth, had broken down nine times before being abandoned – while the camp concert party was cheered chiefly for its courage.

Alternative entertainment was limited, however. You could sit in the huts, with the lights – never very bright at the best of times – turned down when the theatre was in use or the projector was working, and try to write letters, with, of course, a blotter under your hand against the sweat that stuck the paper to your wrist or dripped in steady drops from the end of your nose. You could read a book – if you could find a book. You could wander the camp in search of a beer, but, since it was rationed to a mere three bottles a month and the canteen could never match the ration, anyway, the joy was in the chase rather than the capture. You could – always foolishly but invariably a relief – scratch until they were suppurating the sores raised by the friction of your clothing on your sweat-soaked skin. You could worry about the possibility of dysentery or malaria or the condition of your foot rot. As Squadron Leader Greeno, the camp medical officer, liked to say, 'There are no great athletes here, but there's a great deal of athlete's foot.' Finally you could listen to the ping and whirr of the mosquitoes or the festival chorus of the frogs, have your hair cut in funny patterns such as three dots and a dash or a V for Victory, grow a large moustache, or merely contemplate your navel.

There certainly wasn't much else. There wasn't even a decent war, and the incidence of going round the bend among men brought up in sophisticated cities and flung down in this God-forsaken spot close to the Equator in Sierra Leone was surprisingly high. Life at RAF, Jum, consisted largely of foot rot, gut rot and nut rot.

The more enterprising made something of the place, of course, as they always did, and the theatre was just one example of what they could do when they tried. To give the place the semblance of being a real theatre, one of the headquarters telephone operators, Aircraftman First Class Anthony Derek Tristram, known to all as 'Trixie' because of his slender figure and the fact that he liked to bleach his hair, pluck his eyebrows and tie up his mosquito net with pink ribbon instead of the usual tough white tape, was gracing the centre aisle dressed as an usherette. Trixie never saw anything odd in shaving his legs and wearing women's clothing for a lark, and at that moment, carrying a tray and wearing women's high heels and black stockings, a paper rose behind his ear, and a short fluffy skirt made of mosquito netting, he was mincing up and down with a great deal of hip-wiggling, calling out, 'Cigarettes, chocolates, French letters'. Like many of his kind, he was possessed of a sharp sense of humour, and the idea of dressing as an usherette was unrepentantly his.

Trixie repelled most people and Squadron Leader Greeno had more than once objected to his appearance on this sort of occasion, but he was always overruled by the commanding officer who had served in Iraq and thought it amusing. By this time most of the men at Jum had accepted Trixie and his boyfriends, and mostly they ignored him because West Africa, and particularly isolated Jum, had a strange effect on men so that many on the sexual borderline were touched by the fact that they never ever saw a white woman and very rarely a black one.

And tonight was a special occasion. For the first time in the memory of anyone at Jum – and a few had been there a very long time – a concert party was appearing before them. Not the camp concert party, but a *real* one.

They were under no delusions that it was there for their special benefit. They all knew it was on its way to India but, since the ship that was carrying it had paused in Freetown for watering and supplies, the opportunity had been taken to put on a show for the top brass at headquarters, where the Rev. Daniel Morgan, the padre at Jum, had happened to bump into it and argued fiercely that it was time someone remembered the poor devils in the swamps at Jum.

They couldn't believe their luck and the cinema was packed with impatient men sweltering in its humid confinement, every one of them in the anti-malaria order of mosquito boots, long trousers, buttoned shirt necks, and sleeves rolled down and fastened. As they gazed at the curtains, their clinging garments were black with sweat under the armpits and down the spine.

The lights died and, as the pianist of the Jum Jesters started to pound out an introductory tune, the curtains swung back to reveal a solitary figure on the stage. A real live professional comedian! A man they'd heard of even before the war! He was standing by the footlights, his shirt as soaked with sweat, as anyone else's, the pink blobs of insect bites clear on his arms, dabbing at his damp face with a red handkerchief.

'This,' he said, 'is a bloody funny place to hold a war.'

The quip brought a roar of laughter because it *was* a bloody funny place to hold a war.

Mary Kingsley, the Victorian ethnologist, who knew it well, had once been told, 'When you've made up your mind to go to West Africa the best thing you can do is get it unmade again as quickly as possible and go to Scotland instead,' and it was a pretty fair comment. Early explorers had described crabs standing on their hind legs, oysters growing on trees and fishes walking on dry land. Nobody had believed them, but there was truth in the statements because the land crabs *did* rear upright, oysters *did* grow on the curving roots of the mangroves, and the mudhoppers, small grey creatures like fish, *did* move about on two tiny legs.

The spit of land on which RAF, Jum, was situated, was red and stony and where it ran down to the water the flats at low tide were an ugly expanse of black mud. The nearest civilization, the Creole town of Hawkinge, was several miles up the red laterite road from the camp gates, a collection of native huts, thatched – or tin-roofed stone houses, and ramshackle shops and shacks. Recently, the native population had begun to resent the presence of hundreds of white men in the area and now, for safety, it was out of bounds, and entertainment for the inhabitants of Jum RAF camp was entirely in their own hands and never very easy to come by because after dark there was never enough light to read or write, and never enough to eat or drink – not even fresh water.

The area had once been notorious as the White Man's Grave and there was a mossy tombstone in the local graveyard on which it was recorded that three hundred British soldiers had once died there of fever in three days. The sound of the mosquito that filled the dark hours was always a reminder of past tragedies and tragedies to come, and though quinine had reduced the death rate, that was about all you could say of it, because the climate hadn't changed and there was still malaria, yellow fever, leprosy, consumption and elephantiasis, and above all witchcraft and fetish that made fit black men die when they shouldn't. In Sierra Leone the improbable was normal and even the impossible occurred occasionally. The time to leave, old Coasters liked to say, was after the first hour. Otherwise, you would never go. Unfortunately, none of the men at Jum had much choice. They had been transported there by kind permission of the government because there was a war on and were due to stay until their time was up.

Making a joke of slapping at the mosquitoes, the comedian held up his hand and the laughter faded.

'Before we start,' he said, 'I've got an announcement to make. We're being honoured tonight by the presence of His Excellency, the Governor, his wife, and members of his staff and their ladies.' He indicated the seats at the front where the officers sat around the group captain in command: the wing commanders of the two flying-boat squadrons operating from the station – Molyneux, who ran the Catalinas, and Mackintosh, who ran the Sunderlands; a naval doctor from Freetown on a visit to his brother, Squadron Leader Greeno; the padre; one or two army officers from the West African

Frontier Force; and a languid lieutenant-colonel called Cazalet, once of the Green Howards but since Dunkirk and a severe wound, in charge of security in the area.

The comedian gestured to them to make room and there was a lot of shifting about, to leave a group of empty chairs. Only once before, when the naval depot ship, *Philoctetes*, had sent up a concert party from Freetown, had a woman turned up at Jum. As she had appeared on the stage, somebody had shouted, 'Don't bother to sing. Just stand there,' and even then she had turned out to be a man.

The comedian beamed his approval. 'If you don't mind waiting just a moment or two,' he went on, 'we don't want to start without them, and when they arrive let's give them a good reception because you don't often see people like that up here and they're coming tonight especially to show how much they appreciate what you chaps are doing.'

Touched by pride – martyred pride – the audience responded willingly and eyes began to swivel towards the door. Then the comedian's face changed. 'Here they are, boys! Let's give them a big welcome!'

As he began to clap, accompanied by the audience, every head turned excitedly. The Governor and his wife! His staff and their ladies! This was something to see. Most of them hadn't seen a white woman for over a year.

But the group that swept into the hall were led by a red-nosed man in a travesty of diplomatic uniform, his chest chandeliered with ribbons and sashes hung with old aeroplane parts. His 'wife' was another man enormously padded out with cushions, and his staff and their ladies were the most outrageous group imaginable.

The shout of laughter that rose from the packed benches set the tone of the show. This, they thought, was better than the Jum Jesters, with their tired jokes and smutty jingles about camp life. They settled back to enjoy themselves.

Near the great steel hangar which had been erected on the only patch of flat land near the water's edge, a narrow jetty projected from the concrete apron over the hard mud surface that bordered the creek. It was built of planks and had been patched and repatched with more planks and beaten-out petrol tins. Resting on wooden piles driven into the mud, it supported two huts, both built from aeroplane packing cases and both looking vaguely as if they'd been lost from a native shanty town.

One of them contained the desk of the officer in command of the marine craft section; the other was the duty crew room, with a small section like a telephone booth stuck on the end for the corporal coxswain who acted as piermaster. Past these two huts flowed all the traffic that supplied the servicing, fuelling, arming and crewing of the two squadrons of flying boats operating from the river Bunce.

The men in the crew room, like everyone else at Jum, were lean and thin, their skin the saffron colour that came from the daily intake of mepacrine and salt tablets, their shirts, like those of the men in the cinema a quarter of a mile away, uniformly soaked with sweat. In the middle of the floor, between the three shabby iron bedsteads on which they rested during the night when there was no flying, stood a tall cylindrical coffee can. To replace the moisture they lost as sweat as they worked, it was filled during the day by what the cookhouse insisted was coffee. Nobody thought much of the contents. 'It's all made from army biscuits,' they claimed. 'Thick coffee's porridge and thin porridge's coffee.' It made a good swimming pool for mice.

The interior of the hut was squalid in the extreme. Despite the hole cut in the side which did duty as a window, it was stifling in the still air of the creek, and even the knowledge that their night duty gave them the next day off wasn't much comfort to the duty crew, because they knew there was nothing to do with it when they got it.

On both sides of the jetty there was nothing but mangrove swamps. During the day, though well-stocked with fauna, the swamps were still and silent. At night they came to a clamour of life with the splash of jumping fish, the whirr of crabs, strange groaning sounds from the trees, and the sighing cough of crocodiles. At this moment, however, over the sound of the crickets' perpetual arguing – 'She did,' 'She didn't,' 'She did' – came a clatter of feet on the loose boards of the ramshackle jetty, and the duty crew put out their cigarettes and rose to their feet. One of the Catalina flying boats was about to take off.

'Who is it?'

'Landon. X-X-ray. Sergeant Purdy promised me a tin of peanut butter.'

With an endurance in the region of twelve hours, the Catalinas carried rations and it was sometimes possible to scrounge a tin of something to supplement the wretched food in the cookhouse. With Freetown the only watering place on the West Coast of Africa for the Middle East convoys from England, the Germans had thrown round it a ring of U-boats, and convoys carried only arms and troops and little for the men who guarded the route. Most of them were sick to God's green death of dehydrated vegetables and the canned stew they all knew as dog's vomit, but because of the absence of civilization, there was no hope of supplementing them. So that, with every meal the same, and not much of any of them, and bread – so full of weevils it resembled currant bread, when it wasn't a biscuit – down to two slices a day, devious means had been devised by a few of the old hands to attract the attention of the cookhouse staff while an extra slice was stolen for consumption last thing at night with aircrew margarine or peanut butter from men like Purdy, who was a New Zealander and received it in parcels from home.

At Jum there was a ten-foot difference between normal high tide and normal low tide and a catamaran, built of steel drums and planks and surrounded by old motor tyres, rode up and down on two heavy wire ropes secured to the piles which supported the pierhead. To reach it the Catalina crew struggled down the wide wooden rungs of an improvised ladder and began to toss their belongings into the twenty-four-foot motor dinghy which was to carry them to their aircraft. Two of the marine section duty crew, sailors despite their RAF ranks, climbed in with them and, using an Aldis signalling lamp to show them the way, headed down the dark creek to where the aircraft were moored.

Edging alongside one of the Catalinas, moving warily to avoid damaging the Perspex gun blisters which stuck out on either side of the fuselage, the motor dinghy discharged its cargo of aircrew. As the last item of equipment was handed across the gap, there were a few light-hearted comments from both sides on the joys of night take-offs. Certainly, there wasn't a lot to help. Downstream, three lights – bulbs attached to masts erected in dumb dinghies and powered with motor car batteries – glowed dimly in the darkness to make a flarepath.

In the cinema the concert was just beginning to warm up. The comedian could run rings round his Jum counterpart but he was not above using what local talent there was and a professional pianist, who worked a teleprinter at headquarters, had played a selection of the better known Chopin melodies through which everyone had sat in respectful silence, and a sketch was now just finishing. A man dressed as a nurse was having 'her' hand read by the comedian as she waited for her 'boyfriend' to turn up.

'Here's a bit of luck for you,' the comedian was saying, 'I can see him. He's on his way now. He's just got off at the railway station at Hawkinge Town. He's staggering a bit. I

11

think he's drunk. He's gone in for a beer. No, he's come out again. They don't give credit. He's in the camp. He's coming into this hall. He's at the back! He's coming on the stage!'

There was a commotion by the door at the appearance of a minute airman with shorts down to his calves and the biggest topee in the world covering his eyes. As the audience dissolved into laughter and the curtains came to, the comedian swept everybody away and began to introduce a stout grey-haired man who, judging by his moist features, was suffering a little from the heat. He was long past youth and everybody assumed he was just another eager baritone type who was going to jolly them along with a few rousing songs about the road to Mandalay and Old Father Thames rolling along.

'Ettore Mori-Moncrieff!'

Only a few of the more discerning knew him, but among the ripple of polite applause came one enthusiastic rattle of clapping that sounded like a machine gun and heads turned to where a thickset plump youngster stood up, his eyes shining, his hands going like wasps' wings. Leading Aircraftman Kneller, of the mooring party, the men who laid and maintained the buoys for the boats and aircraft, was one of the few men at Jum who had ever heard Ettore Mori-Moncrieff in action.

His neighbours pushed him down, the pianist tinkled a few notes and the man on stage began to sing. It startled everybody but Kneller and a few others, because the voice that emerged from the bulky body was pure gold.

'Sang at La Scala.' Kneller leaned over to Corporal Feverel alongside him. 'Appeared with Flagstad and Schwartzkopf.'

Corporal Feverel, his immediate superior in the mooring party, was not visibly impressed. He was a short fair young man who looked even shorter because of the width of his shoulders and the sturdy strength of his body.

'Heard him before?' he asked.

'Covent Garden. Used to buy tickets for the gods.'

Feverel smiled. Kneller was something of a phenomenon in that he was one of the few men of the hundreds in the camp who was not lean and emaciated. 'Perhaps he'll ask you to sing with him,' he said.

Kneller grinned in embarrassment. He had a splendid voice and from time to time it could be heard floating across the water as he chased round the buoys in one of the motor dinghies. RAF, Jum, was really rather proud of him and prophesied a great future for him after the war, and when he was dragged on to the stage in the occasional camp concert, he always appeared with a great show of reluctance, but usually had to be almost pushed off.

Mori-Moncrieff had worked his way by this time through 'Questa o Quella' and 'La Donna è Mobile' from *Rigoletto*. He had gone for melodies which anybody could understand and most people knew, and, faced with undoubted talent, the audience responded enthusiastically.

He acknowledged the cheers and began to speak.

'I am told that here in Jum,' he said, 'you have an enthusiast who sings opera whenever he is asked and sometimes even when he isn't.'

There was a shout of laughter and Feverel nudged Kneller.

'I'm also told that it is sometimes hard to stop him.'

'Good old Nellie!' A few yells started. 'Sing us "Your Little Frozen Mitt!" '

Kneller was as pink in the face as a turkey cock, but Mori-Moncrieff was beckoning him to the stage. Pushed up by friends, Kneller stood alongside him, beaming.

'You can sing "Your Little Frozen Mitt"?' Mori-Moncrieff asked.

'Yes, sir.'

'Then, let us hear it.'

Kneller's 'Your Tiny Hand Is Frozen' had always been popular, even with those whose tastes ran to 'The Isle of

Capri' and 'Down Mexico Way' and after one false start and a lot of coughing, he gave it all he'd got. The audience loved it.

'Good old Nellie!'

As Kneller stood beaming, Mori-Moncrieff touched his arm. He had expected an enthusiastic amateur but had got a voice of some quality. 'I think the time has come to sing together,' he suggested quietly. 'I doubt if we shall be perfect without rehearsing or that the accompaniment will be the same as at La Scala – but we must do our best, no? You lead, I'll follow.'

Kneller nodded speechlessly.

'You know "Donna Non Vide Mai" from *Manon Lescaut*?'

Kneller nodded again.

'Then let us begin.'

There was little clapping when they finished because for the most part it had been above the heads of the audience and they were silent out of respect rather than dislike.

And now, what about "The Flower Song" from *Carmen*? You know it?'

'I used to sing *Carmen* with a girlfriend I had. She was in the local operatic society. She preferred "The Desert Song".'

'The Flower Song' gave place to 'The Toreador's Song', then they came down to the level of the audience with 'Come Back To Sorrento', 'Santa Lucia' and 'The Donkey Serenade'.

This time the audience went wild and, instead of allowing Kneller to go back to his place halfway down the hall, Mori-Moncrieff beckoned him backstage.

'What is your name?' he asked, turning to face him in the shadows as the comedian warmed up for another sketch.

'Philip Kneller.'

'How old are you?'

'Twenty.'

'You know much opera?'

'I know all the arias. My mother played the piano for us on Sundays. Her favourite song book was *Gems From The Operas*.'

'Have you studied music?'

'A bit,' Kneller said. 'But not much. My parents died in a motor accident when I was sixteen. I never sang in public till I joined the RAF.'

'You have an ear for music, Philip Kneller. And quite a voice. Did you know?'

Kneller looked at the ageing singer, with his greying hair, pouchy cheeks and the bags under his eyes. 'I have?'

'I was once a great singer. I have sung at La Scala and Covent Garden. In Paris and New York. I know what makes a great singer. I think *you* could be one.' The old man paused. 'If that is what you want, of course. Because to be a great singer you have to wish to.'

'I do wish to,' Kneller said fervently. 'I always did. I even tried to learn German and Italian so I could sing the words. I just never had the money for lessons.'

Mori-Moncrieff smiled. 'You have many faults, of course. But these are the faults of someone who hasn't been taught. You should go to the best teacher there is. Anything less could ruin your voice. Then you could be that rarest of all excitements – a new English tenor. Many Italian opera houses would be glad to have a lyrical tenor of your calibre.'

Kneller blinked. 'I didn't know that.'

'I do. My mother was Italian...'

'Christina Mori, the contralto.'

'I see you've heard of her. Well, Italians know these things. I no longer sing professionally, of course. I teach. And I am here because I felt I had to do something to help. Servicemen are kind to me. They forget I'm growing old and applaud only my voice and the fact that I've bothered to do something for them. Now I would like to do something for *you*. How much longer will you be in this corner of Africa?'

15

'Another two or three months.'

'When you come home, get in touch with me, Philip Kneller.' Mori-Moncrieff scribbled an address on a sheet of paper. 'You need to learn how to breathe. With your chest. Place your hand on your stomach and feel it move. Study it. Watch it. I think it need not be long before you could sing with a company like the Carl Rosa. After that, who knows? Perhaps Covent Garden.'

Kneller was speechless.

'I could get you accepted into the chorus. I know the right people. Then, if you're lucky, someone with the impeccable ear of Sir Thomas Beecham could notice you. Vocal training can be sponsored if the talent, dedication and the voice are there. Would you be willing to work?

'Two years? Four years?' Mori-Moncrieff handed over the address. 'When you come home, come and see me. I think you're far too good to waste.'

As the old singer moved away, Kneller found a hand on his arm and saw the comedian standing by him. His sketch was proceeding at the moment without him and, gesturing with his thumb, he drew Kneller aside, his head still cocked for his cue to return to the stage. 'Ever thought of joining a concert party?' he asked.

Kneller looked puzzled and he explained. 'I've been told to collect twenty-four servicemen. We're going to start a big group in India and we need a good lead singer. Operetta's all right. Needn't be "Roll Out The Barrel", but not opera. Old Hector Moncrieff, bless his cotton socks, is a bit behind the times. The boys don't want that sort of stuff.'

'They seemed to, tonight,' Kneller said, faintly indignant.

The comedian ignored the protest. 'How about it? Plenty of travel. Better conditions.' The cue he was waiting for came and he touched Kneller's arm. 'We'll be here until tomorrow. Leave a message at the officers' mess.'

As he vanished, bursting back on to the stage with, 'What the hell's going on here? That's my wife you're with!' Kneller stood in silence, thinking, unaware of the backchat going on in front of the lights.

He couldn't explain what he felt and didn't really want to. He'd known long since that if he tried he could get himself a place in one of the many concert parties that were going round the Middle East and India but, through some contrary whim, he had wanted to be in the war properly, and had even offered himself for aircrew. Only colour blindness had landed him in what he considered the next best thing – air/sea rescue and marine craft work – and the same contrary whim which prevented him from using his voice to get himself a cushy job had pushed him into the department which in Jum undoubtedly had the hardest job of the lot – the mooring party.

'I'll not bother,' he said aloud.

two

As Kneller slipped back into his place alongside Feverel, his face wore the look of someone who had seen God.

'He told me I could sing,' he said.

'You can,' Feverel agreed.

'He also said he could get me accepted into the chorus at Covent Garden.'

Feverel looked at him, amused. 'Then why the hell are you looking as if you've been struck by lightning?' he asked.

As they whispered, above the laughter and the music from the stage came the intrusive sound of an aeroplane engine. It started, low, metallic and harsh, from the water a quarter of a mile away, and Wing Commander James Molyneux, to whose squadron the aircraft belonged, sat still and quiet, trying to listen. The rest of the audience heard the sound, too, and cocked an ear. Unaware of what was going on, the people on the stage went on with their patter. They didn't know what it meant. To them it was just the sound of an aeroplane engine. To everybody else in the hall it was more than that. To them it was the sound of someone laying his neck on the block.

The river Rokel or Sierra Leone river, the old route of the slavers and the breeding ground for the fevers that ran through the coast's grim history, started in high land up-country and coiled down to a wide delta that was a maze of tufted islands where ancient cannon rusted in decaying fortresses. Its tributary, the Bunce, running south from the delta under the mountains of the Freetown peninsula, became at the end of Jum creek a vast inland lagoon nearly five miles long and over a mile wide.

To the west, beyond the mountains, there was a flicker of purple lightning in the sky and the fitter of the seaplane tender moving slowly through the water, just ahead of where Catalina X-X-ray lay at her buoy, noticed it with pleasure. Lightning meant the rainy season was approaching and after months of unrelenting sunshine, the prospect of grey skies and cooler weather appealed. At the wheel, Corporal Harry Bates had other views. After one rainy season and two doses of malaria, he had hoped to be away from Sierra Leone before the next arrived.

One of the Catalina's crew was standing in the hatch in the bow, wrestling with the slip rope that secured the wire grommet over the metal bitts on the aircraft's nose. The grommet was attached to a wire strop shackled to a red rubber Short aircraft buoy floating just ahead. As the engines started, he cast off and the machine drifted backwards, then began to move forward from among the moored Catalinas and Sunderlands, the pilot working the throttles to give the machine way. In the distance, it was just possible to pick up the glow of light from Freetown harbour.

The big Catalina was moving up the lagoon now, Corporal Bates pleased because he'd scrounged the promised tin of peanut butter from Purdy, the flight engineer. Reaching the end of the lagoon, the Catalina swung again, its engines idling, and the seaplane tender circled slowly, ready to slip in alongside and behind on the take-off run.

Resting over the paddle of a native canoe, Leading Aircraftman Alec Donnelly watched the manoeuvring.

Ginger Donnelly was one on his own. The son of ne'er-do-well parents who had neglected not only his health, his food and his welfare but also his morals, at the age of seventeen he had been so regularly in trouble that, prompted by the police sergeant of his native village who was anxious to see the back of him, the magistrates had given him the alternative of a punishment of their choice or joining one of the services. Ginger had opted for the RAF, and had joined the marine section on the assumption that it was impossible to put a fence round a stretch of water.

Ginger's problems arose not so much because he was dishonest but because he liked women too much. Despite a shock of pale ginger hair, yellow eyes, a face like a potato and a sunburst of freckles that spread across his nose and cheeks like a rash, he had never in his life had any difficulty getting a girl; and, posted to Stranraer seaplane base, he had immediately acquired a dinghy and a woman in Cairnryan. At Jum it had taken him just a fortnight from the date of his arrival to find a fisherman to sell him a canoe and a willing woman at Makinkundi at the head of the lagoon.

By this time, with long service stripes halfway up the sleeve of his best blue, he had been in the marine section for ever, could claim to have worked alongside T E Shaw, the great Lawrence of Arabia, who had been among those instrumental in starting it, and had even gone down in marine section legend as the man who had told his officer while underneath a pinnace with a paintbrush and a pot of anti-fouling that he was 'a fucking deckhand not a fucking decorator'. When the *Duchess of Atholl*, carrying Ginger and many others to West Africa, had been torpedoed, wearing the first mate's uniform jacket for warmth he had taken command of one of the lifeboats and when the submarine had surfaced and demanded, 'What ship?' had replied, 'Duchess of Arseholes. Fuck off, you Nazi bastard!' The navy had been full of praise for his skill when the survivors had been picked up and had liberally entertained the blank-faced Ginger, still wearing the mate's jacket, on gin in the destroyer's wardroom – until they had discovered he was a mere leading aircraftman and not a Merchant Navy officer, at which point he had been hurriedly returned to his friends.

Everybody knew Ginger – even the station warrant officer, the station admin. officer and the group captain – because Ginger was an eccentric and, up to a point, the RAF, like the other services, was surprisingly tolerant of eccentrics of any rank. In addition to managing to look scruffier than anyone else, ashore he invariably carried a long stick with a forked end so that he looked a little like a disreputable bishop with his crook. Having discovered that among his other attributes he could kill snakes, he was unofficially snake catcher to the camp. Someone had once told him a snake could strike only one-third of its length and he operated on that principle. So far it had worked and when some barefooted African set up an uproar among the long grass as he disturbed a sleeping green mamba, Ginger was invariably called on to dispatch it. The stick had come to be his sign of office.

Mostly he worked around the hangar with a gang of Temne and Mende tribesmen who were employed about the base. His duties were not clearly defined – save that he was officially part of the mooring party – and that suited him down to the ground, because it meant he could dodge parades and keep out of the way of the station warrant officer, who knew his reputation and was always on the lookout for him.

Sitting in the canoe, unseen against the shadows thrown by the mangroves in the thin moonlight, he became aware of another boat nearby. It was motionless and there were two men in it, he saw now; he could even hear their voices, though he couldn't make out what they were saying. Since he had no right to be out of camp, it was just possible that the station police had found out about his night-time jaunts to Makinkundi and had commandeered one of the marine section's dinghies to catch him. But Ginger was an expert

21

with the paddle and could move as swiftly and as tirelessly as the Africans themselves. He knew the best places to fish, where the lagoon had no tide race and just where he was sheltered from the swirls and eddies. Dipping the pointed, spade-shaped blade into the water, he moved further into the bank where the stale smell of the mangroves came out strongly to him on the warm night air.

The Catalina was facing Freetown now, its navigation lights on. With its high wing and two Pratt and Whitney engines mounted on a pylon housing the flight engineer, the Catalina was a versatile and reliable aircraft which could fly tremendous distances. Getting it into the air, however, was sometimes a sophisticated pastime. Landing was a test of seamanship as well as of airmanship, but taking off was an art that sometimes bordered on black magic. It needed a quiet prayer and a judicious pull back on the control column at exactly the right moment, because a pull back at the *wrong* moment could ruin any chance of success and, with the moon barely risen in the black night, an old, tired aircraft, a full load of petrol and explosive, nothing but three lighted dinghies to give direction, and a surround of hills, there were all the elements of a disaster. Like everybody else, Ginger always watched with interest when a take-off was in progress.

The roar of the engines opening up rolled along the whole river bank. It could be heard quite distinctly above the noise in the camp cinema where the comedian had now got the audience singing 'Roll Out The Barrel' to the pounding piano. It could be heard in Hawkinge and Brighton, two other military bases in the Freetown peninsula, and in the native villages up-river where fruit was collected and taken in bullom boats down to Freetown market. It had been heard so often and so regularly no one took much notice, though everyone cocked an ear nevertheless.

The big machine began to move forward, its boat-shaped hull sweeping aside the water, the wing floats brushing the surface in showers of spray. As its speed increased and it drew level with the seaplane tender, Corporal Bates opened the throttles and the thirty-seven-foot boat jumped forward, its two diesels thundering.

'He's on the step!'

By the light of the moon, it was possible to see the machine as it lifted out of the water, riding with only the pointed tip of the hull skimming the surface. Then the floats folded outward to become part of the wingtip, a sure sign that the pilot was happy with his take-off, and the machine lifted from the water, leaving a white streak of wash across the dark swirls of the lagoon.

Watching it, Ginger Donnelly glanced round for the other boat but it had disappeared, and as he turned his attention once more to the lifting aircraft, he saw what looked like a faint glow somewhere near the top of the pylon which supported the wing. Then he heard a faint thump over the roar of the engines, and the glow increased to a pinkish light, which swelled and increased.

'Oh, Christ!' he said.

The small thump was followed by a bigger thump and the machine disappeared in a vast flare of flame that shot into the sky, trailing curving sparks as it went. The engines screamed then the Catalina dived abruptly downwards until one wingtip touched the water and it cartwheeled end over huge end, the enormous wing breaking away like a plank flung haphazardly into a pond. The rudder flew off then Ginger saw the machine settle on the water in a huge white wave, surrounded by a sea of burning petrol that lit up the water and the mangroves for miles around. The sudden silence was enormous.

For a second he stared at the crashed machine, then, aware that help would be urgently needed, he dug savagely at the water with his paddle.

In the concert hall, they had all noticed the change in the engine note and the sudden silence. They knew at once what it meant because they'd all heard it before.

Corporal Feverel quietly rose to his feet and began to head for the door because the mooring party were also the salvage party and he'd be needed. Kneller took one last agonized look full of entreaty at the stage, then went after him. Several other men had risen, too, now. Wing Commander Molyneux followed; then, after a while the group captain, a tall, stately figure, rose and walked slowly down the aisle.

The performers on the stage were aware of the drift towards the door and for a moment their singing wavered, but the pianist, who belonged to the Jum Jesters and knew what to do, began to hammer harder at the keys and the singing picked up again.

'It's Landon's crew.'

The muttering flickered in fits and starts about the hall like the fuse connected to an explosive charge. Mori-Moncrieff watched Kneller halt at the door, staring backwards, beseeching him not to forget him, and wondered what had happened. Something clearly had, because the audience's attention was gone. They seemed to be listening to something outside the hall and no longer to the stage.

As the singing came to an end and they moved into the wings they found out what it was.

'Aircraft crashed on take-off!'

The seaplane tender was racing towards the lake of blazing petrol.

'For Christ's sake, Nobby,' Corporal Bates yelled to the airman alongside him. 'What happened? Did he catch a wingtip?'

24

'He was off and clear,' Nobby Clark said. 'Well clear. It seemed to me like an explosion.' His eyes flickered towards the locker in the stern of the boat which contained axes, bolt croppers, fire extinguishers and other tools for use in such an emergency as they faced now. 'I hope to Christ somebody's alive.'

'You must be joking. There never is.'

The aeroplane had settled in the water by this time and only the tail and one wingtip, both hideously buckled, were sticking above the surface. Bates had seen crashes before and knew what hitting the water at a hundred miles an hour could do to the aluminium surfaces of the machine. Torn metal became razor-edged knives and, unlike crashes on the solid surface of the land, injured survivors were all too often swept away and drowned before they knew what had happened.

The flames were just ahead of them now, lighting up their faces. Glancing back, Bates saw the dark shape of the dinghy coming after them, the bow wave pinkish in the glow. He knew what to do. The problem was doing it. In England when night flying was on, a pinnace, a heavy sixty-four-foot boat with a winch and a lifting derrick, was stationed at the end of the flarepath with the duty officer on board, while the tender followed the aircraft with the crash gear. When there was a crash, the pinnace was supposed to keep the aircraft afloat while the tender moved in to cut survivors free. In Jum, there was only one pinnace and it was needed for other things besides flying and there was no duty officer to take control, so that the responsibility rested wholly on Corporal Bates' shoulders. As he skirted the pool of fire, the bow of the tender brushing against a wing float lying lopsidedly in the water, trailing its struts and the pipes of the hydraulic gear, he heard the fitter yell.

'There!'

A hand shot out to indicate a black figure among the flames.

'I'm going in,' Bates said. 'Stand by with the extinguisher.'

He opened the throttles and the boat nosed through the burning petrol to the struggling man.

'Make it quick!'

Closing the throttles, Bates ran back to the well-deck. Clark and the fitter were reaching over the side near the stern where the tender sat low in the water.

'It's Landon!'

As they heaved him up, the pilot cried out, then they had him lying on the well-deck like a landed fish, almost stripped of his clothing, small flames still licking at the collar of his shirt which clung like a blackened cord round his neck. Smothering them with a blanket, they lifted him into the cabin where they laid him on one of the bunks, and Bates ran back to the controls. As the tender emerged from the flames, the paint on its hull bubbling in the heat, it almost collided with the motor dinghy.

'See anybody?'

'We've got one!' Bates shouted. 'Scout round the edges!'

The dinghy's engine roared as it began to circle the dying pool of flames. Its searchlight sweeping the water, the seaplane tender moved in the opposite direction. There were a few floating objects, a cap, a bush jacket, a duffel bag with the air trapped inside it, all of which were quickly yanked aboard, but no sign of any more of the crew.

By the time Ginger Donnelly arrived on the scene the flames were dying quickly in the manner of all petrol fires. Ginger didn't head into them because he was watching how they were trailing downstream on the tide and he guessed that if there were any survivors in the water that was where they would be.

He picked up a floating cap, then a water bottle bobbing on the surface, and he was just about to turn away when he heard a cry. Swinging the canoe round with a couple of expert sweeps of the paddle, he dug at the water.

'Where are you, mate?'

A small white blur appeared on his starboard side and he swung the canoe towards it. It was the face of a man swimming with great difficulty. Blood was streaming from his scalp and gashes in his face to mingle with the water that he splashed over himself in his frantic efforts to stay afloat. As the canoe came alongside, he grabbed it.

'Hang on,' Ginger yelled. 'You'll have the bloody thing over!'

'Get me aboard!'

Reaching over, Ginger grabbed the swimming man whom he recognised as Sergeant Purdy, the flight engineer who was always so free with the tins of peanut butter.

'I was in the pylon,' he panted. 'The wing tore the top off as it went and I floated out.'

Ginger had him across the canoe now. 'Can you get your legs in?' he asked.

The canoe rolled as Purdy made the effort, his left foot swinging loosely in its stocking. 'Marine section's a bit bankrupt, isn't it?' he gasped. 'This the best you can manage?'

He was still trying to get into the canoe as Ginger leaned forward and grabbed his foot. As he heaved, Purdy rolled into the canoe and Ginger stared down at the shoe and stocking he held in his hand, complete with Purdy's foot still inside it.

Another seaplane tender, two more dinghies and the pinnace arrived on the scene, though by this time it was obvious there was little they could do.

As the seaplane tender with Landon on board approached the jetty, a dinghy appeared from the shore containing the station MO, Squadron Leader Greeno. Scrambling aboard the tender, his face grim, he bent over the figure lying on the soaking cushions in a mixture of blood and muddy water and felt for a pulse.

'He's dead,' he said abruptly. 'Is he the only one?'

'Only one we saw, sir.'

As they put Landon ashore, the padre was waiting by the ambulance, a crucified look on his face. Daniel Morgan was older than most men at Jum and had served as a subaltern in the earlier war. Red-faced, black-haired, beetle-browed with vast tufts of hair protruding from his cheeks above a large black moustache, he was tenderer in heart than his appearance suggested. He was generally supposed to be a little mad but the blasé air he affected was Morgan's way of hiding the unhappiness he felt at being involved for a second time in the vast sad business of war. Though not afraid of death himself, he hated it in young men barely old enough to understand what it was all about, who, here in Jum, usually died not because they were standing face to face with the enemy but because of the vagaries of the weather, the climate and a general lowering of standards due to shortages and the conditions in which they lived. He watched the blanketed shape carried down the ramshackle jetty to a lorry, then climbed into the back with it.

Out on the lagoon, the pinnace was still circling the wreck which was now floating half-submerged with the tail and one wingtip in the air. A little further out, two dinghies were moving slowly in the faint hope that someone might still be swimming. As the pinnace's searchlight swept over the black water, it picked up a canoe. The man in it was waving.

'What's that damn fisherman doing here?'

Corporal Fox, the coxswain, peered over the wheel. 'The bastards know they're not allowed on the lagoon when flying's taking place.'

'That's not a fisherman,' one of the deckhands shouted. 'It's Ginger Donnelly and he's picked somebody up!'

The pinnace swung to approach the canoe, and as the two vessels touched, a rope was passed round Purdy's limp shape and he was lifted gently to the deck. As the pinnace crew turned away, Ginger called them back. 'Hang on,' he said, holding up the stocking and shoe with Purdy's foot inside it. 'You'd better have this.'

As the pinnace moved off, he dug at the water and, for another hour, searched the black lagoon before finally deciding there was no longer any point, and began to move upstream to where he had earlier seen the boat. The moon was higher now and the shadows were deeper.

For some time he paddled up and down but there was nothing to indicate what the boat had been or who had been in it, nothing but the moon-touched tops of the mangroves and the few taller trees further inland, and he decided that the boat had been a figment of his imagination, and the voices he'd heard only the chattering of the frogs.

three

The boats were still in the river at daylight. By this time, the pinnace had half X-X-ray's wing lying across the deck. The rest of the aeroplane was marked with a wreck buoy so that the navy could hoist out of the water whatever could be salvaged.

Taking the half-wing back to the base, the pinnace crew and the mooring party watched it dragged, screeching, over the concrete of the slip by the winch that was normally used to haul up the aircraft when they came ashore for major servicing. Very soon they would be moving back down the lagoon, the pinnace this time towing a flat-bottomed punt and carrying a cargo of coffins. When the warm West African water brought bodies to the surface, it was a case merely of removing the identity discs and lowering them into the coffins for a hurried burial at the nearest point ashore. The real problem was getting them out of the water without scratching your hands on splintered bone because, in an area where every small wound festered, a scratch from a fragmented bone could result in gangrene.

In his office at the Catalina squadron headquarters, Wing Commander Molyneux smoked a cigarette as he talked with Wing Commander George Mackintosh, RAAF, of the Sunderland squadron. The two squadron huts occupied adjacent sides of a small spit of high ground behind the hangar and contained the flight offices, the crew rooms, and all the other appurtenances of squadron organization. The two wing commanders' offices occupied opposite ends so they could confer with each other without having to use the telephone.

Molyneux was a man of no particular physical distinction, lightly but strongly built, pushing thirty so that he felt ancient alongside some of his younger pilots, with crisp sandy hair going grey, and indeterminate features that were still attractive because they were lean and strong and there was an alert look in his young-old eyes. He had won the DFC for sinking a submarine off Gibraltar in 1940 when he was still a flying officer piloting a Sunderland, and another for putting his machine down in a difficult sea off Spain to rescue a boatload of survivors from a torpedoed ship.

He looked up at Mackintosh, who was a typical Australian, tall, lean-featured, a grin always ready to appear on his lips. He too, held a DFC – for touching down in an emergency in a river in neutral French Dahomey and, with his Australian cheek, so bamboozling the French harbourmaster that he had been allowed to make repairs to a faulty fuel feed before taking off again over a line of fishing boats which had been strung across the river mouth to stop him. Before arriving in West Africa, they had both done their share of flying in northern hemispheres, guarding convoys, shepherding strays, searching through fog and rain and gusty gale-force winds over miles of sullen grey sea for a periscope or a drifting lifeboat.

'Purdy'll live,' Molyneux was saying. 'He said the engines were behaving perfectly. He's under sedation and a bit dopey, but he insists there was nothing wrong until he heard a loud bang and saw a flash. He didn't know what it was.'

'Fuse of some sort?' Mackintosh looked up from exploring the bowl of his pipe with a penknife.

'He says not. It seemed, he said, to come from outside the machine close to the wing root.'

Mackintosh frowned. 'Anybody else see it?'

'The crew of the seaplane tender saw it, and heard what sounded like a small explosion, then the next minute the whole machine was surrounded by flames. Flames, George! That's something that doesn't usually occur. Whatever it was, it was close enough to the fuel tanks to send them up. There's another witness, too, a chap called Donnelly, also of the marine section. It seems he has a canoe and goes fishing at night round the edges of the creek. He's the one who picked up Purdy.'

'Sounds bloody funny,' Mackintosh said.

'Isn't everything bloody funny here?' Molyneux asked bitterly. 'That comedian chap hit the nail right on the head. Oysters on trees. Fishes that walk. Aeroplanes that crash for no visible reason. I've been here nine months now, you a bit longer, and we've both lost aircraft through accidents.'

Mackintosh frowned and reached through the window to tap the ash from his pipe. 'You know what pilots used to say in the old days, don't you, sport? If they didn't fancy going up, they used to claim there was no lift in the air. I've often thought there's no bloody lift in the air here.'

Sergeant Horace Maxey, of the marine section, three or four spare marine section bods and Ginger Donnelly's gang of black labourers were shifting a cradle containing a seaplane tender suffering from worm and the exuberant marine growth of tropical waters. They were all limp with the heat and Maxey's frantic shouts of 'Two-six! Shove!' didn't stir them much. Maxey was a fretful round little man who, because of his bald head and the fact that he was always lathered with sweat, was known as The Wet Boiled Egg, and it was his job to see boats up and down the marine section slip. On the ramshackle pier behind him, flight mechanics were assembling for ferrying out to the aircraft.

They were dressed in tropical overalls – minus collars, sleeves and legs, so that they looked like khaki combination suits – and their bodies were shiny with perspiration. Their limbs were marked with every colour of the rainbow by the unguents that had been applied to the various kinds of skin rash they had picked up or the minor cuts and grazes that refused to heal. They carried tools or spare parts and wore pith helmets, most of which had long since been sat on accidentally and lost their shape. Alongside the catamaran was a bomb scow full of depth charges because at first light Catalina P-Peter had put down after an unsuccessful attack on a U-boat a hundred miles off the coast and needed bombing-up. A heavy iron refueller trudged past the pierhead to the lagoon, the crew's legs marked by ugly red and green sores caused by petrol or diesel getting into open pores.

Every man was yellow, stoop-backed and slow-moving. It was too hot to move fast and the stoop was as inevitable as the saffron skin. They had arrived from England pink-cheeked and full of energy but after a few weeks of indifferent diet, enervating heat, humidity and mepacrine, all the eagerness had faded into a simple desire to sit still when they were not called on to do anything particular.

It wasn't so much that they were a long way from civilization. As the crow flew, they weren't. But, isolated by the swamps in a breathless sweltering heat in a cleft in the land which halted any breeze or fresh air that might come from the sea, Jum was a lost sort of place. RAF, Hawkinge, and the naval station at Brighton, on higher ground, were quite different. In the creek at Jum, the air was still and full of the acrid smell of mangroves and the stink of diesel fumes from marine engines, which was something everybody connected with flying boats would remember all their lives.

Beyond the end of the creek, one of Mackintosh's Sunderlands was just taxiing in the lagoon for a test flight. The crashing of an aeroplane and the deaths of most of its crew didn't stop the war. U-boats were still ringing Freetown and next week another crew would arrive in a new aeroplane to take the place of X-X-ray so that things could go on as before. With the thousands killed in North Africa and Russia, an accident involving a mere five men was put down as just one of the hazards of flying from a base lacking the facilities of civilized and industrialised England.

The climate was against good and careful workmanship. Men found it hard to remain alert. Aircrew grew careless. Repairs were more difficult. Spare parts were in short supply and you used whatever was to hand. Many a Sunderland or Catalina flew with a Sierra Leone halfpenny – minted with a hole in the middle to be hung on a string round the neck of a black man not in the habit of wearing trousers – substituting for a missing engine washer; while, on the water, the same valuable and desperately needed aircraft often swung to a buoy secured to its sinker by a chain cable whose swivel was held in place by an ordinary four-inch nail because there were no heavy-duty split pins which should properly have been used.

Coastal Command was the Cinderella of the RAF, neglected in favour of her more glamorous sisters, Bomber and Fighter Commands. Even the Germans were said to feel sorry for Coastal Command. Nobody loved them, not even their own side, and in the whole sphere of the Cinderella arm, West Africa was one of the most neglected of all. To the men flying from Jum it seemed a pretty short-sighted policy when shipping losses could lose the war.

As usual after a crash, the mooring party had virtually taken over the pinnace, complete with rations for two days, and four hours later, roughly where Ginger Donnelly said they would be, they picked up two bodies, putty-coloured horrors swollen in the warm water and devoid of hair and fingers because the barracuda had been at them. Slipping blankets underneath them, they hoisted them from the water and searched them warily for identity discs before bundling them up and tying them with rope.

'Sergeant Dugan,' Feverel said as they brought the punt alongside the pinnace. 'And Steen, the second pilot. Steen was split from top to bottom.'

The pinnace crew kept well to the rear as the bodies were lifted on board. The mooring party had done the job before and the pinnace crew were quite happy to let them do it again, because the smell was one which none of them would ever forget, a pungent sweetish smell that pervaded everything and even seemed to have a taste.

Climbing back into the punt, Feverel and Kneller started the outboard and, picking their way round the sandbanks thrown up by the tide, headed for the mangroves, where they shut off the engine and began to use a pole. Finding an opening, they were about to disappear among the curving roots when a native canoe shot round a bend in the river, its occupant waving and shouting.

As they chugged slowly towards him, he indicated that they should follow him. Entering the mangroves, their nostrils caught by the acrid smell of rotting vegetation, they found the third body, an ugly thing that had once been a high-spirited young man but was now minus its head and one leg, draped elegantly, it seemed, across the mangroves that grew out of the mud like the arches of fan vaulting. As Feverel hacked at the roots with a machete the body fell into the water and began to float. Attaching a rope to it, they towed it to the pinnace where the usual blanket was slipped beneath it and it was hoisted on board.

Feverel looked at Corporal Fox and indicated the Mende fisherman sitting hopefully in his canoe alongside. 'Got any money on you?' he asked. 'We usually dash 'em something.'

Fox had no money on him because in Jum there was nothing to spend money on, so instead they gave the fisherman a tin of bully beef from the boat's store cupboard and his face cracked into a delighted smile.

'Another satisfied customer,' Feverel observed dryly.

Everyone put Landon's crash down to the bad luck that seemed to dog everything at Jum. An inquiry was held and the crash attributed to the effects of the climate. No one had been found who could be charged with carelessness, and the usual order was just being written to tighten things up – something which, because of the conditions and the shortages, always had to be tacitly ignored – when O-Orange, Flying Officer Paterson's aircraft, followed.

Paterson was a popular officer with a good crew and he had been in West Africa longer than most. He was an ex-sergeant, yellow and thin like all the old hands, but his skill with an aircraft was greater than many of his fellow officers' and no one worried when he took off or landed because he went by the book and never took risks. His take-off was perfect and, like Landon, he had his floats up even before he left the water.

As the machine lifted over the trees, the crew of the seaplane tender heaved a sigh of relief and turned towards the pier. The lights of the Catalina changed position in the darkness as she swung north along the coast, and she was roughly level with Makinkundi and over the river Bic when the hand who was coiling the ropes in the well-deck of the tender heard a dull thump and, looking up, saw a red glow where he had just seen the Catalina's navigation lights. The glow seemed to expand into an incandescent bubble of light, a chemical colour against the dark sky, billowing larger and larger, vomiting sparks like a roman candle and bursting outwards in a blinding flash of brilliant orange and sulphur yellow. Then the whole lot vanished from sight beyond the palm trees.

'Oh, Christ!' he said. 'Another one!'

The duty officer knew what had happened before the seaplane tender reached the jetty, because a telephone call had been received from the Bic river mine of Jan van der Pas Company, the Dutch-owned group which conducted its operations near Yima. Up there the river split into a series of smaller creeks, and at the end of one of them was a deepwater anchorage and a narrow-gauge railway that ran to a pier at Makinkundi. The mine buildings, the offices, the living quarters, the engineering shops, stood half a mile away from the pier, near the end of another creek formed by the river Bic pushing in from the sea at the other side of the little peninsula on which Yima stood. There they were clear of dust from the mine which would have laid a pink surface over everything they ate and drank and did.

The Dutchmen had seen the aircraft explode and had telephoned just as the duty coxswain was trying to contact the orderly officer to inform him what had happened. The orderly officer dug Wing Commander Molyneux out of the camp cinema where they were having another go at *Blood and Sand*. Molyneux' head jerked up at the whispered information, then he leaned across to Mackintosh, of the Sunderland squadron, who passed the message to the group captain, the MO and the padre, and they all left in a hurry.

The group captain headed for his office to inform the air officer commanding what had happened, the medical officer for sick quarters to prepare his staff in case they were needed, the padre for the telephone exchange to ask air headquarters in Freetown to lay on transport from the harbour to the cemetery on Tower Hill, which was where the bodies would be taken this time – if there were bodies, and he suspected there would be – because it didn't pay in the West African heat to keep them around for long.

Trixie Tristram, who was on the switchboard, eyebrows plucked and wearing immaculately washed and starched shorts, was polishing his nails and was irritated by the interruption.

'We might just as easily get a Creole clerk making a date with his girlfriend,' he said tartly as he reached for the plugs.

JOHN HARRIS

'Or a Syrian trader trying to sell industrial diamonds over the border. I've had them all.'

He pushed plugs in, talking over his shoulder all the time to the padre. 'You know what telephones are like out here. The ants make their nests in the junction boxes or the rats eat the insulation off the wire. I've even heard French and German...'

'In Sierra Leone?' the padre said. 'Do you understand them?'

Trixie tried to look modest. 'I was on the Continental telephone exchange before the war. I often had to speak to Paris or Berlin.'

'What were they saying?'

Trixie backed down quickly because his knowledge of French and German was really limited to demanding telephone numbers or passing the time of day. 'Well, I don't speak them all that much,' he admitted. 'But I can recognize them. German's like barbed wire in your ears. French's different. You...' he listened and worked the plugs again '...you can always enjoy French.'

'What did they say?' the padre repeated.

Trixie looked annoyed at the probing. 'I don't know. It didn't concern me.' He sniffed fretfully. 'We're not supposed to listen in to conversations.'

Molyneux was waiting by the jetty as the padre arrived. The pinnace was just pulling alongside.

'The Dutchmen say she fell into the sea,' he told Corporal Fox. 'But a lot of stuff, including a wing, fell near their landing stage in the Bic.'

The mooring party were already aboard and the little motor punt, dripping water to the deck, had been hoisted to the hatch top. An hour later they were passing Tagrin Point opposite Freetown and heading into the mouth of the river Rokel. If the Bunce was wide, the Rokel was even wider, an enormous expanse of water cutting deeply into the land. By

38

daylight they were off the entrance to the river Bic, which, like the Bunce, was also really only a tributary of the greater river.

Nobody spoke much. Like the marine section men, Molyneux was a sailor as well as an airman, part of a tightly knit community with a highly specialized way of life, web-footed warriors with verdigris on their cap badges and buttons, and a near-naval terminology of speech. Again like the marine section crews, the flying-boat men enjoyed a virtual autonomy of action, and their aircraft, like the boats, were self-contained units with a breadth of possible situations never likely to occur to land-based airmen. They had all worked in England in filthy weather on grey sullen water, in fog and rain and gale-force winds, always operating on unstable platforms, the flying crews regarding the boat crews with more than average warmth because, whatever the conditions, they never failed to put them aboard their machines.

The entrance to the Bic was narrow, with mangrove swamps by the entrance, and turning into it, the pinnace began to move slowly inland. After a few hundred yards, they were met by a launch coming out, a large fast boat with a flared bow and powerful engines. They had often seen it in the Bunce because the Dutchmen sometimes brought it round to Makinkundi or used it for going to Freetown.

A head appeared through the engine-room hatch and the black man on the foredeck tossed a rope. As it made fast alongside the pinnace, a white man climbed out of the cabin. He was fat and comfortable and bathed in sweat. Behind him, to Molyneux' surprise, was Cazalet, the army colonel in charge of security in the area, whom he'd last met over drinks in the mess at Jum before the concert party's performance.

He saw Molyneux' puzzled look and tried to explain his presence there. 'Makin' a few inquiries,' he said. Lookin' for a woman.'

'Aren't we all?'

'This one's a German agent who's been stirrin' up trouble round Kenema. Name of Magda Fallada. A Mrs Geer, wife of a British missionary, got into conversation on the train from Blama a week ago with a Mrs Bowyer, who said she was the wife of a district commissioner at Bo. But there isn't a district commissioner by the name of Bowyer at Bo and we think Mrs Geer's Mrs Bowyer may be *our* Magda Fallada. She's been seen in this area.'

Cazalet's interest in his German agent seemed of small importance to Molyneux in his concern for his missing aircraft and its crew. 'What's more to the point at the moment,' he said, 'is, did you see my aircraft crash?'

Cazalet nodded and indicated the Dutchman. 'Sittin' on the veranda havin' a gin with our friend here.'

The Dutchman pointed. 'She fell in the sea. But we haf here part of the wing. There iss explosion. Much flames and lights, then we hear a crash and realize iss part of the machine which falls into the swamp. We haf find it. Also there are depth charges.'

'I hope you didn't move them,' Molyneux said. 'If they were heading out to sea, they'd have been fused.'

'We do not touch them,' the Dutchman said. 'Because we know they are set to explode at twenty-five feet and the basin where we moor our boats is at high tide almost thirty feet deep. A small coaster can get in.' He gestured. 'Now you must follow me and I must show you where iss everyt'ing. I t'ink also there iss a body. I prefer not to look. I haf not the stomach.'

They followed the Dutchman's launch slowly. Further along, at Yima, the river widened so that a small ship could turn round to make its exit. Behind it the land rose unexpectedly to a flat low plateau where they were scooping out the ore, and the basin, fed by a small stream, looked vaguely like a small man-made harbour. Here the mangroves had given way to sturdy palms and cotton trees, and among them they could see groups of the heavy, short-tailed monkeys of the coast watching the boats like spectators at a football match. Over their screeches came the raucous calls of birds.

Near the end of the creek was a landing stage with steps leading up the steep side to the flat land above. At the top was a large recreation hut on wooden piles hanging over the water to form a boathouse so that in the rainy season the Dutchmen could board their launches without being drenched. Moored near it were a heavy boat like a scow, with which the Dutchmen carried their supplies from Freetown, and a small draught dinghy with an outboard. Further down the creek several boats owned by fishermen from Yima hugged the shore, half-hidden by a high bank that stuck out into the water almost like a breakwater.

Mooring alongside the jetty, the pinnace crew lowered the punt into the water and Kneller and Ginger Donnelly climbed in. The Dutchman gestured to a black man in shorts and shirt standing on the landing stage.

'He go mit you,' he said. 'He show you where.' He turned to Molyneux and the padre. 'Meanwhile, perhaps you will permit me to take you with the colonel here back to our mess? We haf a good Bols gin.'

As Molyneux and the padre disappeared, the black man offered to lead the way among the trees, but Ginger didn't need a guide.

'I know this place like the back of me 'and,' he said contemptuously. 'I often come round 'ere. One of the bar boys lets me 'ave a beer now and then.'

They found the wing of the aircraft without difficulty, a flat surface of aluminium with torn edges. Then the black man pointed and they found a body lying in the grass at the foot of one of the trees.

41

'It's Harper, the navigator,' Ginger said. 'Poor sod.'

They covered the corpse with a blanket, then, as the black man beckoned, they followed him again to where they found two of the depth charges. Ginger held back warily.

'Leave 'em alone,' he said.

'They can't explode on dry land,' Kneller pointed out. 'They're triggered off by water pressure.'

Ginger was unconvinced. 'There's four hundred and fifty pounds o' explosive in them things,' he pointed out. 'An' the bloody plungers what set 'em off are missing. We once jettisoned one in the sea at Mount Batten. The armourers said it had been made safe but it blew up the next day just the same.'

Kneller ignored the superstitious mutterings and, using a machete, cut boughs from the trees to make a stretcher. Rolling the depth charges on to it, they carried them to the edge of the river and left them there.

'The armourers can collect 'em now,' Kneller said. 'Let's get the stiff.'

Ginger nodded. Calling bodies by another name always made it easier.

The black man helped carry the corpse to the water's edge. As they placed it on the deck of the pinnace, a small black boy appeared on the bank from the Dutch mess hut. He was carrying a dripping sack containing bottles of beer and lumps of ice.

They looked at each other and Feverel eyed the blanketed bundle at their feet. 'Sometimes,' he said softly, 'the advantages of this job are hard to distinguish. But there *are* a few.'

four

It was evening when they returned to Jum and, as always at the end of the day, the sun was at its hottest.

As the pinnace put the mooring party ashore and headed for its buoy, Ginger Donnelly paused outside the packing case which did duty as the office of Flying Officer Rodney Hobson, who ran the marine section. Consisting of little more than a table piled with files and a couple of wire baskets, it was illuminated and ventilated by two large wooden flaps which were raised in the morning and let down in the evening.

Hobson could see Ginger standing doubtfully outside, leaning on his long forked stick and wearing faded oilstained shorts fringed like a Victorian tablecloth with too much washing. They were held up by a length of heaving line, and his battered pith helmet had been sat on so often it was now entirely without shape. As Hobson watched, he lifted it to scratch his head, disclosing a dusty-looking thatch that seemed to have been stood on end by an electric shock. Grubby stockings sagged over unpolished shoes made grey by salt water, so that he looked more like a poacher than an airman.

Hobson knew Ginger well. They were both regulars and eighteen months before, near the Horn of Africa, Hobson had been a sergeant while Ginger had been an aircraftman, first class. Providence had finally brought Hobson's long-awaited commission and Ginger's promotion to leading aircraftman and they had celebrated with a few others by being posted to this forgotten corner of the West Coast.

He watched Ginger for a while, drawing slowly on a cigarette. No less than the men under him, Hobson was yellow with mepacrine, had long since lost any surplus fat in the heat, and was suffering from the dust which chafed his neck along the collar of his shirt.

At least, he thought, the Harmattan that came after Christmas and slammed doors and filled the eyes, nose and mouth with grit all the way from the Sahara had now stopped. But if it wasn't one thing it was another, because now the wind had dropped, the flies had started, and soon the rainy season would begin and then it would be mosquitoes, malaria and other assorted miseries.

He sighed. There was no war on in their immediate vicinity but people still died. The latest crashes brought up the number lost during his stay in Jum to three Catalinas and a Sunderland, and in addition there had been one or two drownings as flight mechanics who had fallen from the machines they were servicing were swept away by the swift-running tide. 'A dropped spanner's a lost spanner' was the saying on flying-boat bases, but nobody ever bothered to make sure that the men who worked on the flimsy platforms twenty feet above the water could swim. At Jum the tide ran out at a good ten knots, which to a poor swimmer meant death, and in Hobson's own section two men had also been burned to death when a refueller had gone up in the last rainy season. The big, all-steel, forty-five-foot-long boats carried two and a half thousand gallons of aviation spirit and eight-horse petrol engines to pump it to the aircraft. With the humidity at its worst in the rains, these had a habit of throwing out six-inch sparks, and if fumes had built up in the cockpit that was that. Refueller 62 had vanished in a flare of flame and only the quick action of the fitter who had cut the ropes had saved the Sunderland to which it was tied. The day afterwards, while they were still getting over the accident, a depth charge had fallen from a wing and fractured the skull of the coxswain of the bomb scow who had happened to be standing just beneath.

Hobson had arrived in Jum via South Africa, bringing with him forty-odd men who had served with him in East Africa. One had drowned when a boat had overturned. One had died while a passenger on a test flight in one of the crashed Catalinas; two had been fatally burned when Refueller 62 had exploded; another, brought up in central London among cinemas, dance halls and pubs, had been unable to adjust to Jum and cut his throat; one had lost an eye in a trivial accident involving a fallen tree; and another had died of blackwater fever at a base further down the coast. And all without even the doubtful satisfaction of being properly involved in the war.

As Hobson laid down his cigarette, Ginger made up his mind. Jamming his pith helmet back on his head, he tapped on the door.

'It's hot,' he said.

'Yes, it is a bit,' Hobson agreed. 'Come in, Ginger. In trouble?'

'A bit.' Ginger scratched his crotch. 'I got tinea somethin' awful.'

'Haven't we all? Still, you've no need to worry until it goes far enough down your legs to meet your foot rot coming up. Is that all?'

'No,' Ginger admitted. 'There's somethin' else.'

There was no formality between them. Like Ginger, Hobson had started working boats round aircraft in the days when T E Shaw had still been with them, and there was little either didn't know about the other.

'I was up the lagoon that night when X-X-ray went in,' Ginger said. 'In me canoe.'

'Doing what, Ginger?' Hobson asked.

45

'Just sniffin' round.'

'That woman of yours?'

'Which woman?' Ginger was all innocence.

'I know you've got one.'

'She's only a friend. I'm dead 'ot on friendship.'

Hobson waved away the protest. 'Never mind, Ginger. You shouldn't have been there. You know as well as I do that nothing's supposed to be out there except the duty boats when there's flying.'

Ginger looked indignant. 'I wasn't nowhere near the flarepath,' he said. 'I know what's what. I picked up Purdy.'

'It's lucky for Purdy that Leading Aircraftman Donnelly was somewhere he shouldn't have been.'

'I saw a boat out yonder.'

For a moment there was silence then Hobson lit cigarette and offered one to Ginger.

'Go on,' he said warily, wondering what was coming, because it was unlike Ginger to sneak. 'Somebody been taking one of the dinghies out without permission?'

'It wasn't one of ours,' Ginger said. 'The duty dinghy had put the crew aboard and was heading back here. The seaplane tender was in its proper place wi' the Cat as she started her run. *This* boat was starboard o' the flarepath, up against the mangroves on the side of the river. There was two men in it. I heard 'em talking. They wasn't speakin' English.'

'Did they see you?'

'When I go up-river,' Ginger said, 'nobody sees me.'

'I've noticed. Were they Dutch? There are half a dozen of them working the mine at Yima. They've been there a long time. They go down to Freetown from time to time by the Bunce.'

'They don't go by this boat I saw. It wasn't that launch they use. I know that. I've seen it come up the Bunce. And it wasn't that coaster that comes in from French Guinea to pick up ore – the *Maréchal Grouchy*. I know what boats they have and what they use. This wasn't none of them. And they wasn't wogs.'

'Could they have been fishing?'

'They'd never catch anything where they was.'

'You'd know, of course.' Hobson took a pull at his cigarette and studied Ginger. 'Ginger, you're getting at something. What is it?'

'Sir...' Ginger finally gave Hobson the respect to which he was due and Hobson nodded ironically '...them two in that boat was watchin' X-X-ray.'

'Landon's aircraft? Why?'

'I dunno. When I looked round after the crash they'd gone. As if they'd been waitin' to see it crash and when they'd seen it crash they'd gone 'ome.'

Hobson leaned forward. 'Have you told anybody about this?'

'No, sir.'

'I think we'd better. The Wingco might be interested.'

The Wingco *was* interested.

He listened to what Hobson had to say then slowly lit a cigarette.

'Did anyone else see this boat, Hobby?' he asked.

'I've asked the piermaster and among the duty crew, sir,' Hobson said. 'It seems only Donnelly saw it and even he's beginning to wonder if it was imagination.'

Molyneux puffed at his cigarette. Sierra Leone wasn't the happiest area in the world. The Vichy French who surrounded them were surprisingly hostile and the chief nightmare of the police in Freetown was the possibility of an incendiary bomb in one of the military bases or among the stores that lined the harbour because black Frenchmen never found it hard to cross from French Guinea without passes. Despite the fact that everybody knew saboteurs were being trained beyond the Scarcies river in case the Germans won and it came to invasion, since they often brought smuggled cattle across with them, with food short the police occasionally had to look the other way.

He also knew of an aircraft which had been shot down the previous year while attempting to spy on a British convoy in Freetown harbour. When an attempt had been made to get on friendly terms with the French, he had had to detail several of his officers to attend the ceremony round the hurriedly tidied grave among the ant-heaps in the cemetery at Hawkinge Town.

He hadn't been sure then what it added up to but it hadn't convinced him that all the French in French West Africa were friendly towards the British. Even local problems couldn't easily be shrugged off. Nationalism was growing in Sierra Leone and there was a severe shortage of rice in the colony because Syrian traders kept cornering the supplies and the Africans were restless. Shops had been looted and up-country there had even been a few minor riots which had necessitated units of the West African Frontier Force being turned out to help the hard-pressed police. At Jum the problem manifested itself as raids on the camp. Gates couldn't keep out raiders who swam or paddled round the boundary fence and occasionally Africans, their naked bodies greased with palm oil, slipped into the huts at night to steal whatever they could lay their hands on.

'Well,' he said, 'both these aircraft burst into flames. I've seen flying-boat crashes before but never with flames. Is this chap of yours reliable?'

'As far as discipline's concerned,' Hobson said, 'no, sir.'

'Known him long?'

'We joined up at roughly the same time.'

'Why was he where he was? He shouldn't have been.'

'I know that. He knows it, too, but he's been at this job long enough not to take chances or risk lives. He's just not very good at obeying orders. He has a canoe which he uses when he gets a chance.'

'Fishing?'

'A woman.'

'He's got a woman?'

'Two of coffee, one of milk. Half-African, half-Syrian, I think.'

'How did he manage that feat?'

Hobson shrugged. 'Ginger's quite a character,' he said. 'He's not what you'd call particularly clever but he has a gift for things. He catches snakes and does it surprisingly well. He also picks up native tongues as if he'd been speaking them all his life. In East Africa he was speaking three varieties of Bantu. On the way here, we did a short stint at the Cape and in three weeks he was speaking some Afrikaans and a bit of Malay. He runs one of the shore gangs – mostly Temne and Mende – and he knows what they're saying and they know what he's saying. He didn't recognize what the men in the boat were saying.'

'Could it have been French?'

'It might have been. He wouldn't know French because he's never had occasion to speak it.'

Molyneux stubbed out his cigarette and rose.

'I find all this rather intriguing, Hobby,' he said. 'I think I'll go and see Groupy.'

Group Captain Robert Judd Strudwick, MC, DFC, ought never to have been in West Africa.

He was tall and had conquered female hearts in his youth by his devastatingly good looks. At the age of fifty-two he was still good-looking but they were now the soft good looks of an ageing man who had always been used to the good things of life. He had fought with great skill and determination over the Western Front in the other war and become well-known as one of the great fighter pilots of his day. This skill had stood him in good stead when the war was over and he had remained in the RAF, where he had eventually reached the rank of wing commander. Unfortunately, there he had stuck because it had been discovered that a warrior mighty in battle wasn't necessarily a man capable of organization, something high rank demanded. He had finally retired, not much mourned, in 1937 but in 1939 had grabbed at the opportunity to get back into uniform and, given the acting rank of group captain, had been put in command of a fighter station in Essex. Since during the Battle of Britain he'd had a tendency to disappear into the air in his Spitfire whenever possible, he had never been around when he was wanted and had even managed to get himself shot down near Canterbury, fortunately without much damage to himself beyond a severe shaking which had made him realize he was older than he'd thought.

Deciding he was becoming a nuisance, his superior officers had shunted him to a training command in the West of England, but Strudwick was wealthy and his wife had a title and influence, and his demands to be more actively engaged had finally grown so strident someone had had the bright idea of sending him to Jum, where he was out of the way and could do little harm. He was forbidden to fly in command of an aircraft.

Strudwick didn't like Jum, he didn't like West Africa and he didn't like the ordinance that forbade him flying, but he had always lived in style with servants, big houses and big cars. And, to Flying Officer Hobson's disgust, he had collared for his private use one of the marine section's desperately needed seaplane tenders. He had had it painted white, given it the name *White Bird* and had taken over a complete crew who were expected to be immaculately dressed at all times.

He used the boat to visit the commanding officers at Hawkinge and Brighton and to go down to Freetown. When the heat was particularly oppressive, he could always find an excuse to visit the senior naval officer or the air officer commanding. At twenty knots a boat was a splendid way of cooling off. Group Captain Strudwick had aged in an air force when senior officers were men of privilege, and he believed in exacting his due demands to the hilt.

He listened to what Wing Commander Molyneux had to say, then looked up.

'I believe you're trying to suggest something, my boy,' he said.

Molyneux frowned. He disliked Strudwick and resented him calling him his boy. With a double DFC, he felt he was nobody's boy and didn't enjoy being patronized. 'I feel perhaps we ought to investigate this boat that was seen, sir,' he said. 'I know we've had crashes which can probably be put down to the conditions but it seems to me we ought not merely to accept things that leave us in some doubt.'

Strudwick leaned back in his chair. 'You're surely not suggesting sabotage, are you?'

Molyneux wasn't quite sure what he was suggesting but he certainly felt they ought not to ignore Ginger Donnelly's item of news.

Strudwick heard him out, his expression disinterested. 'Everybody out here suddenly seems to have got the wind up,' he said. 'Sounds a bit like panic to me. And, undermanned as we are, we have better things to do than go sniffing about for non-existent spies. Were you proposing to use people from your squadron?'

Molyneux was not. His squadron consisted of hard-working flying crews and hard-working ground crews, many of whom, suffering from the effects of the climate and indifferent rations, were having a difficult enough time as it was. 'My people are already hard-pressed,' he said.

'How about Mackintosh? Is he prepared to spare anyone?'
'I doubt it, sir.'

Strudwick shrugged. 'Well, the base has no one.' He leaned back in his chair again. 'As it happens, first, I think this man Donnelly's suffering from too much sun. Second, if he *did* see someone, it was a native canoe with a couple of fishermen in it who shouldn't have been there. We'll have the local police go round the riverside villages again, warning them there'll be trouble if they persist. Third, I can't imagine why anyone should wish to be interested in what happens here. God knows, I'm not.'

Molyneux persisted. 'Might we not call in the civilian police from Freetown, sir?'

Strudwick eyed him coldly 'We don't want those chaps poking around here,' he said. 'This is an RAF station.'

It was an old service attitude. The idea of calling in the civilian police was anathema because it suggested some kind of disgrace. Molyneux recognized the way of thinking.

'The civilian police already have their hands full,' Strudwick went on. 'There were rice riots out at Gbani last week. Even shooting. We'll handle it ourselves.'

Molyneux drew a deep deliberate breath. In an ordinary airman, it would have been called 'dumb insolence', which was a chargeable offence, but Molyneux was not an ordinary airman but a wing commander with a double DFC and Strudwick realized he would have to do something.

'You have the station police to draw on,' he said.

Molyneux didn't think much of the idea. The RAF police were usually tall young men who had hoped to be something else – preferably aircrew – but had been drafted into the police branch because of their height. They were invariably unpopular and usually regarded as good at little beyond checking the passes of the natives who worked in the camp. It was probably a gross slander, but Molyneux didn't really think they were the types to produce much in the way of detective work. Especially since the camp had never had a provost officer, merely an RAF police sergeant who, while he was an example to everybody with his smartness, was not considered to be very clever.

Strudwick saw the annoyance on his face and tried to make a joke.

'There's the padre,' he said. '*He's* usually free.'

five

In the end, nothing was done about the two Catalina crashes. Like the crews, they were soon forgotten. What wreckage could be salvaged was dragged up the slipway where it lay for a day or two as a dire warning to all aircrew to be constantly on the alert, then it was hauled behind the hangar where it soon began to disappear under the ever-encroaching undergrowth.

The names Landon and Paterson and their crews were rubbed off the readiness board and yet another new Catalina and another new crew arrived from England. No more concert parties appeared and nobody expected them. Jum was back to normal. Within days it was as if Landon, Paterson and their crews had never existed.

The weather had been growing hotter for some time, the area round the river stifling, the leaves hanging like corpses in the dead, unbelievably humid air. Round the huts the mosquitoes seemed to grow more noticeable, their whirr and ping as loud as the croak of the crickets. The sky remained cloudless but there was a curious fading of colour that changed as the day advanced from blue to steel and from steel to bronze, making the hills behind the camp look like the pale-washed images from a watercolour. As evening approached, nervous little flurries of wind came, raising the dust in tiny whorls that danced across the bare patch of earth that did duty as a parade ground, ballooning the mosquito nets in the huts with an unexpected stirring of air.

The strangeness of the atmosphere made people irritable and tempers became on edge, especially among those who had never seen a rainy season. Eventually the breathless build-up when the lungs seemed to struggle for air changed to an imperceptible darkening of the sky and a silence in which the most unimportant sounds became strident. Then the squalls came, frenzied gales of wind roaring in from every corner of the compass, slamming doors, setting the palm tops thrashing, tearing branches from trees and lifting an opaque wall of red dust. Finally the stillness came again, ominous and frightening, as if there were a spectre waiting in the wings.

New clouds, yellow and muddy-looking, marched over the mountains to the west, then the first electrical storm of the season started with an ear-splitting clap of thunder that startled everybody. It battered at the shuddering earth as if with hammers, and in the drum rolls of noise violent forks of purple lightning played in an incessant flashing and flickering of unearthly light that seemed weird and terrifying.

The first heavy drops of rain spattered the earth as the thunder died, then it came down in a drenching smother which effectively drowned all conversation as it hammered tumultuously on the tin roofs. For three hours a solid wall of rain descended, the whole camp hushed beneath its roaring, so thick, so heavy, you could stand in the doorways and almost see your reflection in the falling water. It didn't seem possible that so much rain could fall in one storm.

If died as suddenly as it had come, leaving the camp like a Turkish bath, and the following morning it was as if the whole world was pale and rubbed out, lit by a pearly radiance whose light seemed to come from an unknown source. Over the land there was a silvery wet haze that drifted like shadows among the trees. Then the sun came out as usual, mocking the distant growl and mutter of thunder that still persisted, but it was watery-looking and cast no shadows, though it started the steam bath again and increased the mist that clung to the ground like grey cotton wool. Eventually the clouds lifted and the mist vanished, and the sun poured down as usual, striking the soaked earth in a sticky breath-catching beat that made every breath feel like a throatful of wet, warm, gasping air, and the mud began to dry with remarkable speed.

A few of those who had been looking forward to grey skies as a variation from the everlasting sun thought it had been a pleasant change, but they began to think differently when another downpour burst on them the following afternoon, shutting out the horizon with its weight and fury, the rain driving across the river in sweeping horizontal sheets that were totally opaque, shuddering against the hangar, the huts, the trees, the thunder and lightning not much less spectacular than the orchestration which had opened the rainy season.

The road to the hangar became a river and the drainage ditches were filled with a boiling torrent, strewn with the wreckage and litter the rain had washed down. In Hawkinge Town there were even dead pigs which had been swept into the swollen channels and, what was worse, the rice shed of the local store had collapsed under the deluge and the rain had got at the stored bags which were now nothing more than pulpy white masses contained in split hessian.

Since there was a war on and aeroplanes had to take off in the gaps in the clouds, the latest storm had caught everybody at work on the lagoon and, shivering despite the stifling atmosphere, they were saturated to the skin in seconds in the deep grey gloom that seemed to shine with moisture in a wet swirl.

'Owing to inclement weather,' Feverel said, spitting rainwater from his lips, 'the war will be held indoors.'

From the ramshackle jetty, the sweeping grey curtain cut off the sight of the moored aircraft. Mr Hacker, the engineer warrant officer, who had served through many rainy seasons in other parts of the world and knew his way about, appeared with a coloured golf umbrella, and the African labourers cut themselves leaves from the banana plants which they held over their heads so that the water ran along the central groove made by the stalk and poured off just behind their heels. Oilskins were available but the temperature was still high and only a few of the more fussy – people like Trixie Tristram and the headquarters clerks – bothered with them, most preferring to be wet rather than suffocated. Cold-weather blue uniforms hanging in the Nissens began to develop mildew and the marine section huts at the lower end of the camp were four inches deep in water.

In addition, they seemed to be losing the war again. The only available radio, situated in what passed as a NAAFI – though there was nothing to buy there – gave them the news. The place filled up every evening, as men, still grimy with grease and mud, and usually saturated, steaming and exhausted, crowded round to listen to the latest gloomy reports.

Rommel had attacked in North Africa and the British had withdrawn. The news reader made it all sound nice and tidy but most of them had seen something of the war and could guess at the shattered wrecks, the smoking ruins, the bodies and the strings of prisoners. Tobruk had been cut off again but to everyone's surprise – because last time it had held out for months against repeated attacks – this time it had fallen and Rommel had crossed the Egyptian frontier. The general in command had been sacked – the second in a year – and it looked very much as though the Germans were going straight through to Cairo and very probably on to India. They were now at the very gates of the Egyptian capital, halted only by lack of petrol, and were simply waiting until reinforcements of men and machinery could be brought up for the next blow which would carry them beyond the Suez Canal.

At home, it seemed, they were once again frantically scraping the barrel. With what could be raised, they might succeed in stopping Rommel. Without it, they could never hope to hold him, let alone throw him back. In Jum, which was never a place to make you cheerful, the news seemed overwhelmingly bad.

Kneller's singing was heard less often these days. Apart from him, everybody had long since forgotten Ettore Mori-Moncrieff and it even began to look as though any concerts that Kneller gave in future might well be in a prisoner of war camp. He still sang to himself when out alone with Scow 14 but these days there was less of the lively 'Questa o Quella' and a lot more of the 'Miserere' from *Trovatore*.

Flying Officer Hobson began to count the days. He was due to go home soon – providing, of course, that his relief arrived and the Germans hadn't already won the war. It didn't disturb him too much because most people who'd left England in the dark days of 1940 and 1941 had expected never to see it again, anyway.

Aware of the importance of the convoys heading past the bulge of Africa towards Cape Town and the Middle East, Wing Commander Molyneux and Wing Commander Mackintosh and their crews flew more doggedly, but the submarines always seemed to know exactly where they were going to turn up and kept carefully out of sight. The mooring party began to worry again about the four-inch nails which held the aircraft in the water. There were no large split pins in the whole of West Africa.

Ginger Donnelly, aware that there was nothing he personally could do to help the war effort beyond what he was already doing, went his way exactly as before.

The disasters in the north had not gone unnoticed at home and the message that was sent from the Commander-in-Chief, Middle East, to London, 'It is unlikely that an opportunity will arise for the resumption of offensive operations before mid-September,' was never likely to be regarded as music in the ears by the aggressive old man at the head of the British Government. He had long since come to the conclusion that the war in the desert had descended into a yo-yo sort of affair with nobody getting anywhere and that it was time for a change.

The new commander was told what was expected of him and once again the barrel was scraped. New formations were put together; newly trained men were marched from their camps; aeroplanes were assembled; tanks, guns and vehicles began their slow movement to the ports.

The ships that awaited them were travel-stained, slab-sided rusty vessels of all shapes and sizes whose speed varied from nine to fourteen knots, though their chief engineers, canny Scots for the most part, were always inclined to play down their real speed so they had a knot or two in hand for emergencies. Some of them flew the red ensign, some stars and stripes, some the pale blue of Panama.

As they began to assemble in England, the American freighter, *George C Grieves*, left Bathurst, in the Gambia, to head independently for Freetown. The navy in Bathurst quite naturally warned Freetown to look out for her but, nevertheless, that night in the darkness, *George C Grieves* was hit by a torpedo and set on fire. Low in the water and on the point of sinking, she struggled to Freetown. The harbour was crowded and, wanted nowhere because she would impede the movement of shipping, a naval tug took her in tow and dragged her up-river to where she was finally allowed to settle on a shoal at a point where there was plenty of room to pass her.

The *George C Grieves* had been carrying food for the colony and how the submarine commander had known she would be where she was it was hard to decide, because only the air officer commanding and the Commander-in-Chief, South Atlantic, and their staffs, knew of her presence.

'This bloody place's rotten with spies,' Molyneux said bitterly. 'Those French bastards north of the border don't like us, and we know they've been passing Frenchmen and natives across the border ever since 1940.'

'Are you suggesting information gets to the enemy, sport?' Mackintosh asked.

'Security seems to think so,' Molyneux pointed out. 'That chap Cazalet was looking for a German agent at Yima when we went up there about O-Orange's crash. It wouldn't be difficult, after all. This place's permanently ringed with U-boats. They're the reason why there are so many wives still in Freetown who ought to be somewhere like South Africa or England.'

'And why refrigerators are in such short supply.'

'He thinks security out here's abysmal. He reckons information goes through Portuguese Guinea every time the navy sends a ship up there – on the excuse of patrolling Bissau – to pick up wine and brandy for the officers' mess at headquarters. The crews talk and he's trying to stop the run. He doesn't even trust the railway. It goes from Freetown to Pendembu, and Pendembu's only twenty miles from the frontier with French Guinea. And you know what it's like: you take your own servant, your own supply of tinned food, your chair, your bed, your ice box, even your own oil lamp. It's almost impossible to check what people are carrying. Even the civil servants are careless. He says the mammies in the market wrap their fruit and vegetables in old confidential papers from the secretariat files, and if they do that, what's to stop 'em sometimes wrapping 'em up in up-to-date ones.'

Mackintosh shrugged and Molyneux went on. 'He's right to be worried, of course,' he said. 'With what's happening in the Middle East, they'll have to send replacements for everything that was lost in the last fiasco and, by God, when they do we'll have to be on our toes, because there'll be a lot of 'em and they've got to get through.'

Mackintosh acknowledged the fact. 'The U-boats are growing altogether too clever for my liking,' he admitted. 'I've got C-Charlie flying this evening. Rendezvous at daylight tomorrow. I wish to God we could catch one of the sods on the surface and nobble it. It would give a boost to morale all round.'

Molyneux frowned. 'The bastards are appearing everywhere along this coast,' he agreed. 'I've had orders to send two of my aircraft down to Takoradi.'

'Snap. Two of mine go to Bathurst with instructions from the AOC to all crews to take extra care. He feels Paterson's and Landon's crashes shouldn't have occurred and points out quite rightly that aircraft don't grow on trees.'

six

The rain came again the following day, this time harder than ever. It fell in straight glassy splinters that shattered as they struck, a devastating deluge that rattled on the tin roofs and thundered in the ditches as it flooded away. The sound on the undergrowth was a steady roar threaded through with the hollow plop-plop of dripping waters, every leaf of every tree streaming like a miniature waterfall, the drips clunking into the puddles in an arpeggio of notes. The river became a muddy looking flood that brought with it small trees, fallen boughs, dried palm fronds and brushwood from the upper reaches in the hills where the falls gushed over the rocks in full spate.

By this time the growth of vegetation from the wet heat-soaked earth was incredible and the wild cucumbers were visibly fatter, the plantain trees near the Nissens had pushed up several notches, and the bush had burst into a delicate new green studded with trumpets, bells and lanterns. The camp had become a sea of mud criss-crossed by wheel marks and, as the thermometer climbed, the foetid air gagged in the throat.

A warning went out to dinghy crews, moving about their business between the aircraft and the trembling jetty, to keep their eyes open for branches swept downstream which could be a menace to the flying boats' fragile hulls, and Ginger Donnelly and four of his gang were taken off the task of clearing the ditches and spraying the stagnant pools with paraffin to prevent mosquitoes breeding and sent upstream in Scow 14 to search for half-submerged logs. Being Ginger, he took it as an invitation to visit his woman at Makinkundi.

Her name was Ili Atu and it had been Ginger who had rechristened her from a song they all sang, called 'The Ballad of Lizzie Morgan'. Her home was near the market-place and opposite her door was the only street lamp in the area. In 1897 the village headman had been one of the chiefs selected to attend Queen Victoria's second jubilee and he had been so impressed by London's gas lamps he had taken one back to Makinkundi where he set it on a concrete plinth to illuminate the village. For the rest of his life it had remained a matter of great surprise and disappointment that it failed to light up regularly after dark like its London brothers.

For a living, Ilu Atu/Lizzie Morgan ran what might, by a great stretch of imagination, be called a bar. Two warped whitewashed doors, one coming off its hinges, opened to reveal a garage-like interior with a wooden counter behind which there was a gin bottle – empty – a whisky bottle – empty; and a brandy bottle – also empty. Her stock consisted entirely of palm wine or bottled beer, bought, scrounged or stolen in Freetown. One or two bamboo tables and chairs stood on the crooked sidewalk and along the rear wall was an incongruous admixture of heavy Edwardian furniture that seemed to add to the gloom and the smell of damp. On one side wall was a gaudy print of the battle of Rorke's Drift and on the other a plan picture cut from the *Illustrated London News* of the British battle fleet of 1939 – much of it unfortunately now victim to U-boats or aircraft – together with a fading picture of King Edward VII and Queen Alexandra, circa 1906. About the room also, in fretwork frames, were seventy-two photographs of black men, women and children all portrayed in their best clothes but all out of date with the tall collars and picture hats of another age. None of them were relatives; Lizzie had obtained them from a photographer in Freetown when he'd cleared out his cupboards, because she'd thought they made the place look respectable. On the corrugated iron roof the feet of vultures scraped and clattered.

On Sundays, to please the minister, Lizzie went to church dressed in an ugly blue serge skirt and jacket with a straw hat decorated with artificial cherries, and vast black patent shoes on her broad flat feet, but now round her slender body she wore only a white lappa of Manchester cotton decorated with huge brown footprints. Despite the coarseness of the design it gave her an innocent dignity that would have appealed to cleverer men than Ginger. On her head was a pink headcloth which contrasted magnificently with her dark skin, and her wide smile showed perfect teeth because she spent an hour each day polishing them with a piece of fibrous tree root.

As Ginger appeared, she closed the garage doors and unhitched the lappa, to stand in front of him, naked, slim and boyish, her skin purple-black.

'One day we marry,' she said.

'Yeh,' Ginger agreed in a flat voice. 'One day.'

Afterwards, she opened the doors again and, as Ginger sat on a horsehair sofa underneath the solitary hurricane lamp she used to illuminate the place after dark, she produced a bottle of beer for him. 'No beer in camp,' she said proudly. 'But Lizzie got beer.'

Ginger nodded and began to pour the beer into the sawn-off bottle she handed him in lieu of a glass. There seemed to be hardly a single glass in the whole of Sierra Leone and most people drank out of cut-down bottles. Ginger eyed the sparkling liquid cheerfully and took a deep swallow.

'Cold,' he said. 'How're you doin', kid?'

Lizzie shrugged. 'Okay,' she replied. 'Except white boss come. I t'ink he Dutch. He get plenty drunk. He humbug me.' She gestured to the back room where she slept when the bar was closed.

Ginger took another swig at the beer, then, noticing the unfamiliar label, held up the bottle to ascertain its origin. Most of the beer consumed in the protectorate was Canadian and much of what appeared in native bars was stolen from the docks. To his surprise, this one was French.

'Who got it for you?' he asked.

'Friend belong me. I got plenty. Soon-soon is bundu ceremony. Afterwards people drink plenty beer.'

Ginger knew about bundu – the circumcision ceremonies practised in the bush on both males and females, and the acrobatic and magician's shows that were put on with the drinking that followed.

'I get him stored in shed,' the black woman said. 'I get boy to carry it for me.'

'I'll carry it,' Ginger said. He was an amiable man and not at all the person to worry about the white man's dignity or the dignity of the RAF.

He carried the boxes of bottles into the bar then sat drinking the rest of his beer, still and silent, his forked stick alongside his feet. One of the village mammies walked past, an earthenware pot on her head. Behind her, aping her, was a small girl carrying on her woolly crown a sheet of paper held in place by a stone. The sun was out again and Ginger stared at the broken step of the bar where a small green lizard was basking in the heat. Startled, as the shadows of the woman and child fell across it, it vanished in sudden zigzag flashes like coloured darts of flame. Ginger wondered if Lizzie's 'friend' was also one of her lovers.

As he made his way back down-river, the tide was running out fast under all the rainwater that came from the hills. Ginger handled the old scow automatically with the skill of someone who had been handling boats for years, his eyes fixed on the empty beer bottle he'd brought away with him.

He had set it on the engine hatch just in front of where he stood at the tiller, and he read and re-read the words on the label over and over again. *'Bière Etoile. Mise en bouteille à Conakry.'*

His attention was finally caught by a Sunderland, towed by a seaplane tender, moving slowly out of Jum creek towards the lines of mooring buoys. Following it were a refueller and a bomb scow. Despite the purple-grey clouds along the mountains which indicated more rain, there was going to be flying, and the view was confirmed when he saw a motor dinghy appear towing a line of masted dumb dinghies for the flarepath.

As he stepped ashore, he noticed that the elephant grass which up to a week before had been sparse, brown and withered at the end of the dry season, was growing rapidly in the steamy heat. It would eventually reach eight or ten feet high and was already tall enough and wet enough to soak him as he pushed through it. As he trudged towards the hut where he lived he heard an uproar among the long grass then one of his Temne labourers appeared with his eyes rolling. 'Boss Ginger,' he said. 'Snake!'

Ginger didn't quicken his steps. Neither did he slow them. Wearing mosquito boots as he was – they were forbidden during daylight hours but that made little difference to Ginger – he was not so vulnerable as the barefooted Africans. The snake was in the centre of the path through the long grass, a six-foot green mamba, its head raised, watching the scared Africans who were staring at it as if hypnotized. Without a word, never taking his eyes off it, Ginger edged round the back of the reptile, and, with a quick jab with his stick, he trapped the snake with the fork behind its head and pressed it down into the damp earth. As the tail lashed wildly one of the black men produced a heavy stone.

Ginger picked up the dead snake by the tail and handed it to the black man who held it as if it were a time bomb, then progressed placidly towards his billet. Reaching his hut, he pushed the stick under his bed and, placing the empty beer bottle on the orange box that did duty for a locker, sat staring at it, a cigarette dangling from his lips.

The rain he had expected started soon afterwards, coming at first in a few heavy drops like bombs, and the mosquito-wired doors of the hut crashed open as Kneller and Feverel fell through, their khaki soaked and mud-covered from working on buoys. Taking the simplest solution, they stripped off their muddy clothes and stood naked outside the door until they were clean.

Entering the hut again, they noticed Ginger. He was sewing by this time. He had acquired a tatty leopard skin from one of his friends in Makinkundi some time before and was engaged in making matching gloves, handbag and hat to take back to England to give to the first woman he came across who looked obliging. The fact that the skin was as stiff as a board and improperly cured and that no woman in her right mind would have been seen dead in what he was making was by the way. Over his head was his selection of *Men Only* pin-ups. The whole wall was covered with breasts, bottoms, thighs and navels. He had stuck them there in the first flush of enthusiasm on his arrival but had long since lost interest in them and now noticed them no more than he noticed the squeak and rattle of the fan that revolved slowly above his head – 'Sssss-ah-phttt, Sssss-ahphttt' – constantly there because of a fault in the hub.

'What's up, Ginger?' Feverel asked ' flinging down the towel with which he had dried himself. 'Got the willies? Gone jungle at last?'

Ginger looked up, unperturbed by the chaffing. He had a strange affection for Feverel and Kneller. It was closely connected with his own ill-spent mismanaged youth and his lack of most of the amenities of civilization. He could write only with an effort and Feverel, who had been a newspaper reporter before the war, had obliged on more than one occasion by writing delicate missives to his girls for him, while Kneller could not only sing but could actually make sense of the little black dots like the trail of a drunken spider across a sheet of music. He lit a cigarette and gestured at the bottle. Kneller stared at it with surprise.

'Where did you get it?'

'Makinkundi. It's French.'

'What's it matter if it's beer?'

As they talked, the rain increased to a steady and sickening descent that hammered on the roof, the brown flood bubbling under the eaves, every blade of grass dripping its weight of water to the sodden earth. With darkness, it slackened off and the sound of an aircraft taking off reached them.

'C-Charlie,' Feverel pointed out.

Ginger said nothing, still smoking, his eyes still on the bottle.

'Why don't you get the photographers to take a picture of it, Ginger?' Kneller asked. 'People would buy it.'

The squadron photographic sections had long since discovered that the unused film from the cameras on the aircraft could be cut off and used to take pictures which could be sold for souvenirs. Naked black girls were especially popular.

Feverel looked at the damp haze outside the window. 'The fitter off the *White Bird's* gone sick,' he said to nobody in particular. 'Malaria again. That means they'll have to supply someone else when Groupy wants to go visiting.'

The weather in England was just about the opposite of the weather at Jum. Jum was sodden and swathed in mist. England was bright with summer sunshine and the fields had never looked more beautiful, so that the ships' captains assembling for the convoy conference were not over-anxious to get back to sea.

The conference was held in a schoolroom, the ships' captains in civilian clothes, in their eyes the faraway look of men used to staring over vast distances. They carried briefcases and as they sat down they began filling in slips of paper giving the number of officers, hands and DEMS gunners in their ships. They had already been informed of the places they would occupy in the convoy – a matter of joy to those on the inside, of great concern to those on the flanks – and been given sealed envelopes containing the stragglers' route they were to follow if they lost the convoy, which were not to be opened until they were twenty-four hours at sea.

The escort commander began to speak.

'As usual,' he said, 'for reasons of security you're not being informed of the route you'll take, but I can say this: for once, you're not going far enough west across the Atlantic to see the Statue of Liberty.' There was a faint ironic cheer and he smiled. 'You'll have noted your convoy number, WS24, and you all know what WS stands for. WS means Winston's Special, and it's usually reserved for fast troopships. This time, though, because of the situation in the Middle East and the need for what you're carrying, it applies to you.'

He explained the need to keep their places, do exactly as they were told, and avoid that most heinous of crimes, making smoke. As he spoke, he looked hard at the masters of the coal-burning ships.

'The chaps in the desert need what you're carrying,' he said. 'To stop Rommel coming any further. With what you've got in your holds, the chances are that they'll even do better than that and might actually throw him out of Africa. But the Germans are as aware of this as we are and they'll do everything in their power to stop us getting through.'

It was a little like a lecture in a village hall, and the escort commander wondered that the merchant captains trusted the navy as much as they did. One day, he felt sure, something would go wrong and then the bitterness and the resentment would be beyond belief.

'We shall need to be alert,' he continued. 'Not just the look-outs. Every man working on deck must keep one eye on the sea, because intelligence has it that the Germans are assembling one of their wolf packs to stop us. Perhaps more than one.'

He paused and looked at his notes. 'For your information, however,' he said. 'We've been thinking ahead a little, too. There'll be air cover well into the Atlantic and a strong escort south. At Gib we'll have air escort to Cape Blanc, which is on the southern extremity of Spanish African territory, where we'll be met by air escorts from Bathurst who'll pass us on to escorts from Freetown. They'll be Catalinas or Sunderlands so don't mistake them for Focke-Wulf Kondors. They'll escort us into Freetown where we shall be watering and taking on supplies over a period of four days. So have your requirements ready. It'll be your last chance until you reach the Cape.'

Twelve hours later the ships put the shore behind them, moving in file along the swept channel. Dropping their pilots, they headed for open water to commence the complicated business of assembling in their proper formation. As squalls of unexpected rain drove from the south, they began to roll and the formations lost their neat shape.

At roughly the same time, another convoy was putting behind it the skyscrapers of Manhattan, heading west for the rendezvous with the ships from the Clyde. There were over a hundred vessels, cargo ships, bulk carriers, tankers, refrigerated vessels, and they came from ten different countries. Together, their gross weight was in the region of a million tons, and their cargoes included oil, frozen meat, food, explosives, detonators, bombs, shells, lorries, aircraft, tanks and men. They would meet more heading south from Gibraltar.

In the corvettes the mess-decks were already a shambles. The chief hope of their crews was never for comfort, just that there might be duff for pudding and that, with luck, they'd be held back for a boiler clean next time they reached their home port. The sailors climbing into their hammocks fully clothed didn't look forward to darkness, but mostly they thought only about sleep, which was the prize they all looked for off watch, and like all sailors they were optimistic enough not to expect trouble.

In that, however, they were wrong, because the staff of Admiral Karl Dönitz, head of the German U-boat service, known to the U-boat crews as the *Stab ohne Bäuche*, the staff without pot-bellies, because of their youth and inexperience, were watching and waiting, one eye on the reports from the *Beobachtungsdienst,* their deciphering service. They knew how important supplies were for the beleaguered British in the Middle East and they already had a *B-Dienst* message containing the sailing date and the convoys' routes, times of departures and meeting places, even the stragglers' route which even the masters of the merchant ships didn't yet know. They had picked it up in a signal from America. With the Atlantic telegraph cables overloaded, the signal had been sent by radio, so that it had become potentially insecure the moment it was transmitted, and they had already moved the *Gruppe Heydt*, a pack of U-boats on station slightly to the north of the expected route of the convoy, further south. A second group, just released from a recent battle in the Atlantic and refuelled from milch cow submarines, was also moving south at full speed. Those with enough torpedoes left were to form a line which would be reinforced by new boats from Germany and older boats from France. The two groups would be known in signals as 'Markgraf' and 'Herzog' and it was expected that it would take several days for them to get into position.

That same afternoon, a signal arrived at Jum addressed to Group Captain Strudwick, the station commander and to Wing Commanders Mackintosh and Molyneux.

Mackintosh received his first and appeared in Molyneux' office a couple of minutes later.

'You were right, sport,' he said. 'Things are happening. Those replacements you were talking about are a fact. Here they are. Due off the coast next month, in our sphere of influence for two days, then into Freetown for water and stores before taking off for the Cape and the Middle East. This is it, sport.'

'Pity there aren't more of us,' Molyneux said.

'Or that Lungi isn't yet operational.'

There was a moment's silence as they thought of the new airfield being constructed just across the mouth of the Rokel for the new four-engined American aircraft they so desperately needed.

'The buggers sank eleven ships – seventy thousand tons – off this coast in March,' Mackintosh pointed out. 'We could do with a few of those long-range jobs Bomber Command's beginning to lose every night over Germany.'

'Or some of these new radar-directed lights we've heard of,' Molyneux agreed. 'They say they're death to a submarine at night.'

'Which is the only time you can catch the bastards on the surface,' Mackintosh said.

'This is our last chance, sport. If the convoy system can't deliver the goods, where do we go next?' He paused and puffed at his pipe. 'Just to help matters, I hear we're losing Warrant Officer Hacker. Going home for a commission.'

Hacker, the engineer warrant officer, was an ex-apprentice, one of that splendid body of men who were the backbone of the RAF workshops, and Molyneux considered the information, hoping that Hacker's replacement would be as good as Hacker.

'He was due home, anyway,' he said. 'Time-expired, like a few more. I hear a ship's due in.'

Nobody ever knew where the news of homegoing ships came from, only that there seemed to be remarkably few of them. The lean stooping men who had finished their tour of duty watched for them like hawks, because though hundreds seemed to pass, going south, none ever seemed to come back. Most time-expired men were bitterly convinced that the harbours of the Middle East were packed with idle ships, and when one – they never seemed to come in twos – arrived, the time-expireds immediately began to panic that they'd be forgotten.

The new arrivals in their unfaded khaki, their skins still pink and white and healthy, wondered what they were getting so worked up about. They couldn't understand the anxiety, because they'd not long come from green fields, English beer, and Vera Lynn on the radio, and had not yet realised that in Jum there was nothing but boredom, heat, sickness and flies, and that the very absence of war was what really got you down so that rumours of homegoing ships and clearance chits became the most important things in life. As the old hands had discovered, there was more to being in a war than facing the enemy with your teeth bared.

And this time, though nobody was yet aware of it, there was even more than that.

PART TWO

Crisis

'...The critical phase of the U-boat war cannot be long postponed. A bolder and more reckless strategy and concentration against shipping of immediate military importance are the keynotes of present enemy policy...'

Admiralty report. 1942

'...General Rommel positively asserts that, providing he can be supplied from Italy and providing the British are prevented from reinforcing their army, he will be able to defeat them again outside Cairo. It is confidently felt that the British cannot be expected to hold their present position without the men and the machines they need. Even with reinforcements, they will have difficulty...'

Intelligence digest of the Kriegsmarine,
9 July 1942

Ginger had not been wrong when he had said that X-X-ray's crash had been witnessed by two other men. So had O-Orange's.

They came from a small group of wooden buildings in the hills near Bonai. The sign on the gate announced that it was the base camp of an iron ore prospecting company. A lot of digging went on in the protectorate, most of it near Pepel on the river Rokel, or nearer the coast and the river Bic at Yima where it was possible to scoop the ore out of the hillside with ease. Mining engineers were always moving about the protectorate looking for new sites, because Sierra Leone seemed to be built on iron ore in thick deposits of rich red haematite, and this group of huts at Bonai had been erected ten years before by the Dutch Jan van der Pas Company which worked the mine at Yima. It had come to nothing, however. The area had yielded little and the huts had been left empty and until recently unused.

Situated in the hills, Bonai was away from the curiosity of the native tribes and the coastal Creoles. There was a stream giving fresh water and it was within easy reach of Freetown. Officially, the men there were the Sierra Leone Land Survey Company. Unofficially, they were nothing of the kind.

Several months before, while running a school for U-boat officers in the Baltic, a Westphalian U-boat expert, *Kapitänleutnant* Gunther Heidegger, had been ordered to Berlin by Admiral Dönitz. Heidegger was one of the lucky U-boat captains from the first wave of lone-wolf operators of 1939 and 1940. His contemporaries, Prien, Endrass, Schepke, Kretschmer, were all gone by this time, either dead or prisoners of war, and only Heidegger and a few more had survived the battle of the Atlantic to teach the newcomers their trade.

As he'd arrived at naval headquarters in the Tirpitz Ufer, Heidegger had been warned by an aide to be careful. Because of the recent British raid on St Nazaire, Admiral Dönitz had had to give up his headquarters near Lorient in France and was temporarily in Berlin.

'And *Onkel* Karl doesn't like it,' the aide whispered.

He had led the way along the corridors past closely guarded rooms where batteries of teleprinters received signals from listening stations all over Europe, from as far north as Finland to a clandestine one operated, with the connivance of the Spanish government, near Seville.

Slightly built and sharp-featured, the admiral was looking irritated and Heidegger had wondered what was coming and if he were to be sent back to sea. Successes came more sparingly these days and perhaps Dönitz was considering using a few of the old hands to stiffen the new boys. Heidegger had no wish to go because he had recently married and marriage was inclined to dampen a man's ardour for taking risks.

Dönitz had come quickly to the point. 'You must be well aware,' he said, 'that General Rommel in North Africa now feels he has the measure of the British there.'

Heidegger had smiled. 'Indeed, sir.'

Dönitz' expression didn't slip. 'It's his intention to throw them out of North Africa,' he went on, 'to occupy the Suez Canal zone and push on towards India. His first move will take him to the gates of Cairo itself.'

After the British defeat in Libya, it seemed very possible and, because Dönitz wasn't a man given to boasting, Heidegger had been prepared to accept what he said.

'But, of course,' Dönitz had continued, 'the British will make every effort to see the *Afrika Korps* doesn't succeed – indeed, that *they* are thrown out of Africa themselves.'

'That would seem obvious, sir.'

'We have news, in fact, that they're already preparing counter-attacks and have been scraping the barrel in England and even in the United States. We have information of new tanks, new anti-tank guns, new aircraft, new self-propelled guns. However, since the Mediterranean was closed to them by the Luftwaffe, convoys initiated in New York, Nova Scotia, and the Clyde now have to go via the Cape of Good Hope and, because they're short of escorts, they meet in the Atlantic and proceed together to the only good watering and supply harbour on the West Coast of Africa – Freetown, in Sierra Leone. I need hardly say that these convoys are of vital importance to the British.' Dönitz sat back in his chair and gestured. 'Though the air cover provided – over the Atlantic by the British is still incomplete, Hudsons and Catalinas are now operating from Gibraltar, and Sunderlands and Catalinas from Freetown, so that sinkings off the bulge of Africa have declined. However, I expect this to be only temporary because escorts are not always provided just there and ships are still sometimes routed independently, and I intend an offensive off Cape Town to draw away more ships of the Royal Navy.'

Heidegger had listened quietly, wondering how all this affected him.

'British naval resources,' Dönitz went on quietly, 'are already fully strained by the Atlantic and, with the war now extended to the Far East, they can't expect much help from the Americans, so that, with demands from other theatres, their long-range aircraft in West Africa have been reduced in numbers.' He leaned forward. 'Meanwhile the Vichy authorities in French West Africa, Guinea and Senegal are growing concerned about the shortage of supplies from Europe and would be glad to see the war brought to an end.

'General Hatziger, the Commander-in-Chief, in Southern French Guinea, is a known sympathizer. Moreover, black French subjects move regularly across the border into Sierra Leone and, since the British there seem to take little notice of them they obviously include some of our agents. And, because there's still a telephone service between Sierra Leone and French Guinea, the problems of communication don't arise. There are high hills along the coast, and a coast-watching service and a listening station have been established near Freetown. Now, as you doubtless know, British codes and ciphers are being read by the *Beobachtungsdienst*, our deciphering service, so that we know the position, course and speed of all British convoys and are reading their Admiralty U-boat situation reports, even to the point of knowing where the British *think* our boats are. With the Middle East as important as it is, so too are the military convoys round the Cape.'

Dönitz sat back and stared fixedly at Heidegger. 'It will be your job,' he said, 'to see they don't arrive. The coast of West Africa has become crucially important. You're being sent there to organize things.'

Slipping through Vichy France with a few others, all English speakers – naval men, one or two members of the Dutch Nazi Party and anglophobe Frenchmen who knew Senegal, Guinea and the Ivory Coast – Heidegger had not found it difficult to reach Algiers and Morocco. From there, he and his companions had made their way to Casablanca and finally to Conakry in French Guinea. The British navy's destruction of the French fleet at Oran in 1940 had created many enemies there and the French general in Conakry had been notorious for his dislike of the British even before Oran and the Gaullist fiasco at Casablanca, so that it was a simple matter to slip across the Great Scarcies river into Sierra Leone. The coastal watching station and the radio station were already functioning under the guise of the Sierra Leone Land Survey Company and Heidegger's first job had been to open an office in Freetown, from whose windows there was a view of the harbour.

In the meantime Rommel had struck again and at that moment the British were heavily involved in trying to hit back with a counter attack. So far, it had seemed, things were not going well for them and convoys were hurriedly assembling in New York and the Clyde to carry whatever could be spared from Europe. The problem for the Germans was not the discovery of their dates of departure – *B-Dienst* was able to do that with ease – it was aircraft. When submarines operated in wolf packs, the first boat to sight the intended victims radioed position, course and speed for the rest of the pack to move in, but this was something which, because of their low speed when submerged, had to be done on the surface and aircraft could force them to dive and lose contact. Without aircraft, however, it was the British who were fighting blind, and it had seemed at once to Heidegger that Dönitz' plan was incomplete and that he could do far more than merely report movements.

With the reports he had sent to Berlin had gone a plan of his own. Attempts to sabotage ships were never easy, since they had to be made in the middle of a crowded harbour, but the flying boats at isolated Jum, on which so much depended, were only too vulnerable.

The plan had gone first to an agent at Pepel and from there to another agent at Kambia, which was close to the Great Scarcies river. From there it had crossed into French Guinea by runner on one of the ferries over the river. The agent in neutral Conakry had radioed direct to Berlin. It had taken no more than twenty-four hours and within a few hours more the answer had come back by the same route.

'Operate!'

They had put the plan into operation at once and X-X-ray and O-Orange had proved its efficiency.

The destruction of X-X-ray and O-Orange had been no accident, any more than the discovery of *George C Grieves* en route for Freetown. The Royal Navy's signal about her from Bathurst had been easily intercepted by Heidegger's listening post and almost at once a message about the arrival of 'a lorry carrying supplies and travelling alone' had been passed by telephone to Pepel and passed on again to Kambia and across the ferry on the Great Scarcies river. Even her limping passage up the Bunce hadn't gone unnoticed by the two men who ran the office of the Sierra Leone Land Survey Company in Freetown. Both apparently Dutchmen, they had debated for a while, then, after allowing a little time to pass to allay suspicion, had sent a guarded message by telephone to Heidegger who sent off a further message to Berlin via Pepel and French Guinea. He was well pleased with his organisation and that night they celebrated with whisky bought openly in Freetown from the United Africa Company.

'A total write-off!' The man who spoke was pink-faced and good-looking in a hard, thin-lipped way. He gestured at the man alongside him, a youngster with clean-cut features, handsome – almost beautiful – in the blond blue-eyed manner so admired by German exponents of Aryan philosophy. 'Willer and I saw it.'

'You went to look?' Heidegger's smile had vanished.

'From the river.'

'Then you are stupid, Lorenz. You might have been noticed. Anyone watching such things too closely could be suspect.'

'There were others watching. Half the people from the river villages were there. Half Freetown turned out, I gather, when they passed through the harbour.'

'It was still dangerous.' Heidegger frowned. 'And when you speak – even to me – I would prefer that you speak in English. It must become a habit. We never know who might be listening.'

Lorenz frowned. As *Kapitänleutnant* Heidegger was well aware, Lorenz was at Bonai not only to perform specific duties, but also to watch the others and report on them.

'I'm sorry, *sir*.' Lorenz switched to English and stressed the word very deliberately to show he had no fear of Heidegger. 'I was merely enthusiastic. And excited at our success.'

'Excitement's a luxury we can't afford,' Heidegger said.

The steward refilled their glasses. He was thickset but not ill-looking, though heavy eyebrows gave him an intimidating appearance.

'Whisky, sir?' he asked. 'On the bill of the Sierra Leone Land Survey Company.'

Heidegger accepted the drink without comment and used his finger to pick out an ant's wing. Just behind him, Lorenz nodded at the steward.

'Thank you, Pfitzner.'

The two men smiled at each other, and Heidegger frowned. He disliked Lorenz but he regarded *Obergefreiter* Pfitzner, who he knew had been sent as Lorenz' assistant and handyman, ready to run his errands and to toady to anyone on his behalf, as nothing but an unthinking lout. He liked to get drunk, even on native palm wine; when he ate his manners were those of a pig; and Heidegger knew he was growing desperate for a woman. Any time now, he thought, Pfitzner would break out and, if he behaved as stupidly as Heidegger expected him to, he could be the end of them all.

'There's one other thing, Lorenz.'

Lorenz turned. As he did so, the door opened and a woman entered. Young Willer's eyebrows shot up and the smile on his face grew wider to one of sheer delight.

'This is *Fräulein* Fallada. Magda Fallada. She arrived while you were away.'

Lorenz was beaming now with undiluted pleasure. 'This is an honour, *Fräulein*,' he said. 'To what do we owe this delightful intrusion?'

'*Fräulein* Fallada is part of Dr Goebbels' organization,' Heidegger explained. 'She arrived in Sierra Leone via Senegal in 1940.'

'To do what, *Fräulein*?' Lorenz asked.

'My job's trouble.' The woman said coolly.

'We've made a study of it. We find local grievances and use them to the advantage of the *Führer*. I was in Sudetenland before the war. There the grievance was the German minority's lack of power. Here it's rice and the mixture of nationalities. The tribesmen are against the Creoles. The Creoles are against the Syrians. And the Syrians are against everybody. I've been up-country near Kenema and Port Loko. The British want to put right the troubles caused among the different ethnic groups by the shortage of rice. It was my job to exacerbate them.' She smiled. 'We win *our* battles with words, not guns.'

'Guns are still useful when the words run out,' Lorenz said. 'The essence of war is violence.'

He was putting on the act of a tough warrior, a German superman, and Heidegger interrupted before he could say any more. 'Until we can get her safely across the border to Conakry,' he said sharply, '*Fräulein* Fallada will remain here out of sight of the authorities. It's our duty to make her comfortable.'

Despite his words, he wasn't happy to have the woman there. She was tall, blonde, and well-made, but there was the same assured look on her face that there was on Lorenz' heavy features. Somehow they went together.

Lorenz was still smiling. 'I hope your departure won't be too soon,' he smiled.

'It will be as soon as possible,' Magda Fallada admitted. 'I don't like Sierra Leone.'

'As far as the British are concerned,' Heidegger interrupted, '*Fräulein* Fallada, like the rest of us, is Dutch. She is the widow of Dirk Fallada, one of our engineers.' He gave a thin smile. 'You'll remember he died last year. Because of the U-boats, she has been unable to go home.'

Lorenz' grin seemed set in plaster. 'I remember,' he said. 'Such a sad end. And widows need consolation, don't they? Perhaps we'll be able to take her mind off her sorrows, won't we, Pfitzner?'

Pfitzner grinned back at him. His heavy eyebrows gave him an evil look. 'That we will, sir,' he said.

Willer, twenty years old and beautiful as a girl with huge eyes and long dark lashes, moved forward, his expression eager, to replenish the woman's glass. He was slight and small boned, and Heidegger had often wondered if he were a homosexual. His interest in Magda Fallada seemed to suggest he wasn't, but Heidegger didn't think he'd get far with her because he was too young, too idealistic and too inexperienced, and the Fallada woman had a hard, knowledgeable look about her. Lately Heidegger had been watching Willer closely because his face had been wearing a strained look so that Heidegger had a suspicion he wasn't as fit as he pretended and that West Africa didn't suit him. Like Lorenz, Willer was a good Party man, completely sold on the Nazi cult, and Heidegger suspected he might be hiding some illness so as not to let the *Führer* down.

At the moment, his face was flushed and his eyes were bright. Watched by Pfitzner, he and Lorenz were manoeuvring round each other like cocks round a barnyard hen. The woman's eyes were on Lorenz. Clearly some chemistry between them was working already, and Heidegger didn't like it. There was no place for a woman in what they were doing, and he watched them quietly, a tall intellectual-looking man, his fair hair brushed flat against his narrow skull.

As other men appeared, Heidegger gestured to them to drink with them, and for a while they stood discussing what had happened. As they finished their drinks and left one by one, the black man who looked after the bar disappeared to wash the glasses, but not before quietly pouring a bottle of beer for himself in the security of his little cupboard-like bar. When he'd finished, he picked up a little raffia bag containing more stolen bottles of beer, well-padded so they wouldn't clink, and set off at a jog-trot down the hill to Hawkinge Town. He had nearly seven miles to go.

t w o

The presence of Magda Fallada at Boina had created a different atmosphere at once.

Heidegger was aware of it as soon he appeared for breakfast the morning after her arrival. Lorenz, who was never very good at getting up, was already in the dining hall, dressed in freshly washed and starched khaki.

'The very picture of a successful geologist,' he crowed.

The other officers were also considerably smarter and cleaner than Heidegger had seen them for some time, Willer prominent among them with his girl's complexion and shining handsome face; all carefully shaved, their hair plastered down in spikes; even *Obergefreiter* Pfitzner, with his dark eyebrows and evil eyes, was wearing a clean white coat and had polished his shoes.

Magda Fallada's entrance would have made a film star jealous. Everybody snapped to their feet as she appeared in the doorway and several heels clicked. Heidegger frowned. He'd warned them against the habit long since. If anything gave away a German it was the damned heel-clicking.

He rose and was about to gesture to the empty place alongside him when Lorenz yanked out the chair next to his. Magda smiled at him, gave a little bow towards Heidegger in greeting, and accepted. Lorenz pushed the chair in and sat down alongside her.

'Pfitzner! Coffee!'

Pfitzner's move forward was more a sidle than a stride and he was leaning over her with far more enthusiasm than he ever showed towards anyone else, taking a quick glance, Heidegger noticed, down the open top of her shirt as he did so.

After breakfast, Heidegger took her on one side and told her what they were doing and what his plan consisted of.

'Why try to get at the ships in the harbour,' he said, 'when it's easier to destroy the aircraft?'

'There are many ways of killing a cat,' she agreed. 'As you doubtless know, we've investigated the possibility of stirring up trouble in British-dominated areas. Canada, New Zealand and Australia are out but South Africa has a strong anti-British element and Sierra Leone is another place with a great potential for disaffection.'

He didn't reply and she decided he was stuffy and frigid. 'We have agents in all the big townships,' she went on. 'Sefadum. Kabala. Makeni. Bo. Kenema. Port Loko. To say nothing of Freetown itself. In Freetown, though, we found, like you, that we couldn't do much because it's been British so long they think British. But there *are* nationalists and we've been using them. Trouble disrupts the supplies of bauxite, diamonds and iron ore, and disruption's as much a part of war as shooting.'

During the morning, *Obergefreiter* Pfitzner produced coffee, something that hadn't happened for some time because of the shortage of coffee beans, and he hovered round Magda with his tray, breathing heavily, his eyes on her figure and legs. Heidegger watched him coldly. It was part of Pfitzner's job to buy food and it had been noticed that he always took his time, returning later than he should. Despite his look of evil, he was a handsome enough man, strong and with good features, who claimed to be able to get any woman he wanted. He had been a steward on the *Bremen* before the war and Heidegger had once heard him boasting of his conquests among the first-class passengers. He'd been in and out of French ports a lot, picking up a facility in the language and a habit of smoking French cigarettes, and claimed he had learned his technique with women from the French pimps in Marseilles.

Aware of the danger, he had warned Pfitzner about his behaviour but the petty officer had stood in front of him at attention, his face blank, his eyes masked, giving nothing away. Heidegger had always accepted that his loyalty was first to Lorenz but now, with the arrival of Magda Fallada, he was doubtful even about that.

When the group broke up, Magda Fallada was complaining of the heat. Arriving at the door of the hut she'd been given, she found Pfitzner waiting.

'Thought you might like an iced drink,' he suggested.

'That would be very pleasant. But not now.'

'It won't take a minute. I'll knock on your door.'

'I'm going to shower.'

Pfitzner's smile came. 'Nothing better than a cold drink under the shower, *Fräulein*,' he said. 'I can pass it to you. I'll not look.'

She gave him an icy stare. 'I'd rather you went away,' she said.

Pfitzner was still arguing when Lorenz appeared. 'What do you want?' he demanded.

'Just asking if *Fräulein* Fallada would like a cold drink,' Pfitzner said smoothly.

'He's being a nuisance,' Magda grated. 'I'd be glad if you'd get rid of him.'

Lorenz turned to Pfitzner. 'Clear off, Pfitzner,' he snapped.

'*Obergefreiter* Pfitzner, *sir*.'

Lorenz scowled. Having travelled with Pfitzner as a civilian across Occupied France, he had listened to his stories and bought him drinks. Perhaps he had allowed the easy manner to go too far and Pfitzner was taking advantage of it, treating him differently from the other officers – a little more familiar, a few too many smiles. It seemed to be time to bring him up sharply.

'Away you go, Pfitzner,' he said. 'And don't bother *Fräulein* Fallada again!'

Pfitzner gave him a sour smile. 'I bet *you* won't go,' he said quietly.

'That'll be enough of that. Remember I'm an officer.'

Pfitzner was unperturbed. 'And *I* know why you were sent here' he said. 'One of your duties is to watch Heidegger. Well, let me inform you, *Herr Leutnant*, that one of *my* duties is to watch you.'

Lorenz had realized this all along. 'Push off, Pfitzner ' he snapped, and stepped through the door where the woman had disappeared, closing it firmly in Pfitzner's face. As he turned away, Pfitzner's eyes were glowing with anger.

Every man in Boina was eager to be with Magda Fallada but because of their duties most of them had little opportunity and Lorenz was leading the field.

She was something to relieve the tedium of West Africa, he decided, and was built for it, too, and the fact that she made no attempt to repulse him convinced him that he wouldn't have to try too hard. The Tropics affected women as much as men and he ran his tongue over his lips as he watched her moving about.

'What are you thinking?' As he caught her eyes on him, amused and interested, he jumped to attention.

'I wouldn't have thought I'd have needed to tell you that,' he said.

She smiled. 'Perhaps it's a good job I'm not staying too long. You're a good-looking man.'

'You're good-looking yourself.'

'This climate strips the body of surplus flesh. I have a better figure now than I've ever had.'

'I wouldn't mind running my hands over it.'

She stared at him mockingly. 'You know where my hut is.'

He swallowed. 'I have things to do,' he said gruffly. 'Things to organize. I have to leave Boina for a reconnaissance with Paul Willer. RAF security's been tightened up and we need to find out a few things. But I'll be back. Then there'll be time to relax.'

She laughed. 'I prefer more spontaneity,' she said. 'I don't like being placed on the agenda for when time becomes available.'

When Lorenz returned, he drew Pfitzner to one side.

'I want some whisky,' he said. 'No more than a few tots. What's left of the bottle will do.'

Pfitzner frowned. 'Whisky's hard to get,' he growled.

'I'm entitled to my ration. You can knock it off that.'

Pfitzner stared back relentlessly. 'Why is it an officer can chase women out here and a petty officer can't?'

Lorenz turned. 'Have a care what you say, Pfitzner.'

'And you have a care what *you* say – sir!' Pfitzner snapped back. 'You might be starting something. I've been warned by the commanding officer to keep away from women. If it applies to me, it applies to you, too.'

Lorenz was wondering how to react, but he wasn't sure of his ground and in the end he decided to let the disrespect pass. Carrying the bottle with the remains of the whisky, he strolled off through the darkness, trying to affect indifference. Reaching Magda's quarters, he scratched at the door with his fingernail. It brought an immediate response.

'Who is it?'

'Me. Karl Lorenz. I'm back. Can I come in? I've managed to get hold of some of Pfitzner's whisky.'

The door opened and he slipped inside.

'I won't turn on the lights,' she said quietly.

'Then we shan't have to close the shutters. It'll be cooler.'

There was still a moon and he found her hands and pulled her towards him. She didn't resist and he felt her body against his.

'I'm not sure it isn't too hot for this sort of thing,' she murmured.

'It's never too hot,' Lorenz said.

'I'll bet you were a devil with the girls in Berlin.'

He didn't say anything, allowing her to think what she wished. As he kissed her, her head went back and she sighed, leaning back in his arms. 'We've got too many clothes on,' she whispered.

Lorenz' hand lifted to the opening of her shirt. As he undid the buttons, her lips parted and she gave a little gasp.

'For God's sake,' she said abruptly. 'Let's stop behaving like children. All this damned fumbling and mumbling. We both know what we want. The temperature reduces you to the level of a bitch on heat.'

Snatching at their clothes, throwing them to the floor, they clutched each other in the semi-darkness and stumbled towards the bed, to fall on it with a twang of springs. The sound didn't go unnoticed by *Obergefreiter* Pfitzner in the shadows outside.

Heidegger didn't take twenty-four hours to become aware that Lorenz was visiting Magda Fallada's hut.

He had deliberately given her the cabin next to his own, feeling she was safe there; but, late at night heading back to the office for a file he had left behind, he heard voices.

Abruptly, he realized he was jealous and in that moment that he hated Lorenz. It was ridiculous that he of all people should be so concerned, but the thought of the two of them together in bed, naked, perspiring, panting, made him think of his wife in Germany and he almost groaned aloud.

Every sailor knew the Tropics as the fornicating latitudes. When it was hot and the moon was huge, lonely men at sea always thought of the women they'd left behind. Once, years ago now, before he'd joined the *Kriegsmarine* and been only an apprentice in the merchant service, he'd been moved enough by the moon, the heat and his longing for women to write a passionate letter to an old girlfriend he hadn't seen for months. After he'd posted it, he'd been horrified by the things he'd put in it. It seemed he still wasn't too old to be affected and, despite his wish to remain faithful to his wife both in thought and deed, the idea of Lorenz with Magda Fallada brought to his mind visions that were grotesque in their obscenity.

When he got the opportunity, he drew Lorenz to one side to warn him.

'If I can see what's going on,' he said, 'so can the others.'

Lorenz studied him with amused eyes. 'You jealous, sir?'

The girl was sitting at the other side of the living quarters, listening to the gramophone played by Willer, who looked like an ardent young god. She was sitting back in her chair, her skirt pulled above her knees, and Heidegger could see her thighs, warm and soft and enticing. The sight made him swallow uncomfortably and he frowned because he *was* jealous.

'Need you flaunt her?' he asked.

Oh, it's nothing.' Lorenz was enjoying tormenting him, he knew. 'We simply have the same political views. We discuss things a lot.'

As they were talking, the naval telegraphist who handled their radio traffic was busy over his set. As the thin cheeping of Morse stopped, he signed off, threw down his pencil and headed for Heidegger's quarters. Heidegger examined the message carefully. It had come from the *Beobachtungsdienst*, and had been passed on by the *Operationsabteilung Befelshaber der Unterseeboote*. It was marked '*München Blau*', which referred to U-boat positions, course changes and the sailing dates for convoys, and it told Heidegger exactly what he'd been expecting – that the British had been assembling convoys of men and materials for the Middle East – and gave dates, times of departure and projected courses.

He studied the signal then pulled forward a map. The area between Sierra Leone and Pernambuco in Brazil represented the narrowest portion of the Atlantic, the funnel through which, with the Mediterranean forbidden to them, all Allied Middle East convoys had to pass. If the Atlantic could be compared to a city, he thought, this was the one area where density of traffic could occur and U-boats strategically placed across it could do tremendous damage.

Because of its undeveloped state, he knew Freetown was not a satisfactory convoy assembly point or command head-quarters, yet since the fall of France and the loss to the Allies of Dakar and Casablanca, it had had to be used by the British because it was strategically well placed and no better base existed before Cape Town. Every supply ship and troop transport bound for the Middle East had to pass through the area and most had to call at Freetown for fuel, water and stores. Despite this, the whole South Atlantic Command at that period in time possessed only one destroyer flotilla, five sloops and some dozen serviceable corvettes, together with one or two armed merchant cruisers, anti-sub trawlers and small auxiliary vessels.

He glanced again at the signal. *Wolf packs Bennigsen and Heydt are being moved into the area. You will give them every assistance by halting the aircraft which might impede them. Possible British might try to use Lungi field, at present incomplete. Up to you to do all you can to hinder them.* It couldn't have been plainer.

He sent for Lorenz and the two of them began to study the charts. Lungi, on the flat land across the river from Freetown, was being built to take the big American Liberators, which could fly there directly from the States but, though the field was not yet complete, there was always a possibility the British might push in something smaller to help the flying boats.

'I'll send Willer in again,' Lorenz said. 'He studied in London and Paris and can pass as English or French without trouble. For someone as pretty as he is, he's remarkably efficient. He can do the job at Jum first.'

'By boat as usual?'

'Oh, no.' Lorenz smiled confidently. 'They've tightened their security since our last success. An RAF launch makes an hourly patrol during the night these days. He'll have to get into the camp.'

'Can he?'

'There are lorries going in and out all the time, always full of men.'

'...who need identity cards.'

'There are ways of overcoming that. As I discovered at cadet school, and doubtless you did, too, sir.'

Heidegger acknowledged the point. 'How does he get away from Jum?'

'We've thought of that one, too.' Lorenz smiled. 'Willer's a strong swimmer. We can have a canoe waiting down-tide for him. It'll be fitted with shaded lights. We'll put him across the river where he'll be picked up and taken to Lungi. He knows what to take out. You can't level a runway without diggers.'

'It's a lot for one man.'

'Willer's keen.'

'Is he all right?' Heidegger asked. 'He's looked ill for some time and I hear he's been complaining of a pain in his abdomen. Perhaps we ought to have him looked at.'

'Where?' Lorenz demanded. 'There'd be too many questions asked. He'll have to take his chances like the rest of us.'

'What's his trouble exactly?'

'Usual West African trots, I suppose. It's nothing and I have everything set up. He'll be driven to Kumrabai, if possible as far as Aku Town, and go the rest of the way on foot. There are no guards because Lungi's not working yet and the place's smothered with black and white labour. Nobody will question him. He can always get in touch with our man at Mahera along the coast if anything goes wrong. And if he's in trouble we have a sympathizer at Gbabaj who'll hide him. Witte and Johansen in Freetown are also in contact and when he's finished he can hide with them. He could be useful. Witte reports there's a mine and depth charge dump at Giuru that it's possible to get inside.'

Heidegger frowned. Lorenz' enthusiasm was wearing and he was beginning to wonder if the occasional destruction of a flying boat was the best method of completing his task. Despite their aircraft shortages, the RAF always seemed able to dredge up a new one from somewhere. It was beginning to seem, in fact, that when the expected convoys arrived the best way to prevent action against the U-boats was not to destroy the machines in ones and twos but to prevent the use of the whole station at Jum.

Calling for a map of the area, he sat down to study it. Pfitzner placed a cup of coffee alongside his elbow but he didn't seem to notice his nod of thanks so that Heidegger wondered what was going through his head. Once thick as two thieves, he and Lorenz now hardly spoke.

Bending over the map, he studied the line of the Bunce and the five-mile-long lagoon where the flying boats were operating. The land on both sides was edged with mangrove swamps but here and there they narrowed where the higher land pushed into the river. Tracing his finger along the shore, he stopped at a point between Disp and Kumrabai. Machine guns at that point could command the take-off and landing area and the outside trots where the flying boats were moored. There were the remains of a native village there by the name of Minga – emptied of its inhabitants since the British had cleared the area to cut down the breeding grounds of the anopheles mosquito. It was now only a group of dilapidated mud and wattle huts on a spit of land with the remains of their little plots of cultivation and a few neglected banana and pawpaw plants. It would make a good base and two machine guns there could stop all flying from Jum.

Heidegger began to make notes. For the time being they would remain at Boina where they were safe and move down to Minga when they received news of the approach of the Middle East convoys. He looked at the map again. He was under no delusions that the British would not react quickly. Perhaps he needed somewhere stronger where he could hole up. His finger moved over the map again and stopped over the red spot that marked the Jan van der Pas Mining Company's workings at Yima. There was a railway there which ran to Makinkundi on the Bunce and a clear means of retreat to the sea down the river Bic. He moved his notes and papers for a moment. The *Maréchal Grouchy* could be off the coast if they needed her. Her captain was in the pay of the German agent at Conakry and they could escape via the Bic at night and be in Vichy French waters fifty miles to the north before the British realized they had gone.

He leafed through his code books for the name of the German agent at Conakry and began to draft a signal. For the first time he began to feel confident. The period of small enterprises was finished, he decided. They were going into the problem properly. With the flying boats grounded and the convoys largely destroyed, Rommel could move with safety in North Africa, through Syria into Iraq, Persia and Northern India. With the victorious German army still sweeping forward towards Stalingrad, the Russians would be in no position to stop them and the British had plenty of enemies in India who were itching for freedom.

He sat for a long time, lost in his thoughts, before he realized it had started raining again. It drummed and hissed outside, and a flash of lightning lit the tossing trees and the shuddering leaves of the undergrowth. A fly, caught in a spider's web, buzzed in a useless attempt to release itself, the sound coming above the drumbeat of the downpour and the ragged drip-drip on the leaves alongside the hut.

He moved to the open window and stared out at the sliding shimmer of the rain. It blew in as mist to leave a damp patch on the floor and make his clothes clammy, but his mind was busy and he barely noticed.

He became aware of the damp at last and hurriedly shut the window, then he turned and stared at the charts again before slapping his hand down on them and calling for Pfitzner.

'Pfitzner,' he said. 'Bring me a brandy.'

As Pfitzner vanished, he smiled to himself. It was amazing how much could hang on so little. A destroyed convoy off West Africa, lost because it lacked support from the air, could change the whole shape of the war.

three

The rumours about a homegoing ship were finally confirmed when the time-expired men – Corporal Fox, Corporal Feverel, Corporal Bates, Kneller, Ginger Donnelly, Nobby Clark and all the rest of them – were told to collect their clearance chits.

Holding the magic slip of paper at arm's length, Kneller couldn't stop smiling. 'If there were some beer in the camp,' he said, 'I'd get drunk.'

'If we had some ham,' Feverel said dryly, 'we could have some ham and eggs if we had some eggs.'

As he appended his signature to their slips, Hobson looked up at them. They were a scarecrow lot in their frayed shirts and shorts, lean, stooped and yellow as canaries, and at that moment soaked with rain. He'd known them a long time and he regarded them with affection.

'I'm glad I'm going home, too,' he said. 'Because I should hate to run this place without you lot.'

They bridled, still dazed at their good luck and pleased with the compliment.

'On the other hand,' Hobson went on, and they guessed there was a catch to it, 'you've not finished work as usually happens with clearance chits. The new lot who've arrived to take your places were all trained or promoted in the last year and they've all got white knees and know about as much about marine section work as my Great-Aunt Fanny knows about steam navigation. So I shall expect you to carry them until you leave. However, for your information, there's a lorry going to Freetown tomorrow morning, so you'd better make sure you're on it if you want to buy presents to take home. We'll manage for a day. I hope you find something. I never can'.

Warm thoughts of home in their minds, the time-expired men took down their thick blue uniforms from where they had hung for months on the walls of the huts. They could just see themselves getting the glad eye from the girls in their native towns. Unfortunately, to their dismay, they found that the rats and the moths had chewed holes in their trousers in the most unexpected and embarrassing places.

However, for their trip to Freetown they were lucky.

Getting out of camp was a rarity these days and going to Freetown was virtually unknown, so that to find a fine day for it in the middle of the rainy season was a gift from the gods.

The skies had cleared and they had all put on clean khaki, washed and ironed – scorched a little here and there, too – by the dhobi boys. Even leading Aircraftman Alec Donnelly looked clean for a change.

'If the Duke of Windsor had joined the Raff,' Feverel told him cheerfully, 'he'd have looked like you, Ginger.'

The journey to Freetown was hot and dusty because there were too many men crammed in the back of the lorry and they had to stand up all the way, clutching the stanchions that supported the canvas cover, rolling and swaying together as they swung round the corners and the hills.

Trixie Tristram, as time-expired as the rest, his bleached hair combed, his starched khaki immaculate, enjoyed himself enormously as he bounced against Feverel's sturdy shape.

'And there was this German singing this song, ducky,' he was saying to one of his boyfriends. ' "Lili Marlene", it's called. The Germans are all at it these days. There's one group that sing it falsetto. I bet they've all got blond hair and blue eyes. I told the padre. Honest, I think he's going round the bend. He thinks he's some sort of secret service and I'm Mata Hari.'

In the end Feverel gave him a shove. 'For God's sake,' he snapped. 'Lean on your breakfast.'

Trixie turned to look at his hot angry face. 'I think you're gorgeous when you're cross, Fevvy,' he said.

On arrival, the first reaction of the lorryload of men, saffron with mepacrine and for the most part devoid of excess energy, was to go to the harbour. From the wall above the market – a riot of Technicolor where the mammies sold pawpaws, bananas, limes and green oranges – you could see everything that was happening.

There were two vessels moored one behind the other, both converted liners. One was the naval depot ship, *Philoctetes*, which had been there ever since the war began and was said to rest on a reef of empty bottles; the other was an armed merchant cruiser which had limped in after a fight with a German raider the year before. There were no means of repairing her in Freetown and she lay low in the water with flooded holds, the corpses of many of her crew still bobbing against the bulkheads. What made their eyes shine, though, was a group of strange ships laying well out, surrounded by bumboats and canoes whose occupants were offering to dive for shillings while wearing top hats, frock coats or even water wings.

'That's it,' Corporal Bates said enthusiastically. 'That's the convoy for England.'

They were easily persuaded and, feeling better, set off past the stained green statue of William Wilberforce, the law courts, the cathedral and the enormous cotton tree that threw its shade over almost a hundred yards of pavement and had been a meeting place for the freed slaves when they had first arrived nearly two hundred years before. Sierra

Leone took its name from the shape of the hills behind, which resembled a lion in repose, and the thunder which rolled round them like a lion's roar in the rainy season, but the town, so fresh and green-looking from the sea, was a disappointment as usual when seen from close quarters. Hot with a breath-catching closeness, it wore a jaded midday look, drab and drained of energy as it huddled under the hills like a shabby old beggar. Every street had its reminder of the old days, and guns from the slave ships were embedded in the pavements in all sorts of odd corners.

Feverel, Kneller and Ginger found themselves in a native bar. Next door was a carpenter's shop with outside a masterpiece of West African advertising expertise: 'Bungie, Sympathetic Undertaker. Coffins supplied with hearse and uniform men at all moments. Been born sympathetic. Promise to carry on that function.'

Trixie was at the other end of the bar with his friend, and Feverel glanced at his own bottle of beer and a sticky-sweet gin and orange. 'Why is it,' he asked, 'that at headquarters and all military, naval and air force establishments in Freetown they have as much beer as they can drink and that even the bloody native bars can produce gin and whisky, while up at Jum, no more than fifteen miles away as the crow flies, we're rationed to three bottles of beer a month – when they can get it?'

It was something that never failed to puzzle them.

Afterwards, they pushed through the crowds outside the flat, unshaded façades of Syrian shops. They were situated in a mass of buildings from a dead era and were backed by the unpainted box-wood houses and the mud-and-beaten-out-tin dwellings of the poor with their rusting roofs and their air of unwanted junk. Sizzling in the sun, the sweat trickling from armpits and down spines and legs, they pushed through the brightly-hued chattering black people, their ears filled with the high-pitched sound of an African crowd – self-important clerks, mission-educated and stiff in starched linen suits; Hausa traders wearing robes of striped pyjama cloth and gold-embroidered smoking caps; labourers with twanging voices heading for the waterfront with slapping bare feet; farmers with trussed live pigs on their heads; mammies in chemise-like Mother Hubbards and gaudy Madras handkerchiefs, bearing baskets of paper-stoppered ginger beer bottles; Creole girls trying to look European, their faces ghostly with white powder, their dark lips lavender under red lipstick.

It was a riot of breathtakingly crude hues, smells and sounds. Two vultures in the centre of the road tug-of-warred over a dead pi-dog; an overloaded bus wobbled by, its African passengers chirruping like a lot of monkeys; smug cyclists worked at their bells as if they drove Rolls-Royces. The noise and the colour hit them like a hammer blow and for the first time since he'd arrived Feverel began to wish he were not going home. There was nothing in England resembling this and he knew he would never see its like again.

Everywhere in West Africa, he had to admit, wasn't like Jum. After the war, he decided they'd all exaggerate the miseries of Jum, but there were some places further south, he'd heard, where life was said to be quite bearable, even, he supposed, a few in Sierra Leone – especially round Freetown where headquarters was situated and there were beaches and bars and something to do besides twiddle your thumbs.

Refreshed by the beer, they headed for a building of whitewashed brick and corrugated iron that went by the name of the Mi-Ami Restaurant. On the wall some Creole nationalist had written 'English Go Home' and beneath it some disgruntled British serviceman had retorted, 'I wish to Christ I could.' A black figure inside the door, like a disembodied smile in the shadows, took their order and indicated a table in what looked like the loft of a barn. There was only chicken on the menu and, as they sat down, the chickens were dragged squawking from a cage by the door, slaughtered and plucked. The entrails were slung on to the tin roof to be fought over by the waiting vultures, their feet clattering on the corrugated iron sheets, right alongside the bemused customers.

Trixie Tristram was once more there, this time with a new friend, a blond blue-eyed pretty young man, deep in conversation.

'You say there's a lorry going back?' the young man was saying.

'Of course. Join us, dear. Are you time-expired, like the rest of us convicts?'

'No. Just been down to HQ to deliver some papers. From Hawkinge.'

'Didn't they lay on a car, ducky? They *are* a mean lot, aren't they? They're just as bad at Jum.'

'If I can get a lift back to Jum, I know someone in Transport who can fix a lift to Hawkinge.'

'Well, just tag along and pile on board,' Trixie said. 'Don't mention my name, though, dear, because it's supposed to be only for us old lags. What's your name?'

'Paul.'

'Mine's Derek. This is Arthur.'

By late afternoon they had all managed to fill themselves with drink and food. Trixie set off to buy lengths of material – not for female relatives in England like most of them but for himself, less intrigued for a change by the texture and the value than by the blond blue-eyed young man he'd picked up. Corporal Bates, inflamed by thoughts of home, unwisely allowed himself to be persuaded by a small boy offering his sister – who, he claimed, was that West African symbol of purity, a schoolteacher – into a native brothel that looked like a stable. Outside the door, under a roaring cloud of flies, stood a mountain of used bottles and opened tins. The

104

others, arms full of newspaper-wrapped parcels, succumbed to the blandishments of the sidewalk salesmen selling wallets, purses, writing cases and leather pouffe covers decorated with palm trees and elephants. Nobby Clark bought a splendid suitcase which he filled with lengths of Indian silk, nightdresses and pyjamas so out of date they were Edwardian, and everything else he could think of for the women of his family. As he humped it to the lorry for the return journey, he was greeted with jeers by Ginger Donnelly who, after ten years in the RAF, had seen it all before.

'Them suitcases,' he said, 'ain't leather at all. They're cardboard underneath. Chap in our 'ut bought one when the last ship 'ome came in, in February. The 'andle came out as 'e was going up the gangplank and the lot went into the 'arbour.'

Clark eyed his suitcase with considerably less enthusiasm than before and decided, when the time came, to tie it up well with rope.

The lorry was waiting near the cotton tree and they set off on the long drive back to the camp. Corporal Fox and Corporal Bates had elected for a lark to take the narrow-gauge railway that ran past Brighton and Hawkinge Town on its way to Pendembu and the borders of Liberia and French Guinea. It was quite an experience with its miniature engine and miniature carriages, and you could always rely on the driver stopping en route to buy dried fish or provide hot water for some mammy who was waiting to make coffee. Sometimes they even had beer to sell.

The lorry was free but more wearing because where the macadam ran out the red laterite surface on the road was appalling, and every few miles there were gullies crossed by bridges wide enough only for single-file traffic, and the native drivers of the West African Frontier Force liked to race for them so that most of the gullies contained the rusting wreckage of vehicles which had met in the middle.

The bush started as they left the town. The streets didn't just peter out; they stopped dead, and from then on the trees were like a solid hedge all the way to Jum. A mile or two from the town, everybody started singing, even Trixie and his boyfriend, both a little high on gin and orange. 'Bless 'em All' inevitably, because it was the song of time-expired men the whole world over.

> There's a troopship just leaving Bombay,
> Bound for old Blighty's shore,
> Heavily laden with time-expired men
> Bound for the land they adore...

The marine section sang it with special gusto because it was supposed to have been written by that predecessor of theirs, Lawrence of Arabia himself. Who else, they argued, would have had the brains to put into words so exactly the emotions of servicemen a long way from home?

Always at its hottest before it finally disappeared, the sun fried them as they clung to the lorry's stanchions, rocking and bumping and swaying as they sped up and down the hills and round the winding curves. Red and gaudy green, the land seemed to enclose them, the trees brushing the sides of the vehicle as it swayed.

A few black men waved and cheered as they passed, but there were no horses or mules, because horses and mules couldn't live in Sierra Leone. A company of native soldiers of the West African Frontier Force, tall, strong men in shorts, shirts, and huge boots designed like boats for their broad flat feet, grinned as they tramped past, and a lorryload of time-expireds from RAF, Hawkinge, exchanged insults and ribald gestures.

Dropping into a valley, they passed a stream running over a cluster of rocks where African women from a nearby village bent over the water, naked to the waist, slapping and hammering at their washing. It was a place that had already entered into poetry and song and Ginger got them singing again.

> ...And if you think that Africa calls,
> Just take a look at Swinging Tit Falls...

He was conducting his choir with a leather-handled bundu knife he'd bought as a souvenir, pretending to bring in first one side of the lorry then the other. The blond-haired airman Trixie Tristram had picked up watched him warily and Trixie gestured.

'Make up your mind, dear,' he giggled. 'This side or that.'

The blond-haired man moved to the left and Ginger swept him in.

> There's lizards, mosquitoes and snakes green and black
> And bloody great scorpions that fall down your back...

At Giuri the road curved close to the Bunce. The creek was navigable at this point for flat-bottomed craft, and on the hill nearby, well away from military installations, a mine and depth charge dump had been set up by the navy. It was fed by a winding road from a landing stage in the creek where lighters from Freetown could come alongside. A flag flapped against the greenery and there was a glimpse of a West African sentry and a few bored sailors in white shorts.

They were still singing as Hawkinge Town came up and they roared cheerfully between the dark masses of cotton trees and palms whose curving boles slashed the sky, their fronds rustling in the hot wind. Mud-and-wattle huts huddled among the banana plants in aromatic air heavy with the smell of wood smoke and vegetation, the ancient smell of Africa, so that a few of the men in the lorry wrinkled their noses and wondered if, after so long, they could ever live without it.

As they waited for a group of children to cross the road, two mammies, naked to the waist, waved from where they were selling mangoes from calabashes and in the open doorway of a wood-and-tin dwelling, a tailor crouched over an ancient treadle sewing machine looked up and grinned. From somewhere among the trees came the monotonous plink-plonk of a single-octave tune on an instrument made from a biscuit tin and, like a bass accompaniment across the hot still air, the thud of a bundu drum in the steady throb of a pulse.

Ginger's woman was outside the store buying tinned peaches for the celebrations that would follow the coming bundu ceremony, and, because one or two of them knew her bar from the days when they'd been allowed out of camp, they started to sing.

> Go home, Lizzie Morgan,
> Go home, Lizzie Morgan,
> You gone done put your Mammy to shame...

She smiled and waved, but Ginger kept his head well down, pretending to fasten his shoe lace, because he had no wish for her to know he was going home.

As the lorry joggled along the rough road to the camp, the singing died. They were all tired now and feeling the effects of the heat and the first real drinking for months. At the gate, a service police corporal, all smart, starched khaki and blanco'd belt, was checking the native workers as they left the camp, poking his fingers through their carrier bags and satchels to make sure they'd stolen nothing. The men in the lorry started to sing 'Why Are We Waiting?' and 'Why Was He Born So Beautiful?' and the corporal gestured angrily at them. The blond young man alongside Trixie blew him a loud raspberry and Trixie giggled. Eventually, the flustered policeman decided to forget the passes and waved them through.

They climbed down with their newspaper-wrapped parcels and brand-new leather-covered cardboard suitcases, not sure whether to regret the amount of liquor they'd drunk or the fact that there was nothing in the camp to provide a hair of the dog that bit them. Hot, stooped, and beginning to wonder in a curious sort of way if they really wanted to go home, they stumbled towards their billets. They'd all heard the saying that if you stayed too long the Coast got you, and several of them were wondering if it had.

Men were heading for the water bowser to fill bottles for the night. A few others, still grimy from the day's work and trembling and fatigue and hunger, were heading for the cookhouse. A few were kicking a ball about on the uneven patch of red earth that did duty through the year as a football and cricket pitch. It wasn't too bad for football but it wasn't much good for cricket. The wicket was matting on a stretch of concrete which had a crack at one end that one of the Australians in Mackintosh's squadron, a fast bowler of no mean repute in New South Wales, could hit three times out of four so that the ball – if it didn't half-kill the batsman – went clean over his head and the heads of the wicket-keeper and the longstop for four byes.

In the huts, stifling after the day's sunshine on their iron sides, bored men with a long time still to serve were wondering how the hell they were going to occupy themselves *this* evening and if the rats that inhabited the roof spaces were likely to be having a noisier circus than usual. The question defeated many of them so that they lay on their beds in the suffocating atmosphere, stupefied, miserable, thinking of home and mentally totting up the months that lay ahead. It wouldn't have been so bad if there'd been a war. As it was, there was nothing, nothing at all. Jum was a rotten place with no beer, no women, and unbelievable heat. Rain or fine, it never let up and the thought of the evening stretching ahead made them wonder what was the point of knocking off work because there was nothing to do when you did.

A few of the more self-reliant like Feverel, Kneller and Ginger sat outside on home-made stools to watch the red laterite roads change to a delicate pink in a splendid sunset as the day disappeared. The old hands – and Feverel, Kneller and Ginger had been away from England a long time – had developed a considerable skill at filling in their time. In the early days, before it had been placed of bounds, they had explored the back-alleys of Hawkinge Town where most white men never went. Nearby, a man with the look of a farmer was gazing fondly at a solitary half-grown chicken in a small wire netting compound he'd built. He was feeding it breadcrumbs he'd saved from his meal, his eyes always on the sky for the kite hawks that hovered ready to snatch it up. Satisfied there were none within reach, he turned away for a water bottle to fill a rusty tin lid, and as he did so a hawk, appearing from nowhere, swooped. The chicken fancier danced with fury.

'The bastard's pinched my last one!' he yelled. 'I had six when I started! To fatten up! To lay eggs! The buggers have taken 'em all!'

Ginger sympathized, blank-faced. 'When we first came here,' he said, 'you could buy eggs a tanner apiece from the dhobi boys. I used to fry 'em in a old sardine tin. But then the price went up so I got me own chickens. Kept 'em in a run wi' wire nettin' round, just like that.'

The chicken fancier studied him, tears of rage still in his eyes. 'What happened?' he asked.

'Shite 'awks got the lot,' Ginger said. He grinned. 'But don't let it get you down,' he added. 'The worrying keeps you fit.'

'I *am* fit,' the owner of the chicken growled. 'This is the fittest place in the whole bloody world. It has to be. No self-respecting germ would tolerate our living conditions. They should send out a few political fat-bums from the House of Commons and then they'd improve a bit, I bet.'

Ginger listened to the bitterness placidly. 'It'll be nice to go 'ome,' he admitted.

'It'll seem funny,' Kneller decided.

They thought about it for a moment and realized it *would* seem funny because they'd almost forgotten what home was like. When they'd left England in 1940 the chances of ever returning had been so remote as to be non-existent, and the best way to deal with it at the time had seemed to be to forget all about it.

'What do you think of most about going home, Ginger?' Kneller asked.

'Going to bed with a white bint 'stead of a black 'un. What about you?'

'Going to Covent Garden and hearing *Rigoletto*.'

Feverel had no doubts about what *he* wanted. 'A bath,' he said. 'A *hot* bath. For three years, ever since we left Blighty, I've had cold showers and swills in buckets. I've washed in the sea and I've washed in the river, but I've never – not once – had a sit-down hot bath. Never. I dream about it like an alcoholic dying for a drink. I want to sit with scalding water up to my neck and luxuriate for an hour. It's the first thing I'll do.'

Within minutes the light faded to the violet ambience of evening. Moths, big as small birds, appeared among the elephant grass, and then the fireflies, while the gaudy little toads that lived under the stones added their song to the night-time chorus of frogs, mosquitoes, bats and owls. In trousers and mosquito boots, Feverel began to search the camp for a book while Kneller doggedly played dominoes

111

with Nobby Clark as he had every evening for months now, both of them dedicated to avoiding boredom.

Corporal Bates was studying his beer coupon. He'd heard there was beer in the NAAFI but every one of the three spaces on his coupon had been marked by the NAAFI corporal with an inked cross, and he was wondering if he could successfully use some of Trixie Tristram's hair bleach to get rid of them. It had been done, he knew, and he was wondering if the NAAFI corporal had spotted the dodge yet.

The heat stood in the huts like an assassin and occasionally you could hear the rats making love in the roof or the noise of a flying beetle roaring along between the beds. Ginger busied himself over a little electric stove he'd made out of wire from the aerial of a wrecked Catalina which he'd wound into spirals round a four-inch nail and screwed to a piece of asbestos set in a tin and fed with electricity from the light switch. It was highly dangerous and thoroughly illegal but it enabled him to make a piece of toast from a slice of stolen bread.

One of his hut mates, still with several months to do and bored to the point of suicide, watched him listlessly, wondering how he was going to get through the rest of his tour. A few men hunted for cockroaches, the enormous spiders that appeared spasmodically, or the rats which the Africans called pigs and liked to eat roasted in mud cases. But these pastimes were considered a sign of going round the bend and newcomers avoided them like the plague. If there'd been a war, it wouldn't have been so bad because the danger would have given them something to think about. But there was nothing, nothing, nothing at all.

Darkness came. The first mosquito droned and eventually they were whirring like sewing machines wherever there were men. The news went round that the camp cinema was showing.

'What's on?' Bates asked.

They were having another go at *Blood and Sand*, and a few men headed for the cinema. As others drifted in and out of the huts, the news arrived that the ships they'd seen in the harbour weren't going home after all. They'd just come from home and were going the other way. Flying Officer Hobson, who'd been down to see the navy about a new set of mooring buoys, had passed the news to Sergeant Maxey who'd passed it to Corporal Feverel.

'At least they brought mail,' Feverel pointed out. 'Transport's sent a lorry to collect it.'

The time-expired men didn't believe him, because they didn't *want* to believe him, and they tried to avoid contemplating the blankness of what could easily be another month or more. The cinema finished early because the projector had broken down again. A few began to pull down their mosquito nets, crawled inside and lay wide awake, unable to face people and preferring the opaque cocoon-like anonymity of their beds. The cleverer ones shared a stolen slice of bread. One or two, worried about their possessions and thinking of the raiders who came up the creeks in canoes, began to arrange elaborate booby traps with string and tin cans. Drawing on his experience, Ginger had only a ju-ju of shells and feathers.

Eventually the lights went out without warning. A few arguments started. A few listless dirty stories were told. Apart from the duty crew at the jetty, the service policemen on the gate, the radio operators, the duty officers and NCOs, the stewards clearing up in the officers' and sergeants' messes, the camp was silent.

It was then that the place was shaken by a terrific jolt that seemed to shudder the whole coast. Those men still not asleep saw the sky light up with a flare of red and heard the long roar of a multiple explosion. For a second, as it died away, they lay still under their mosquito nets.

'What's that?' Kneller asked.

113

'Thunder,' Nobby Clark said. 'I saw the lightning.'

Feveral wasn't convinced. Standing outside the hut he stared at the sky. The moon was low over the horizon and against its glow he saw a monstrous cloud of smoke curling and coiling, touched on its underside by flame, thrusting upwards as though alive to a height of around five hundred feet where it began to spread outwards like a vast mushroom.

Feverel studied it for a moment, trying to get his bearings.

'It's the mine dump at Giuru,' he said. 'It's gone up.'

f o u r

Within minutes, a camp policeman was at the door of the hut, shouting for the mooring party, the pinnace crew and any men not due for duty.

'Report to the base at once,' he said. 'Mine dump's gone up and there are casualties. The road's been destroyed so they're going to take 'em out by water.'

The pinnace crew were already being ferried to their boat when Feverel's group arrived on the jetty.

'I'll take Scow 14,' he said. 'She doesn't draw much and there'll be room to take stretchers.'

Scow 14, ugly and unloved, hadn't carried depth charges or ammunition for a long time and didn't even possess a hatch cover, but the mooring party were used to old boats. They'd worked with a mobile squadron in Saldanha Bay where they'd had to manage with civilian craft and a couple of discarded navy whalers with Kitchener rudders. With Catalinas, you couldn't get anything more difficult than that.

As Kneller cast off, Ginger busied himself with the engine. Inevitably it refused to start, so he hit it with the hammer from the tool bag and, as it began to chug, they trudged downstream after the pinnace and a seaplane tender carrying Squadron Leader Greeno, the MO, and a couple of orderlies from sick quarters.

As they edged into Giuru creek, they noticed that the smell of oil, sweat, human effluvium, cooking and rank vegetation which was the normal bouquet of the river bank was overlaid by a new smell compounded of charred wood, explosives and burned flesh. Seeing that the landing stage had been reduced to matchwood, Feverel placed the scow's nose on the shelving mud. Someone had laid down planks as duckboards and, even as they arrived, men appeared carrying a stretcher. On it was a sailor, the remains of his scorched white uniform clinging to his body. He was terribly burned and writhing in agony. As he was placed aboard the scow another stretcher appeared. When the stretchers occupied the whole centre of the scow, Feverel put the engine into reverse and, with Kneller and Ginger up to their waists in muddy water pushing of, he edged astern until he could swing round and go alongside the pinnace.

'We've room for more,' Fox called.

Feverel nodded and headed back inshore under the overhanging trees. The bridge that the lorry carrying the time-expired men had crossed only hours before had also disappeared and there was a great gap in the road where the blast had roared down the cleft in the hills to remove everything in its path. As they nosed ashore again, a dazed petty officer wearing nothing but his cap and a blanket stumbled down the duckboards and was pushed on to the deck. Squadron Leader Greeno, already covered with mangrove mud, straightened up from a stretcher as it was lifted and taken down to the boat.

Three times the scow headed out to the pinnace before the bigger boat weighed anchor and began to head for Freetown. By this time naval boats were beginning to appear from downriver but none of them had the shallow draft of the scow and they could only be used for ferrying to the hospital.

With dawn they began to see the devastation that had been caused. Everything within five hundred yards of the dump had vanished. Native huts stood roofless and all the foliage had disappeared so that there was nothing but scorched earth littered with scattered thatch, sheets of corrugated iron, beaten-out petrol cans and tar barrels and splintered planks. A few African soldiers searched among the debris for the bodies of their comrades. Directing them were officers of the West African Frontier Force, among them Cazalet, the languid lieutenant-colonel Feverel had last seen on the Dutchman's launch up the Bic when they'd gone looking for what was left of O-Orange. He was poking about with his swagger stick, bending down almost as if he were sniffing the earth.

As the sun rose, the injured appeared more rapidly – African soldiers, villagers, white sailors. The column of smoke had dispersed now, but the air was still full of the smell of explosive. All round the area where the dump had stood trees lay flat, palm trees, eucalyptuses, jacarandas, even huge tulip and cotton trees, all radiating outwards like the spokes of a wheel. A few dazed Africans from the nearby village picked over what was left of their homes.

The houses nearest the explosion had simply disintegrated, their wattle and mud sides vanishing under the blast in a torrent of dirt and dried palm leaves. The zone of destruction seemed to stretch for a quarter of a mile in every direction, the fringes still crackling under small licking fires. A bucket chain and a pump had been set up from the creek and, even as the injured were taken down to the boats, water went up to put out the last lingering flames.

There were already vultures in the trees. Where they came from nobody knew but they were always the mourners at any disaster, squatting on the branches with their dusty black mourning clothes, their naked red heads moving as they watched, their scabby necks twisting, the light catching the vicious curved beaks and amber eyes. They reminded you of the harpies who had knitted round the guillotine in the French Revolution. Then, suddenly, as one of the lorries backfired, they lifted off with a slow flap of wings, not all together as you might have expected, not in a panic, but one after the other as if to show their unconcern.

In a state of shock, staggering, weeping, gasping, more survivors appeared. There were dozens more beneath the wreckage, and men and women, still stunned by the disaster, were scrambling among the debris to pull them out. The bodies were being placed near the road. They seemed to be coming from every direction, all sizes, all ages, all colours, though sometimes it was difficult to decide what colour they'd been originally. Every surviving tree, even beyond the immediate impact of the explosion, had been stripped of its foliage and stood up stark and bare, while near the crater a lorry lay on its back, the stumps of its axles in the air, its tyres burned away. By the look of it, the place would never be green again.

It started raining in the afternoon and when the scow returned to Jum it was dark and they were all saturated and covered with mud. The pinnace and the seaplane tenders were still on their way back from Freetown where they had been ferrying the last of the injured.

As they tied up to the buoy, Feverel was frowning.

'Wonder what happened?' he said.

The same concern, but with different connotations, was being expressed by Wing Commander Molyneux and Wing Commander Mackintosh.

'It makes a big hole in our attack potential,' Molyneux said. 'We're going to have to either go easy for a while or aim better. There's going to be no dropping of depth charges on suspicion. We've got none to spare.'

'How did they get the bloody things up to Giuru, anyway?' Mackintosh asked.

'Lighter from an ammunition ship at Freetown. They were carried ashore by native labour.'

'Christ,' Mackintosh said. 'What a way of doing things. If it's the wrong way, that's the way the jokers out here'll do it. What do they think caused it?'

'The navy puts it down to deterioration. But as everybody near the seat of the explosion's dead and the whole of the watch that was on duty's just vanished into thin air, it's hard to be certain. They're a bit concerned. It's going to leave *them* short, too.'

'It's going to leave a few families short as well, sport,' Mackintosh growled. 'What's the butcher's bill?'

'Ten naval men, fourteen privates of the West African Frontier Force and about twenty-seven villagers. They haven't got the tally of the injured yet. When I went down there that army chap, Cazalet, was rooting about. He didn't seem to agree with the navy and he's insisting on guards on all important installations.'

Mackintosh struck a match and applied it to his pipe. 'Well,' he said, 'it wasn't us for a change, thank God. Perhaps our crook luck's left us and gone to the navy.'

In that, Wing Commander Mackintosh was dead wrong.

The following morning, with the sky still sombre and threatening and the clouds ragged-edged and yellow-grey, so low that the tops of the trees were hidden in a muddy-looking fog, the road to the hangar was a ribbon of red mud after the rain, and the undergrowth, dripping diamonds in the strange light, was bright green now that the dust of months had been washed away. The wild cucumbers were suddenly almost fully grown and the plantain trees had pushed up another notch to the windows. The lizards looking for moths and cockroaches on the sills seemed to be studying them with jaundiced eyes.

The mangroves held wraiths of mist that never seemed completely to disappear. Sometimes it could play weird tricks, coming out of the trees and gathering on the water to form itself into a ball, or show ghostly white in the moonlight, even bursting into thousands of wisps when the breeze got up. The palm trunk supports of the ramshackle jetty shuddered under the weight of the torrent of brown water coming from the hills and the walls of the crew hut were wet with moisture.

C-Charlie landed, and almost immediately F-Fox left to take its place. During the day the sky darkened again, and a storm of particular intensity broke over the camp. Then it stopped abruptly, leaving only the weeping leaves and an atmosphere that was heavy, humid and depressing. Orders came for the duty refueller crew to turn out.

'K-Katie,' they were told. 'She takes off an hour before F-Fox lands.'

Corporal Herbert Bunting and the two men who comprised the crew of Refueller 81 slithered down to the base and were taken by dinghy to where the refueller was moored just down the creek. Starting the engine they trudged slowly to the lagoon where the aircraft faced every way possible on the slack tide.

Refueller crews were supposed to serve only a matter of a month or two before being changed. Tricky to handle, the big iron boats were very heavy and very hard against the fragile aluminium sides of an aircraft, and they needed skilled boat-handlers. But there was something very special about refuellers and it was generally accepted that refueller and bomb scow crews were mad, anyway, because they always seemed to be at the centre of any mischief that was going and they clung to their unwieldy charges as long as possible.

Working his way carefully alongside K-Katie, Bunting made fast and waved to the flight engineer waiting on the wing to sign for the petrol and make the test for water. A heaving line was flung, the pipes were hauled up, the caps were unscrewed and squares of chamois leather produced. The decks of the iron boat were covered with cocks and valves that controlled the flow of petrol through filters and lengths of wire-reinforced pipes, and the after bulkhead of the cockpit supported a large rotary pump which delivered vast quantities of lubricating oil – by hand, in order, it was claimed, to keep the refueller crews from becoming too bored. There was no breeze and the air was heavy and still after the storm.

'Let's have it.'

His eyes alert for sparks, Bunting reached to the starboard side of the cockpit where the eight-horse engine connected to the pump was situated. His best friend had been one of the men fatally burned in Refueller 62 and he had no wish to join him.

Looking about him, one eye open to make sure his escape route was clear, he leaned on the starting handle. With the heavy air and the vents open, the cockpit seemed full of petrol fumes and he noticed that the fitter and the deckhand were watching carefully from the deck just above him. As the motor started, he breathed a sigh of relief. No sparks. No explosion. Nobody hurt, thank God!

He had just climbed out of the cockpit to the iron deck when he heard what sounded like the click of a mousetrap going off. He swung round, wondering what it was, just as a roaring, rending explosion engulfed the refueller in orange flame. The blast flung Bunting overboard and before he knew where he was, he was swimming and an iron hatch cover which had torn a great gash in the leading edge of the Sunderland's wing as it was wrenched off, splashed into the water nearby.

To his surprise the fitter was alongside him. The deckhand was still aboard struggling with a rope, his hair on fire though, finally, he decided not to bother and, running along the iron deck of the refueller, now denuded of its fittings, he jumped overboard. On the wing of the Sunderland, the flight engineer was yelling for help.

As he trod water, Bunting dazedly came to the conclusion that it might be a good idea to put some distance between himself and the aircraft and, turning on his back he began to kick away from it, followed by the fitter and the deckhand, whose face was bright pink where it had been seared by the flames.

Dinghies and a seaplane tender working near the other aircraft had stopped what they were doing and were swinging in tight circles. A bomb scow cast off its ropes and, though still laden with depth charges, began to trudge round to help. The pinnace was working at the far end of the trot of buoys and Corporal Feverel, in a dinghy under a dripping iron Munro buoy hoisted clear of the water by the pinnace, had just finished replacing the four-inch nail which held the shackle with a new one. Once the job had had to be done from Scow 14, heaving the chain in hand over laborious hand, and he was just reflecting how much easier it had become since the arrival of the pinnace when the refueller went up. He knew at once what had happened because it had happened twice before. As he scrambled back aboard the pinnace, the fitter leaped towards the controls of the winch, the buoy splashed back into the water and the pinnace began to head after the other boats at full speed.

By this time the aircraft itself was caught in the mass of flames from the refueller and somewhere inside a man was screaming. The door in the side opened and the wireless operator, who had been carrying out a check on his set, started yelling for a dinghy, before deciding it was wiser not to wait and jumping into the water. The flight engineer was shouting, 'I can't swim, I can't swim,' and had just begun to run along the wing when the tanks went. There was a tremendous 'whoomph' and, as the aeroplane vanished in a huge flower of yellow flame, he was lifted into the air, his legs going as if he were riding a bicycle.

Because it hadn't occurred in the air but on the water and while the aircraft was moored to a buoy, Group Captain Strudwick conducted the inquiry into the loss of the Sunderland himself. He had already made up his mind about the reason for the explosion and fire and it didn't take him long to inform Flying Officer Hobson what he thought.

As an orthodox airman, he didn't like the marine section. They were a queer group of men – airmen, yet not airmen: sailors, yet not sailors – men who didn't fit into what he considered a proper RAF structure.

They had always been unpopular with the more formal minds in the RAF, and the service police actively loathed them because not only did they never polish buttons or cap badges, but they could claim – and always did – that the resultant months of verdigris was only because the salt spray had ruined hours of hard work the night before. Even in Jum they seemed out of place. The station warrant officer complained that, because they claimed to work with the tides, he could never get them on parade and they always seemed twice as scruffy as everybody else with knives at their waists and speaking a different language that no one understood. In addition, Group Captain Strudwick was well aware of the feelings they had for him for taking one of their precious seaplane tenders for his own use, and was never quite sure how much sarcasm there was in it when Feverel and Kneller, working on a new buoy in the water by the slip,

123

gave him guardsmen-like salutes while stark naked but for sweat rags and pith helmets.

'Those men of yours must have been smoking,' he announced.

The suggestion was so patently silly Hobson wasn't sure what to reply.

'Sir, with respect, I don't think they'd dream of smoking while refuelling.'

'I prefer to dispute that,' Strudwick said sharply. 'During the Battle of Britain, I came across a group of recruits in a garage who were emptying tins of petrol rescued from France into an open tank to be pumped into aircraft bowsers and I actually caught one of them lighting a cigarette. If men can be that stupid in England, they can be that stupid in West Africa.'

Hobson's expression became dogged. 'Sir. Again, with respect. These men aren't recruits. They're old hands. Corporal Bunting's been working with flying boats for two years. He was on refuellers at Stranraer and he's been doing the job out here for five months. He's a very experienced and careful man.'

Strudwick gestured. 'They *must* have been smoking,' he insisted.

'Sir – ' Hobson took a deep breath, realizing he was laying his head on the block by his refusal to agree '...it's impossible. Out here, where the air's still and heavy and the fumes hang about, it would be committing suicide.'

'Two men are dead: a man working inside the aircraft who was trapped by the flames and the flight engineer who drowned. Why were rescue craft not available to pick him up?'

'It isn't standard procedure, sir, for refuelling and bombing up.'

'Then I think you'd better *make* it standard procedure,' Strudwick snapped. 'This isn't England, you know. This is West Africa. Anything can happen here – and usually does.'

Nothing was said about putting the refueller crews on charges and Hobson realized that, despite Strudwick's conviction about their guilt, he wasn't prepared to go so far as to press the point. To allow the matter to quieten down, however, he appointed a new crew to the spare refueller. Bunting needed a little placating.

'I wasn't smoking, you know, sir,' he protested. 'And neither was anybody else.'

Hobson waved aside his objections. 'I know that,' he said. 'But there's nothing I can do about it. At least you're not on a charge and for a time I thought you might be. Be thankful for small mercies. You'll run a duty crew. At least there's not much wrong with a seaplane tender.'

'No, sir,' Bunting agreed stubbornly. 'Except that it isn't a refueller.'

Hobson was irritated and angry and that evening he took his problem to Wing Commander Molyneux.

'Could they have been smoking, Hobbie?' Molyneux asked.

'I don't think for one moment they were smoking,' Hobson said. 'Bunting's a responsible chap. He was a policeman in Civvie Street and you can't get much more responsible than that. Besides, he's been doing the job for five months and wanted to do it for his whole tour.'

'Martyr type?'

Hobson shrugged. 'I think it's a pride in doing a more dangerous job than anybody else,' he said. 'And out here it *is* dangerous. There are already two burnt-out refuellers on the mud. Now there'll be a third.'

While they were talking, Mackintosh appeared in the doorway and Molyneux waved him to a chair. Hobson eyed him warily. After all, Mackintosh had just lost a valuable aircraft and one of his aircrew and he might be taking the group captain's view that it was Hobson's fault.

Mackintosh studied Hobson, then managed a smile. 'Take it easy, sport,' he said. 'Nobody's blaming you.'

They were still talking as the sudden darkness fell.

Normally they would all have been in the mess having a pre-dinner gin – if there *were* any gin – but they were grim-faced and preoccupied and indifferent to the fact that the office was full of the whine and whirr of mosquitoes. In the ceiling the fan moved slowly, stirring the air, but only, it seemed, to give them a variety of hot blasts. They were worried, not merely because of what had happened to K-Katie, but also because the AOC had indicated his intention of paying them a visit.

'After all,' Mackintosh said, 'this makes three aircraft in less than two months. That's a lot of aircraft.'

'It seems to be pretty bloody general, too,' Molyneux growled. 'Takoradi's lost one. Crash on take-off. I've been told to detach G-George.'

Mackintosh struggled to get his pipe going to his satisfaction. 'At Bathurst,' he said, 'the bloody U-boats are coming so close inshore they're expecting to see 'em cruising up the main street. I've got to send another Sunderland. L-Leather caught one on the surface but it fought back and filled the hull full of holes.'

'Write-off ?'

'They got the plugs in and she was beached in shallow water. She'll fly again but it'll take time. R-Robert's taking her place.'

Molyneux frowned. 'This place's beginning to look bloody empty,' he said.

'Times change, sport,' Mackintosh commented. 'Six months ago we were on top of the U-boats and even got a few nice words from the Admiral. It seems to be different now. There are more submarines these days and a lot less aircraft.'

'And you can bet your bottom dollar they'll be reinforcing. Rommel's only just outside Cairo now. Christ knows what they're doing up there in the desert.'

Mackintosh smiled. 'Probably wondering what the hell we're doing down here in West Africa.'

They were beginning now to find problems with the over-worked aircraft, and the fitters in the hangar were having to go all out to get the machines back in the air quickly when they came in for servicing.

Bringing a machine in was never easy. Sunderland A-Apple was towed from the lagoon down the narrow creek, all eyes on the wingtips in case they were damaged by the tough mangrove branches. As she was made fast to the buoy that lay just off the end of the slip, men began to wade into the water – not particularly willingly because there were jigger worms there, and if you were unlucky they laid their eggs under your toe nails so that your foot swelled painfully and a minor operation had to be performed in the sick bay to remove them. As the aircraft rose on her cradle and was edged into the hangar, a vast machine with flat grey sides like cliffs, the fitters fell on her like flies.

The rain came once more that afternoon, putting a grey curtain over the whole base so that from the piermaster's office it was impossible to see the trots of aircraft. Dinghy drivers, refueller and scow crews, fitters, riggers and flight mechanics returned soaked. The camp these days was surrounded constantly by the misty miasma from the swamps, and the huts on the lower side of the camp filled with water again while drainage ditches became potential death traps. The mosquitoes were biting like mad dogs and malaria, dormant during the dry season, had increased suddenly so that shivering men were being carted off every day to the sick bay. The chorus of frogs and toads grew deafening and Ginger Donnelly killed two mambas in four hours among the long grass. The hatred for the narrow spit of land was almost tangible.

However, mail arrived and though it proved Feverel and the prophets of gloom correct, at least it was a consolation. It included a parcel for Ginger from the pub he'd frequented in England and, scanning through it quickly to find it was full of dubbin, shoe polish, laces, a packet of washing powder, shaving soap and such articles as were considered by civilians to be of prime importance to a serviceman, he hurled it into a corner in disgust. Bates' wife had sent him a fruit cake, but the large box of talcum powder – a great necessity where you sweated buckets and broke out in rashes – that he'd begged her also to include, had burst out of its wartime utility packing and he was trying to convince himself that if he scraped off the thick perfumed white layer and washed the cake under the shower it would miraculously become eatable.

'The water wouldn't go in far,' he explained, staring at it frustratedly.

'You got anything, Nellie?' Feverel asked.

Kneller held up a letter. It came from Ettore Mori-Moncrieff and was addressed from India where he was now entertaining troops.

'I hope,' he wrote, 'that you believed me when I said you should become a chorister at Covent Garden. I enclose my address and when the war is over – and I pray God it will not be too long – please write to me. If I should not, for some reason, still be around – and I might not, because I am no longer young and am finding this tour exhausting – then get in touch with the chorus master there. I have written several letters on your behalf to a number of people, a list of whom I include. Any of them should be able to help you, and I name several because in wartime one never knows the future. I trust you will not fail me because someone with an ear for music such as you have should not neglect its possibilities.'

Kneller was touched but Feverel didn't seem very surprised.

'It's only what everybody's been saying,' he pointed out.

That evening Kneller's voice could be heard through the mist as he took out Scow 14 to check the strops and grommets on the aircraft buoys. He was tough and brave, and despite his voice, a good worker who had learned to splice wire the hard way and could now keep up with Feverel and Ginger Donnelly.

A-Apple was lowered into the water the following morning, her service completed, towed back to the lagoon and secured to a buoy – one of those buoys that gave Feverel and Kneller nightmares with their four-inch nails. During the afternoon, Flying Officer Knight, her captain, was informed he would be taking off in the early hours of the next morning to be in position a hundred miles out into the Atlantic at first light. The crew were given their course and rendezvous, and, as the flarepath dinghies were towed into place, they scrambled into the lorry that took them to the jetty. As they climbed into the interior of the Sunderland, there was a lot of chaffing.

'Don't keep us waiting when we land,' the Australian navigator said, 'and there'll be a jar of peanut butter for you.'

'You can stick your peanut butter.' Corporal Bunting was still disgruntled at being taken off refuellers. 'Only Australians would eat that stuff.'

There was a last-minute hitch as it was found one of the dashboard light sockets was faulty and a message was sent ashore by dinghy. An electrician appeared with a new socket and fitted it as the crew chafed and waited, and it was growing dangerously late as A-Apple prepared for take-off, because they had also had to wait an extra half-hour for the

Catalina they were supposed to be relieving to come in and land.

As the returning Catalina arrived with a tunnelling 'swoosh', taxied and made fast, Flying Officer Knight started A-Apple's outer engines, let go her mooring and swung away to the holding area. There, her engines idling, the last checks were made, then he swung her to face into the stream and called base for clearance.

'Roger,' he said as base replied. 'Here goes!' And he slammed open the throttles of the four great Pegasus engines.

The metal propellers bit at the air and the huge machine began to move forward. They were in for a seven-hour flight.

There was a slight breeze blowing and the water was stirred by small wavelets. They weren't high enough to damage the always-fragile floats but were high enough to help the take-off, and Knight stared ahead, confident there would be no trouble. The week before, on a dead still day, he had ploughed, fully loaded, up and down the five miles of lagoon three times before finally bumping into the air from artificial waves created for him by the wash of the seaplane tender. The breeze was slightly across his path and he began to adjust the outer engines, keeping one at full revs, the other slightly throttled back to keep the aircraft straight. There were no rules. It was always a case of suck it and see because water made everything different.

Knight liked his Sunderland, despite her shabby appearance where paint had been peeled off by flying in tropical rain. They would live on Machonachie's stew and coffee until they returned, but the Sunderland was a magnificent machine to handle, especially at the end of a trip when, lightly loaded, he liked to do steep turns and sideslips to show what she was capable of.

The great square fuselage began to cut through the water, throwing out a flat spray on either side and trailing a deep white wash behind it through the brown surface of the river.

The mangroves moved past faster and faster until they became a blur, then, as the enormous wing began to take her weight and she moved on to the step, Knight pulled gently back on the stick.

Moving through the water behind her at full speed, the throttle wide open, the seaplane tender in the hands of Corporal Bunting held her position until the Sunderland began to draw away from her. Then, just as she was on the point of lifting off, there was a bang, the aircraft's tail came up until it was almost vertical, and the nose of the machine dug into the water in an enormous cloud of spray and flying water.

'Christ, another!'

On the point of closing the throttles, instead Bunting slammed them with the heel of his hand to make sure they were fully open and swung the wheel so that the boat slid into a skidding turn at full speed.

As the searchlight flared, sending its ice-white beam across the dark lagoon, they saw the mountainous wall of water flung up by the aircraft, and a huge mist of spray drifting away. What looked like a tidal wave was moving, ahead of where the aircraft had disappeared, then it seemed to surge back on its tracks, just as the aircraft bobbed up, tail first, like a fisherman's float, before settling back and sliding out of sight.

The water was littered with floating wreckage, an aileron and one of the elevators laying flatly on the heaving surface, then a wing float bobbed up and joined them. There was no sign of any member of the crew until the fitter, who was in the stern of the boat, yelled and pointed. A man was struggling in the water, drifting rapidly downstream on the tide.

Opening the throttles, Bunting swung the boat round in a tight circle that threw up a large wave, and stopped her dead within a yard or two of the swimming man. A rope was thrown and the shocked man grabbed it and was able to swing his arm so that it twisted round his wrist. The fitter and the deckhand were unable to haul him aboard so Bunting left the wheel to join them and, between them, they had him gasping on the well-deck. It was the rear gunner and he appeared to be uninjured.

'What happened?' he asked. 'Am I alive?'

'Yes.'

'I'd just got in the turret when I heard this bang and the kite stood on its nose and started filling with water. I jettisoned the doors and fell out. I didn't know where I was.' The dazed man looked up anxiously. 'You sure I'm alive? Am I the only one?'

'It looks like it.'

The rear gunner looked at his rescuers for a moment with blank eyes then put his hands over his face and started to weep.

There were celebrations at Boina that evening as the news of their latest success reached Heidegger. Following the disaster at Giuru and the incident with the refueller, it seemed a triumph. As the reports came in, Lorenz could hardly contain himself.

Much as he disliked Lorenz, Heidegger had to admit he was very capable and the men under him liked his tough approach. The only fly in the ointment seemed to be the absence of young Willer. Their contacts at Kumrabai and Mahera had not heard of him and it worried Heidegger. Had he been injured? Had the British picked him up? Were they questioning him?

'He's lying low,' Lorenz insisted. 'He's after the petrol, at Lungi. He's just waiting his chance.'

Heidegger nodded. 'I think we'd better have a toast to that,' he said.

They started drinking before the evening meal – French brandy from Senegal and Scotch whisky stolen from Freetown docks – and one or two of the younger men grew noisy. The meal was a rowdy affair with a lot of shouting and bread throwing, and Heidegger at the head of the table noticed that Pfitzner, supervising the serving of the meal, was watching Lorenz with angry eyes as he talked across the table to Magda Fallada.

He was outlining the year's successes for her, his face alight with hope and ambition. '*Schaarhorst* and *Gneisenau*,' he was crowing. 'Escaped from Brest. *Tirpitz* at Trondheim to stop any attempts by the British and the Americans to supply Russia by North Cape. Britain hit by the U-boat campaign. Singapore gone. The Philippines gone. The Japanese running riot across the Pacific. The American fleet sunk at Pearl Harbor. Rommel at the gates of Cairo. German soldiers at Sevastopol, Rostov and Stalingrad.'

It was an impressive list, Heidegger had to admit. He saw Lorenz raise his glass to the Fallada woman and she returned the gesture with a look in her eyes that confirmed his suspicion that she and Lorenz were lovers. As he watched them, Pfitzner moved behind Lorenz and Heidegger saw him deliberately spill coffee across his knees. Lorenz' rapt look vanished at once as he swung round and glared.

'My apologies, sir,' the steward said blandly. 'An accident.'

Lorenz subsided as damp cloths were brought but, watching, Heidegger suspected that the time was coming when he'd need to do something about Pfitzner. He had been brooding for some time now, withdrawn and angry, his heavy brows down, his eyes always on Lorenz and the Fallada woman. He'd been warned again by Heidegger to keep away from the woman he was chasing in one of the villages at the head of the river but – Heidegger found himself feeling guilty – if he himself could feel stirred by the thought of Lorenz and Magda Fallada naked on her bed, then doubtless so could Pfitzner, the boastful lover of women. The spilling of the coffee seemed to spell trouble and, despite the successes at Giuru and Jum, Heidegger was conscious of a chilly uneasiness.

s i x

The trots in the lagoon, which had been looking bare for some time, were looking even more bare now.

The stand-by crew had been called out and a boom defence vessel was now anchored over the spot where A-Apple had gone in, for a diver to go down to attach strops to haul her to the surface. Because of the faulty light socket, the convoy that had been expected had been without air escort for two hours and it had been enough for the U-boats to take advantage of it. Two ships had been sunk and another was being towed by a naval tug towards Freetown harbour. The navy were understandably annoyed.

Molyneux and Hobson sat in Mackintosh's office, Mackintosh frowning at the service sheets of the lost machine.

'The bloody thing had just gone down the slip,' he was saying. 'Hacker swears she was in excellent condition.'

'He's got some good chaps in the hangar, too,' Molyneux said slowly. 'We've never had much fault to find.'

'We've lost a lot of aircraft all the same, sport,' Mackintosh pointed out.

'Perhaps they weren't all due to bad servicing.'

Hobson looked up, startled, and Molyneux shrugged and pushed a packet of cigarettes forward.

'This is an important base,' he pointed out. 'And, what with detachments and accidents, we've nearly been wiped off the map.'

Nobody spoke and he expanded his theme. 'We provide cover for the whole Sierra Leone area,' he pointed out. 'From south of Bathurst down to Takoradi where they're also having unexplained accidents.' He lit a cigarette slowly and thoughtfully. 'At the moment we're managing to keep our machines in the air – just – but some of the most important convoys of the war are due past. Without them, Uncle Erwin up in the desert could push through to the Canal. When shall we know what caused it?'

'As soon as the boom defence vessel starts lifting,' Hobson said. 'I've got a tender alongside her with a radio. As soon as they know, they'll call headquarters who'll ring us.'

Towards midnight, Corporal Feverel, Kneller and Ginger Donnelly were awakened and told to report to the base.

'Now what's on?' Feverel asked.

'Sick man to be taken off the beach at Lungi.'

They knew the water at Lungi well. They had laid a triangular bombing target just offshore and had taken advantage of the opportunity to spend a whole joyous day there with the pinnace crew away from the suffocating confines of Jum, with a breeze fresh from the sea and only the possibility of sharks and the vicious stings of the Portuguese men-o'-war to mar the swimming.

'Who is this chap?' Feverel asked. 'The King of England?'

'One of the foremen, I heard,' the service policeman who had wakened him said. 'You're a dab hand with a signalling lamp, they told me.'

Feverel acknowledged the fact and the policeman went on cheerfully, 'Perhaps they think you might be attacked by the Scharnhorst as you go across the bay. They were going to do it by ambulance, but it's too far round so they're going to do it by boat.'

Feverel began to dress, wishing he hadn't been so good at Morse as a Boy Scout. Corporal Bates was waiting with a seaplane tender alongside the catamaran when they reached the base and as they climbed aboard, Squadron Leader Greeno, the medical officer, arrived. He was followed soon afterwards by Molyneux, whose thin face looked angry and puzzled.

'It's not one of the foremen,' he said. 'They think now he's a foreigner. If it's true I want to know who he is.'

The tender was just about to leave when they heard a car brake to a stop in the darkness. A torch flashed and, as feet clattered down the jetty, Morgan, the padre, appeared.

'Thought I might be needed,' he pointed out. 'They said he was in a bad way.'

As the boat moved out of the creek into the river, picking out the buoys with its searchlight, they could see the glow of Freetown in the distance. It wasn't very bright because the glow of Freetown never was, but on the hill behind the town they could see the sparkle of lights from the hospital.

The padre was still recovering his breath. 'Dhu, man,' he said, lighting his pipe and filling the cabin with acrid smoke, 'even if he is a poor benighted foreigner I suppose he's still entitled to a prayer when he's dying.'

'*Is* he dying?' Molyneux asked.

'I gather he's in a bad way,' Greeno said.

'He slipped across the border from French Guinea,' the padre added. 'Wanted to join De Gaulle's lot.'

'Who says?' At that moment, Molyneux wasn't much inclined to trust foreigners.

'*They* said,' Morgan pointed out vaguely. 'I heard them tell the doc.'

Molyneux wondered if his normal enthusiasm was running away with him. Morgan was an odd character. He had come from a country parish and Molyneux never quite knew what to make of him because he seemed to spend all his time in the mess drinking his ration of whisky and that of

137

any non-drinker he could persuade to hand over his allocation. Nevertheless, he was far from a normal run-of-the-mill vicar because he was an Oxford scholar, had won a gong for bravery in the other war, spoke excellent German and French and had travelled extensively in Europe. In fact, he'd been in some doubt in 1939 as to whether to become a padre or an interpreter and even now was called on occasionally by the navy to translate when they picked up U-boat signals in clear.

The boat was thrusting through the water at a good speed now, Corporal Bates nursing it because they had a long way to go. As they approached the river mouth the waves coming in from the sea through the wide entrance of the Rokel caused it to lurch and the doctor reached out suddenly for a handhold. The boat's crew were in the wheelhouse with Bates, the mooring party sitting on the hatches over the noisy diesel engines in the well-deck.

There was nothing to see in the darkness and Ginger began to yawn. He was just on the point of curling up on the deck for a sleep when they noticed that the stars and the lights of Freetown had disappeared.

'Rain,' he said.

A few minutes later they were hit by a squall that slashed at the windscreen and drove them all into a crowded group in the cabin. Then a message came from forward that a light was flashing from the naval signal station on the hill.

'What's he saying?' Bates asked.

The Aldis clattered and the light started again, a winking pinpoint in the blackness high in the sky.

'He says, "You are..." He says, "You are in the middle of" ' Feverel looked at Bates and grinned. 'He says, "You are in the middle of a minefield." '

'Oh, charming,' Bates said. 'Bloody charming!'

'If the navy bothered to tell us where they were it would help,' Molyneux growled.

'We don't draw much water, sir,' Feverel reassured him. 'We ought to go over them.'

'Unless they're floaters with the old glass horns. In Sierra Leone they could well be. What do we do? Turn back?'

'Dhu, boy,' Morgan said. 'If we're in the middle of it, we might just as well keep going. I'll say a prayer.'

It was in the early hours of the morning when they reached the beach at Lungi and Bates closed the throttles so that they drifted with idling engines.

'Can't we go further in?' Molyneux asked.

'No, sir,' Bates said. 'It's hard to see in the dark but I think we're as far in as we dare go.' He pushed forward the chart for Molyneux to see. 'It varies between three feet and two fathoms and the chart doesn't say where because it changes every year. There are also rocks.'

Molyneux frowned. 'Well, we can't get at the bloody man unless we do go in,' he snapped.

Bates agreed to move in a little further but he was worried. He had his clearance chit and an inquiry into a lost boat would mean missing the troopship home which, after two doses of malaria, was something he didn't look forward to. He shut down the engines again and dropped the anchor. As they began to discuss what to do, a light flashed from the shore.

'They're telling us to hurry,' Feverel announced.

'Ask them if they've a boat.'

It appeared there was a native fruit boat but because of the hour there were no oars and no crew. Molyneux began to look angry but Morgan quietly started unfastening his shoes. Stripping off his stockings and shorts, he dragged at his shirt. His body was covered all over with black hair.

'How far is it to the shore?' he asked.

'Around a hundred yards, sir,' Bates said. 'Bit less now, I imagine.'

'Can we make up that much in rope?'

139

Ginger and Kneller had already seen what he was up to and they were unhitching the mooring ropes and bending them together. Attaching a length of grass line from the locker, they added the springs and the heaving lines. As Morgan dived in and reappeared at the side of the boat, blinking in the glow of the searchlight, his moustache dripping like an elderly seal's, he reached for the end of the line.

'Can you swim that far?' Molyneux asked.

'Used to do my twenty lengths of the baths regularly at school, man.'

'You're a bit older now.'

Morgan gave a small smile. 'There's caution for you. Perhaps you could help by making sure the line runs freely. And this time *you* could offer up a small prayer. I shall need my breath for swimming.'

Kicking off from the side of the boat, he headed into the darkness. After a few yards, it was impossible to tell whether he was still afloat or not apart from the fact that the coils of line on the deck gradually grew less. Eventually they stopped.

'I hope to God he's reached the shore,' Molyneux said, 'and not just sunk to the bottom.'

After a while the light ashore began to wink.

'He says "Haul",' Feverel called out, and they began cautiously to pull the wet line aboard. Eventually, they made out the shape of a wide-beamed bullom boat emerging from the darkness, the padre pushing at the stern with a long bamboo pole. As it bumped alongside, Molyneux climbed in with the doctor. 'Come on,' he said to Ginger and Kneller. 'Better have you two, as well. This thing's heavy.'

The padre had collected three or four other poles and they thrust at the sea bed until they began to make way towards the shore. There was a strong swell running and the tide was setting down the coast, but eventually, soaked with sweat, they ran the boat on to the sand and Ginger and Kneller jumped over the side to hold it steady.

The water was deeper than they had expected and, now they were out of the river and into the sea, considerably colder. Two black men appeared and indicated that they were willing to carry anyone ashore on their backs who didn't wish to get wet. Molyneux and Greeno accepted the offer and vanished into the darkness. Morgan jumped back into the sea. 'I'll find some trousers and come back here,' he said.

As he vanished Ginger and Kneller looked at each other. Up to their chests in the sea, they could just see each other in the spill of the tender's searchlight but couldn't see the water's edge or anything of the land beyond. They had no idea where the others had gone and could only concentrate on holding the boat beam on to the current. How long they remained there they had no idea and they began to grow cold.

'Sing us a song, Nelly,' Ginger said sarcastically. 'Cheer us up.'

'What would you like? "Roll Me Over In The Clover" or something of Vera Lynn's?'

' "Your Little Frozen Mitt" wun't come amiss just now.'

They were almost asleep when voices ashore brought them back to life and they saw lights moving down to them as though they were descending to the beach from the higher land where the airstrip lay. Eventually figures appeared from the darkness, a few white men with Molyneux and Greeno, followed by the padre wearing borrowed shorts and a pair of old tennis shoes. Black men were carrying a stretcher. As they lifted it into the fruit boat the man on it showed no sign of life.

They all climbed aboard, together with two of the Africans, who were to pole it back to the shore, and began to lean against the bending bamboos. As they bumped alongside the seaplane tender the laborious business of getting the stretcher aboard began. A wind had risen and there was a swell running so that the boats went up and down against each other like horses on a fairground roundabout. Then, just to improve matters, a downpour started, and by the time they had the unconscious man inside the cabin everybody was soaked to the skin.

'Freetown,' Greeno said as the engines were started. 'I've arranged for an ambulance.'

There was still a journey of twelve miles ahead of them and the cabin was packed with people as they crowded in out of the rain. The unconscious man, a blond handsome youngster, they saw now that they had him under the cabin lights, began to mutter.

'He'll be lucky to survive the night,' Greeno said. 'Let's have the best speed we can.'

Morgan paused as he dragged on his shirt. 'What's wrong with him, anyway?' he asked.

'Burst appendix, I suspect. He'll be lucky if he makes it. He was just conscious enough to talk to me. He'd had a pain in his belly for some time and it had moved down towards the ileac fossa. At first I thought it was plain appendicitis but the pain had become much worse and now it's diffused. All the signs. It seems he tried to carry on too long...'

'Doing what?' Molyneux rapped.

The doctor was silent for a moment then he shrugged. 'Whatever he *was* doing. Those chaps ashore said he managed to talk a bit before he lost consciousness and he told them he'd slipped over the border from French territory to join the Free French. He thought he might be welcome. Whatever it was, he should have reported sick long since. I think he's left it too late.' Greeno frowned. 'He's also got first-degree burns on his hands.'

'Burnt hands and a burst appendix?' Molyneux said. 'They don't seem to go together, do they? Especially in a Frenchman trying to join the Free French.'

The unconscious man was muttering again and Morgan bent over him, frowning, his ear close to his lips.

'Give him air, padre,' Greeno said.

'I'm trying to catch what he's saying.'

Molyneux was examining the sick man's possessions, half-hoping they might disclose something dramatic. But they consisted of little else but a webbing pack containing spare socks, a towel and toilet materials. 'Well,' he pointed out slowly, 'his papers *say* he's French.'

He was frowning deeply and Greeno looked at him. 'Think he might not be?' he asked.

'I'm wondering, Molyneux admitted. 'Especially as the site manager was telling me they've just had a couple of their machines damaged by what he felt was sabotage.'

Greeno looked startled. 'Who do his papers say he is?'

'Paul-Marie Weiler, born in Mulhouse, Alsace, working as a mechanic at Kissidougou. There's also a slip to say he served his period of conscription in the French Engineers in 1939 and 1940.' Molyneux looked up sharply. 'Doc, when he told you about the pain in his belly, how did he do it? In what language?

Greeno looked puzzled. 'Oddly enough, in English.'

'A Frenchman who speaks English. Here in Lungi? Where he shouldn't be? Isn't it a bit odd?'

Morgan straightened up from the muttering, half-conscious man, a curious expression on his face. 'It might be odder than you think,' he said flatly. 'Because, at the moment, he's speaking German.'

seven

As the seaplane tender, returning through the early morning mist hanging over the river, turned into Jum creek, it ran straight into a new panic.

Molyneux, Greeno and the padre were lolling in a doze in the cabin where, despite all their efforts, the man from Lungi had died before they had even reached Freetown. Ginger was curled up in the well-deck, and Feverel and Kneller were somehow managing to sleep on the hatches above the roaring diesels. It was Bates' startled shout that brought them all to their feet, and they saw him pointing through the veils of mist to where they could just make out one of Mackintosh's Sunderlands stranded on the mud at the entrance to the creek, her port wing canted up in the air, the big letter M on her side catching the early light. Immediately, Molyneux knew it was another in the chapter of strange incidents that was plaguing the base.

The crews of the pinnace and a dinghy were struggling to stop the aircraft slipping off the mud into the water and they were all cursing, blinded with sweat and covered with black mangrove slime. The pilot was standing in the forward hatch and the rest of the crew were on the wing, apart from the flight engineer who appeared to have been doing aircraft guard duty and was in the dinghy with Mackintosh and almost in tears.

'What the hell's happening?' Molyneux demanded as they slipped in under the huge wing.

144

'The bloody thing's sinking,' Mackintosh snarled. 'We're trying to keep her on the mud until we've got C-Charlie off the slip and she can go on in her place at high tide.' He wiped a muddy hand across his face to remove the sweat. 'How about giving us a lift to the jetty? She'll be all right now, I think.'

As they headed for the base, Mackintosh filled in the details. 'I was asleep when the panic button was pressed,' he said. 'About two o'clock in the morning. The duty coxswain telephoned the mess. I got the crew down to the base and Hobbie got the pinnace on the job. Just in time, too.'

At the jetty, sending the land crabs and mud hoppers scattering from under the resounding planks for their holes in the mud, he set off for his office at a furious pace that indicated the temper he was in, the flight engineer almost running behind. As the questioning started, Molyneux leaned on the door jamb, I smoking, his face taut and narrow with his thoughts.

The flight engineer insisted no one had boarded M-Mother and he had been sleeping when he had heard a sharp report. He had thought the guard on one of the other aircraft had his revolver with him and had fired at a crocodile or something.

'You were a long way from the bank, sport,' Mackintosh snapped. 'And crocodiles don't normally operate in the middle of the river.'

'No, sir,' the flight engineer agreed. 'But I couldn't think of anything else. I had a look round but there were no marine craft nearby...'

'Native canoes?'

'The duty coxswain saw none,' Hobson said.

'Neither did I, sir,' the engineer went on. 'But it was a dark night and a black skin on a dark night's hard to spot. I decided it wasn't important because it had come from outside. But then I heard water and realized she was filling

145

up. The hole wasn't very big – the noise I heard wasn't very big either – but it was letting in water, in gallons. I stuffed it up with a wooden plug wrapped in a towel and flashed the pierhead with the Aldis. The pinnace managed to get her nose on the mud.'

A lot of people missed their breakfast as the hangar crew were called out, and C-Charlie was put into the water, her service only half-finished. M-Mother, the hole plugged, her pumps going and watched on either side by dinghies, was towed at full speed to the slip. Warrant Officer Hacker, up to his knees in water, was examining the hull even before she left the river.

Molyneux and Mackintosh stood on the ramshackle jetty outside Hobson's office, watching as the slipway crew worked.

'Anything heard of A-Apple?' Molyneux asked.

'The navy's got their diver down now,' Hobson said.

Molyneux looked at Mackintosh. 'I don't know who's behind all this,' he said. 'African nationalists, disaffected airmen or what. But from now on my aircraft guards will not only carry weapons but will also stay awake.'

The telephone went and Hobson snatched it up through the open window of his office. As it clattered he handed it to Mackintosh who leaned forward abruptly, listening. 'You sure?' he said.

There was a moment's silence then he nodded. 'Well, that gives the AOC something to chew on,' he said.

As he put the telephone back on the rest he looked at the others.

'The navy's got her up,' he said. 'The diver says there's a bloody great hole in the hull at just about the point where it breasts the water on take-off.'

A-Apple, it seemed, had torn open her hull on a floating log and that was that. Floating logs were an occupational hazard with flying boats. Ship's timbers, fallen overboard or drifting in from some torpedoing in the Atlantic, had caused more than one sinking in places like Calshot, Stranraer, Mount Batten and Lough Erne back in Blighty, and with the flying boats in Africa using all sorts of strange stretches of water, from the lagoon at Langebaan in the south, Santa Lucia Bay close to the border of Portuguese East, Takoradi, Bathurst and Jum, which wasn't a bay anyway but a river, accidents were bound to increase. Here, where the lagoon was fed by fast-flowing streams which widened waterfalls and washed away bridges, the rainy season occasionally brought down whole huge trees, and some of them – old half-submerged ones blackened by long soaking and with their branches worn to stubs – were hard to spot in the dark.

Not entirely convinced, Hobson gave instructions that the whole stretch of water was to be thoroughly searched and allocated the pinnace, two dinghies and the mooring party in Scow 14 to the job. He was a little worried that he and his section would be accused of carelessness or indifference.

None of what the pinnace, the dinghies and Scow 14 brought in, however, was big enough to hole a Sunderland and Hobson began to feel a little better. But he was still not satisfied and, worried they hadn't searched far enough, he personally took the pinnace as far as Freetown for another search. There was still nothing.

The AOC arrived that evening. He was a brisk man and he wasted no time. He let it be known that while he was worried about the accident rate he blamed nobody.

'There seems to be something wrong with our bloody aircraft these days,' he said. 'Five, isn't it, in six months? To say nothing of one up in Bathurst and one in Takoradi. London's wanting to know what the hell's happening.'

'If they came out here, sir, and looked for themselves,' Molyneux said gently, 'they might understand. We still haven't got split pins for the mooring swivels.'

'Haven't those bloody things arrived yet?' the AOC growled. 'How do you manage?'

'Four-inch nails, sir. At least the marine section changes them regularly.'

'We need better than that,' the AOC growled. 'I suppose by the time the war's over, this place will finally be organized. It's a bit like Topsy. It just growed without much thought for sanitation, comfort or anything.

'As for replacements...' the AOC paused for a moment before continuing '...we're not likely to get much from England for a while. They're too concerned with the Middle East. Everything that works, everything that lives and breathes, in fact, is being sent there. When they pass this place it'll be the most important convoy that's ever left England. With what it'll contain, we could knock the Germans out of Africa for good. Without it, we might lose the whole Middle East. I want a clamp-down on carelessness or indifference.'

'There's not much wrong with my chaps, sir,' Molyneux said.

'Hangar?'

'First rate, sir.'

'That's what Mackintosh said. How about the marine section? Are they supporting you properly?'

'I'm not only satisfied, sir, I'd go so far as to say they're very good. They're a funny lot, sir – neither fish nor fowl nor good red herring. They don't like being associated with ordinary people and I'm inclined to let them be. Independence of spirit's a good thing if it's accompanied by efficiency.'

The AOC frowned. 'The navy's talking about enemy agents, but perhaps that's because they don't want to admit carelessness at Giuru.'

Molyneux described the precautions that had been taken and the AOC nodded and drew the interview to a close.

'Well, I want very tight security,' he said. 'I want everybody on the top line and I want every aircraft brought into service – *and kept in service!* We can expect soon to learn dates. I was half-hoping for a few American Liberators at Lungi but they're fully occupied with the North Atlantic and West Africa's always the last place anybody thinks of.'

The following morning, Colonel Cazalet, of Security, appeared outside Mackintosh's door while he was discussing the latest disaster with Molyneux. He was immaculately dressed and looked so cool, so distant from disaster, Molyneux found himself wondering resentfully how the hell he did it.

'Hear you've been havin' a bit of trouble,' he said. 'Aeroplanes and all that.'

Molyneux looked at Mackintosh.

'How did *you* know?' Mackintosh demanded.

'My job to know,' Cazalet said. 'Quite a casualty list, isn't it?'

They admitted it was. 'This bloody place seems to be accident-prone,' Mackintosh growled.

Cazalet blinked. 'If they *are* accidents,' he said.

Mackintosh scowled. 'And what precisely do you mean by that?' he growled.

Cazalet blinked again. 'Thought of sabotage?' he asked.

'Should we?'

'Might be a good idea.'

Mackintosh's eyes narrowed. He had an Australian's dislike for languid Englishmen and Cazalet seemed to have a gift for not saying everything that was in his mind.

'What are you getting at, sport?' he demanded brusquely.

Cazalet wasn't the slightest bit put out by his tone. 'Remember that strip cartoon before the war?' he asked. 'Kids' thing: *Pip, Squeak and Wilfred.* Chap in it went around planting bombs.'

149

'You think it might be bombs?'

Cazalet smiled. 'Not that sort, of course. They were round like a cannon ball with a fuse sendin' off sparks. I'm thinking of a small charge placed where it might do a lot of damage. A Catalina's wing's got quite an overhang aft of the pylon.'

'You've done your homework,' Molyneux growled.

Cazalet shrugged. 'Good place to put it,' he said. 'Wouldn't be spotted and it's close to the petrol tanks and the fuel feed lines.'

'You think my Sunderlands were done that way?' Mackintosh asked.

Cazalet shrugged. 'Can't tell. Probably something a bit cleverer, because yours were later and you've been taking precautions.'

'Nice of you to say so. You jokers down at headquarters must be bloody busy working out conclusions like that.'

Cazalet held up his hand in protest. 'Just my job, that's all. Been makin' a few inquiries for some time. Something was probably attached to them.'

'It wouldn't be magnetic. Magnets don't stick to aluminium.'

'Other things do.'

'The bastard who did M-Mother would have had to get away pretty smartly.' Mackintosh's temper was still working on a short fuse.

'No problem at all,' Cazalet said. 'Such a thing as time pencils. Tube with acid in. Acid eats away the wire that sets off the detonator. Gives a chap time to get clear. Developed by the soft-shoe boys who go ashore in enemy territory. Italians used them when they fixed charges underneath *Queen Elizabeth* and *Valiant* in Alexandria harbour. They'd actually picked 'em up from the water and put 'em ashore when the charges went off.'

'I hadn't heard of that.'

'You wouldn't have, would you? Not many people did, because they compensated the list in *Queen Elizabeth* by flooding the opposite compartments so that any German aircraft that came for a look-see would report her still upright, and the admiral went on living on board as if nothing had happened. Even had a photograph taken of the hoisting of the colours, complete with guard and band and the admiral himself on the quarterdeck, especially for the foreign press. She's been out of action for months but they've been keeping the Eyeties who did it incommunicado and so far nothing's leaked out. They did it with some sort of submersible motor boat and diving suits. If they could do it there, they could do it here.'

'With a submersible motor boat?'

Cazalet smiled. 'Something a bit less sophisticated than that, shouldn't wonder,' he said. 'After all, everything here's a bit less sophisticated than anywhere else, isn't it? Suppose he was already in the camp.'

'One of our chaps?'

'Didn't say that! But it isn't hard to get inside a camp surrounded on three sides by water, is it? Might even have walked through the gate. As we've just decided, things out here aren't as sophisticated as they are elsewhere. Goes for camp security, too, perhaps?'

Mackintosh and Molyneux eyed each other silently.

'He must be still here then,' Molyneux said.

'Doubt it. They don't work like that. He'd get away by river. Swimmin'. They'd pick him up.'

'It'd be bloody chancy,' Mackintosh said.

'Sabotage's a chancy business.'

'Did he cause those explosions at Lungi?' Molyneux asked.

'Could have. He could have been picked up by boat and put ashore on the opposite side of the river to cross to Mamo where there could be another boat to take him to Pepel.

151

From there he could get to Lungi easy. It's less than thirty miles. That chap you picked up there, shouldn't wonder. I've seen his papers. They're dud.'

'Where are they operating from?'

'That's somethin' I'd like to know.'

'It would need some organization.'

'What makes you think they haven't got an organization? I heard that chap you picked up was speaking German.'

'That's what the padre said.'

'Is he good at German?'

'He's an expert. He was in Munich at the time of the Nazi Party rallies. He entertains the mess from time to time with imitations of the bastards he met there.'

'How about me having a word with him?'

The padre arrived within five minutes of Molyneux' telephone call. He hadn't changed his mind. 'He was speaking German,' he said.

'His papers said he was an Alsatian,' Molyneux pointed out. 'Don't they speak German in Alsace?'

The padre frowned. 'Not the sort of German *he* was speaking. He had a north German accent. He was from Hamburg or somewhere like that.'

'Could you tell anything he said?' Cazalet asked.

'He seemed to be talking about ships. He mentioned *"Flugboote"* – which is "flying boats" and something about, *"Es liegen sehr viele Schiffe im Hafen."* That means, "the harbour's crowded with shipping." '

Molyneux frowned. 'What,' he asked, 'would an Alsatian whose home's about as far from the sea as you can get in Europe and whose papers say he'd been living at Kissidougou, which is a hundred miles inside French Guinea, be doing talking in German about ships?'

'Come to that,' Cazalet said, 'if he *was* a Frenchman and *was* wanting to join the Free French, which I gather he claimed before he became unconscious, why was he at

Lungi? The nearest place in Sierra Leone to Kissidougou is Sefadu and that's only fifty miles from the railway at Pendembu. So why didn't he go to Pendembu or Bo and take the railway to Freetown, instead of turning up on the wrong side of the river at Lungi? What else did he say?'

Morgan smiled. 'I thought someone might ask questions,' he said. 'So I wrote it down.' He fished out a sheet torn from a notebook and placed it on the table. 'It was all a bit disjointed but he said something I didn't catch which was to happen "*im August*". "*Zehnte August*". Tenth of August. Then he kept repeating numbers – AS29 was one. Another was WS24. There was also an RS number and an OS number. I didn't get them properly. What are they? Cyphers?'

Molyneux frowned. 'They sound to me,' he said, 'like convoys.'

Although Ginger Donnelly was by no means a fast thinker, he was also no fool. He had kept the bottle of *Bière Etoile* on his locker ever since his visit to Makinkundi and now, following the rescue of the dying man from Lungi, he began to think about it again.

As he had listened to the comments of the medical officer, the padre and Wing Commander Molyneux, the thing had begun to hang together. Men in a boat on the night X-X-ray had crashed, speaking a language he couldn't recognize; a bottle of French beer turning up in Makinkundi, which was only around eighty miles as the crow flew from the border of French Guinea; and now an unknown man at Lungi claiming to be French but speaking German.

He made up his mind in the middle of directing his gang of Africans in the pushing of a seaplane tender on its cradle towards the slip. He simply stopped what he was doing and, leaving the sweating Sergeant Maxey yelling, 'Come on! Two-six! Shove!' just walked away. When Maxey turned round to look for him he was halfway to the hut where he lived. Ten minutes later he was outside the door of Hobson's office. It had been raining again and the airman who clerked for the section, a neat young man who had once worked on the stock exchange and preferred pushing a pen to handling a boat, looked up to see Ginger's pale-lashed eyes blinking at him through the drips that fell from the roof. Ginger could never have been called handsome and, with the mepacrine yellow that stained his skin, and the soaked overalls that clung to his scraggy frame, he had the appearance of a wet evil sprite. The clerk frowned. He didn't like Ginger. Ginger didn't like him. It made everything very easy.

'Op it,' Ginger said, jerking his head.

'This is my office.'

'I said 'op it. Go and 'ave a drink. They got a barrel of water in the 'angar made all nice an' clean wi' purifyin' tablets. Go and 'ave a swaller. It's stopped rainin'.'

The clerk eyed Ginger for a moment then decided that discretion was the better part of valour. Pretending unconcern, he vanished and Ginger pushed through his office, knocking to the floor with his stick a pile of papers and the clerk's tin mug. He didn't bother to pick them up.

As he placed on Hobson's desk the empty beer bottle he'd been cherishing, the sun, which had been struggling to pierce the rain clouds, managed it at last in a waft of heat, and the ray of light fell on it as if it were a spotlight.

Hobson studied the bottle gravely, then looked up, never very surprised by any action of Ginger's. 'Ginger,' he said, 'I didn't know you cared.'

The attempt at humour passed over Ginger's head. Reaching forward he turned the bottle round so that the label faced Hobson. 'It's French,' he pointed out.

Hobson studied the label. Its significance struck him at once.

'Where did you get it?'

'Upriver. Makinkundi.'

'Girlfriend?'

'Yeh, I been out 'ere a long time now. I've drunk beer in Freetown bars. I've drunk beer in 'Awkinge Town and Brighton. I never seen that one afore.'

'No, Ginger.' Hobson said quietly. 'Neither have I. Where did your – er – your girlfriend get it?'

'Boyfriend, I reckon.'

'I thought *you* were her boyfriend.'

'She's got one or two others.'

Hobson pushed a cigarette packet forward and Ginger helped himself.

'You're telling me something, Ginger,' Hobson said. 'It might help if you'd use words.'

Ginger was unoffended. He indicated the bottle. 'There's a bundu ceremony coming off soon. She bought it for the booze-up they 'ave afterwards. Somebody musta slipped it over the border. Somebody where this feller who got it for 'er works.'

Hobson was still staring at Ginger's bottle as a smart naval launch from Freetown turned into the creek and headed towards the base. Its crew were putting on a good show, clearly determined to show the junior service how to do things, and as it approached the deckhands were standing stiffly to attention with ropes and boat-hooks in the best naval fashion.

Unfortunately, the tide race at Jum was tricky – especially after the rains – and as the launch did a smart swing-to with its stern, the bow whacked unexpectedly against the catamaran with a crash that sent the crew staggering to one side. The passenger in the well of the launch, a commissioned engineer with a weather-beaten face, who had once been a chief petty officer, snarled something under his breath about 'bloody 'am-fisted matelots' and scrambled ashore, a magnificent figure in white against the gaunt, sweating, muddy men who worked and lived in the swamps.

He had half-expected to be received in naval fashion – not exactly a red carpet or even a bos'n's pipe because the RAF were a bloody uncivilized lot who didn't know how to go about things – but at least someone to salute. Nobody took any notice of him, however, until he found himself looking through the open window of Hobson's shabby office. Hobson was still looking at Ginger's bottle and, seeing the spectacle in white outside, neater and tidier than anything he'd seen for months, he rose to his feet.

'Looking for somebody?' he asked.

The naval man was just about to bark at him when he spotted the blue stripe on Hobson's shoulder and changed his mind.

'Wing Commander Mackintosh?'

'Up the hill there,' Hobson said.

'How do you get there?' The sun was blazing down now and the naval man, used as he was to a breeze blowing off the sea, was beginning to feel the sticky heat of the creek and was wondering where the transport was.

'Usually,' Hobson said, 'we walk. I'll walk up with you, if you like. I'm going that way.'

He picked up Ginger's bottle and led the way down the rickety jetty. The naval man stared down his nose at the jetty, and Hobson smiled.

'We're supposed to be having a decent place built for us,' he said. 'Unfortunately it never seems to get started.' He indicated a group of concrete piles lying on the mud surrounded by land crabs and mudhoppers. 'One day,' he said, 'they'll bring a pile driver down and start knocking them in, and then we'll get a proper jetty and some decent housing here. As it happens, though, it won't affect me much. I'm due for home.'

'You're lucky.' The naval man spoke with feeling because he'd only recently arrived and he didn't like Sierra Leone very much.

They continued talking as they headed along the jetty and Hobson couldn't resist getting in a dig, because the people in Freetown, who complained about conditions louder than anyone else, always collared everything worth having – including the drink. 'Unfortunately,' he said, 'there always seems to be something more important to do down in your neck of the woods. It's amazing how much they seem able to provide for headquarters in Freetown where the air's salubrious, and how little for us unhappy lot up here in the swamps where it's not. Perhaps it's because headquarters esteem their comfort more than they do ours, or perhaps it's because the builders don't like swamps and mosquitoes.'

Despite his teasing, Hobson's manner was gentle and by the time they had climbed the hill the naval man had thawed a little. He had discovered that, like himself, Hobson was a Yorkshireman and they were on friendly terms as they approached Mackintosh's office.

'Purvis.' The naval man introduced himself. 'If ever you're down in the harbour, find your way aboard HMS *Gleaner*, boom defence vessel. We hoisted your aircraft up, I can promise you a gin.'

'I'd like to do the same for you,' Hobson said. 'But unfortunately up here it's harder to get. The mess runs out occasionally and I couldn't guarantee it.'

Molyneux was in his office, reading Hacker's first report on M-Mother. Hacker was in no doubt that M-Mother's near-miss had been due to some sort of explosion near the waterline. This was clearly what Cazalet had been suggesting and now, it seemed, they had proof.

He looked up as Hobson appeared, then frowned as he placed Ginger's bottle on the table.

'What's this, Hobbie?' he said. 'Are we celebrating something?'

"Fraid not, sir,' Hobson said. 'In fact, it's empty.'

Molyneux looked puzzled and Hobson explained. 'Nothing very special about it, sir,' he said. 'Just an ordinary beer bottle. The only thing that makes it different is that it's French.' He turned the bottle round so that the label faced Molyneux. 'It came from Makinkundi. One of my chaps got it.'

'The one with the girlfriend?'

'Exactly. She got it from a boyfriend. Now, what,' Hobson asked, 'would a French beer bottle – it was full when Ginger got it – be doing at Makinkundi where there are no Frenchmen?'

As they sat studying the bottle, the corporal clerk from Mackintosh's office a few yards away, put his head round the door.

'Sorry to interrupt you, sir,' he said, 'but Wing Commander Mackintosh wonders if you could step into his office for a minute?'

Molyneux looked at Hobson who shrugged. 'The navy's visiting,' he said. 'Probably the boom defence vessel's report on A-Apple. Brought by a commissioned engineer working with the naval diving teams.'

Molyneux rose, then he frowned. 'Why the hell would he bother to bring it personally?' he asked. 'If it didn't contain anything special, he'd have sent it by teleprinter. Come on, Hobbie, this sounds interesting.'

Commissioned Engineer Purvis had laid a folder of photographs on Mackintosh's desk and he and Mackintosh were bent over them, studying them.

'Mr Purvis,' Mackintosh said, 'has something interesting to tell us. Not at all what we expected.'

Purvis was sure of his facts because he'd been fishing wreckage out of the sea for a large part of his naval career.

He pointed to one of the photographs. It showed the hole in Flying Officer Knight's A-Apple.

'Sea water does funny things to aeroplanes,' he said heavily. 'But I've never seen it do that before.'

He indicated the photograph again. 'It puzzled me,' he went on, 'so I took it to our salvage experts. They had no doubt. They said it was an explosion and that it came from inside the aircraft.'

Molyneux's eyes widened. 'Inside?'

'That's what they said.'

'But there's nothing to explode there,' Mackintosh pointed out. 'That hole's in the hull, sport. Beneath the floorboards. Somewhere under the galley near the drogue stowage. There's no machinery there and no depth charges.'

Purvis was unmoved. 'They reckoned something in the region of a five-pound charge,' he went on. 'It blew out the hole and, since the aluminium was bent outwards by it, it acted as a scoop.'

'And with the aircraft at take-off speed,' Mackintosh said slowly, 'it would shovel up tons of water in seconds. No wonder the poor bastards stood on their nose and went in.'

Purvis' report, coming on top of Hacker's report and the appearance of Ginger's beer bottle, changed things at once.

Mackintosh immediately obtained the name of every man who had worked on the aeroplane and questioned them all at length about their movements on the day of the crash. It proved only that they were all in the clear. This left the crew – who were not available for questioning because they were all dead save the rear gunner who was still in hospital – or somebody unknown who had been aboard the machine when he shouldn't.

It was at this point that Ginger remembered an extra man in the lorry that had returned from Freetown full of time-expired men on the afternoon of the explosion at Giuru.

'That blond feller,' he said to Feverel. 'The one 'oo wouldn't sing. 'Oo was 'e?'

'I didn't know him,' Feverel admitted. 'And if he's time-expired, it means he's been here as long as we have and we should have done. Didn't Trixie Tristram know him?'

They sought out Trixie in the snug bower he shared with one of his friends in what had originally been a storeroom in one of the Nissens. It was surprisingly colourful, with pictures on the wall and pink ribbon on the mosquito nets, and smelled of perfume.

'That feller in the lorry coming back from Freetown,' Ginger said. " 'E was standing next to you. Did you know him?'

Trixie hedged. After they'd returned to the camp, the fair-haired boy had disappeared and, to his great disappointment, Trixie had never seen him since. 'No, dear,' he said cautiously. 'I never saw him before in my life. He asked me in Freetown if the lorry was going back to camp and I said it was, so he hitched a lift. That's all I know. He said his name was Paul.'

'Paul what?'

Trixie looked coy. 'I don't bother with the "what" part, dear. Paul's enough for me.'

They passed on the information at once to Hobson who passed it on to Molyneux and Mackintosh. A check was immediately made of everybody who'd returned to the camp in the lorry, and the police corporal in command at the gate at the time of the return was put on a charge for permitting it to pass inside without identity cards being checked.

A search for the missing airman was immediately set in motion but, as Molyneux had expected, he wasn't turned up, though, when questioned, more than one man of those in the lorry from Freetown mentioned him and none of them knew him, which was odd, because, as Feverel had said, if he were

160

time-expired, *everybody* in the lorry ought to have known him.

'I think we're trying to bolt the stable door after the bloody horse has bolted,' Mackintosh growled.

As the inquiries about the unknown airman increased, one of the dinghy drivers recalled taking out a man to A-Apple in the early evening. He didn't know his name, however, and lists of passengers weren't kept, but the piermaster remembered someone asking him which aircraft was due to take off that night and recalled that he had said A-Apple. There was no reason why he shouldn't have done. Similar inquiries were normal enough from the odd people who appeared with equipment to do a job. The man who had asked him, he remembered, like the man who had been taken out to A-Apple, had worn normal short-legged, short-sleeved, collarless overalls like anybody else and had said he was going to check the drogues.

Mackintosh and Molyneux looked at each other.

'What was he like?' Mackintosh asked.

The piermaster thought for a while. 'He was slight and fair, sir,' he said. 'And good-looking. Very good-looking. Like a film star.'

Molyneux looked at Mackintosh. 'The chap from Lungi,' he said.

eight

The AOC's request for every aircraft to be in service kept the whole of Jum busy, particularly with the implications of what Cazalet had said and what the padre had offered.

It seemed to Molyneux, in fact, that they ought to press their inquiries further, but Cazalet was up-country investigating a sudden upsurge of unrest over rice at Miteboi and Kabauka, and in the end Molyneux decided that, in view of the beer bottle Ginger had produced, it might be a better idea to make their inquiries at Makinkundi. As he turned the idea over in his head, his thoughts fell on the padre. It was really a case for the civilian police or the CID department of the RAF police, which Molyneux knew existed, though he'd never come across it in Sierra Leone, but it occurred to him the padre might do the job more efficiently than anybody. He was a devout enough man who conducted his sparsely attended services every Sunday, struggled against the odds to provide a reading room for the bored occupants of the camp when there weren't any books, and was always available to anyone with a problem such as deaths at home or a wife who had gone off with another man.

But he was also unorthodox; though his habit of doing what he could for his spiritual flock in the way he did rather than pound their ears with prayer had always seemed to Molyneux to be the right one under the circumstances. The previous Christmas he had obtained several pigs to provide a Christmas dinner and when volunteers to guard them against

162

the depredations of the natives – who were also keen to have a Christmas dinner – had not been forthcoming due to the normal indifference of the lower ranks, it had been Morgan who had sat every night on top of the pigsty with a shotgun fighting off the mosquitoes to make sure they weren't stolen. His efforts had done more for the Church than a couple of dozen sermons.

'Dhu, man,' he had said, 'the strength of Christianity lies not in its divisive denominations but in the behaviour of those who practise 'em, and I always did think singing "Nearer, My God, To Thee" as the ship sank was a pretty impractical solution to the problem.'

Bored like everybody else and restless because he was blessed with a great deal of energy and little on which to expend it, when Molyneux put his idea to him, he jumped at the chance.

'Sure, boy,' he said. 'Just leave it to me.'

Molyneux' next recruit was Hobson. 'I want a boat upriver with a radio receiver,' he explained. 'I think somebody's hacking down our aircraft and, if they are, they're probably using a radio somewhere and I'd like to pinpoint where it is. And since, if I'm right, there are likely to be Germanic undertones, we need someone up there who not only speaks German but also understands the Germans. The padre.'

He frowned. 'I also want someone to find out more about the origin of that French beer. Although it came from French Guinea it arrived here from somewhere nearer than that. How about sending this chap Ginger, who seems to know everything that's going on at Makinkundi, up there to collect fruit for the mess – together with those other two who went to Lungi? There's a bundu ceremony coming off and it'll need someone with a bit of a head on his shoulders.'

During the night, one of the signals sergeants installed a brand new radio aboard the pinnace and the following morning before the day's work had properly started Corporal Fox brought the boat alongside. The padre climbed aboard and she was out of sight round the corner into the lagoon when Corporal Feverel brought Scow 14 from her buoy.

'Sing us a song, Nelly,' someone called from the jetty and Kneller, always obliging, offered his imitation of Bing Crosby singing Bing Crosby's favourite and the favourite of everybody at Jum, 'I'm Dreaming of a White Mistress'.

As the old scow trudged up-river, Kneller indicated a group of crocodiles basking on the mud, yellow-brown and hard to spot in the sunshine, one of them with its mouth open so they could see the yellow gums and saw-edged teeth. Crocodiles always intrigued. They seemed the very essence of evil, and though for the most part they moved slowly, that they could move fast the mooring party knew well because they had once seen one snatch an unwary dog from the water's edge. Further upstream a huge lizard walked in slow motion among the mangroves and terns splashed like dive-bombers into the river after fish, while pelicans, beaks tucked into chests, took off and landed like clumsy grey Sunderlands. Cranes, herons and bright kingfishers hunted among the shallows, and the air was alive with the screech of monkeys and birds, while occasional eruptions on the surface of the muddy water indicated where a shoal of small fish fought to avoid the jaws of a barracuda. A native fisherman, balancing incredibly upright in his pencil-slim boat, flung a circular net touched to meshes of gold by the sun, and a great Susu canoe roared past under a bellying sail towards the fruit market at Freetown. The helmsman, a grinning cage of white teeth showing in his black face, held up a wicker basket as he leaned on the heavy steering oar on the poop. 'Egg, boss?' he yelled. 'You want egg for cook?'

The pinnace was anchored at the head of the creek, bright in the glare of the sunshine against the dark mangroves, and

Corporal Fox was on the foredeck with a hand compass taking a sight on one of the hills. The crew watched the scow move inshore, wondering what was going on. They knew something was. Nobody normally operated at that end of the lagoon and there were extra aerials slung from the pinnace's mast while the padre was below with the wireless sergeant, their heads together, listening all the time as they fingered the dials.

The scow edged in near the loading jetty belonging to the iron mine. It rested on concrete piles that supported a narrow-gauge railway. Halfway along were three or four of the tipper wagons that brought the ore down from Yima for the little coaster, *Maréchal Grouchy*, which came from time to time from Conakry.

The smell of hot earth, sweat, river mud, decayed fish and excrement came from the land like the fumes from the open door of an oven, breath-catching and stifling as the sun rebounded off the ground with a violence that was almost physical. Makinkundi, half-hidden among the trees, looked lush and brilliantly green after the rain. As they climbed ashore, the women left their corn-pounding to crowd round, grinning and chattering and smelling of charcoal and perspiration, their bare black breasts rubbing against the white men's arms.

Then the inevitable wide boy arrived, full of sly, smutty jests and convinced he knew how to deal with white men. There was one in every village, always full of smiles, always able to speak better English than the rest, though inevitably in the end they all resorted to the pidgin that was common to everybody. This one was small, his lower limbs swathed in a length of coloured cotton wrapped round him like a towel beneath the umbilical hernia which, as with so many of his kind, was the result of a wrenching village birth.

'Boss come for kill crocodile?' he asked.

The Africans liked to see crocodiles dead. That way they were safer and, skinned, crocodiles meant food. Occasionally the officers' mess at Jum organized shoots from a motor dinghy with an Aldis lamp and a rifle, and the back of the hangar contained several neglected skins for which, in the shape of handbags or shoes, women in England would have given their right arms.

'No come for crocodile,' Feverel said.

'Crocodile bad ju-ju,' the black man complained. 'Plenty magic. Humbug fisherman.'

The river villages attributed unearthly skills to crocodiles and before they would touch the flesh, even when they were dead, the village constable had to be fetched to cut out the spleen which they regarded as a fetish. When one was killed at Jum, the uproar as they pounced on the gutted carcass with their knives was as good as a circus and one of the camp's free entertainments.

The black man was looking puzzled, then he grinned as light dawned. 'Boss come for *banana*!' he yelled and Feverel nodded. 'Boss, I got banana! Also mango and pawpaw and orange! Lime very good for gin!'

As they stood in a group in the middle of the village, surrounded by shabby brown-thatched huts and circled by piccaninnies wearing nothing but ju-jus of bells or feathers to keep away the evil spirits, the fruit began to appear. So did the fruit flies.

'Let's leave it to him and go and find a drink,' Feverel suggested. 'Ginger knows where it's lying around loose, I'm sure.'

Ginger led the way to Lizzie Morgan's bar. As he put his head inside, he called out and a black face topped by a pink headcloth appeared. Feverel found himself approving of Ginger's taste.

'You got beer, Lizzie?' Ginger asked. 'French beer?'

'I got.'

The beers appeared and Feverel paid with a Sierra Leone banknote as big as a bed sheet and a few washer-like coins. He looked round at the rows of black faces peering from their fretwork frames.

'Relations?' he asked. He sank half his beer and looked at Lizzie. 'Where you get beer?' he asked.

Lizzie shrugged. 'Friend belong me.'

'What him name him?'

'Him name Brima Komorrah.'

Feverel looked at Kneller. Half the males in Sierra Leone were called Brima Komorrah in one or another of its variations.

'What him do?' he asked.

'Him houseboy. In hills. Boina. Good job. Get plenty dash.'

Ginger wondered again if Brima Komorrah was one of Lizzie's lovers. 'Live 'ere?' he asked.

'No. Him live Hawkinge Town. All men know Brima. He big man. Strong like buffalo. Come Moa river way.' As they sat on the edge of the dusty patch of earth edged with sunken beer bottles that Lizzie called her garden, she began to sing in a thin high-pitched voice. *'I be sleepin' tonight where de moon shines bright, on the banks of Moa ribber.* He bring plenty food. He dash me money. Brima good man.'

'Yeh,' Ginger said thoughtfully. 'He would be.'

'What do white bosses at Boina do?' Feverel asked.

Lizzie shrugged. 'Brima say dey look for iron.'

'That all?'

'He say dey send messages. He hear dem.'

'What sort of messages? Radio messages?'

'Brima say dey got big mast. Like ship.'

'To search for iron ore deposits?' Feverel, looked at Kneller. 'What else have they got up there?'

'Lorries. Plenty lorries.'

'How many white bosses? Dis Brima, him know?'

'He say many.' Lizzie held up her hands with her fingers outspread – one, twice, three times.

'Thirty men?' Feverel looked again at Kneller. 'To look for iron ore? I'd have thought half a dozen could do the job easily.'

The French beer was cold and Feverel held up the empty bottles. 'You got more?' he asked. 'For take back to camp.'

Half a dozen more bottles arrived, to disappear unopened into the webbing side pack Feverel carried. As he was tucking them away, the black woman whispered to Ginger.

' 'Oo was it?' he said.

She whispered again, her eyes flickering over the other two in an embarrassed way. Ginger finished his beer and stood up. 'I'll be back,' he said, jerking a hand at the black woman. 'Got somethin' to do.'

Feverel and Kneller were just finishing their beer when Ginger returned. He nodded to the woman and squeezed her shoulder.

'Okay,' he said. 'It's okay.'

As they left, Feverel looked back. The black woman was looking nervously after them.

'What was all that about?'

'She's bein' 'umbugged. Some white bloke.'

'Where from?'

'Boina.'

'What's he after?'

'What you think 'e was after?' Ginger looked angry. 'It'll be all right now though. I fixed 'im.'

'How?'

'She's got eight brothers.'

Taking the scow with its load of fruit into the river, they lashed her alongside the pinnace and got the pinnace crew to row them back ashore with the inflatable dinghy.

'Where are you lot going?' Corporal Fox demanded. He was an amiable easy-going man but the mooring party seemed to take over the pinnace so often and so completely he was always inclined to be suspicious of their motives.

Feverel smiled. 'We're going to the bundu celebrations,' he said. 'Ginger got the chief to send us an invitation. Lovely pasteboard card, RSVP and everything.'

Fox frowned. 'Well, watch your pockets. It'll be like fight night at the Dog and Duck at Wapping Steps.'

The bundu ceremony took place in the early evening at a place called Aki in the bush, then the population of Makinkundi swept back and the native beer and the palm wine started flowing. Tall young palms, stripped of their leaves, had been hauled down and secured to the ground like great bows, and, as the celebrations began, youths clinging to ropes while the lashings were cut made forty-foot leaps into the air as the trees sprang upright.

A magician, dressed in strips of monkey skin, seemed to drive a feathered arrow through his cheeks and, with a scalpel-like knife, slashed at his tongue and chest until the blood flowed. Tumblers and acrobats were followed by jugglers who put on a hair-raising performance, using four-year-old piccaninnies flung from one to another over whirling razor-sharp swords that flashed within a fraction of an inch of the small spinning bodies, then an old evil-looking man wearing nothing but a triangle of cloth and a jumper of fishnet decorated with jangling bells made of shells, appeared, his whole body enveloped in snakes. Two great pythons formed the foundation but on top of them were layered puff adders, cobras and green and black mambas and dozens of smaller snakes. He draped the mambas over the body of a small boy assistant with a whitewashed face, wearing little else but beads and a straw-and-feather head-dress, then allowed himself to be bitten all over his body.

Finally, by way of light relief, he pushed one of the smaller snakes up each of the boy's nostrils, for the heads to appear a second later from his mouth while the tails were still hanging from his nose.

One of the villagers made an audible remark about the venom having been extracted from the snakes' fangs and in a flash the snake charmer was in front of him offering him the chance to test them for himself.

As the man vanished to the shrieks of delight of the other spectators, the snake charmer grinned at Ginger. 'You want 'em bite, *you*, Boss Ginger?' he asked. 'You want, I let 'em.'

'They couldn't bite their way out of a rice pudden,' Ginger said scornfully. ' 'Ow's business, Luki?'

The old man shrugged and Ginger went on. 'You all right for snakes?'

'You got some for me, Boss Ginger?'

'I can catch 'em if you want 'em.'

Finally the witch doctors started their ju-ju. As the chanting began, the women turned away but the men, eager to see, pressed forward and within minutes a dozen of them were shuffling about in the crowd, hypnotized and indifferent to the blows and pushes that kept them stumbling along. It was only when half a dozen of them started fighting, stolidly clubbing at each other with wooden stakes as thick as their arms, that Ginger touched Feverel's arm. 'I reckon we'd best be off,' he murmured.

None of them had any fears of staying the night in Makinkundi. Ginger knew the place inside out and they had no doubts that he would know where to go.

When he had first arrived in Africa he had been severely lectured on the proper attitudes to take towards black men, and earnest officers concerned with racialism had instructed him how to behave to the natives. It had all gone in at one ear and out at the other, and he still called them wogs, blackies and niggers and, against all the predictions of the experts, wasn't left for dead. The sheer inexplicability of it might have worried the experts, but it never entered Ginger's head that it was at all unusual.

Establishing themselves at Lizzie Morgan's bar, they ate a meal of rice and fish and Lizzie kept them supplied with the French beer she had acquired. With the seventy-two black portraits staring at them, high stiff collars, picture hats and all, it was like eating a meal in the middle of a football crowd.

As it grew dark, they began to hear drums, throbbing and insistent as black hands fluttered over the skins. The excitement of the bundu ceremony and the beer and palm wine were getting hold of the crowd now and the drunkenness increased. Among the trees, the sky was bright with the glare of fires and occasionally it was possible to get a glimpse of torches and kerosene lanterns, while the black shapes in the darkness seemed to be nothing more than half-moon grins, eyes and a pair of shorts or a lappa. As the gaudy stars pricked their way through the palm fronds, the biscuit-tin zithers began their flat plink-plonking and more drums started, bigger than before, interspersed with shrieks of laughter and the monotonous tinkling of native xylophones.

Inevitably the rain came, falling heavily in an unexpected thunderstorm that drove everybody indoors, and the mooring party took shelter in a large square hut constructed of straw, palm fronds and mud. It had three rooms, all dark and smelling of woodsmoke, and the owner, who knew Ginger, produced a bottle of palm wine which Feverel and Kneller drank to the accompaniment of the spat and trickle of rain, while Ginger pretended to be a monster and chased the owner's wife and daughters in and out of the rooms, the women shrieking with mock terror while the owner gave shouts of twanging laughter at their antics.

As the rain stopped and they headed back to Lizzie's bar, they could see the lights of the pinnace, which Corporal Fox had moved further out into the river in case some drunk with a canoe decided it was worth setting up a raid. Then, abruptly, they were aware that the whole of Makinkundi seemed to be in the open space in front of Lizzie's bar, a mass of agitated figures and wavering torches that etched highlights on black faces. The voices seemed suddenly to have become angry and Lizzie was beginning to look worried so they closed the garage-like doors and placed the bars across, watching through the cracks as the crowd swept past. A small boy was knocked down and trampled on and a hut was shoved over. Banana plants were broken and they could see the women edging to safety as the crowd pushed by.

Then, for a brief moment, they saw a white man outside, yelling angrily as the crowd washed over him like a tide.

'That chap's in trouble,' Feverel said.

They wrenched the door open to go to the rescue but the white man had vanished and the crowd was milling round the square, so that it was clearly impossible to move among them. As they dispersed, there was no sign of the white man and the whole place seemed to be on the move, a mass of running figures and wavering torches. The mood of the crowd had changed completely. From being full of high-pitched African laughter and deep banjo-voiced singing, it was suddenly filled with menacing shouts and the deep baying sound of anger, and people started to run along the road by the edge of the river, dozens of dogs and small boys leaping back and forth across the drainage ditches as they went.

'Was that the bloke who was humbugging your girlfriend, Ginger?' Feverel asked.

Ginger nodded. 'Yeh. Reckon so.'

'Well, he won't be humbugging anybody else for a bit,' Feverel said grimly. 'I reckon he'll be lucky to get out of this lot alive.'

Ginger nodded again, his face expressionless. 'Yeh,' he said. 'Reckon 'e will.'

nine

Africa looked its age and Makinkundi seemed to wear a guilty expression as the mooring party went to the river's edge the following morning. A house had been set on fire and the rain, which had come again during the night, had washed the embers into sooty puddles. But it was as though it had sluiced away the violence of the villagers and brought them to their senses, and they were moving about sheepishly in the bright morning sunlight, curious to see what the night's depredations had brought, but not *too* curious because the police had arrived from Hawkinge Town and too much curiosity could seem like guilt.

The climbing sun drew steam from the earth to mingle with the thin wisps of blue smoke that still curled lazily from the burned-out house. There was a strong smell of crushed grass and the spicy aroma of burned vegetation but no sign of the white man they had seen the night before, and their questions brought no response so that they could only assume he'd got back into the car which had undoubtedly brought him to Makinkundi and headed back to where it was safe. The familiar smell of charcoal, the smell everybody who served in Africa would remember to the end of his days, was stronger than ever and the deep red of the road to the river's edge was touched by the bright bronze-yellow of the new day.

The pinnace crew responded to the yells from the shore and the inflatable dinghy took them off. Fox watched them

174

approach. The noise ashore the previous night had worried him a little and he had moved the pinnace still further out into the river and had stood on deck, watching the flames and the torches and the moving crowd ashore with narrowed eyes.

'Bit of fun and games here last night,' he said as they climbed aboard. 'You're lucky to be still around.'

'We was all right,' Ginger said.

Fox watched as Scow 14 was cast off and headed downstream, its hold filled with the fruit collected the previous day. He had an idea something very odd was happening because the padre was still below with the sergeant wireless operator, their heads together, listening all the time as they moved the dials. Neither of them had had much to say and they took their meals without leaving the set.

Jum was inclined to be gloomy after all the accidents that had occurred. The officers' and sergeants' mess, both somewhat thinned out by the deaths of the crews of X-X-ray, O-Orange and A-Apple and the postings to Takoradi and Bathurst, were most affected, but even those men who lived in the ugly Nissen huts and remained bound to the shabby uncomfortable base were concerned too.

The aircrews trusted the men who worked on the engines, cleaned the bilges and made sure everything functioned on their long trips over the sea. They were all part of the same esoteric community and there was a considerable rapport between them. The practice of slipping small items of oversubscribed flying rations to flight mechanics, fitters, riggers and marine craft men was far from unusual, and everybody shared the common indignation when accidents occurred which shouldn't have occurred.

Molyneux was intrigued to hear of the white man in Makinkundi.

'Know who he was?' he asked Feverel.

'No, sir.'

'Serviceman?'

'He looked like it, but his clothes weren't uniform, though it's a bit hard to tell, because everybody wears what they like out here.'

Molyneux nodded agreement. He was wearing civilian-cut shorts and a South African bush jacket himself.

'Did he say anything?'

'We saw him yelling, sir, but there was so much noise going on we couldn't make out what he was saying.'

Molyneux didn't ask whether Feverel thought the Africans he'd questioned had told him the truth, even though most of them must have been pagans and hadn't sworn on a Bible. As the padre liked to say, it was almost too easy to become a Christian in Sierra Leone because the missionaries, both black and white, made converts just for the sake of the thing and they'd often discovered that pagans could be just as honest – and sometimes more honest – than someone who called himself an Anglican or a good Baptist.

However, he contacted the police at Hawkinge Town and asked them to find Brima Komorrah. They knew of him but knew nothing of his background save that he came originally from up-country, had filed teeth and a skin marked by lines of healed knife cuts that the Africans called 'tattooing'. He lived at Hawkinge Town, and Boina, where he worked, was in the Occra hills where a land surveying company was searching for new veins of iron ore. The police seemed a little preoccupied and it came out eventually that they were busy because of the near-riot at Makinkundi that Feverel had described. They had heard a white man had been attacked but they hadn't yet found him and the sergeant was still investigating.

Intrigued by the thought of a single white man in Makinkundi, Molyneux initiated a little cautious counting of noses to find if anybody was missing from the camp. Nobody was, so he rang RAF, Hawkinge.

Hawkinge had also heard the news but couldn't account for any absentees either, so he tried Royal Navy, Brighton, with the same result. Deciding that the man must have been a civilian, he tried British Overseas Airways, whose Sunderlands occasionally flew into Jum where they were serviced as if they were normal RAF machines. Since there was nowhere for civilian passengers to stay overnight, the corporation was organizing a few rest bungalows near Hawkinge Town and some of the bricklayers and carpenters they employed, not being under Service discipline, were inclined to break out occasionally.

Once again he drew a blank, so he decided to try Lungi. It was just possible that one of their employees, taking the long way round to Freetown, could have found himself in Makinkundi at an inopportune moment. It took him almost half an hour to contact Lungi and he could hear Trixie Tristram complaining shrilly as he picked up a variety of wrong numbers. The site manager was inclined to be short-tempered because his work was still hampered by the sabotage of his machines.

'You're sure it was sabotage?' Molyneux asked.

'Sure, I'm sure. African nationalists, I expect.'

Molyneux decided differently and, since unattached white men were difficult to explain and the one he was seeking didn't seem to fit into any known pattern, he decided it might be a good idea to go and see for himself. He was just on the point of leaving when the pinnace returned.

The padre's face wore a secretive expression as he walked up the hill from the jetty with the wireless sergeant. For the next hour he was closeted with the signals section then he headed for Molyneux' office.

'What kept you?' Molyneux asked. 'The riot?'

Morgan didn't answer directly. 'There's noisy for you,' he said. 'Worse than an eisteddfod with a gorsedd of bards all fighting drunk. I've got a few things to show you. I've been up at signals digging them out. Take a look at this for a start.'

He laid in front of Molyneux a sheet of paper on which he had written what looked like two lines of German poetry.

... Diene Schritte kennt sie, dienen zierlichen Gang,
Alle Abende brennt sie, doch mich vergass sie lang...

'What is it?'

'It's a song. A German song.'

'What's it mean?'

'Not much in itself. But it's significant, isn't it, in view of the amount of German that seems to be floating about round here at the moment?'

Molyneux looked puzzled. 'Is that what you picked up?' he asked.

'Yes,' the padre said. 'But not on the wireless. On the telephone.'

Molyneux sat bolt upright. 'On the bloody telephone?'

'Some time ago as a matter of fact. I was talking to one of the telephone operators at HQ. The one who dresses as an usherette when the concert party's on...'

'A bloody bad influence, in my opinion,' Molyneux growled.

'That's my opinion, too, to say nothing of the medical officer's. But that's by the way.'

'For God's sake, Taff, come to the point! What happened at Makinkundi?'

'I'm coming to it. Just be patient. I'm putting things in the right order. This telephone operator chap speaks a little German – not as much as he pretends, but some – because he was on the Continental telephone exchange before the war and he told me he'd occasionally picked up German in his

178

headphones while trying to get numbers for Groupy or other people.'

'German? Here?'

'You know what the telephone lines are like. They're about as efficient as everything else and you can just as easily speak to the Scarcies ferry operator as the commissioner of police. I told him to call me if any more came in. He did. Just before we left for Makinkundi. That's what I heard. No more. Just that. Then it went off and we picked up the United Africa Company ordering rice. Eventually, he got what he was after, which was British Overseas Airways in Freetown.'

'Well, go on. What is this song?'

'It's one the Germans sing. It's called "Lili Marlene". He'd got a crossed line and was on to someone who had a radio going in the background. It's a catchy tune you don't easily forget and I recognized it at once because I know it well. I believe it was written during the last war and I heard it first at one of those ex-servicemen's reunions the Nazis liked so much. As an ex-soldier, I got invited and we spent the evening wallowing in nostalgia, and for nostalgia "Lili Marlene" has Vera Lynn beaten to a frazzle. The signals officer's also heard it. Not only on the forces network in English but also in German on the telephone like me, which seems to indicate that somebody round here who isn't aware of what the telephone can do makes a habit of listening to German radio.'

The padre paused and smiled. 'It's a good song, mind, and I gather it's becoming popular in the desert, with everybody singing their own version. South Africans in Afrikaans. Poles in Polish. Even the Indians in Urdu and Hindi. I'm told the first time they heard it in Italian they thought it was Mussolini's National Anthem.'

Conducting himself with the stem of his pipe, the padre offered the tune.

Vor der Kaserne, vor dem grossen Tor,
Stand eine Laterne und steht sie noch davor…

He had a surprisingly good baritone voice but Molyneux stared at him as if he were mad. Morgan guessed what he was thinking.

'Trust a Welshman to spot a good song,' he said cheerfully. 'I tried it on young Kneller, that singer chap we have. Man, there's a voice for you. He knew it, too. He'd heard it on the pinnace radio. He sang it for me.'

'He would. Is that all?'

'I think it's a lot, because it fits with what we heard at Makinkundi, which is why I brought it up first. We picked up transmissions that the wireless sergeant couldn't account for.

'In English?'

'That would be too much luck.' The padre gestured with a handful of signal flimsies he held. 'This is everything we took down. We kept a listening watch the whole time, the sergeant taking down the Morse and me listening on a spare set of headphones for anything in plain language in German. There wasn't much. The sergeant said they were on the same wavelength as the navy and that it was hard to separate them. But every time the navy blasted out, so did they – underneath. He couldn't separate them because there was a lot of what he called mush, but I bet their friends could.'

'What was it?'

'Numbers mostly.' The padre waved the signal flimsies again. 'They were the same ones we picked up from that feller at Lungi. The plain language was isolated words and phrases – all meaningless. But there were some I recognized.'

'Such as?'

' "*Abteilung*", which means "section, division, unit". And "*B-dienst*", which I gather from the navy is the deciphering service the Germans use against British signals. We also picked up some French, too. The name Hatziger, for a start. And that, in case you don't know it, is the name of the Vichy general in French Guinea who doesn't love us very much because there's a grave in Hawkinge Town cemetery that contains his son.'

Molyneux' eyebrows shot up. 'Does it? I didn't know.'

Morgan fished in his pocket and produced a sheet of folded paper. 'Run your eye over that, boy.'

Molyneux picked up the sheet. It was dated *May 1941*, and was from the then air officer commanding to the then C-in-C, South Atlantic.

'Subject,' he read. 'Destruction of French Dewoitine aircraft, 16 May 1941.'

'This machine,' the message read, 'was shot down by naval anti-aircraft fire. Both members of the crew were killed. Papers found on them indicate they had come from French Guinea and were intending to overfly the harbour of Freetown, where Convoy AS 11 was watering en route to the Middle East. Pilot was *Commandant* Charles-Christophe Hatziger, a regular officer of the French *Armée de l'Air*. His passenger has been identified as Jean-Pierre Dufy, a civilian and a known German agent in Conakry. Both men have been buried at Hawkinge.'

Molyneux looked up. 'Where did you get this?'

'Signals office. They're a pretty ungodly lot here and since there isn't much call for my services in church, I get employed around headquarters in a variety of ways whenever anybody's short of a pair of hands. Censoring mail. Tidying drawers. Just the job for an active man. We were clearing the files to make room for the new bumph that comes in when I saw this. I remembered it when we picked up the name last night so I dug it out again for you.' Morgan touched the message. 'I know the grave, because I've been looking after it. Group captain's instructions, in case Vichy changes sides, as they undoubtedly will if we start winning.

181

'One last thing.' The padre looked smug. 'With the aid of signals, we got a fix on the transmitter for you. It wasn't very exact, of course, because we were a bit close to each other, but the lines we drew meet somewhere around Boina in the Occra hills.'

Molyneux was still staring at the padre, his heart thumping suddenly with excitement, when the telephone rang. He listened for a while then he put it down and told his clerk to get him a car.

'Things seem to be happening,' he said.

'Police Sergeant Momedu of the Hawkinge Town police has picked up this Brima Komorrah who provides the French beer I'm interested in. He should be useful. Care to come along?'

Together they drove to Hawkinge Town. The police station was a bustle of efficiency with self-important black constables moving in and out. Sitting on a bench just inside, looking terrified, was a large African, his hands clasped on his knees, his eyes rolling.

'This is the chap?' Molyneux asked.

'Dis de chap.' Sergeant Momedu spoke passably good English, having once served in the Sierra Leone Regiment. 'He Brima Komorrah from Moa ribber. Him Sherbro boy. We pick him up dis mornin'. Plenty trouble Makinkundi las' night. Bundu ceremony at Aki. Plenty drumming. Plenty dance. Everybody laugh. Den white boss come. Get drunk. Fight start. Boy pour petrol over white boss and set him fire.' Momedu's eyes rolled towards a nearby door and he jerked his head. 'He in dar.'

They had noticed the smell when they'd arrived but had thought nothing about it.

'Is he the one we heard about?' Molyneux asked. 'The one who was attacked.'

'Yassah.'

'Is he badly hurt?'

'Boss, he dead.'

Molyneux' heart sank. He'd been hoping the white man, when he found him, might be able to tell him a few things.

'Who is he?' he asked.

Momedu had no doubts. 'He got Dutch papers, sah, but I t'ink he mebbe French.'

Molyneux looked quickly at the padre. 'Why do you think that?'

Momedu placed a dirty rag on the table and opened it out. It contained a scorched blue packet of cigarettes.

'*Caporal*, sah.' He pointed to the cigarettes. 'Dutch boss no like *Caporal* cigarettes. Only French boss smoke *Caporal*.'

'How do you know that?'

'Sah, one-time me small boy belong Guinea.'

'Were you, by God? Did you hear this chap speak French?'

'No, sah. He speak somet'ing I no know. I speak him English. Den he speak me English.'

'What did he say?'

'He bad hurt. I tell him I take him hospital. He no wan' go hospital. So I send boy for doctor.'

'And did the doctor talk to him?'

'No, sah. He dead. Chop-chop. I got all his t'ings 'longside next door.'

'Any papers?'

'No, sah. No papers. Bunch keys. Coins. West African coins wit' hole in middle for string, for Mende boy to put round neck. And cigarettes, sah. Also, him shoes plenty muddy, Boss. But mud not from here. From up-country. In hills. I t'ink.'

'Boina?'

Yassah. Boina way. We find motor car belong him. I t'ink dat from Boina way also.'

Sergeant Momedu not only had a knowledge of things French but he also appeared to have the makings of a detective.

'You want to see him, sah? Soon dey take him away.

'Anything to see?'

'No, sah. Much burn. No hair. No eyebrows. Not'ing.'

'I'll see him,' Morgan said. 'If he *is* French, then he'll more than likely be a Catholic, but, dhu, man, I don't think the Lord would object if he has a Protestant prayer said over him. I seem to be doing this a lot lately.'

As Morgan vanished, Molyneux turned to Momedu again. 'What about this Brima Komorrah? What did he have to say for himself?'

'He say beer come from Boina.'

'Lots of things come from Boina, eh?'

Yassah. I t'ink he steal. He mess boy dar.'

'Would *he* know that chap you've got in there?'

'Yassah. He know. I take him look-see. He know. He say he from Boina.'

'What about the other men there? How come they have French beer?'

'Boss, he don' know.'

With the aid of Momedu, Molyneux managed to question Komorrah but the African knew nothing. He admitted stealing bottles of beer from where he worked, and he was scared stiff because he thought it had been bought from a Syrian who had arranged for it to be stolen from the docks and he was afraid of being implicated. Occasionally, he said, other beer appeared, though he had no idea, not being able to read, that it was French. All he knew was that it was different, and he thought it came across the border.

Molyneux' mind was busy. 'What'll happen to him?' he asked.

'He be charged,' Momedu said. 'He t'ief.'

Molyneux frowned. 'Can you hold him for a while, Sergeant? I don't want anybody to know I'm interested in Boina.'

Momedu smiled. 'Sah, we hold him plenty good. We say he arrest for humbugging policeman. We take him Freetown. Nobody palaver him there.'

Morgan was grave-faced when he reappeared. He said nothing as they left the little stone police station and climbed into Molyneux' car. Carefully, he lit his pipe and puffed at it for a while. Eventually he spoke. 'I think Momedu was right,' he said slowly. 'At least, part right. He certainly wasn't British. But I don't think he was Dutch or French either. I think he was German.'

'Another of the buggers?' Molyneux' head jerked round. 'Why do you think that?'

Morgan opened his hand. 'This,' he said. 'It was among his money.'

In his palm was a small metal badge, almost circular and not much bigger than a large coin. It was blackened by the flames that had killed its owner but as Morgan rubbed it with the hall of his thumb, Molyneux saw it was fashioned like a laurel wreath surmounted by an eagle. On the other side were a few embossed words and a swastika.

'What is it?' he asked.

'It isn't a coin,' Morgan said. 'That's for sure. But I do just happen to know what it is.'

'Come on, Dai. Don't be so bloody modest.'

Morgan smiled. 'Well, I've seen one before because, as you know, I was in Germany in 1932. It's a medal. There were a lot about in those days. They were given to young Nazis who attended the Party SA Rally in 1931. The Brownshirt boys were very proud of them.'

185

ten

It seemed to Molyneux that he finally had enough proof to translate his suspicions into action.

When he took his story to Strudwick, for once the group captain seemed impressed. 'Unfortunately,' he said, 'the air officer commanding's in Takoradi. Which leaves me as senior group captain in charge of the command. In addition, it looks as though we're going to have our hands full. There's been a riot in Freetown and two companies of the Frontier Force have already been sent to deal with more trouble at Miteboi and Kabauka. The commissioner considers it's organized. I'll send a signal to the AOC in Takoradi at once, though, informing him what you've turned up, and I'll warn the navy to be careful with their radio traffic. As for Boina, I'll get in touch with Cazalet. In the meantime, go and see the police in Freetown. You'd better take the *White Bird*.'

Molyneux was overcome. He wasn't to know that Strudwick was hoping to get his broad stripe when the AOC went home and was eager to show he'd been helpful and intelligent.

The river was shrouded in mist and, as the *White Bird* came alongside the Portuguese Steps, Tower Hill beyond the town was hidden by low cloud. Freetown was seething with people. Half the population seemed to be on the streets and they all seemed to be yelling insults. The din from the fruit market was deafening, and, because of the crowds,

186

Molyneux decided to try the C-in-C, South Atlantic, first. The marine guard at naval headquarters was uneasily watching the mob, his hand near the webbing holster that housed his revolver.

The admiral agreed to see Molyneux at once and an aide appeared, a lieutenant with a blond beard big enough to make Molyneux feel hotter than ever. 'Anything important?' he asked.

'I think so,' Molyneux said.

'Anything to do with that lot out there?'

'No.'

'Hmm.' The aide sniffed at Molyneux' laconic replies. 'Thought it might be. It's a bit like the Zulu War, isn't it?'

The admiral was a small man with fierce eyebrows. He indicated a chair as Molyneux was ushered in.

'You've picked a splendid time to come and see me.' He gestured at the open window. Outside it sounded like a cup final with the favourites a goal down and ten minutes to play.

As he pushed a packet of cigarettes forward Molyneux began to explain why he was there.

'We brought a man off Lungi beach a few nights ago,' he began.

'Heard about that.' The admiral's eyes twinkled. 'Got yourself in a minefield, I heard. Should leave these things to the navy.'

Molyneux went on to describe what had happened and that the hospital had confirmed the medical officer's opinion that the dead man, despite his burns, had died from peritonitis following a burst appendix. 'It's my view, sir,' he said, 'that he was responsible for the explosions at Lungi, but that he was already in great pain and, because of that, was careless and was caught by one of them.'

Finally he outlined what Morgan had told him, and asked if any of the numbers they'd picked up had any significance.

The admiral listened carefully, his elbows on the desk, his white shirt so dazzling it made Molyneux feel scruffy.

'Yes,' he said. 'They do. They're convoys. And that raises a point: They haven't come within our sphere of influence yet. We've only just heard of them ourselves.'

'The dead man's papers,' Molyneux pointed out, 'said he was a Frenchman but the sky pilot says he's German – a North German.'

'Wasn't there another of these strange Franco-German bods picked up at Hawkinge?'

'Makinkundi, sir.'

The admiral sat back in his chair. 'Seem to be rather a lot of Germans about at the moment, don't you think? Think there's something in the wind?'

'You doubtless know that better than I do, sir,' Molyneux said. He pushed across the slip of paper on which Morgan had scribbled down everything he'd heard, together with its translation. The admiral studied it then he looked up.

'AS 29,' he said quietly, 'is an army convoy. UK-Freetown, en route for the Middle East. WS 24 is a UK-Middle East convoy also via Freetown and Cape Town. RS stands for Gibraltar-Sierra Leone and OS for UK-West Africa.' He stared under his heavy eyebrows at Molyneux. 'You, my lad, have stumbled on something important. What else do you know?'

'Not much, sir,' Molyneux admitted. 'But that Dutch land survey company in the hills at Boina seems to keep cropping up.'

The admiral's brows came down so fast they seemed to click. 'Don't they have an office in Freetown?'

'They do, sir. In James Street.'

The admiral slapped his desk. 'Let's get the police on to 'em.'

He picked up the telephone and demanded police headquarters. As it chattered back at him, he slammed it into its rest with a frown.

'They're surrounded by a crowd of bloody Africans all yelling their heads off,' he said. 'This place's gone mad and we're kidding ourselves that it's all just about rice.'

It was almost midday when the police car arrived. It contained a police sergeant driver, an African constable, and a thin-faced inspector with pale hostile eyes who said his name was Yorke. Like most British officials in the colony, he looked overworked and drained of energy. Also inside the car was the ubiquitous Colonel Cazalet back from the north. He looked languid, self-possessed and, despite the stuffy heat, as cool as ever. As they nodded to each other, Inspector Yorke tapped the sergeant driver on the shoulder.

'Get going, Laminah.'

The driver turned a broad Mende face to him. 'Fast, sah?'

'No, you idiot. Normal speed.'

They were driven at what, nevertheless, seemed to Molyneux a reckless pace through the city, and Yorke managed a shaken grin.

'Trouble with my driver,' he said, 'is that he can read and unfortunately he's read all the wrong papers. He was given some old copies of *Motor Sport* and, ever since, he thinks he's Fangio or somebody. The only way to stop him is either to demote him, which would be a pity because he's a good sergeant and the bugger can drive. Or hit him over the head with the jack handle.'

He didn't seem over-keen to be involved. The police, he said, already had their hands full. On the other hand, since their job largely consisted of watching the docks and the ships and the Syrian traders for smuggled diamonds, it wasn't often that anything broke their ordered and boring routine, and this sounded a whole lot better than searching the cisterns of ships' lavatories for illegal mail.

Roaring past the old cotton tree, the car slid to a stop outside a shabby block of offices where it was immediately surrounded by Africans eager to know what was happening. Yorke pushed his way into the building, followed by Molyneux and Colonel Cazalet. The place was like an oven so that Molyneux' khaki was saturated with sweat within seconds.

The door of the survey company's premises was stained wood with a large frosted glass panel, and, leaning on the wall outside, were two Africans – clerks judging by their glasses and their white suits, shirts and pith helmets. There were also two African girls, both in gaudy European dresses, their faces purplish under the white powder they wore.

'You work here?' Yorke asked.

'Yes, sir,' one of the clerks said. 'Ever since the company opened.'

'When was that?'

'Jan van der Pas and Co. started the land survey company in Boina in 1939, sir. Very important.'

'That wasn't what I asked you. I asked when did you open *here*?'

The clerk's self-importance remained undisturbed. 'The company closed down when the war started, sir. It opened again this year. Under new management.'

'And this office?'

'Four or five months ago, sir. This is a very important office, sir. We have agents in Sweden, Switzerland and the USA.'

'Doing what?' Cazalet seemed to wake up for the first time.

'Iron, diamond and bauxite mining goes on all over the protectorate, sir. We send reports all over the world. I am Mr Henry Wilberforce Brahima Lucas, chief clerk. I was educated at the mission church at Kimbo and the Fourah Bay College. I almost passed my examinations.'

Yorke remained unimpressed. 'Who has the key to this place?' he asked.

'Mr Johannes de Wit, sir. He keeps it very carefully because he says we have too many secrets.'

'Surveying reports can't be all that secret,' Cazalet said. 'Where does he live?'

'Cape Station on Lion Hill.' Yorke seemed to have come to life at last. 'I have the address. Lives with the other white man who runs this show. Chap called Ubert Jansen. Must have influence. *I* can't get a house there.' He swung round to Lucas. 'Why haven't you been to see why no one's come down?'

'Sir, it is not my business.'

The inspector sighed. The educated Creoles, descendants of the ex-slaves who had first peopled the colony, were heavily involved with the administration and liked to put their spheres of duty into rigid patterns. He studied the locked door with a jaundiced eye as if he disliked it. 'Break it open, Constable,' he said.

Lucas stepped forward, full of indignation. 'Sir, you cannot do that!'

'Oh, yes, I can, my lad. Step aside.'

'I cannot permit it, sir.'

'I'll give you just two seconds to get out of the way,' Yorke said flatly, 'then I'll arrest you for impeding the police in the performance of their duties.'

Reluctantly, the clerk moved and the constable stepped back. As the door swung open, the constable fell into the room. Yorke, Cazalet and Molyneux followed, trailed by Lucas and the other clerks who immediately filled the air with gasps of horror and wails of protest. The floor was littered with scattered files and someone had been burning papers in a steel waste-paper basket. Yorke bent over it, poking about with his stick, then he crossed to the desk where the drawer stood open.

191

'I think someone knew we were coming,' he said.

Lucas stepped up to the inspector. 'I wish to report a burglary, sir,' he said.

Yorke looked at him as if he were mad.

'Someone has broken and entered this office, sir, with burglarious intent.'

'I can see that, you ass! What did you keep here?'

'Nothing, sir.'

'No money?'

'Just a little for postage.' Lucas crossed to the drawer and produced a tin box, which he opened with a shout of delight. 'And that, sir, they have missed!'

Yorke glared. 'They weren't after that, you fathead,' he said.

'These tribal people will steal anything, sir.'

'There speaks a bloody Creole,' Yorke muttered.

Cazalet was rubbing his nose. He looked at Molyneux. 'Who knew about this body of yours?' he asked.

'Which one?'

'The one from Lungi'll do.'

'A far as I know only the police, the people at Lungi and us.'

Yorke frowned. 'Wonder if that was what the bloody riot here was for. To keep us busy while someone cleared this place out. Certainly the people we picked up didn't seem to know what they were objecting to. Hang on a minute.'

He disappeared and Molyneux heard his shoes on the stairs. Cazalet leaned on a metal file. He was just too languid to be true.

Yorke was away long enough for Molyneux and Cazalet to smoke a cigarette. Cazalet also offered one to the African policeman but, as they heard the inspector returning, the policeman hurriedly tossed the butt through the open window where it was pounced on by a small boy who shot off with it between his lips, puffing like a train.

Yorke was frowning and looked hot. 'The bastards were here first thing this morning,' he said. 'Let's go and look at this house of theirs.'

'Fast, sah?' the driver asked as they climbed into the car.

'*My* fast,' Yorke growled. 'Not yours.'

They shot off with spinning wheels to Cape Station where most of the senior white officials lived in the cooler air of the hills. There was rain in the offing as they climbed into the grey mist of the clouds. Yorke glared at it.

'This bloody place!' he said bitterly, clearly hating every inch of it with a resentment that had built up over years.

They were looking out over the Creole houses now, a mass of decaying tin-roofed buildings with Victorian lace curtains set in damp gardens crammed with hibiscus and wide-leafed banana plants. A few military lorries churned past towards a Nigerian transport camp where the vultures strolled about like a football crowd looking for cookhouse refuse. It was raining again.

'Ruins your uniforms,' Yorke observed sourly. 'Mould collects on anything that isn't in constant use. You can't hang a thing up for twenty-four hours without being able to graze a cow on it.'

As the car halted outside a large house, a houseboy in a cotton robe came forward.

'Who owns this place?' Yorke asked.

'Boss Solomon, sah. He Syrian trader.'

'He's doing time for smuggling diamonds.' Yorke growled. 'Who did he let it to?'

'Boss de Wit and Boss Jansen.'

'Thought so. The bastard's probably in league with 'em. Where are they?'

The boy shrugged and Yorke looked at Molyneux. 'Somebody certainly got wind of your body,' he said. He pushed the houseboy aside and went into the house. There was a bookcase loaded with books and magazines, native rugs on the floor, a native mask on the wall with a couple of crossed stabbing spears and an arrangement of bundu knives in red leather sheaths. The food safe stood with its legs in small basins of paraffin to keep the ants from getting inside.

Yorke moved through the house, followed by the protesting houseboy, but there was little to be found and all the drawers seemed to have been emptied.

'Did the white bosses take away any papers?' Yorke asked.

'Sah, I t'ink so.'

Yorke frowned, then abruptly he turned and went outside. Standing in the middle of the road in the rain, he stared up and down the hill. Returning, he lit a cigarette and stood frowning again.

'This is about the only house in the district that isn't a bungalow,' he pointed out. 'I wonder why.

Going to the hall, he stared up at the ceiling. Above the stairs was a trapdoor, secured by a large padlock.

'What's up there?' he asked the houseboy.

'Boss, I don' know. Boss de Wit tell me I no go up there.'

'In that case,' Yorke said, 'we'd better have a look.' He turned to the black constable. 'Have that thing open, Suri.'

The constable found a pair of steps and a long screwdriver. Placing the steps under the trapdoor, he forced the lock. As he pushed the trapdoor open, Yorke passed him a box of matches and they heard him strike one.

'Sah!' His voice was excited. 'I t'ink you come.'

The inspector didn't hurry. He took a couple more puffs of his cigarette and turned in leisurely fashion to the houseboy. 'You got a torch?' he asked.

'Yassah. I got.'

Taking the torch, Yorke climbed the steps. For a moment he was silent then he turned to look down at Molyneux and Cazalet. 'You'd better come up here,' he said, and, hoisting himself up, disappeared into the loft after the policeman.

The other two climbed after him. The loft was like the inside of an oven and Molyneux broke into a fresh sweat at once. Yorke gestured with the torch.

'No wonder they kept the bloody place locked,' he said.

In one corner stood what was clearly a radio set waiting to be assembled. It was of ancient vintage and appeared to have valves as big as goldfish bowls.

'Receiver-transmitter,' Cazalet said. 'Don't need a thing like that in the land surveying business. Not even with agents in Switzerland, Sweden and the USA. Works on storage batteries.' He indicated a heavy wooden box alongside. 'Range up to four hundred miles by voice, I'd say; more by key. That's enough for the U-boats.'

Yorke was eyeing the set with interest. 'I bet it weighs nearly three hundred pounds without the batteries,' he said. 'And sends out blue flashes when it's working. Typical Sierra Leone lash-up. God knows how they got it up here without being spotted. Broken down to its component parts, I suppose. Like everything else out here, it probably dates back to Victoria.'

PART THREE

Operations

'...Agents in Dublin, Belfast and Glasgow report the departure of ships for the Middle East. It is expected that US convoys will join off West Africa. Large quantities of the new six-pounder anti-tank gun and Sherman tanks, together with the new Priest self-propelled heavy gun, and other vehicles, are aboard. Troops have been assembled at camps in and around Liverpool, Manchester and Glasgow and it is believed that these troops are also part of the convoy, which is without doubt intended to reinforce the British Middle East Forces...'

Dispatch to Führerhauptquartier *from German Minister in Dublin via Madrid, 11 July 1942*

'...It is reported from Rome that the Anglo Saxons may be preparing to land a force in western North Africa, whence later on they intend to launch their first blows against Europe. It is believed at Naval Headquarters, Berlin, however, that this force is an operation for the provisioning of Malta. Whatever the truth, it is clear that the success of such an operation will depend on the British in the Middle East being reinforced to the point where they can not only resist General Rommel in Egypt but can also drive him back in sufficient disarray as to make a landing or an attempt to relieve Malta feasible. In view of this, every attempt must be made to prevent the British being reinforced in the Middle East...'

To Kriegsorganisation VI *from Dept IVF (Navy), Berlin, July 1942*

At Boina Heidegger had been worrying for some time about the bar boy, Brima Komorrah. He had failed to turn up and Heidegger had been wondering if the British had picked him up and questioned him or whether he was merely suffering from a dose of malaria, what the Africans called 'belly palaver'.

One of the petty officers was singing in a nearby bath-house, his voice soft and nostalgic.

> Es geht alles vorüber
> Es geht alles vorbei
> Nach jedem Dezember
> Gibts wieder ein Mai.

After every December there'll always be a May.

Heidegger's eyes were distant as he listened, then he remembered his instructions that they weren't to speak German in the camp and made a mental note to reprimand the singer. He was still thinking about it when a message arrived from a Syrian at Hawkinge Town to inform him about Pfitzner's death. Pfitzner had been missing with one of the vehicles for two days now and Heidegger had been concerned that he'd done something stupid. The message seemed to indicate that he had, but under the circumstances it didn't seem to matter. Dead, Pfitzner could hardly be questioned on where he'd come from, and Heidegger

attributed his death directly to the Fallada woman. Since her
arrival the dissensions and jealousies had been obvious.

'The man was little better than a pimp with a swastika
stamped on his backside,' he said.

'He was a good Party man,' Lorenz growled.

'It's a pity he wasn't as good at his job,' Heidegger
snapped. 'Get in touch with Suleiman at Hawkinge Town.
Find out everything you can.'

Lorenz had barely vanished when another signal arrived.
B-Dienst was watchful and had missed nothing. Even the
British admiral in Freetown didn't yet know the facts. It came
via French Guinea, and was concerned with positions,
courses and numbers.

'Wolf Pack Herzog,' it ended, 'will be moved to position
Lat 151° 30' 20'' N, Long 191° 21' 30'' W. Wolf Pack
Markgraf will move to position twenty miles south.'

Heidegger reached for a chart and a pair of dividers. The
position he'd been given was roughly opposite Cape Verde
and a hundred and fifty miles out to sea west-north-west of
the Gambia. The courses and times of the convoys had
originated in England, he knew, so there could be no mistake.
He looked at the message again. Three convoys, one from the
States, one from England and one from Gibraltar, were all
due to come together within six hundred miles of where he
stood before heading south. One hundred and forty ships,
excellent pickings for the U-boats. The supplies Rommel
feared would never get through.

He looked at the convoy numbers, made a note of them,
and sent for Lorenz. When he appeared, Heidegger tossed the
signal across. 'We move down to Kumrabai tomorrow. Find
Willer and let him know he's to make his own way there.'

Lorenz grinned and vanished. Pfitzner was forgotten.
Passing out the necessary orders, he headed for Magda
Fallada's quarters. She was asleep, wearing nothing but a
sheet. Bending over her, he ran his hands along her body so

that she sighed and stirred. As her eyes opened, she saw Lorenz above her and put her arms round his neck.

'Not now,' he said. 'Save it for later. It will seem better in the safety of French Guinea.'

Her eyes widened and she sat up so that the sheet slipped from her. 'We're going? At last?'

'Looks like it. We have a little job to do first. When we've finished, the British will be running in small circles wondering what's hit them.'

'What *will* have hit them?'

'Machine guns.'

'A battle?

'Not really. Just that all their aircraft will be full of holes and sinking. The Middle East convoys will then be wide open to our U-boats and, while the British are sorting that lot out, we shall doubtless be heading for French Guinea.'

'When do we leave?'

'Tomorrow. So start packing. We'll be taking over the mine at Yima for forty-eight hours.'

She was on her feet now, stark naked, moving about the room and reaching for her belongings.

'We're travelling light,' Lorenz warned. 'No unnecessary baggage. The lorries will be full of weapons and ammunition.' He grabbed for her and kissed her. 'You'll travel with me,' he said. 'Out of Heidegger's way. I'll go and arrange it now.'

He went out, slamming the door. As he started for his quarters, a shout stopped him dead in his tracks. He turned and saw the telegraphist hurrying towards him.

'Not now,' he said. 'Not now!'

'I think you'd better see it, sir!'

Angrily Lorenz snatched the signal flimsy and began to read.

'*Gottverdammt!*' The fury broke out of him in a shout and he spun on his heel and began to run for Heidegger's office.

Heidegger was collecting his papers. At his feet, the native houseboy was burning papers in an old oil drum. The hot oil filled the office with a sickly stench. As the door burst open, Heidegger looked up.

'Willer's dead!' Lorenz said.

Heidegger jumped to his feet. 'When?'

'Three nights ago, it seems. Witte telephoned from Freetown. He's had to bolt. They were expecting a raid.'

'Did the British catch Willer?'

'No.' Lorenz' expression was without pity. 'It seems he was suffering from a ruptured appendix and was trying to get to our contact at Mahera. He was found and evacuated to Freetown, but he died on the way. They don't know who he is, though, and his papers are in good order. As far as they know he's an Alsatian hoping to join the Free French.'

'What about Witte and Johansen?'

'They've shut down and are heading north. They expect to make it because they've got half the population of Freetown on the streets. They'll be taking a boat across to Pepel to pick up the railway. They'll cross into French Guinea at Banguraia. They've destroyed everything and burnt their papers. There's nothing to give the game away.'

'Don't be a damn' fool, Lorenz!' Heidegger snatched the signal. 'There's everything to give the game away! That office's supposed to be a subsidiary of this place. The police will signal Banguraia and be up here in a matter of hours.'

Lorenz looked scared. 'I'll warn Magda.'

'For the love of God, Lorenz, get your mind on your job! We weren't sent here just to get *her* across the border.'

Lorenz swallowed. 'What do you propose?'

Heidegger dropped the signal on the desk in front of him. 'How many of us are there?'

'Thirty-nine. All trained men.'

'Weapons?'

'Enough to make a nuisance of ourselves. Heavy machine guns as well as rifles.'

'Very well, we'll move at once. The plan remains the same. We simply move a day earlier.'

'And the getaway? To the border?'

'There won't be time if they've broken Witte's cover. We'll use the river Bic. The Dutchmen at Yima have a fast launch, which should be big enough for the lot of us. Inform the *Maréchal Grouchy* we shall need picking up two miles out between Lungi and Tagrin Point. They're to wait there with steam up, ready to set a course at once for French Guinea. We can be inside Vichy waters in four and a half hours. It'll take the British that long to wake up to the fact that we've gone.'

When the police arrived at Boina, armed to the teeth and ready for action, they found the place deserted. In Yorke's car the drive had been a wild one.

The air had seemed to be full of flying ants which smeared themselves on the windscreen and deposited their wings inside the car, and once, as they had begun to climb, they had seen a prowling leopard, two yellow eyes and the flash of a spotted body moving rapidly into the trees. Turning off the main road, they began to climb more steeply, moving higher and higher, to where the low bush gave way to taller vegetation – baobabs, eucalyptus and cotton trees. The air was chillier here and – the movement of the car created a draught that cooled their bodies and dried the sweat on their clothing.

The hills were full of colour, ranging from yellow to pink to purple. There had been another downpour and the place was covered with a thin mist as the vehicles came to a stop, but there was no sign of life except for two or three black men from Boina village, complaining that they hadn't been paid.

Cazalet was standing alone, gnawing the end of his swagger stick as he watched the policemen move through the deserted bungalows, his yellow eyes cold and watchful. 'They must have bolted for the border,' he said to Yorke.

Reaching inside the car, he fished out a map and, spreading it on the bonnet, began to trace with his finger the route north. 'We've got to watch the Scarcies. You'd better ask your people to keep a look-out for any unexplained vehicles.'

As Yorke started radioing orders, Molyneux watched uneasily. Having started up the hare, it seemed to him that his place was now with his squadron.

'Mind if I borrow your car?' he asked Yorke. 'I need to get back.'

'Help yourself. We'll be here some time.'

Scrambling into the car, Molyneux tapped the driver on the shoulder. 'Jum,' he said.

Sergeant Laminah rolled his eyes and grinned. 'Fast, sah?'

'Fast as you like.'

The journey was something Molyneux was to remember all his life and fully explained why Yorke tried so hard to keep his driver under control. They hurtled down from Boina on a winding road awash with red mud, sliding round the corners and sending goats, chickens and children scuttling for the undergrowth. Once on the tarmacadam, Laminah really put his foot down and the car headed north-west as if the devil himself were on their tail.

Screams and jeers followed them as they roared round corners and leaped over the brows of hills. At the narrow bridges over the gullies, Laminah didn't bother to wait. The drivers of vehicles coming in the opposite direction, suddenly aware that the madman approaching them at speed intended to dispute the bridge, slammed on their brakes. Laminah slithered past with inches to spare.

After the rain, the country looked fresh and iridescent butterflies lifted from the bush. The clipped simian cries of monkeys and the shriek of parakeets rose in alarm and a cloud of glossy purple starlings and lemon-coloured weavers exploded into the air as the car sped past. A woman in a scarlet lappa carrying on her head an umbrella and a Bible turned away and cowered to avoid the wave of muddy water Lamina threw up.

Holding his hat on with one hand and clinging for dear life to the side of the car with the other, Molyneux breathed in a series of gasps as the car hit the bumps. Then they slithered round a corner and found themselves face to face with an army lorry driven by a black soldier just as it was approaching yet another of the endless narrow bridges. The driver's eyes almost popped from his head as he slammed on the brakes and yanked at the steering wheel. As Laminah slipped under his nose, the lorry's front wheels dropped from the road and it began to roll slowly down the steep bank towards the creek.

Molyneux had never arrived at Jum in such style. As they roared down the road from Hawkinge Town, the crowds of black labourers heading home at the end of the day began to scatter. Laminah seemed intent on crashing through the painted barrier, but, slamming on the brakes in the last few yards, he slithered the car sideways, straightened out, and came to a stop with the bonnet inches from the pole.

A shaken-looking RAF police corporal appeared. 'What the hell are you trying to do?' he demanded.

'Open the barrier, Corporal,' Molyneux shouted.

The corporal looked worried. 'Sir, I shall have to see your identity card.'

'Open the bloody barrier!' Molyneux snarled. 'It's an emergency.'

The corporal tried to throw up a salute, changed his mind and leaped for the barrier, his right arm still performing

205

JOHN HARRIS

indeterminate movements by his ear as the car roared into the camp and headed for headquarters.

Mackintosh was just leaving his office as they slithered to a stop, and Molyneux panted out what had happened. Followed by the Australian, he dived into his office and, crossing to a chart of the river hanging on the wall, he ran his finger along it. He had long since decided that Cazalet and Yorke were wrong and that the Germans hadn't bolted for the border. If someone wanted to disrupt flying at Jum – and it had become pretty obvious that that had been the intention for some time! – they wouldn't give up at this point. They would stick a machine gun or two on the river bank opposite the mooring trots. It only required a hole or two in a flying boat at water level to make it unserviceable, and from the bank opposite a heavy machine gun could polish off the lot.

'Between Disp and Makinkundi,' he said, half to himself. 'From there they could tie the whole thing up.' He swung round to Mackintosh. 'Get on the blower, George,' he said. 'We're probably in bad trouble! They've just unearthed a bunch of German agents. I was there. I think our kites are about to come under fire.'

Mackintosh looked startled and he went on hurriedly, his hand still on the map. 'They'll go to Kumrabai, then down the spine of land between the swamps to Makinkundi and Yima.'

'What the hell are you talking about?'

'The Germans! We've got to clear this place! I'll get in touch with Bathurst and Takoradi and see how many kites they can take.'

Mackintosh stepped forward. 'Listen, sport...'

Molyneux was reaching for a signal pad when Mackintosh snatched it away. 'For Christ's sake,' he yelled. 'Listen! There's not a snowball's chance in hell of moving!' He flourished a signal flimsy he was holding. 'Look what's just come in! Those convoys we've been expecting are on the way!'

'Have you heard from the admiral?'

'No. Nothing. But, listen, sport, our kites are going to be needed *here*, not in Bathurst or Takoradi. The AOC's even trying to bring *more* kites in to help because the navy says *this* is where the danger's going to be and we've got to be on the top line.'

Molyneux gave him a worried glance and made up his mind quickly. 'Right,' he said. 'Then let's shift those slabsided monsters of yours over to the east side of the river out of danger. Get in touch with Hobson. We're going to need every man he's got, to say nothing of every man we've got. I wish we knew where they were, so we could try dropping a bomb on the bastards.'

In fact, the Germans had already reached Yima. The lorries had swung off through Hawkinge Town while Molyneux was still on his way back from Boina and had headed into the bush towards the coast. The sight of the sun on the sea cheered Heidegger.

The mine buildings were in the middle of a large area of muddy earth criss-crossed by wheel marks. The bush had been cut well back to keep the mosquitoes at a distance, and the only shade in the whole area was from a single eucalyptus tree that threw a thin shadow in the direction of the river Bic. The main gate of the mine was open and they drove straight in, to draw up outside the door of the office. There was only one man, the manager, there, and he looked up, puzzled, at the arrival of half a dozen unfamiliar lorries.

'Attend to him, Lorenz,' Heidegger said. 'But no killing. We don't want the alarm raised. I'll secure the gate.'

As Heidegger began to gesture at the armed men tumbling from the vehicles, the Dutchman inside looked alarmed and, as he approached, without warning Lorenz hit him over the eye with the pistol he held in his hand.

'Get him out of sight,' he snapped.

As they occupied the offices, a car containing two more Dutchmen appeared from the quarry face, the expression on the occupants' faces at the sight of the strange vehicles as puzzled as that of the manager. They were rounded up and locked with him in a storeshed. Soon afterwards, a lorry appeared from the mine workings driven by another Dutchman, followed by a car containing two more. They, too, were marched away and locked up. Inquiries revealed that they now had everybody.

'What about the mineworkers, *Herr Leutnant?*' Lorenz turned as one of the petty officers questioned him. 'There must be sixty or seventy of them.'

'Forget them,' Lorenz said. 'Nobody's going to start shooting at us with that lot in the way. The British are too sensitive about African reaction, especially after the troubles in Freetown.'

There was a lot of grumbling at Jum because no one knew what the panic was all about and Molyneux hadn't the time to tell them. He was trying to contact the AOC to warn him of the danger.

By this time flying crews were being pushed aboard their aircraft from dinghies, and checks were hurriedly made and the rakes that held the controls taken off. As the grommets that held the aircraft to the buoys were unlashed and slip ropes put on, engines were started, outers first to bring the buoy into view.

As her mooring was slipped, Sunderland C-Charlie, the first machine to move, began to taxi, the pilot frowning as he stared about him and tried to think ahead to avoid tight positions; because, like boats, Catalinas and Sunderlands didn't have brakes but, unlike boats, couldn't go astern.

208

Fortunately, the wind was light and the machine swung easily and headed downstream to turn round the rear of the trots, the flight engineer cursing as he did his acrobatic act on the ladder with the slip rope in his hand. No two approaches were ever the same and if you missed and had to go round again it was drinks all round for the crew.

They made the buoy at the first try and the flight engineer shoved the slip rope through the buoy's harness and shot back up the ladder to the bollard, cursing as he trapped a finger. Even as the next machine began to get under way, a bomb scow loaded with depth charges slipped alongside C-Charlie and, while two armourers knelt on the wing with a winch, a wire was passed to the scow. In the old days they had had to use five-hundred-pound anti-submarine bombs which were as useless as Christmas puddings unless dropped straight down a U-boat's open hatch, but things had improved with the arrival of aircraft depth charges, especially since they'd learned to fuse them for explosion at twenty-five feet and catch the U-boats as they were submerging. But they were still in short supply – shorter still since the explosion at Giuru.

As the depth charges were hoisted into place and secured to their racks, a refueller appeared on the other side of the machine. The sense of tension was touching everybody. Most of the men doing the work weren't quite clear what the fuss was about but a few rumours had started and they were all aware that they had to work fast and accurately. The aircraft were going to be needed before long.

By the time they had finished the AOC's signal had reached every base on the West Coast and they were all preparing to move aircraft towards Freetown, while their own moorings were readied for the arrival of other aircraft from further south. It was a case of when-father-turns-we-all-turn, all the way back to South Africa and round the corner to Santa Lucia Bay in the Indian Ocean.

As he watched his machines taking up their new positions, Molyneux decided to contact Inspector Yorke. Yorke remained silent for a second or two after Molyneux had finished but, when he finally spoke, even over the assorted cracklings and whistles of interference he sounded worried.

'I think you're probably right about those machine guns,' he said. 'None of my people report seeing lorries on the move north. I'll try to contact Cazalet but until I do I think we're going to have to do something on our own. I'll get the navy to land a few chaps at Mamo across the river to work north. Can you get a few to Makinkundi to work south?'

'We're hardly trained for that sort of thing,' Molyneux pointed out. 'But I'll see what I can do.'

two

'I want volunteers,' Molyneux said to Hobson. 'What have you got in the way of time-expired men?'

Hobson listened as he explained and as usual promptly offered the mooring party and the pinnace crew. 'I expect we can find a few more, too,' he said. 'How are you going to get them up there?'

'What about Groupie's boat?'

'He'll never permit it.'

But he did. The AOC arrived in a bad temper while they were discussing the matter and made his decision at once.

'The *White Bird*,' he said emphatically, 'is to be returned at once to the marine craft section, where it will remain henceforward.'

By getting Sergeant Maxey to push back into the water a tender that had been up the slip for service, Hobson raised two tenders, a scow and the pinnace. Twenty-odd time-expired men of all trades, including even a few clerks from headquarters and main stores, were stuffed aboard the *White Bird*, most of them complaining loudly because carrying rifles and wearing webbing in a temperature that was enough to suffocate an ox wasn't what a decent clean-living time-expired airman ought to expect when he was awaiting a ship to take him home. Sergeant Maxey, no less time-expired and no less indignant, was stuffed aboard after them, sweating like a fountain as he pushed his way into the cabin.

'Make sure you don't get too near to him, dear.' Trixie Tristram, also time-expired and spiteful at having to dress up and look like a soldier, leaned towards one of his boyfriends. 'He gets a bit high when he's warm.'

Standing on the jetty, Molyneux tried to explain just what they were expected to do.

'You're not supposed to be commandos,' he explained.

'You're telling us, dear,' Trixie's acid voice came from the back.

Molyneux' grim look stopped any laughter. 'West African troops are being landed opposite Pepel and will approach from that side. More will approach from Hawkinge Town as soon as they arrive. You can leave the serious fighting to them. All you're supposed to do is keep your heads down and keep them busy. Their intention's to prevent our kites stopping their submarines sinking ships – and one of those ships might well be the one that's due to take you lot home.'

It was a shrewd point because to the time-expireds the idea of someone sinking their ship was enough to stiffen anybody's determination, and they frowned at each other, trying to see themselves as warriors.

The *White Bird* was just on the point of casting off when Hobson saw Ginger Donnelly leaning on his stick by the pinnace. 'You, Ginger,' he said, jabbing a finger. 'Go with Sergeant Maxey. You know Makinkundi and seem to have influence there. He might be glad of help.'

As the *White Bird* drew away, Molyneux stared after it. One boat and twenty men didn't seem much and the party for the second seaplane tender looked like being even thinner on the ground because with the big anti-submarine operation just over the horizon, he knew he couldn't expect men to be taken off boats or aircraft maintenance. Then Warrant Officer Hacker pointed out that a new draft had just arrived from England and were at RAF, Hawkinge, awaiting posting to Takoradi and Bathurst.

'How many?' Molyneux demanded.

'Forty-nine, sir.'

'Grab 'em.'

'They're all flight mechanics, fitters and riggers, sir. All white knees. Brand new in the service even.'

'I presume they've all been taught to fire a rifle.'

Hacker held back a smile. 'Probably not with much success, sir.'

'We're not looking for snipers,' Molyneux said. 'Just someone to make a lot of noise.' He looked at Hobson. 'How long would it take to go round by sea to Bic creek?' he asked.

'The pinnace does it in a couple of hours.'

'Right. Let's have some of this new lot round there. Then we'll be on three sides of the bastards and they might just decide to throw their hands in.'

Molyneux was just wondering whom he could put in charge when the padre appeared. 'I was beginning to think there was never going to be any excitement round here,' he said.

By now darkness was almost on them, and Molyneux heaved a sigh of relief. Darkness would give them a few hours' respite and instructions were issued that no lights were to be shown. Orders had also been given that dinghies carrying armed men should patrol the lagoon, while full aircraft crews, save the captain and navigator, who could well be needed at any moment for briefing, were ordered aboard with waist guns cocked and ready to fire.

The new arrivals from England, snatched from what had appeared to be a reasonably comfortable billet at Hawkinge and brought in lorries to some God-forsaken place which seemed full of mosquitoes, surrounded by water and mud and occupied by savages, were beginning to gather near the pier in front of the hangar, bewildered and perspiring under rifles, ammunition and water bottles. They were all freshly in the RAF and brand new to West Africa, and were wearing the new-issue shirts that were a cross between a bush jacket and a shirt and were a dead loss in either role. They hadn't even yet thrown away the vast heavy solar topees that were issued in England by some idiot who'd doubtless never had to wear one, and they were all wondering what the hell was happening, because in England ground crews weren't usually involved in shooting and getting shot at.

Hobson counted them and ordered half of them aboard the pinnace. Fortunately, there was rain about and it was cooler than normal with brooding clouds clinging to the hills, but the pinnace was so packed with humanity it seemed that if anyone moved too suddenly half a dozen would fall overboard; and to add to the crowding they had hoisted the punt inboard, its outboard detached for safety because it would more than likely sink on tow beyond the mouth of the river.

They had rounded the corner of the creek and begun to head north when the remainder of the party of armed men were ordered aboard the second seaplane tender, and the first man had just put his foot on the rattling boards of the jetty when firing started from across the river. Lorenz had found a point on the west bank from which he could see the trots of aircraft and two automatic weapons had been hurried forward. They were placed in position just as it began to grow dark.

At the sound of the firing, Molyneux swung round and, pushing past the crowding airmen, ran to the end of the jetty. Hobson was there to superintend the loading, because everybody at Jum wasn't a sailor and some were distinctly ham-fisted in boats.

'What's happened?' Molyneux asked.

Hobson gestured out towards the river. 'Seems to be coming from the other side. Somebody's flashing.'

He had grabbed the piermaster's Aldis and was watching the signals.

' "Machine gun fire," ' he read. ' "From far side of river." '
'Ask him what they're shooting at.'
The lamp clattered and Hobson turned. 'He says, "Me." '
'Ask him if there's been any damage.'
The Aldis clattered again and Hobson turned once more.
'He says there are holes in the hull. Near the tail.'
Molyneux frowned. 'Who is it?'
'T-Tommy. There he goes again. "Do we return fire?" '
Molyneux frowned. He was in a difficult position. T-Tommy, like all the other aircraft, had been bombed-up and ammunitioned for early take-off. If they used their ammunition firing across the river they would have to be resupplied.
'Tell them to try to keep their heads on. Then ask Hacker to get airframe fitters on those holes. And pray for rain, Hobbie.'
By a miracle Molyneux' prayer was answered and when the rain came a few minutes later it put a curtain of water across the river and the firing stopped. There had been little damage but it had proved that the Germans meant business.

There was no sign of hostility as the *White Bird* came alongside the loading jetty at Makinkundi. Half a dozen tipper wagons, plastered with mud, stood forlornly on the rails above their heads. Moored alongside was a heavy motor lighter.
At Maxey's signal, the airmen scrambled ashore, their khaki black with sweat under the rifles, fifty rounds of ammunition and water bottles. They were followed by Maxey, looking more like a wet boiled egg than ever. This, he decided, was a job for the RAF regiment but, since nobody expected bases in West Africa to be attacked and there was no RAF regiment there, it had been dropped in the lap of Horace Maxey, a first-class coxswain who not only wasn't a soldier but wasn't even really an airman but a sailor.

It was growing dark and he was uncertain what he should do. In the light of the hurricane lamps and naphtha flares from surrounding houses, a few small boys appeared, begging cigarettes, then the know-all wide boy offering his sister. 'Very good jig-jig,' he said. 'No mammy sickness. She schoolteacher. All clean and white inside.'

'Who wants her?' Trixie observed to his neighbour. 'Mind you, the little boys look nice.'

A black policeman shooed away the children. A few mammies, smelling of sweat, charcoal and palm oil, called out softly, laughing at the burdened white men and, feeling fed up and far from home, Maxey was just wondering what to do next when the firing towards the aircraft started. Heads jerked up and the laughter of the mammies stopped at once as they hurried to scoop up their children and bustle them away to the safe side of the houses. It was at this point that Ginger Donnelly decided he was being pushed about by too many people, and as Maxey looked round for a safe spot, he slipped off quietly towards the village.

Lizzie Morgan was still shaken by the uproar that had resulted in Pfitzner's death and Ginger put his arm round her as she started shivering again.

'What happened?' he asked.

She pointed to the door. 'Brudder belong me come. Plenty palaver.'

'Good for brudder,' Ginger said. 'Where brudder now?'

'Brudder at mine. I tell him, "You go work, police no find. De Lord Jesus look after."' She remained worried and explained what had happened. 'Many men come. I see guns. Boy tell me dey done got mine bosses locked up. If army come, mebbe brudder get hurt.'

'Why don't he do a bunk?'

'He scared. Mebbe he get shot. Dey all scared.'

'Of comin out?'

She nodded and Ginger frowned. 'Mebbe we ought to make 'em more scared o' stayin' in,' he observed.

As he set off through the trees and past the scraggy little patches of barley and Indian corn, the stunted mangoes and the banana plants, the fact that a man had died there three nights before didn't worry him at all; everybody in Makinkundi knew Ginger well enough to ignore him. Beyond the palms the whitewashed stone houses were like old bones in the fitful moonlight, and round the roaring naphtha lamps the foliage glowed unnaturally green. He could hear crickets and frogs, and a few dogs burst from the shadows towards him, barking with lunatic frenzy before disappearing just as quickly.

Reaching the edge of the village, he stopped at a shabby hut that looked as though it had mange. Its thatch was untidy and there were holes in the walls. The man who appeared from the dark doorway was old, his kinky hair grey, his face lined, his body stooped, his legs thick with elephantiasis. He wore a mangy-looking leopard skin and about him hung an assortment of ju-jus – a child's finger bone, a chicken leg, a bunch of feathers, a snake's skin, all the appurtenances of a witch doctor with a large clientèle. He beamed a welcome at Ginger.

' 'Lo, Ibrahim,' Ginger said in an offhand manner, never one to show too much enthusiasm. ' 'Ow's the old fetish these days?'

The old man indicated a gaudy red, black and yellow basket of cane and raffia with a tightly fitting lid tied with a twisted straw cord. 'I busy, boss Ginger. I got snakes.'

Ginger prised open the lid a fraction, then shut it again quickly at the ominous rustling sounds inside.

'Dem snakes be for Luki, de snake man. I go take 'em.'

'I'll take 'em for you,' Ginger said. 'Save you a walk with them old legs of yourn. 'Sides, old Luki keeps a nice palm wine. I've got me stick in case one of 'em gets out. I got

217

something I want you to do, see. Special. For me. As a mate, like.'

As Ginger moved about his private business indifferent to the war, the rain came, noisy and drenching. The spasmodic firing stopped and Maxey heaved a sigh of relief and went once more over his instructions. The job wasn't likely to be difficult, he'd been told. The army would be along eventually to take over. All he had to do was make a lot of noise and be a nuisance to this group of Germans who were supposed to be somewhere on the spit of land between Makinkundi and Mamo. When the firing had started he had done what he considered the most sensible thing and got his men to cover, but now that it had stopped it seemed less important to advance with flying standards and shouts of 'Hurrah!' than to find some sort of shelter from the bloody rain.

Spitting the water from his lips, he formed up his party in threes, and marched them to the centre of the village, where, finding the thatched shelter where the market was held, he got his men underneath. It was a large square construction on poles with low structures like sawing horses set in the ground where on market days the mammies rested their baskets. Wet through and weary, Maxey's men used them as seats.

Maxey frowned. The chief snag, as he saw it, was that he didn't know where the enemy was. Neither, it seemed, did anyone else. Not Hobson, nor Molyneux who had set the thing up, nor the group captain. Not even the AOC.

But, though Sergeant Maxey didn't know it, they were on the point of finding out.

Catalina B-Beer – known to its crew as B-Awful, because the port engine never delivered the correct number of revs and the automatic pilot was faulty – had landed from her patrol just as darkness came. She approached from the north and, turning over the mine at Yima, swung round to land against the tide.

Her pilot, Flying Officer Kitchen, a twenty-one-year-old with curling hair, innocent blue eyes, and one of the most extensive vocabularies of oaths on the station, was cursing his luck. For the most part the Catalinas had the respect of their crews but they required plenty of muscle and pilots dreaded handling them when the automatic pilot went out. After twelve hours of it Kitchen was exhausted because he'd been flying for the most part at five hundred feet and, with the temperature in the nineties, the sun through the Plexiglass had left him drained.

'Pity we can't crash the bloody thing and get a new one,' he complained.

'We could try pawning it,' the navigator suggested.

'She's too bloody old. Nobody would have her.'

'She always gets us home, Skipper,' the navigator said soothingly. Kitchen wasn't noted for the smoothness of his landings and the navigator always kept a drawerful of freshly sharpened pencils to plug the holes when the rivets popped out of the hull during his worst efforts.

The dinghy appeared alongside as they made fast to the buoy, and they climbed in, tired, sweating and fed up after twelve hours of boredom looking at nothing but empty sea. Kitchen was still complaining as he made out his report in the squadron office.

'I've flown hundreds of bloody hours,' he was saying 'and I've never fired a gun, dropped a bomb or even seen any sign of the enemy. He signed his report sourly. 'Not a damn thing all day,' he went on. 'Not even a bloody seagull. There's more activity going on at that mine at Yima than *we*'ve ever seen.'

Molyneux, who was just inside his office heard him and swung round at once.

'What *did* you see?' he demanded.

'Nothing, sir,' Kitchen said. 'It's in the report. Just miles and miles...'

'At Yima, man!' Molyneux snapped. 'At the mine at Yima!'

Kitchen looked puzzled. 'Dozens of chaps, sir. Running about like a lot of blue-arsed flies.'

'What else?'

'Nothing else, sir.'

'Dammit, man, you know how to make a report! Make one!'

'Yessir.' Kitchen stiffened. 'I saw a string of lorries as we came over – just before the rain arrived. We were a long way away and it was dusk but I was using the binoculars and I could see movement. There were a lot of men.'

'How many?'

'About thirty, sir. But nobody seemed to be doing much work. They seemed to be preparing for a siege, if you ask me. I saw guns.'

Molyneux headed for his office. 'Get me Cazalet,' he said to the clerk.

Kitchen stared after him. 'What's got into the old man?' he asked. 'He sounds as though he's got something on his mind.'

The station intelligence officer, busy with Kitchen's report, looked up. 'So he has. And so will you have before long. You'd better nip off and get some grub. You might be flying again in an hour or two's time.'

three

Lorenz was still cursing the rain and the onset of darkness when he became aware of the approach of soldiers from the south. He was wet through after the downpour and wondering if they dared light a fire to dry themselves when one of his men brushed through the dripping foliage.

'*Herr Leutnant!* There are troops moving through the bush towards us.'

For a moment Lorenz wondered if it were Heidegger joining him, then he realized it couldn't be, because his informant was pointing to the south. He remembered then that he'd seen a lot of activity among the flying boats across the lagoon and realized that somehow someone had guessed Heidegger's plan and had landed troops at Mamo. Any moment now, they could expect them where he'd set up the machine guns – perhaps even at the mine at Yima!

He glanced at his watch, suddenly nervous. It was dark now, humid shadows filled with the musky smell of crocodiles and the steady drip of rainwater from the trees. There would be no more firing until daylight, he realized, and obviously the most sensible thing was to return to the mine and warn Heidegger.

He arrived in a hurry. Carrying the heavy Spandaus, he and his men were sweating profusely and covered with mud.

'Troops,' he panted. 'Moving up from Mamo! We had to pull back!'

He caught Magda Fallada's eyes on him and put on a little act of courageous desperation, the look of a man facing terrible odds.

'Does that mean we're no longer within range of the flying boats?' Heidegger asked.

'It means just that,' Lorenz said. 'We ought to be heading for French Guinea, not hanging about here.'

Heidegger gave him a cold look. 'We haven't finished our job yet,' he said. 'We'd be failing in our duty if we gave up now.'

'Are you hoping for a Knight's Cross, *Herr Kapitän-leutnant*? We can't hope to hold this place.'

'We can do quite a lot,' Heidegger snapped. 'We have the men. We also have diggers, lorries and tractors. Have them parked about the buildings. They're heavy and will give us armour-plate shelter. And be quick. If they're already organizing against us, I'd like to know what they intend. Get along towards Makinkundi. The Dutch normally keep a lighter alongside the loading jetty. We could rig a machine gun on that and move downstream. We could do a lot of damage before they became aware of us.'

'It would take us all night to get everything aboard,' Lorenz said. 'And we couldn't do it after daylight. It would be suicide in daylight.'

Heidegger looked at him coldly. 'If dying worries you, Lorenz,' he said, 'there's always the escape route down the Bic.'

In fact, the Bic was already occupied.

The pinnace had made good time downstream with an ebbing tide and they had progressed round the corner opposite Kupr into the entrance to the river Rokel until they had arrived at its tributary, the Bic.

Against the dark background of the hills, the entrance to the river looked like a cave, a black hole in the searchlight's beam among the paler shadows of the crowding mangroves. As the patches of mud were picked up, Corporal Fox eyed them dubiously from the wheelhouse.

'I'm not going in there till daylight, sir,' he said to the padre. 'It's too tricky.'

It was pitch dark as he shut down the engines and dropped the anchor. As they swung on the lifting sea, the rain that had frustrated Lorenz reached them. At first it was just a few heavy spots plink-plonking on the roof of the wheelhouse, then the heavens opened and, the men crowded on deck, new to this sort of weather, tried to cram below. Fox quietened the grumblings by offering tea, and the few mugs they had on board were handed round and shared, though it was impossible for more than a few to sit down.

Eventually the rain stopped and they could see the stars and Fox ordered everybody out on deck again. One of the new arrivals promptly celebrated the event by falling overboard, and only Feverel's quickness with the boat-hook prevented him from being drowned. He was shoved below and given another mug of tea to quieten his complaints.

'I've lost my specs,' he said loudly. 'I had 'em on when I fell in.'

Fox sighed. It was always the same with flight mechs, riggers, fitters, photographers, electricians, wireless ops and clerks. They were always falling in the water. Normally it stopped everybody getting too bored, but they could have done without it at this moment.

The day came suddenly. A bright blinding glare rose behind the hills and sent a shaft of flame to touch the high misty blueness of early daylight, then the sun itself appeared, a yellow eye staring across the curve of the earth. As it grew lighter, they saw the tide had covered the narrow mud-flats and then that a small ship was lying a mile or two offshore.

'Where's she come from?' Fox asked. 'What's she doing there?'

There was no sign of life ashore, though they could see crocodiles on the mud further up the creek and could hear the screams of monkeys and the raucous cries of birds. The sun beat down on them like a brassy gong, swallowing all the moisture that had been left on the decks by the rain.

The padre, who was supposed to be in command, held what he tried to think of as a conference on the foredeck with Fox and Feverel. The operation was supposed to be an inter-services affair. The navy were looking after the entrances to the river Bunce. The army at Mamo were to advance at first light along the river bank towards Yima, while more soldiers – when they arrived – were to push down from Hawkinge. The RAF were watching Makinkundi, while the pinnace, carrying thirty five men, was to poke its way up the river Bic from the sea. The operation had been buttoned up quickly enough, but it was still a typical West African lash-up that went with the four-inch nails through the swivels in the chain cable of the aircraft buoys. Telephones were non-existent and the radio linkage was uncertain, but at least all the aircraft had been refuelled and bombed up, though to get them off the water and into the air when the panic button was finally pressed was going to be a full-time job. The alarm had come at a distinctly inconvenient time, and it was a strange sensation to the padre – to be acting as a general.

None of them was sure what they were supposed to do but it was finally decided that they should move further up-river and that Feverel should explore ahead of them with the little punt. They were just lowering it into the water when they discovered that the falling tide had stranded the pinnace with its bow on an unexpected mud bank.

'Oh, charming,' Fox said bitterly, staring at the chart with a frustrated expression. 'There's no bloody mud bank marked here. We'll have to stick out a kedge. There's plenty of water around if we can reach it.'

The boat-hook and the lead line appeared and, watched by their landlubber passengers who were intrigued by these nautical mysteries, they went round the pinnace taking soundings. It was hot now and the men sitting on the hatch cover, many of them beginning to suffer the first tortures of prickly heat, couldn't rouse much enthusiasm for what was going on.

'We here for keeps?' one of them asked, scratching at the livid red rash that had appeared on his chest.

'Not on your life,' Feverel said, mud-spattered but brisk despite the temperature.

They found a channel from the stern to deep water, and an anchor was lowered to the punt and attached to the winch hawser, then the punt chugged away and the anchor splashed down.

As the pinnace's six-cylinder diesels went astern, the winch was also started. The sound of the engines grew louder and the watching airmen, puce in the face under the heavy equipment, moved nearer for a better view.

'Keep away from that hawser,' Fox shouted. 'If it parts, it'll have your goolies off.'

There was a hurried shuffle forward to safety and Fox groaned. 'Not *forrard*,' he said. 'That's the bit we're trying to get off the mud.' He gave the padre a harassed look. 'Sir, can you get 'em in the hold? As far aft as you can. It might raise the bow.'

The telegraph pinged and the bight of the hawser leading to the kedge lifted from the water with a spatter of drops and a loud twang as the strain came on. As the engines went full astern a dirty grey-looking froth floated forward from where the screws churned uselessly at the mud. Fox cut the engines and went aft for a look. In the hold, the padre had everybody lined up, harness, rifles, ammunition and all, and a lot of hot bewildered faces stared up at Fox.

'Try jumping up and down,' he suggested.

'What for?' The inevitable question came.

'It might help get us off,' the padre said. 'Now be quiet and do as I tell you.'

Feeling stupid, they all jumped together.

'Again.'

'Side to side now, sir,' Fox said. 'Might roll the bow in the mud and clear a passage.'

In no time the padre had the bewildered landlubbers moving from port to starboard and back again. As the engines and the winch started once more, the wire tautened slowly again and then came out of the water, vibrating madly. The splice began to twist and the wire was like a thin steel bar, humming and singing over the towing horse. The pinnace trembled and the water from the stern raced along the side as if she were moving, rushing and boiling as it surged forward.

'Come on, you bastard bloody boat!' Fox was muttering savagely to himself in the wheelhouse, imagining the shame of having to admit spending the whole period of the operation stranded on the mud. 'And let's have those stupid sods jumping again, you silly little vicar!'

A message, somewhat more polite, was passed to the padre and, as the airmen started to jump up and down again, a shout came from the punt.

'She's moving!'

There was a different kind of shiver from the pinnace this time, then the hawser dipped suddenly, splashing into the water with a loud whack.

'Haul it in,' Fox shouted, weak with relief. 'She's moving!'

He shut down the engines and they began to haul themselves off with the winch alone, the pinnace moving quite distinctly now, sliding off the mud, slowly at first but gathering speed all the time. Then, settling herself like a duck taking to the water, she was finally properly afloat and swinging round, alive once more.

A faint derisive cheer came from the hold.

Because Cazalet was off the air, to Molyneux there seemed no alternative but to go to Makinkundi personally and let the men there know exactly what to expect.

'Keep your ears open, George,' he warned Mackintosh. 'I'm taking a radio. Inform me if anything happens. I can be back in three-quarters of an hour if necessary.'

With daylight, Maxey had brought his men back to the loading jetty to join the party from the second seaplane tender. From the jetty, Molyneux could just see the roofs of the mine through the trees. He looked at his watch. The biggest anti-submarine sweep they'd ever been called on to deliver was just over the horizon and he was terrified of losing his machines. But he was also worried that the signal to go would arrive at any moment and he had the uneasy feeling that he was in the wrong place again. His position was at the base but, since he'd started this half-baked operation, he felt he ought to have some part in it.

He turned to the men carrying the radio. 'How about setting it up in that bar there?' he said. 'Then we can be in contact with the base.'

The two wireless operators, both new to West Africa, placed the set on a table just inside the doorway. One end of the aerial was attached to a pole in the roof and they were looking round for somewhere to attach the other end when Ginger's Lizzie gestured to a gas lamp in the middle of the village.

The wireless operators stared in amazement. 'Does it light?' they asked.

They were still wondering when the set came to life. It was Mackintosh.

'We've just had that chap Cazalet on the telephone,' he announced. 'There's no sign of the bastards headed north. I told him we'd been under fire and that we thought now that they were holed up at the mine. He decided we were dead right. He's already on the way back, but he's having trouble.

227

There's a bridge washed out at Kamimbo but he'll have the
West African boys there as soon as he can. He asked if you
could keep the bastards busy.'

Molyneux frowned. 'Who does he think I am?' he asked.
'Rommel?'

Cazalet arrived with a rush. The lorries were packed with
eager black men in the khaki uniforms and bush hats of the
West African Frontier Force. The rear was brought up by a
British sergeant in a Bren gun carrier – old because all the
new ones were in North Africa, but still serviceable, its gun
capable of doing a great deal of damage.

As they stopped, the radio started cheeping and the British
sergeant took down the message and headed for Cazalet's
car. Cazalet glanced at the flimsy and looked up at Hubbard,
the lieutenant in command of the black soldiers who was
bending over a map spread on the bonnet. 'Done it,' he said.
'The chaps who were landed at Mamo from Freetown
flushed out the buggers with the machine guns. They stopped
firing.' He lifted his head to cock an eye at the first streaks of
daylight appearing over the cotton trees and palms.

'Right,' he said. 'Let's go.'

He stood back, watching the black soldiers climb into the
lorries. They arrived in the army straight from the bush,
brave, loyal, superstitious and childlike, qualities they soon
lost when they reached the ports where the coastal Creoles
carried their Bibles to hide their breaches of the law. They
were proud of being soldiers and enjoyed showing their paces
on the dusty parade ground where, every evening, an African
sergeant drilled them fiercely. The watching black crowd
enjoyed it, too, and it was Lieutenant Hubbard's habit to
punish his men for their misdemeanours by striking their
names from the drill roster so that they sulked in their huts
until allowed to join in again.

Growling slowly down the road, the lorries stopped fifty yards short of the mine and the soldiers deployed on both sides of the road that ran up to the gate. It was constructed of heavy timbers criss-crossed with barbed wire and was firmly shut and locked. Beyond it, the mine buildings reached out towards the river Bic.

Cazalet was still studying them when Inspector Yorke arrived, Sergeant Laminah grinning all over his face at the speed at which they had travelled. As Yorke informed him of what had been done, Cazalet studied the barbed-wire fence. Yorke watched him, wondering what was in his mind. 'Are you going in?' he asked.

'That's the general idea,' Cazalet said. 'There's bound to be a bit of old iron flying about.'

'Well,' Yorke said, 'that creates a bit of a snag. We want no more riots and a few dead men could start one. I'm told there are fifty or more Africans from Makinkundi of yesterday's shift still in there.'

'Not now there ain't,' a voice said from behind them. 'We've got 'em out.'

As they turned they saw Ginger Donnelly watching them, his ugly face interested, as shadowy, dusty-looking and scruffy as usual. He was leaning on his long forked stick and under his arm he held a deep gourd-shaped raffia and cane basket in red, black and yellow patterns within which it was possible to hear something moving.

'Where did you come from?' Cazalet asked.

'Just passin',' Ginger said. 'On me way down the road there.' He indicated the basket. 'Got this to deliver.'

'And what did you mean when you said you've got them out. Whom have you got out?'

'The shift workers.'

'Where've they gone?'

Ginger gestured. 'Up there. Makinkundi. They waded through the swamps. They've gone 'ome.'

'Who sent them home?'

'I did.'

Cazalet looked at Ginger's grubby figure. He wore no badges on his muddy khaki and it was impossible to tell whether he were military or civilian. 'And how did you accomplish that miracle?' he asked.

'Put a fetish on the place,' Ginger said. 'They was scared of bein' shot if they nipped outa the gate.'

'Why didn't they go out by the river then?'

'Scared o' crocodiles.'

'They've seen crocodiles before.'

'Yeh, but in Makinkundi they think they're magic. So we told 'em a curse 'ad been put on the mine and if they stayed where they was their arms and legs'd fall off and they'd break out in warts or turn into frogs.'

'You can do that?'

Ginger shrugged. 'Not reelly. In fact, there wasn't no curse. I just got the witch doctor to say there was. He's a pal o' mine. I know all the witchies, snake charmers, magicians and ju-ju boys round 'ere. They decided to take a chance on the crocs. They're all in Makinkundi now. It wouldn't work for me, o' course. I don't believe in curses. But they do. They drop dead if the old witchy says they've got to. I expect we'll 'ave to get the fetish took off when you've finished or they'll never go back.'

Cazalet eye him for a moment. 'Well,' he said, 'that seems to be that worry disposed of.' He turned to the British sergeant. 'Ask Lieutenant Hubbard to let me have the loud-hailer, Sergeant, please.'

The loud-hailer was brought up and he blew into it a couple of times. 'Hope they're not difficult,' he observed. 'But I think I'm being optimistic. I notice they've parked all their diggers and lorries very strategically, and it's a good bullet that'll go through a bulldozer. Ah, well...' he raised the loud-hailer and directed it towards the group of huts '...here goes!' He blew twice more and began to speak into the microphone.

'Jan van der Pas Company!' His words boomed out, echoing among the trees. 'This is the British army. We wish to enter your compound. Please open the gate.'

He lowered the loud-hailer and waited. There was no sound and no movement from the other side of the gate.

'I'm not deluding myself that they've left,' he commented. 'They're there all right. What's more, while we can't see them, I dare bet they can see us. I'll give 'em another go.'

'This is the second time of asking,' he said. 'We have no wish for trouble and don't wish to put anybody's lives in jeopardy. This is private property but we wish to make a search. Open the gate.'

Again there was silence and in the still, humid heat that was held close to the earth by the low clouds it seemed menacing. The palm fronds hung listlessly and the British sergeant's shirt was black with sweat. Cazalet still contrived to look cool.

'Last time of asking,' he said.

Lifting the loud-hailer, he tried again. 'I shall not ask again,' he said. 'I'll give you five minutes to open the gate, then we shall pull it down.'

He looked at his watch and waited. Inspector Yorke offered him a cigarette which he smoked quietly. He seemed to have the gift of remaining perfectly still, which was probably why he stayed cool when the others showed the effects of the heat.

After a while he nodded to Lieutenant Hubbard. 'All right, Nick,' he said. 'Have it down.'

Hubbard turned to where an African sergeant was standing. 'Have it down, Sargy,' he said.

The sergeant and half a dozen men approached and a pair of wire cutters appeared. As the sergeant lifted the cutters, however, they heard a voice give an order from the huts half-

JOHN HARRIS

hidden beyond the diggers and bulldozers. The sergeant jumped as bullets kicked up the dust by his feet, and one of his men spun round and fell to his knees. Grabbed by his arms, he was dragged into the trees and they all looked at Cazalet for orders what to do next.

'Damn,' Yorke said. 'I didn't want to start a bloody battle here.'

Lieutenant Hubbard eyed the open expanse of earth in front of the huts. The solitary eucalyptus tree threw a long pale shadow in the watery sun.

'There's not much cover,' he pointed out.

Cazalet agreed. 'This ought to be a combined services operation,' he said to Yorke. 'All the rage just now. Suppose those chaps at Makinkundi and Mamo and in the river Bic all started getting aggressive and pushing forward? The old Huns in there would find they'd got their hands a touch full. And that,' he concluded, 'might enable us to get among the bastards without having too many of our chaps hurt. Let's put it to Molyneux.'

As the sound of the firing reached the river Bic, Feverel looked up.

'That's a machine gun,' he said. 'It seems to be developing into a battle.'

Looking up at the trees on the land above them, the padre hoped it wouldn't mean more funerals. If it weren't flying crew then there was invariably somebody whose constitution or mental attitudes couldn't support the heat and the conditions, and funerals always seemed out of place in this forgotten corner of Africa.

Fox, who had had himself put ashore by the punt with a pair of binoculars, was just returning with the identity of the ship anchored offshore.

'*Maréchal Grouchy*,' he said. 'Registered at Conakry. She's lying almost stern-on and I could read the name.'

As he climbed aboard the pinnace, Feverel and Kneller took over the punt and chugged slowly up the winding creek.

It was quite narrow at the entrance, with other narrower creeks leading off into the mangroves. Two crocodiles watched them, their heads turning slowly as the boat pushed further into the narrow cleft in the land. The water was black with mud and stank of decaying vegetation, but as they turned a corner, the river began to open out. Turning into the bank and cutting the engine, they cautiously began to pole themselves forward. The heat among the overhanging foliage had a choking quality.

From behind a projecting spit of land, they could see two native fishing boats moored against the bank with, just behind them, the Dutchmen's big launch. In the basin alongside the landing stage was the supply scow, secured with the little outboard-powered dinghy beneath the piles of the boathouse.

Feverel blinked the sweat from his eyes, then he took off his pith helmet and mopped at his face with the rag he wore round his neck.

'Last time we were here,' he reminded Kneller nostalgically, 'we were given iced beer.'

They had just returned and were scrambling aboard the pinnace when Molyneux came through on the radio.

'They want us to do something active,' the padre explained.

They looked at the bewildered white-kneed men clutching their rifles on the stern of the pinnace.

'With that lot?' Fox said.

'There are three dozen rifles.'

'Fat lot of good they'd be against a machine gun, sir.'

Feverel was frowning. 'I reckon it's less a case of us going in,' he said, 'than of them coming out.' He explained what he meant. 'There were boats moored up the creek and that seems to indicate what the *Maréchal Grouchy's* doing out there. I bet she's been sent down to pick them up when they've finished. Once aboard that thing, they could be in French waters in an hour or two.'

The padre looked puzzled.

'We could stop 'em, though, sir,' Feverel went on cheerfully. 'If they're going to use that launch we saw up there, we have one splendid weapon. We've got a wire hawser in the hold that we used to tow a target down to Lungi. Attached to the winch wire and a set of strops we've got down there, it'd stretch across the creek.'

The padre was uncertain. 'They asked for something positive,' he said doubtfully. 'They want us to put our chaps ashore.'

'Then let's do both, sir.'

The narrowest part of the river was near one of the bends and the pinnace was moved up and, out of sight from the boathouse, nosed into the bank. As he appeared from the wheelhouse, Fox looked round at the deck crowded with bewildered landlubbers wondering what the hell was going on. He was an indolent man who always felt harassed when the mooring party started getting ideas, and he took it out on his passengers.

'Get these stupid sods below,' he snorted. 'They're in the way!'

Sweating profusely and tripping over their rifles, the airmen were pushed into the forecastle, the radio cabin, anywhere there was room, and told to stay out of the way. It was stifling below and there was a chorus of dismay. Fox glared at them. 'If you don't shut up,' he snarled, 'I'll close the bloody door and lock it! Then it'll be *really* hot!'

As the pinnace moored fore and aft, the punt was worked alongside and wire strops and shackles were dragged from the hold with the wire towing hawser and lowered into it. Starting up the engine, Kneller and Feverel chugged across the river, and, dragging the strops ashore after them, shackled one of them round the bole of a large palm tree. Trudging back to the pinnace, they attached a heavy rope to the end of the winch hawser, dropped it into the punt and climbed down after it.

'What's going on now?' one of the airmen asked, his head above the hatch coaming.

'We're making a mousetrap,' Feverel explained.

One or two men offered to help but Feverel pushed them away with a protest that they'd get their fingers caught, and settled for two of the time-expireds.

The punt low in the water with four men on board, they headed back across the river, paying out the rope as they went. Reaching the shore, they moored the punt and began to haul in the rope. The winch wire, attached to the other end with the winch in neutral, began to follow it. By this time they were all plastered with mud.

'This is a bloody mucky job,' one of the two helpers complained.

'The mooring party's never been noted as the glass of fashion,' Kneller agreed cheerfully. 'We'll make you honorary members.'

Eventually the end of the winch wire appeared from the water and they dragged it across the mud and shackled it to the towing hawser and the strops, and attached them to the wire round the palm tree. Then, standing on the mud, Feverel took a look round him and began to make circles above his head with his hand.

With Kneller up to his knees in the water watching it, the wire was hauled taut and the brake applied.

By this time Cazalet was beginning to grow annoyed. What he had expected to be a neat little operation was turning into a major battle.

'We'll have to rush the place,' Yorke said.

'Not so easy as you'd think,' Hubbard pointed out. 'As usual the bush's been cleared because of mosquitoes and that gives them a bloody good field of fire. There's no cover at all except one tree fifty yards from anywhere. You can't approach from any side without being spotted, and I'm not going to have my chaps all knocked off for a lot of bloody Huns who are well and truly bottled up.' He turned to Lieutenant Harder, his second-in-command. 'Let's have the Bren set up, Frank, and give them a burst or two to show we mean business.'

The Bren was brought up between the trees and gave the huts a couple of long bursts. The firing started the birds shrieking and set the monkeys jumping and screaming in the trees. There was no sign of life from the buildings beyond the gate and Cazalet frowned.

The African soldiers, joined now by the party that had pushed up-river from Mamo, were dispersed among the trees and the firing started again. They could see bullets chipping splinters off the wooden huts and hear them whining into the air from the parked diggers. Then, as one of the African lance-corporals, too enthusiastic for his own good and seeing an opportunity to get nearer, led three of his men between the trees, a burst of fire from the buildings brought down two of the men at once. The other two dived for shelter as the lashing bullets cut down twigs and leaves and set the whole population of the forest dancing with rage.

Standing near the gate, Hubbard received the news with an angry frown.

'Corporal Luke,' Harder reported. 'Hit in the head. Private Malaki in the hip. Malaki's all right. I'm not so sure about Luke.'

'Blast,' Hubbard said. He'd grown surprisingly fond of his black soldiers and, knowing they trusted him, he didn't like them getting hurt. 'That means we've got to do the thing properly now. The buggers can't go shooting at the King's men.'

Heidegger was growing worried. He was well aware, even before Lorenz had returned from his reconnaissance towards Makinkundi, that they were surrounded and that an attempt to secure the lighter in the Bunce and shoot up the aircraft was futile. They'd probably not even reach the water's edge. And any moment now the RAF would start dropping bombs. It seemed to be time to check on their escape route because he had no wish to spend the rest of the war in a British prison camp.

The mine buildings had been built close together so that moving between them in the rainy season wasn't too hazardous. Under cover of the strategically parked diggers, it wasn't difficult to slip from one to the other despite the firing, and Heidegger moved through them, past the men standing behind doors clutching their weapons, his eyes flickering over the open space in front.

'It's up to us,' he encouraged. 'We mustn't let the Fatherland down.'

Nobody answered him and he realized that the old out-of-date cult of the Fatherland had given way to the new cult of the *Führer*.

The telegraphist had set up the radio in one of the central buildings which had been arranged as a reading room. It was a bare whitewashed place with only African masks and spears as decorations. There were a few brightly coloured mats on the floor and several leather-covered armchairs which in the dry season would be covered with dust but now, with the rains, showed a grey film of mould over their polished surface.

'Try to contact the *Maréchal Grouchy* again,' Heidegger said. 'We may have to leave tonight.'

As the operator bent over his set, Heidegger sent for the mine manager to find out from the Dutchmen whether their boats were fuelled. The man he sent reappeared in a hurry.

'They've gone, *Herr Kapitänleutnant!*' he said. 'They unscrewed the window frame and escaped.'

Heidegger frowned and, picking up a pistol, moved through the huts towards the Bic. The last hut had been built over the river to form a boathouse and the room above had been turned into a games room. There was a table-tennis table and a radio and, as he walked towards the window, his feet echoed hollowly on the boards. The place smelled of the damp which came through the floorboards from the river beneath. A man stationed by the window turned.

'Take care, *Herr Kapitänleutnant*,' he warned. 'The English might be trying to get in through the back door.'

From alongside him, Heidegger studied the Dutchmen's boats below. Surely, he told himself, they would never leave them with empty fuel tanks. A boat with empty tanks was as good as no boat at all but it was still just possible the Dutchmen themselves might try to use them for their own getaway.

'It's your duty to stop anyone taking those boats,' he pointed out.

The man nodded and Heidegger edged forward warily for another look.

The padre had finally got his party ashore. It had been a lengthy business and he had begun to realize that, despite the purple and white ribbon that graced his best tunic, it was harder to run a battle than he'd ever thought. His ideas were out of date and it was largely thanks to Corporal Fox, Feverel and Kneller that they'd been able to achieve anything at all.

Even putting the ham-fisted newcomers on to the mud had been a difficult business because, with Kneller at the tiller, the punt would carry no more than three at a time and had to go backwards and forwards, its passengers eyeing the three inches of freeboard like rabbits eyeing a snake. As the group gathered onshore, already well plastered with mud, they began to work their way forward over the flats to the trees with the instructions to try a few pot-shots at anything they could see. The new arrivals clearly didn't like this part of the operation but the padre got them spread out and told them to work their way nearer and fire when they got the opportunity.

Untrained for this sort of thing, however, they clung together, watching the padre nervously and it occurred to him that it wasn't all that different from Ypres in the winter of 1917–18. The only change was the smell, and he remembered how he had felt the first time *he* had heard firing.

As he turned, he saw the end of the boathouse in front of him, the water sparkling on the underside. For a moment he stood still, wondering what to do, then he saw a man standing in the shadows by the window and wondered if he could hit him.

It didn't worry the padre that he held a rifle. When the war had broken out, among other things he had considered forgetting his cloth and joining an active regiment again, and had reached France in 1940 just in time to take part in the evacuation of Dunkirk. Arriving to comfort the wounded and dying, he had ended firing a Bren gun as the Messerschmitts came over. It had cost him not one minute of repentance. To Daniel Morgan, the Nazis deserved none of the sympathy that he had in abundance for other men. Wounded, he would have done everything in his power for them. Clutching a weapon, they were a threat to the bewildered youngsters with him and he knew he was a good shot with a rifle.

Remembering the words of an American chaplain at Pearl Harbor – 'Praise the Lord and pass the ammunition' – without hesitation he lifted the weapon and fired.

four

By the time Lorenz returned from his sortie to Makinkundi, it was afternoon. Like Heidegger, he was well aware by now that they were surrounded and that the British, assuming that escape was impossible, were in no hurry. Nevertheless, he decided, someone would eventually think of bombs and the wooden-huts at Yima didn't seem to offer much in the way of protection from high explosive.

As he struggled back through the undergrowth, he heard a shot from the direction of the Bic, then a wild fusillade. It was difficult to tell where it came from and he assumed that the British were making another attempt on the mine. The need for care slowed him and the heat was stifling. When he reached the safety of the mine buildings he could see no sign of Heidegger and one of the men gestured with his head. Heidegger was in the reading room, stretched out on a settee where the medical orderly was trying to pad a wound in his shoulder.

'What happened?' Lorenz asked.

'It's not too bad,' the medical orderly said. 'He was hit from the river Bic.'

Heidegger looked pale and shaken but he was still busy with the defence of the mine.

'What did you see?' he demanded.

'Makinkundi's swarming with troops,' Lorenz said. 'We'll not get out that way.'

241

Heidegger frowned. 'Then we must try to keep them occupied here in the best way we can in the hope that the U-boats can handle the convoys.' He had changed his mind with his wound and had accepted that escaping via the Bic was going to be more difficult than he had expected. 'We shall have to wait until dark before we can move out, and in the meantime we have to assume that the Dutchmen are probably giving all the details of our defences to the English.'

Lorenz frowned. 'Which Dutchmen? I locked them in the storeshed.'

'You obviously didn't lock them carefully enough,' Heidegger said coldly. 'They removed the window and escaped.'

Lorenz scowled. 'We should have got rid of them in the beginning,' he snapped. 'We should have shot them.'

Heidegger ignored him. He was preoccupied with the defence of the mine and Lorenz turned to the radio operator. 'Are we in touch with the *Maréchal Grouchy*?' he asked.

'She's waiting off the coast, *Herr Leutnant*.'

'Warn them to stand by.'

Magda Fallada was sitting in the office hidden from the firing by the bulk of a Euclid. Lorenz picked up one of the tommy guns. An idea was forming in his mind. He could see no future in Heidegger's forlorn hope and the chances of holding on until dark seemed slim. With the resources at their disposal, he couldn't imagine that the British would be prepared to sit on their backsides and wait for surrender. And – once more the thought of bombs came to his mind – they had aeroplanes.

It had never been his wish to die bravely for the Fatherland. There was still too much to do and it seemed to him that Heidegger might even be seeking a heroic death in the best traditions of the German navy's officer corps – which wouldn't do him much good, anyway, because there would be no one to witness and report it. It might be good sense to see for himself what the possibilities of escape were.

He knelt beside Magda. 'I'm getting out of here,' he said quietly.

She looked up. 'Heidegger thinks it's going to be difficult.'

'For him perhaps. It needn't be for us.'

'What do you mean?'

'Two could get out where twenty-two couldn't. That lot in there with Heidegger: what are they? Seamen and petty officers for the most part. French traitors, Senegalese, dissident Dutch. They're not even all Germans. *We*'re the élite. We're the ones who're needed back in Berlin. You and me.'

'What about Heidegger?'

'He's finished.'

'Dying?'

'Yes,' Lorenz lied. 'He'll never move from this place. It's up to us to save ourselves. There are boats in the creek and the *Maréchal Grouchy's* waiting off the coast. We can slip down there and get out as soon as it's dark.'

She said nothing for a moment, then she nodded. 'Very well,' she said. 'I'll go with you.'

Hubbard had finally decided to tackle the line of buildings from the side and capture them one by one. They all seemed to be of wood, plasterboard and mosquito wire set on low stone frames so that where they adjoined it ought to be possible to hack their way through from one to the next. The nearest one, furthest from the parked diggers and bulldozers, a low flat building that looked like a dining hall, seemed the most vulnerable.

The wire fence had been cut by this time and his men deployed among the thick bush that surrounded the open space in front of the buildings. He called Harder to him.

Harder was an ex-sergeant recently commissioned and he had a tough capable look about him.

'Right, Frank,' he said. 'Let's have the Bren playing on that main building from the other side while we go in at this end. Have your chaps fire at any windows you can to make them keep their heads down. Pass out what grenades we've got. We'll open the bowling from this end. Wait until you hear us then let go with everything you've got. Try not to hit us. We'll give you ten minutes.'

As Harder disappeared, Cazalet smoked a cigarette quietly, then, just as unhurriedly, looked at his watch. 'Time's up,' he said.

As he spoke, there was a clatter of firing from the opposite end of the group of buildings, and one or two overs whined above them.

'That's Harder,' Hubbard said. 'Off we go!'

Stepping out into the sunshine, he waved to his men and they crashed out of the bush and started running across the open space, followed at a walk by Cazalet.

The high-pitched tribal yells of the soldiers were sufficient to warn Harder's party that they were on their way and the firing rattled out more strongly from their left. As he raced across the open space in front of the buildings, Hubbard saw two men fall, then he was up against the bole of the eucalyptus tree. Pausing for his men to catch up, he set off again, jinking to right and left, aware of little spurts leaping from the muddy earth around him, then he flung himself down alongside the low stone wall that supported the wood, plasterboard and mosquito wire construction of the hut.

Over his head a light machine gun was firing, whoever held it within a foot or two of him. Pulling the pin from a grenade, he reached up and tossed it through the open window.

'Oh, well played,' Cazalet said aloud as he watched.

The roar as the grenade went off stopped the shooting long enough for the West African soldiers to reach the wall. Without pausing in his run, one of them leaped through the open window, swinging his rifle as he went, and Hubbard scrambled up and vaulted after him. The plastered walls inside were pockmarked where the grenade had exploded and in one corner where he had been flung lay a black-haired man who looked French. He still clutched his weapon but his body seemed to be oozing blood from a dozen points. Another man lay in a huddle in a corner holding his head, watched by the grinning West African. There seemed to be nobody else.

Cazalet was well satisfied. At least they were into the buildings now and under cover. 'Very pretty, Nick,' he said as he climbed inside. 'They'll be making you a general before long.'

The firing behind him had made Lorenz stop. He pulled Magda into the bush and waited, aware that they'd escaped just in time.

He gestured with his head and they moved towards the path to the landing stage. As he studied the basin with the moored dinghy and the heavy supply scow, he decided that neither of them appealed to him much as a means of escape. The scow was too slow. The dinghy was too small. Then he noticed the dinghy had an outboard motor attached, which was odd because, left unguarded, the fishermen would undoubtedly steal it.

It seemed unimportant, however, and he had just decided to use the launch tucked behind a projecting spit of land further downstream and that it would be possible to board her with the dinghy without being seen, when he saw movement in the bush a few yards away. Immediately, he understood the significance of the outboard motor and, pushing Magda down among the foliage, he lifted his head cautiously.

'It's the Dutchmen,' he whispered. 'They're going to steal the boats.'

'What are you going to do?'

Lorenz smiled. 'What we should have done long since,' he said.

The Dutchmen were moving cautiously through the bush but, as they reached the path leading to the landing stage, they straightened up and began to run. They were halfway down, backgrounded by the red earth of the low cliff, when Lorenz stood up and fired the tommy gun from the hip. It was as if a giant hand had hurled the hurrying men aside. One of them was flung against the cliff, his clawing fingers drawing agonized lines in the muddy soil. Another fell from the path to the catamaran below, to roll over the edge and splash into the water. The others slumped down, blocking the path. One of them, a fat man with a pink face and heavy stomach, dragged himself up, tried to crawl, and finally fell back.

Magda's eyes were horrified. 'You killed them,' she said, her voice shocked. 'You killed them in cold blood!'

Lorenz' face was taut and angry. 'We're fighting a war,' he snapped. 'We're in no position to take chances. Taking chances won't get you to Berlin. Come on, let's get away from here. I'm not staying to be captured or killed. Heidegger's ideas of gallantry aren't mine.'

Leaving her on the bank at the top, he set off down the path. Reaching the Dutchmen, with his foot he tipped them from the edge of the path so that they rolled into the foliage. One of them fell to the catamaran and sprawled there. Climbing into the dinghy, Lorenz slammed the oars into the tholes.

Magda watched silently, horrified by what had happened. She had never seen men killed in battle and it had shocked her. Slowly, she headed down the path towards the Dutchmen. One of them was still alive and, wrenching at her skirt, she tore a strip from it and tried to staunch his wounds.

'Come *on*!' Lorenz called.

She stared at him angrily, suddenly, stubbornly, against him for his lack of compassion. 'This man's hurt,' she said.

'So what?'

'He needs help.'

Lorenz sneered. 'You're a damn fool! Germany will never win the war if we allow our feelings to direct us.'

'You have no feelings, it seems.'

Lorenz stared at her for a moment, his, eyes cold. 'Make him comfortable then,' he said. 'I'll start the boat and come back for you.'

He headed downstream to the launch and she watched him climb aboard and disappear below. As she bent over the Dutchman, he gave her a look of loathing that shrivelled her soul but she tried to ignore it and went on working, her hands red with his blood.

For some time she crouched over the injured man, trying in a hopeless sort of way to help, until, abruptly, she realized there had been no movement from the big launch lying behind the spit of land. Looking up, she was just in time to see Lorenz climbing back into the dinghy, his face furious. Reaching for the oars, he headed back to the catamaran.

'That damn' boat only has throttles and a telegraph by the wheel,' he snarled as he scrambled ashore. 'The starters and gear levers are in the engine room.'

She looked up and said nothing.

'I need you, Magda,' he urged. 'Quickly.'

'I'm not interested.'

'All you have to do is stand in the engine room, and when I ring the telegraph, press the starter and work the gear lever. One engine would do until we're out of the river.'

'I'm not going out of the river.' She indicated the wounded Dutchman. 'I have work to do here.'

He didn't seem to hear her properly. 'We'll do it the other way then. You can stand by the wheel and *I*'ll start the engines and put her in gear.'

'I'm not going!'

Lorenz' face grew red. 'I can't do it on my own!' he shouted. 'If I put her in gear without someone on the wheel, she'll run aground.'

'That would be too bad.'

'Listen, Magda…!'

'I'm not coming!' she stormed. 'This man's badly hurt!'

Lorenz stared down at the Dutchman who was sitting up now, his back against the cliff. 'Can he stand up?' he asked.

'No.'

'I don't believe you. Get him on his feet.'

She stared at him in horror. 'You're mad!'

'Get him on his feet! He's going in the engine room of the launch to work the gear lever and you're going to see he does.'

'It'll kill him!'

'I don't give a damn! Get him up!'

The Dutchman clearly understood what they were saying because he looked at Magda and shook his head, his fat chins wobbling.

'Get him up!'

The Dutchman spoke, enunciating painfully 'I will not come,' he said.

'You'll do as you're told,' Lorenz snarled.

The Dutchman shook his head again. 'Your nation has destroyed mine. I will not lift a finger.'

His face furious, Lorenz reached into the dinghy and picked up the tommy gun. 'On your feet,' he said.

'*Herr Leutnant*, I will not do it.'

'Then I'll shoot you!'

'Karl!' As Magda moved forward, Lorenz flung her aside and she fell to her knees.

'Get up or I shoot!'

The fat Dutchman stared calmly at the gun and shook his head. Lorenz' eyes seemed to grow red with rage as he pulled the trigger. The earth jumped and the Dutchman fell back, blood welling from his mouth.

'You oaf!' Magda screamed. 'You lunatic! You're not fit to live with decent human beings.

The gun swung round. 'Get into the dinghy,' Lorenz snarled. '*You're* going to do the job!'

She rose slowly to her feet. Her face was pale and her eyes were glittering with hatred. 'No,' she said. 'Never. I'll stay and take my chance with the others. I wouldn't lift a finger to help you.'

'I'll shoot!'

'Then shoot!'

For a long time, Lorenz' finger hovered over the trigger then, abruptly, he swung away and climbed back into the dinghy. As he turned, she gave a choking cry, sank to her knees and began to sob.

five

The signal the admiral had been awaiting for days dropped on his desk even as Cazalet gained the safety of the mine buildings.

'Dates, times and courses, sir,' his aide pointed out. 'New York–Middle East, Gibraltar–Sierra Leone, UK–Cape Town. A hundred and forty ships.'

'Inform the senior officer afloat,' the admiral said. 'He's to pick up the convoys as soon as they come within our area. Pass it on to the air officer commanding and to RAF Jum. You can also inform Hawkinge and Brighton, too, though God knows what they can do with their Stringbags.' He reached for his pipe, tobacco pouch and matches and stuffed them into his pocket. 'I'm off to see the port supply officer,' he said. 'You'd better inform the hospital, too. There's usually an odd case or two for them and this time there could be quite a few, judging by the number of men these ships are carrying.'

It was like a damn' big game of chess, he decided as he headed for the door. The British and the American naval staffs were working as hard as the Germans to forecast positions and numbers. Each side had an idea of the other's intentions but neither had a complete knowledge of what they were. Though the Germans had had some successes, and had obviously picked up information on the convoys moving south towards Freetown, the British were listening just as intently to German radio traffic, and had already diverted the convoys further west so that the wolf pack known to have been across their original course was doubtless now trying to re-establish contact, shifting to a new patrol line across what Berlin thought would be their new path.

The officer commanding the Freetown destroyer flotilla called his captains on board.

'Being in all respects fit for sea and ready to engage the enemy...' Wrapped in traditional wording, the written instructions were handed out and explained. Bos'n's pipes wailed and shouts echoed along steel corridors. 'Watchmen and special sea duty men close up! Secure all scuttles and water-tight doors!' In mess decks and passageways, men lashed hammocks. Communications were tested and stokers, telegraphists and artificers hurried to their positions. Underfoot there was a faint trembling as engines began to turn.

The flotilla leader slipped her buoy within half an hour and headed north past Lungi towards Sallatouk Point. Her captain, who was also the senior officer afloat, studied the charts, already aware that somewhere up ahead of him at least two wolf packs were waiting for the approaching convoys. His eye moved over the list of ships available in reserve. There weren't many and with the shortage of depth charges after the explosion at Giuru there would have to be no mistakes.

'It would help if we knew where the buggers were,' he said.

Worried and uncertain, as the telephone rang Wing Commander Mackintosh snatched it up and barked his name. It was the admiral's aide.

'The convoy's due in our area within twenty-four hours,' he warned. 'Are your people standing by?'

'Yes. But we've had a few problems. Our aircraft have been under fire.'

'Those Huns from Boina? What are you going to do? Put your kites in the air?'

Mackintosh's voice was sarcastic. Trust the navy to put its big feet in the custard. 'We can't have the bloody things floating round the sky doing nothing,' he said.

'Why not?'

'Because they'll be no bloody good to anybody, sport, if they have to come down to be refuelled and serviced just when they're needed.'

As he slammed down the telephone, Mackintosh swore. Whatever the Germans intended, he decided, they'd certainly picked a crook time for it.

U-1761, one of the boats from *Gruppe* Herzog assigned as *Vorpostenstreifen*, or picket line, had only three torpedoes left, one of them defective, was low on fuel and, with her port diesel causing concern, had finally given up the struggle to take up position and was heading northwards towards the Bay of Biscay and the safety of the pens at St Nazaire.

Nobody on board was pleased, the captain least of all. He had not had a successful voyage and had headed south as ordered, hoping, with all he had gleaned from the signals about the coming clash, that his chances would be good and might finally make the voyage worthwhile. But he had lost an officer and two ratings overboard in the Atlantic and now had a petty officer ill below with pneumonia and had finally given up the struggle.

As the U-boat made its way northwards on the surface, the look-out wasn't being particularly alert because he wasn't expecting to see anything. Though the wind was negligible, the night before the moon rose was pitch black and it was with great surprise that he suddenly saw a light directly ahead. It appeared only for a matter of two seconds but he recognized it immediately as a careless sailor lighting a cigarette on the deck of a ship. He leaped for the button of the alarm and heard it sounding below in the control room. By the time the captain reached the bridge there seemed to be ships across the whole horizon. Quite accidentally U-1761 had stumbled on Convoy WS24.

It was with some pleasure that U-boat headquarters in Berlin received U-1761's report and the position of the huge convoy. It had required considerable courage to keep every available U-boat tied to this one operation when they could well be used in the North Atlantic, and U-1761 was ordered to remain on station whatever the difficulties, no matter who was ill, shadowing the convoy while a signal went out ordering *Gruppe* Markgraf, fifty miles south of where the convoy had been sighted, to proceed northwards at top speed, while the boats at the western end of *Gruppe* Herzog's line were ordered to turn east. Within an hour twenty-four U-boats were making their way towards the convoy. They were expected to meet each other a hundred miles south of their present position and a hundred and fifty miles west of Sierra Leone. More boats operating to the south-west of Freetown in the southern half of the Gulf of Guinea were ordered to head west and north at speed and as close to the Sierra Leone bulge as possible to shorten the voyage.

Inside the hut they had captured, Cazalet was studying his surroundings. The concrete floor was covered with scattered cartridge cases and items of equipment.

They moved warily through the building. It seemed to be a dining hall, and there was a large room with a small corrugated shack alongside where the cooking was done. Reaching the other end of the building, they paused on the wire-meshed veranda that ran round it to keep it cool. There seemed to be no one about but the minute Cazalet put his head out, a storm of bullets came from the next building and he withdrew it quickly and turned to the British sergeant.

'Outside, Sergeant,' he said. 'Round the back. Set the Bren up on the corner and be ready to give those windows opposite a good pasting. I'll give you two or three minutes. You'll see where to fire.'

As the sergeant disappeared, Cazalet warily studied the next building. It was made chiefly of wood and the outside wall consisted of the same wire mesh in frames on a low stone construction to keep out the mosquitoes as that of the building he was in.

Taking off his cap, Cazalet placed it on the end of his swagger stick then, ducking behind the stone-built lower half of the wall, he crawled along, holding the cap on the stick so it could be seen through the mesh.

Immediately two men rose from behind the low wall of the building opposite and there was a roar of firing. The mesh above Cazalet's head twanged and pinged and the cap flew into the air as a cloud of dust and dozens of dead flies, mosquitoes, spiders and other insects showered down on him. At once the Bren started and he heard someone scream, then he heard Hubbard's men shouting and the pounding of feet.

This time they found two men, one dead, one a black man with a terrible wound in his head, muttering in French. They seemed to be in a group of offices but beyond there was a central chamber from which they could hear muttering and they knew that there were men waiting to ambush them as soon as they appeared opposite the door.

They were standing now pressed hard up against the whitewashed wall in the corridor. Positioned as they were the men in the central chamber could stop them on their route towards the next hut. Cazalet stared at the white-painted wall, frowning. The only entrance to the room was via the open door, behind which the enemy waited.

Hubbard was fingering a grenade when Cazalet put a hand on his arm.

'Not that,' he said. 'Not this time.'

Hubbard frowned. 'What other way do you suggest, sir? A grenade in there will stop the lot.'

'It might kill the lot, too. And I'd prefer a few of them alive. That way we might learn a few useful names.'

'I'm not having my men throw their lives away, sir.'

'No need,' a voice behind them said and Cazalet turned. A scruffy shadow stood beside them, the same scruffy shadow they had seen earlier, ginger hair on end, grubby shorts drooping over sagging stockings and scuffed shoes. He still carried the large cane and raffia basket and forked stick.

'Where did you come from?'

'I stuck around,' Ginger said. 'I wondered if you could use these?'

He held up the basket and Cazalet eyed it, intrigued.

'What have you got in there?

'Snakes. Green mambas. Big 'uns, too. Right poisonous.'

Cazalet was curious. He'd already learned that this strange grubby creature carried surprises up his sleeve. 'What have you got in mind?' he asked. 'We can hardly train 'em to attack an enemy.'

'Oh, no!' Ginger seemed shocked at the suggestion. 'Just unfasten the lid and chuck the basket inside. Seven mambas ought to put 'em off a bit. Good as a grenade, you ask me.'

Cazalet stared at Ginger, then it occurred to him that Ginger had the glimmerings of an idea.

'Go on,' he said.

'It's surprisin' 'ow scared folks are of snakes. All you got to do is wait for 'em to start yellin'. And they will, because these is big snakes and they're pretty mad at the moment. They didn't want to come to this 'ere party and they're feeling a bit spiteful. They'll be madder still if they get chucked ten feet through the air to land on their 'eads in there. They'll come out fightin' and while everybody's yellin' and dodgin' the bites, you'll be able to go in.'

Beyond his concern to get the job done, Cazalet was even amused.

'Where did you get 'em?'

'I told you. I know the snake charmer.'

'You seem to know a lot of people.'

'Yeh, well, I do, don't I?'

'Well, *I* don't know much about snakes and I doubt if Hubbard here does either. Will you be coming with us?'

'I might as well.'

'Like a gun in your hand?'

Ginger produced a club. It was made of iroko wood and was as hard as iron and heavy as lead. 'This'll do me,' he said.

Cazalet nodded. 'All right,' he suggested 'Let's give it a go. Are you sure those snakes are in a bad temper?'

Ginger grinned. 'Never seen worse,' he promised.

As they stood pressed up against the wall, Ginger unfastened the cord that held the lid and lifted the basket. Hubbard had a look of contempt on his face.

'It'll not work,' he said.

'You wait,' Ginger retorted. 'Nobody I've ever met takes well to 'avin' 'alf a dozen big mambas chucked at 'im. You ready?'

'As ready as we'll ever be.'

'Right. 'Ere goes.'

Swinging his arm back, Ginger hurled the basket round the corner of the open door as hard as he could. There was an immediate burst of firing that removed chunks of plaster from the wall opposite, followed by a dead silence. Then there was a yell of fright, followed by more yells, and a rifle was thrown out. A man appeared and one of Hubbard's men grabbed him. The second man to appear tried to bolt but Ginger kicked his feet from under him and, as he fell, hit him at the side of the head with his iroko-wood club. He was flung against the wall and as he bounced off Ginger hit him again. This time he fell to the floor and didn't move.

As the last man appeared, his hands in the air, Cazalet eyed Ginger. 'I begin to understand,' he said, 'why the African native tribes were such formidable enemies when we opposed them in the last century. You don't have a blow-pipe, do you?'

Ginger wasn't very quick to latch on to jokes. 'No,' he said, busy with his forked stick rounding up angry snakes and dropping them back into the basket. 'I don't 'ave a blow-pipe.'

They were hidden from Harder's group now by the parked diggers and bulldozers and seemed to be in the main office. There were files, typewriters and desks, a waste-paper basket containing the charred remains of documents, and in the corner a radio transceiver on a bench. On one of the desks there was a list of names and addresses, some of them in Freetown, some of them in the villages along the border and, guessing they were the names of agents, Cazalet slipped the list into his pocket. Underneath it was a chart of the coast of Sierra Leone and a copy of the *West African Pilot*. Positions were marked on the chart and passages ringed in the book. Comparing the two, Cazalet decided the marks on the chart indicated the positions of submarines, so he folded the chart, placed it inside the book and tucked the lot under his arm.

Hubbard was peering warily from the hut towards the last big building, a thatched structure overhanging the edge of the river Bic. 'Some time soon, sir,' he ventured, 'they'll start throwing their hands in.'

Cazalet frowned. 'There may be one or two at first,' he said. 'But nothing worth a damn. From what I saw of the buggers in France, if there are Nazis among them – and there will be, or they wouldn't be here – the bastards will be fanatics and try to fight on. I'm going back to the radio. I think someone ought to see this chart. It might be important.'

Inspector Yorke was still waiting near the radio link for instructions and he grasped at the list of names and addresses Cazalet had found with a whoop of delight.

'These bastards are agents,' he said. 'German agents.' He jabbed with his finger. 'We've suspected this chap, Suleiman, at Hawkinge Town, for instance, for months but have never been able to get anything on him. I must get this down to the commissioner as fast as possible and set up an operation to round the sods up.' He stared at the list again. 'That one,' he said, his voice awed. 'I'd never have believed he was one.'

He was about to turn to his car when Cazalet stopped him.

'Hang on a moment,' he said. 'There are other things to go to Freetown besides your precious list.' He gestured with the chart he held. 'I imagine this is what the admiral's been panting for, for days. I'm going to see if we can get it down by boat.'

Concerned that the operation was becoming too long drawn out, Molyneux was beginning to contemplate the use of aircraft with bombs to clear it up but, as soon as he saw the chart, its importance was clear at once. The small circled crosses could only be submarines, because there were numbers alongside them and what looked like radio call signs. Curving towards them from the north ran a long red arrow-headed line, joined by another line, which began over in the west, together with the numbers AS29 and WS24. Marked in the margins were the numbers RS15 and OS12. The Germans had amassed their information without error.

As the seaplane tender swung away from the loading jetty and headed downstream, the radio operator turned from his set to Molyneux. 'Wing Commander Mackintosh, sir,' he announced. 'He wants to speak to you.'

Mackintosh sounded excited, his voice coming from the radio strained and metallic. 'It's on!' he said. 'Those bloody convoys of ours are sailing straight down our throats! Date of arrival – the fourteenth!'

Molyneux explained what had happened. 'I'm on my way now,' he said. 'With a chart showing everything. We've Just picked it up. I count twenty-four U-boats across the route to Freetown harbour and others moving up from off Takoradi. Ask the admiral or the AOC to have the boat met in Freetown. They'll want to act on it. You got all that down?'

'Sure have, sport.'

'Right. Have a car meet me and warn the boys to stand by. We've got the bastards this time, George, and I think we're *all* going to be flying.'

six

By this time, Lorenz had left the area of the mine behind him and, edging down the Bic, heaving the dinghy across the black water, it occurred to him that it wouldn't be long before it was dark. If he were to go, he realized, that would be the time to do it. He remembered the launch and scowled at the memory of its uselessness. He was soaked with his own sweat by this time but he knew he must continue rowing. If the British he guessed were down the river heard the outboard engine, they'd be waiting for him.

The water was not moving, covering the mud and lapping well up the mangroves so that he knew it must be around high tide, so he shipped the oars and allowed himself to drift *under* the boat's momentum, keeping close to the shore among the shadows of the overhanging trees.

It *was* dark now, with the swift darkness of the Equator, and to *his* surprise as he steadied the boat, he saw a light flash *through* the mangroves ahead of him. It was Fox examining the *h*awser they'd strung across the river, to make sure it was not too low in the water, and Lorenz actually saw the shallow curve of *wet* wire as the light fell on it.

The light remained *on* for a moment or two and he decided he could cross the *wire* if he stayed in the centre of river. At that point the *h*awser would be below the and the dinghy surely *did*n't draw much more than metres. It would have *to* be done fast, however,

260

and he stared at the outboard, suddenly realizing it could be his salvation.

Drawing a deep breath, he reached towards it, switched on the petrol, and primed it. Then, winding the rope round the flywheel, he grasped the toggle, set the motor central, and heaved. As it failed to respond, he cursed and with trembling fingers wound the rope on again. This time, it coughed but still failed to fire, and, with the perspiration in his eyes and dripping from his nose, he wound the rope on again in a panic of frustration.

'Gottverdammter Aussenbord,' he snarled.

Twice more, the motor refused to fire and, cursing, the sweat running off him, he almost dropped the rope in the water. Forcing himself to control himself, he paused, drew a deep breath and decided to try once more before he drifted on the tide within sight of the waiting British. Going through all the motions, slowly and painstakingly, carefully advancing the throttle, he wound the rope on yet again, praying silently that this time it would work.

The engine fired unexpectedly and, because the throttle was advanced, started to scream as the propeller thrashed the air. His heart leaping, Lorenz flung down the starter rope and dropped the propeller into the water. It was revving so fast the boat leaped forward with a jerk that nearly flung him over the side, then began to head smoothly down the river, the bow lifting with the speed.

Blinking the sweat from his eyes, Lorenz sat back, trying to peer through the darkness.

'Gott sei Dank,' he said aloud. 'Thank God for that!'

'They're coming out!' Kneller's tenor voice, coming over the buzz of the outboard, was almost falsetto with excitement.

Fox was in the wheelhouse talking to the padre, who had had himself brought back on board the pinnace to discuss what they might safely do next, and for a second they stared at each other. Then, while the fitter dived for the winch brake, Fox leaped for the deck and started shouting to the men with rifles still ashore to shoot.

Their eyes narrowed, they waited as the searchlight came on. But Lorenz, roaring out of the shadows at speed, the outboard howling, the bow of the dinghy high, knew exactly where the hawser was. Swinging the tiller, he swept out of the darkness to the centre of the river.

'There he is!' Feverel yelled, his arm flung out.

The men with rifles on the opposite shore started firing and a few bullets whined over the pinnace. One of them, better aimed than the rest, whacked into the wheelhouse above Fox's head.

'Christ!' he said, diving for the deck.

None of the bullets went where they should. The dinghy was moving swiftly and the men with the rifles weren't trained marksmen.

'He's going to run smack into the wire!' Kneller yelled.

They could see the dinghy now, its bows wet with spray from its own bow wave and gleaming in the light, and they all became silent as they waited for the crash as the propeller was torn off.

'He's hit it!' Fox yelled.

But, just as the dinghy swept over the wire, Lorenz lifted the outboard from the water. It screamed as the propeller whirred free and he heard the wire scrape along the bottom of the boat as its forward momentum carried it over, then he knew he was past and let the motor drop back. It went in with a flurry of spray and the dinghy immediately picked up speed again, followed by a few badly directed shots from astern.

'The bastard's got away!' Kneller was almost dancing with rage.

'It's only one man,' Fox yelled.

'How do you know it isn't bloody Hitler?' Kneller spluttered and began to scramble into the punt.

'What the hell are you up to?' Feverel demanded.

'I know what I'm doing,' Kneller yelled furiously. 'Leave it to me! Just pass the torch and keep the searchlight on until I can get ashore.'

Feverel handed over a heavy rubber-covered torch. 'What the hell are you going to do, you mad idiot?'

'There won't be any more Germans coming down here. You see.'

Put ashore by Feverel, Kneller began to push through the undergrowth. He knew exactly where he was going and a few minutes later he was staring with the torch down at O-Orange's two depth charges which he and Ginger Donnelly had placed near the bank some time before.

Studying them, he saw that the fins had broken off, leaving canisters two foot long, their noses concave, looking no more deadly than two small oil drums. Dragging them to the edge of the basin, where it needed no more than a push to roll them down the bank and into the water, with the torch he inspected the basin. The tide was up and he knew that at high water it was around thirty feet deep and that the pistols went off at twenty-five.

The capture of the last building had been held up again and, growing bored with the slow progress, Ginger had wandered off. Moving through the bush at the back of the buildings, he delivered the basket of angry mambas to their rightful owner then, pushing through the trees, headed for the Bic. There might, he decided, be something worth pinching.

As the trees thinned, he saw the glint of water and realized he was close to the artificial lagoon that the Dutchmen had constructed at the end of the river. He couldn't imagine what he might find there, but at least it was better than ploughing round Makinkundi with the Wet Boiled Egg ordering him about. Ginger had never been able to accept being ordered about.

As he stepped out of the trees, he stopped dead. To his surprise, over a slight rise in front he could see a woman not far ahead of him. And, by the look of her, she was a bit of all right, too. Blonde, plenty of before and plenty of behind, and very interesting-looking. He wondered what she was doing there.

Magda Fallada was still kneeling on the path alongside the catamaran. Around her sprawled the bodies of five dead Dutchmen. Another was in the water, trapped beneath the catamaran and ever since Lorenz had disappeared she had stared numbly at the hand that protruded from beneath it as if appealing for help.

Shocked and dazed, her mind crawling with loathing for Lorenz as she churned over the tragedy, she began to see for the first time that the driving force that propelled Lorenz came from the principles of the régime for which he worked. She had been only a girl when Hitler had come to power and had seen only the good he had done and the fact that Germans, humiliated by the earlier war, were once more able to hold up their heads.

She had not been aware of the other things but now, kneeling on the bank alongside the silent basin at the end of the Bic, unaware of the smell of mangroves or the waning heat, unaware of the whining mosquitoes and the raucous clatter of the frogs and crickets, it dawned on her that she had not been aware of those other things because she hadn't *wanted* to be aware of them. Like many other German women who had idolized Adolf Hitler, she had shut out of her mind the things that were done in his name, and, on the occasions when she'd been unable to do so, had told herself that he could never have known about them. Now sitting by the dead Dutchmen, her mind stiff with the memory of the butchery, it dawned on her that she had been deceiving herself. The demi-god *knew!* He must have known. Everything that had been done in his name he must have condoned and perhaps even ordered. Thinking about the men who surrounded him, she began to feel a repugnance she had never felt before. She had heard rumours about perversion, corruption and cruelty, but had forced herself not to believe them. Now she knew she'd been deluding herself for years.

It had grown darker as she turned over her weary thoughts. As she heard the dinghy's outboard start, she remembered Lorenz, but only dully, as if he were someone she had met in a nightmare. Then she heard the motor grow louder and heard scattered shooting and found herself praying that he had been killed.

Still kneeling there, her thoughts leaden, she was just beginning to wonder what she could do to put right the great wrongs she had allowed when she became aware of a light moving among the trees that grew along the side of the basin. She stared at it for a while, wondering what it was, until slowly it penetrated her shocked intelligence that it must be one of the British airmen from Jum. Rising to her feet, almost as if she were another being watching herself, she began to move towards him.

The man with the torch seemed to be struggling to move something heavy, and she could hear him panting as she stood near the dead Dutchmen, staring upwards, wondering whether to call out.

On the lip of the land above, Kneller looked down into the water. The launch was behind the spit of land out of danger but he could attend to that later. The motor lighter could carry a good thirty men and here, above it, the bank had been cleared so that the African labourers could carry boxes and crates and drums up without them snagging on branches.

It was difficult in the darkness to see what he was doing but, near the path that led down to the catamaran, he thought he saw something move in the shadows. Vaguely aware of a woman's voice calling him as he pushed with his foot, he stopped dead, wondering who it was, and saw her below him to his right. But when he looked down, intending to check the depth charges, he saw it was too late. They were already rolling down the bank, bumping and leaping over small obstructions, until they disappeared from sight in the shadows below him, and with a yell he slithered down to the water's edge and began to run along it to push the woman to safety.

It had never occurred to him that the effect of the depth charges with their four hundred and fifty pounds of Torpex, falling into the narrow confines of the basin, would be different from the effect of a depth charge falling into open water where the blast could go downwards and spread outwards. Here, in the shallow water and contained by the high sides of the basin, the result was unbelievable.

There was a glow and a terrific double jolt that seemed to shake the universe, then the river bed seemed to lift to meet him and he saw the piles supporting the overhanging boathouse snatched away by an invisible hand as the whole building collapsed. Almost as if in slow motion, it burst apart, planks and timbers flying outwards.

A tree by the water's edge fell with a crash and he saw the remains of the boat shed drop into the water in a ruin of splintered wood. The scow was also disintegrating in a welter of planks and pieces of iron and, faintly, he saw the launch, protected by the protruding bank, lift and roll. It bumped on the bottom as a whole tidal wave of water was swept away and a few moments later was lifted violently as the sea poured in to replace it and the water now floating through the air above his head in a cloud of misty spray.

The explosion had lifted him towards the screaming woman. Flung into her arms, the two of them were carried onwards, clutching each other like lovers, before slamming against a tree. Around them, a roar like an incredible thunderstorm was going on and Kneller's lungs emptied with a rush and a cry of protest burst from his lips. He tried to shout for help but his mouth seemed to be filled with sawdust and all he could get out was a cross between a sigh and a whisper. As the two of them huddled together, their arms round each other, things seemed to be dropping all round him and he was surrounded by a wet inky cloud. In one horrifying moment as the blast snatched at his clothes, the world seemed to have been jolted off its axis and, his head full of pain, he felt like a man voyaging through space.

The darkness had helped Lorenz, and he had managed to leave the mouth of the Bic in complete safety.

For some time, he held the dinghy steadily out to sea. The *Maréchal Grouchy* was out there somewhere and he was making sure that he'd be aboard her. He felt in his pocket for the heavy rubber-covered torch he carried. He would need to signal well ahead or the waiting Frenchmen might well imagine it was a British attempt to board them.

After a while, the outboard spluttered and died as the petrol ran out. Scrambling about the dinghy, he found a spare can and managed to slop most of it into the tank. It wasn't easy without a funnel but the sea was like a millpond, with nothing but little ripples to stir the surface. As he wrenched at the toggle of the starting rope, the engine caught at once and he chugged further out to sea. He had a long way to go and he had no wish to have to row.

Eventually, however, the engine began to run raggedly and finally it died. It was too hot to touch and he could only imagine it had seized up completely. Cursing, he reached for the oars. He was far enough now from the shore for safety but the *Maréchal Grouchy* was nowhere in sight and the moon had not yet risen. A few outriders of clouds darkened the sky and he cursed again, wondering where the Frenchmen had got to. He was almost in despair when he heard the gurgling of air bubbles and the gushing of water in the darkness.

Swinging round, wondering what was happening, he was startled to see a submarine rising to the surface. He could only just make it out in the darkness and if it had been a little nearer, it would have risen under the dinghy. He laughed out loud. That would have been a splendid way to get aboard, he thought. Not even wet feet. He heard the clang as the hatchcover in the conning tower was thrown back and the rush of air into the boat, then he was reaching frantically for the torch.

'SOS, SOS,' he flashed, and almost immediately he heard German voices. A second later a searchlight came on, wavered a few feet from him then dropped on him, blinding him with its ice-blue light.

''S ist ein Beiboot,' he heard someone say. 'Ein Mann. Allein.'

Grabbing the torch tighter. Lorenz began to signal again. 'Deutscher Offizier. Deutscher Offizier.'

There was a babble of voices then a different voice called to him.

'Identify yourself.'

'Leutnant Karl Lorenz. Vertrauensmann. Fernmeldeaufklärungskompanie, Freetown.'

The searchlight went out and a smaller signalling lamp fell on Lorenz.

'Come over here!' he was ordered. 'And no nonsense. You're covered by a machine gun.'

Almost hysterical with delight, Lorenz began to pull towards the stark black shape just visible in the spill from the beam of the signalling light. As the bow of the dinghy ground against the curved tanks, he tossed the painter to a sailor standing on the narrow deck. The disembodied voice from above him came again. 'Come aboard. You're still covered, so do it carefully or you're a dead man.'

Grinning all over his face, Lorenz scrambled to the deck of the submarine and made his way to the conning tower.

'*Leutnant* Lorenz. Karl Lorenz,' he announced himself. *Kriegsmarine*. I was sent here to provide you people with information on convoys.'

'We've heard of you,' the submarine commander said. 'I'm *Kapitänleutnant Zur See* Schutze. This is U-1022. Let's have you below.'

Climbing through the hatch. Lorenz followed Schutze to the tiny wardroom where Schutze sat down and held out his hand.

'Papers first,' he said. 'Something to identify you.'

Lorenz produced his papers and Schutze studied them before handing them back, satisfied. He reached into a locker and produced a bottle.

'You'd better have a drink,' he said. 'What about the rest of you?'

Lorenz explained how the *Maréchal Grouchy* was to have picked everybody up but that it had become impossible.

'Somebody got on to us,' he said. 'We had to take over a mine at Yima. They were attacking it when I left.'

'What about *Kapitänleutnant* Heidegger?'

'He's holding the Tommies off to make sure I got clear. I was ordered to go, to make sure there was someone to tell the story.'

'On your own?'

'On my own.' The lies came easily now. There might be explaining to do later but Lorenz felt he could get away with it. 'I stole the boat. I was hoping to find the *Maréchal Grouchy*.'

Schutze smiled. He was young and tired looking with a fuzz of half-grown beard on his face. 'Well, now you'll have the pleasure of seeing what your information can do,' he said. 'We were watching the southern flank below Takoradi with U-997 and U-1113 when we were ordered to join *Gruppe* Herzog. They're across the route of the British convoys. We were told to make all speed on the surface. You must be the luckiest man alive. This operation could mean the end of the war.'

He poured drinks and swallowed his own quickly. 'And amen to that,' he said.

Jum was like a stirred ants' nest. Leaving Sergeant Maxey and all the men who had been sent up river kicking their heels in Makinkundi, scared stiff their ship would arrive and leave for England without them, all the boats with the exception of the pinnace, which was still in the Bic, were withdrawn to stand by to re-arm, refuel and service the aircraft.

The first machine took off towards midnight to search ahead of the approaching convoys. The destroyers from Freetown were already moving to a position where they could join the escorts which had brought the convoys south. Together, they provided a formidable barrier, never big enough when the submarines had their information ahead, but more than enough when the boot was on the other foot as it was now.

Jum was full of controlled movement as men hurried out to aircraft. Catalina T-Tommy had been towed to the slip and hauled on to the concrete apron where the airframe fitters had descended on her like locusts to repair the holes made in her by Lorenz' machine gun. As Molyneux stepped ashore, Mackintosh was heading out towards his Sunderland.

'The Navy are on their way,' he said. 'We'll hold the fort. I've got two aircraft up.'

Minutes later, looking like a huge grey pelican, Mackintosh's own Sunderland lifted majestically off the water and disappeared into the sky towards the north.

T-Tommy was ready for lowering into the water within two hours. After her went, M-Mother, the hole in her hull repaired. As she slid down the slip and was towed back to her moorings, the hangar crew wiped their sweaty faces and stood back. Every machine on the station was available for flying.

Mackintosh's Sunderland had picked up the convoy by this time. Like all Sunderlands, she was a dream to fly, very stable and with fingertip control, and they cruised along at a hundred and twenty knots, having set the two inner engines by ear and synchronized the outers by the Aldis from the window. Navigation was by dead reckoning and there was no panic. They had done the job too often before, watching convoys, rounding up scattered ships, and, here on the Equator, they had little to fear from German aircraft. Even in the north where there was the possibility of attack, they had always felt secure because the Germans were wary of the bristling guns of the Sunderland and had christened it the *Fliegende Stachelschwein* – the Flying Porcupine.

There were two men in the galley preparing coffee at dawn when the first sighting came. As the alarm klaxon went for action stations, they dropped what they were doing and rushed to the bomb room to grab the handles of the bomb doors, praying Mackintosh wouldn't bank suddenly and leave them swinging in mid-air. They wound the doors down and slid the loaded racks out under the wing, and the radio operator was banging out his sighting report to the navy as Mackintosh came down astern of the submarine which lay on the surface, its decks awash, following the convoy.

Ahead they could see the ships like rows of black dots on the water which was just beginning to sparkle with the sun. The Germans seemed to be occupied with getting into position and were not watching out but, as they drew nearer, Mackintosh saw one of the men in the conning tower turn. Immediately, men began to run towards the gun on the platform behind the conning tower. The German commander had decided the best tactics were to fight back with the impressive battery of weapons he carried, but the front gunner of the Sunderland opened fire and one of the Germans rolled over the side.

As the Sunderland came in, the starboard engine was hit and she faltered, but Mackintosh was in position now and he let go his salvo of depth charges. As he turned away, he saw one actually bounce off the submarine's casing, then the surface of the sea seemed to shudder and heave for yards around. The submarine was wallowing in the middle of the foam, its decks awash, and, as it sank, Mackintosh came round again and dropped another salvo. The submarine reappeared then seemed to lie wearily on its side and vanish amid a wild turbulence of bubbles and masses of oil.

'Jesus,' Mackintosh said in an awed voice.

Mackintosh's sighting report arrived in Jum as Molyneux watched the first of his crews return. They were standing at the end of the wooden jetty waiting for a lorry to take them away, laden down with the trappings of their trade. One of them wore a girl's silk stocking round his neck as a good luck charm and they were all chattering excitedly because they had picked up Mackintosh's signal just as they had landed.

A motor dinghy on a cradle, pushed by a group of black men led by a new sergeant with a white face and white knees who had arrived to take Maxey's place, was moving slowly towards the marine section slip. One of the black men wore a ju-ju at his throat – a bunch of bird's feathers to ward off evil spirits – and Molyneux reflected that there wasn't a lot of difference between white and black men. Black men wore birds' feathers, pebbles, a bit of rag, a withered dog's leg, anything they fancied to keep them safe from evil spirits. White men wore a girlfriend's stocking or a favourite scarf. Black man's ju-ju and white man's ju-ju were very much the same.

The first report came in as Molyneux reached his office, then a few minutes later an excited and triumphant message arrived to say that Mackintosh had straddled a submarine with depth charges and it was believed sunk. Not long afterwards, operations room telephoned to say that the navy had caught another on the surface trying to edge in to the convoy in the last of the darkness and had attacked at once. Two survivors had been picked up.

Forced by the patrolling aircraft to submerge, the submarines were losing contact with the convoy and, knowing they could only regain it by moving on the surface, they were rising again only to be found once more. But Molyneux was under no delusions. The fight was going to go on all next day and into the next night. Fortunately, there was a moon, which would help, but it would take twenty-four hours for the convoy to make the last two hundred miles to safety and they would have to struggle every bit of the way.

In the Bic, the pinnace was taking on board the men it had put ashore the day before. When the depth charges had gone off, the boat had rolled violently as a vast tidal wave had come rushing down the river towards the sea, and they had heard fragments of wood and metal dropping into the water alongside them. The wave had lifted the pinnace, rolled it violently, shaking it like a terrier with a rat, sending the masthead sweeping across the sky, emptying the cupboards, clearing the bunks and the chart table and flinging men against hard and heavy objects, and they had heard an ominous clank from the winch that indicated that the strain on the hawser strung across the river had done some considerable damage. They were just recovering when there had been a second huge wave, this time in the other direction, as the sea had rushed back to fill the void the depth charges had caused, and what the first wave hadn't scattered the second one had.

Despite the shouts of the men ashore, they had spent the night sorting things out, picking up the smashed crockery and scattered equipment, trying to repair the winch and putting a bandage on the head of the fitter which had come into violent contact with the starboard engine, and it was only with morning that Fox had agreed to take any notice of the indignant men ashore.

By this time, tired, hungry, thirsty, daubed with black mangrove slime and damp with sweat, they had come down from the higher ground and were beginning to gather among the mangroves that fringed the river, complaining that when the tide came in again they would drown without fail.

Dropping the rescue nets over the side, Fox sent Feverel ashore in the punt to bring them aboard in groups of three.

'I saw a crocodile,' one of them pointed out.

'I've seen dozens,' Feverel said.

'They could have your goolies.'

'They wouldn't bother with yours. Not enough of a meal.'

As the men were dragged up the sides of the pinnace they were noisy and excited and loud with claims of having shot Germans. Most of them hadn't seen enough to shoot at, but all of them had fired and they were all certain they'd destroyed the enemy opposition. Kneller hadn't returned, however, and Feverel wondered what had happened to him. Enough had occurred in the last twenty-four hours to make him worried. Kneller was a brave youngster, even if a little naïve, and he was anxious to know where he was.

'I'm going ashore,' he told Fox. 'I want to know what's happened to Nellie.'

There had been silence at the mine for some time now. Hubbard had advanced to within striking distance of the big building near the water's edge. Its walls were starred with bullet marks and its windows had fallen in, the construction beyond gone in a shattering unexplained explosion in the river, leaving the big building isolated, one end part-collapsed, the wire mesh torn and battered looking. There was no sound from inside and Cazalet guessed it was full of frightened men. He had rejoined Hubbard for the final operation and was staring thoughtfully at the partially stripped thatched roof.

'I wonder,' he said slowly, 'if we could set fire to that lot with a Very pistol.'

Their first shot landed in the middle of the damaged thatch, a white ball of light trailing a coil of smoke, then it changed to a red glow and a moment later the straw started to burn.

'That ought to make 'em think a bit,' Cazalet mused.

Almost at once a man with a white flag appeared and ran across the space between the big building and the hut where Hubbard was directing operations. He was French and was bundled away by the sergeant. Then several more men appeared and fell through the door.

'*Je me rende*,' the first man shouted.

'*Vous êtes français?*' Cazalet fancied his French.

'*Oui.* Charles-Richard Piccard, *ancien officier de l'Armée de l'Air.*'

'And a bloody traitor, too, I've no doubt,' Cazalet commented. 'Take the nasty little thing away, Sergeant.'

There were several Germans among the Frenchmen, one of them an ex-U-boatman.

'Now we're beginning to see daylight,' Cazalet observed. He gestured back at the building. 'How many more?'

'*Fier und Zwanzig,*' the U-boatman said.

There were a *Kapitänleutnant*, another officer and several men still in the building. Cazalet was doing quite well with his limited German, and it seemed that the decision had been made for the most experienced men to escape by boat with their report while those who were left were to hold off the attackers as long as possible.

Even as they discovered what was about to happen the firing started again. The roof thatch was burning furiously now, the flames devouring it and sending up a huge column of brown smoke into the air.

'I'd better get back to the radio,' Cazalet said. 'And warn those chaps in the river Bic.'

He was just about to turn away when they heard the roar of an engine from the other side of the burning building.

'I think you're too late, sir,' Hubbard said 'That's from the river Bic.'

Feverel was surprised at the damage he saw. The boat shed and the building above it had collapsed into the water in a scattering of planks, timbers and thatch. The bush lining the creek had been flattened and crushed and there were dead fish floating in the water, even a dead crocodile.

As he stared at the ruin, he could see the two native fishing boats he had seen the day before, aground on the bank, surrounded by fishermen from Yima, chattering like monkeys and gesturing at the flattened trees by the water's edge and the scattered planks of the boathouse. Near them, half-hidden by the bend of the river, he could see the Dutchmen's big launch. The mast had fallen, but she was still afloat and still moored to the bank by a single unbroken rope. Even as he looked at her, a man appeared from below, then two or three more and he heard the engine start.

He watched, unable without a weapon to do a thing as the remaining mooring rope was cast off and the launch swung away from the bank, edging past the native boats to pull away from the shore. The engine sounded uneven, as if the tidal wave which had deposited it on the bottom had damaged the propellers.

As it vanished, he turned back to his task, suddenly uninterested in the escaping boat because he could see Kneller. He was huddled at the bottom of a palm tree near the water's edge but, though all the firing seemed to have stopped, he didn't lift his head as Feverel approached.

As he reached him, to Feverel's surprise Ginger Donnelly rose from alongside him, and then he saw there was a woman holding Kneller in her arms, her clothes like Kneller's, saturated and in rags.

She gestured at the ruined hut and at the catamaran upended on the bank, and Feverel saw bodies lying in the undergrowth and one floating in the water nearby. The woman's jaw worked. She was spattered with mud and her eyes were wild.

'It was the explosion,' she said in English.

To the men on the pinnace the roar of the launch's engine came quite distinctly across the mangroves. Almost at once the bow wave was seen through the trees, then the boat itself, roaring down the creek towards the open sea.

Faintly disappointed at his share in the battle, the padre had been on the point of withdrawing from the Bic, but now he swung round and started to shout.

'Haul up that wire,' he roared and the fitter and one of the deckhands leapt to the winch and started turning by hand.

Intent on escape, the Germans never even saw the hawser. The launch swung round the corner, tilting to the turn, its nose lifting as it increased speed. As it ran on to the wire, the bows leaped high out of the water and there was a twang, a metallic crash and a scream of engines as the propellers tore themselves to pieces. As the bows flopped back into the water in a growing circle of ripples, the launch lay stopped, dead, her rudders caught, her propellers stripped. The screaming died as the engines were cut, then men came pouring from below, and the airmen on the deck of the pinnace, bewildered at being once more involved in a battle when they'd thought it was finished, began to fire. This time it was hard to miss. One of the Germans fell into the water

278

and began to swim slowly and painfully for the shore. After a little more sporadic firing, the rest flung down their weapons and raised their hands.

The padre stared at them, startled. 'I think we we've won,' he said.

eight

The sea seemed to be covered with ships. In the distance a Sunderland was just swinging into its last run in front of the convoy before turning for base and the radio operator reported that he'd just picked up a contact. As Molyneux took the Sunderland's place, he saw one of the destroyers from the starboard side of the convoy put on speed and race ahead, then it swung sharply to starboard and a second or two later he saw the sea heave astern of it as its depth charges exploded.

The radio was filled with excited chatter. The destroyer came round, leaning to the sea, and this time Molyneux actually saw the depth charges falling through the air. As the sea heaved again, he watched closely, then he saw a black thing like a whale rise out of the water, obscene and menacing, lifting slowly, almost perpendicularly, before sliding back into the darkness, great spouts of water and air rising where it had disappeared.

'We seem to have got among them,' he said.

Almost immediately, they picked up a contact and dropped their depth charges. Whether they were effective or not it was hard to say; they were unable to remain in the vicinity because the navigator spotted a submarine astern of the convoy. As they raced towards it, they saw it dive hurriedly and by the time they arrived at the spot where it had disappeared, the swirl of sea made by its dive was dispersing, and Molyneux dropped only two depth charges.

'Just to let 'em know we're here he said. 'It'll keep their heads down.

By this time there were three aircraft circling the convoy as it moved sedately beneath them, and they searched carefully in the increasing daylight. As the flight engineer announced that their fuel position was reaching the danger point, Molyneux turned for home. Thirty miles from the convoy, he saw Catalina B-Awful on her way out to relieve him and the two aircraft passed so close it was possible to see Flying Officer Kitchen's innocent young face quite clearly. As they touched down and moved to the buoy, they were met by a dinghy which rushed them ashore, while other boats brought out the maintenance crews, fresh depth charges and petrol.

Mackintosh was in his office, smoking a cigarette. 'How's it going?' he asked.

'We had a few contacts,' Molyneux said. 'Nothing more. Gather you got one.'

'We put in a claim. The navy got another. That makes two of them and one to us, so far. It ought to help. No reports of any ships being sunk either. I'm off again soon.'

Molyneux nodded and Mackintosh vanished. Molyneux made his report, then headed for the officers' mess for a meal and a sleep before he took off again in the evening. The coming night would be the danger period because it would be the submarines' last chance and they would inevitably be taking risks, especially as they had been unsuccessful so far.

His sleep was fitful and, only half-refreshed, he was back at the rickety wooden jetty in the late evening waiting to be ferried out to his machine. His crew were all looking tired but they were buoyed up by the successes. Reports had been coming in all day of submarines forced to submerge, though one had tried to fight back and had hit B-Awful's starboard fuel tank so that petrol had flooded the flight deck and the navigator and the engineer had been wounded. But Flying Officer Kitchen, his innocent blue eyes hard for once, had dropped depth charges and seen the U-boat sink by the bows before he had had to put down on the sea within reach of naval help.

Flying Officer Hobson was in his office as Molyneux reappeared. He, too, looked tired. 'It would be nice to go home feeling we'd done some good,' he said.

As Molyneux climbed down to the catamaran and into the dinghy with his crew to be ferried out to his machine, Hobson watched him from the end of the jetty. As he stood there, he became aware of Ginger Donnelly, back at last with the men from Yima, busy below him on the mud, surrounded by half a dozen of his labouring gang. He was holding the limp shape of a green mamba and, remembering hearing a lot of shouting not long before, he realized one of the Africans must have seen the snake wriggle from the river under the hut and summoned Ginger.

'Big one, Ginger?' he asked.

Ginger held the snake up in a muddy paw for him to see. 'Nah. Just a tiddler.'

'I gather you had them in the front line at Yima.'

Ginger nodded. 'They did all right,' he agreed. 'But they didn't bite nobody, I reckon they was too scared.'

Hobson gestured towards the aircraft trots. 'Your inspired guess over that beer bottle seems to be paying dividends now,' he pointed out.

Ginger nodded again, unmoved. He tossed the dead snake into the river and watched it drift downstream on the tide. 'Yeh,' he said. And that was all.

Half an hour later, in the growing dusk, Molyneux opened the throttles of his aircraft. As they headed down the strip of water, rattling and bumping as the Catalina lifted to the step, he had to control his excitement. Then the bumping stopped and they lifted into the air over the growing darkness of the land. Almost immediately the radio operator picked up the naval report of another success.

'I think we're bloodying their noses a bit,' Molyneux said.

In U-1022, there was an atmosphere of despondency. All day and all the previous night they had kept edging in to the convoy but again and again had been spotted and forced to dive. Even during the hours of darkness, they had had no success because of the moon and the radar with which the aircraft were fitted.

Schutze was irritable and Lorenz found it wiser to remain out of his way because the feeling that they were failing when they ought to have been succeeding was clear. There had been immense excitement at the first glimpse of the convoy and Lorenz had been on edge as U-1022 had moved in. It had been growing dark and it had seemed easy but, as they had headed in on the surface, there had been sudden panic as everyone on the bridge had fallen through the hatchway and the submarine had been rushed into an emergency dive. The depth charges which had followed had shaken them. Light bulbs had been broken but they had not been much hurt, though they had had to lay low long enough to lose contact with the convoy.

When they came cautiously to the surface again, it was daylight and the convoy had vanished. But they had picked up a directional signal from another submarine and had moved in again. Long before they were within reach, however, the lookout had given the alarm and they had all piled below again and Schutze was swinging off to starboard, hoping to throw off the attack. The depth charges had not been near enough to do any damage but they had sounded horrendous to Lorenz.

'Is it always like this?' he asked.

Schutze gave him a cold look. 'When they pick us up,' he said. 'And they seem to be picking us up rather more than normal at the moment.'

Throughout the day they had been forced to remain submerged. Towards evening they had picked up another message giving the convoy's course and speed, but the other boat had gone off the air in the middle of its transmissions, which seemed to indicate she was under attack, and they heard no more of her.

When they came to periscope depth again, the moon was out, filling the sky with pearly light, and the sea was like a silver sheet. Studying it, Schutze could see nothing. The convoy seemed to have disappeared and he was just trying to swallow his disappointment when he saw a black speck on the horizon against the moon. As he moved the periscope, he saw there were more black specks, then more and more. The horizon seemed to be filled with ships. Warily, he studied the sea about them. There were no signs of escorts and he assumed they were all closed up on the convoy which had surely now almost reached the safety of the river Rokel. This was his last chance and the only hope he had of catching them was to surface.

'Take her up,' he said.

By this time, the navy was filled with euphoria. Six submarines had been claimed as sunk and only one ship, a straggler, had been caught, its attacker destroyed within minutes of its triumph.

'Jerry seems to be having a hard time of it for a change, sir,' the flight engineer said as he brought a mug of coffee to Molyneux. Sitting with the machine on automatic pilot while he held the mug between his hands, Molyneux nodded, remembering the lean years from 1940 when the Germans had acquired their bases on the French coast so that their U-boats didn't have to emerge into the Atlantic via the North Sea and the north of Scotland. It had put two hundred miles on the distance they could cover and reduced by a hundred per cent the risk of being caught. The shipping losses that had resulted had been enormous and only rarely had they been able to catch them at it. In those days it had been a long and unsatisfactory war for the crews of the flying boats, and even during the last year when conditions and equipment had improved with radar, it had remained a boring business. It was hard to remain enthusiastic and eager when you searched for months without success.

The moon was just rising and the stars were hanging in the heavens like lanterns so that he could see occasional patches of silver on the water. The roar of the engines filled his ears but everything else was still and silent. Below him the sea to the horizon seemed empty but the radar man had his eyes glued to his set, hoping for a contact. The convoy, a mere grouping of shapes on the horizon, was virtually safe and they were searching round the tail end of it in the hope of frightening off persistent last minute attackers. The first ships must be just beginning to enter safe waters by this time and the chances of a contact were slight as the patrol reached its limit. Any minute now they would have to turn for home, but Molyneux decided to stretch it out as far as he could by throttling back the engines. In the distance a frigate, chivvying on a straggler with a faltering engine, was moving slowly, leaving a white wake which they could see quite clearly in the moonlight that laid a brilliant pathway across the sea. As the moon rose higher, the pathway widened and Molyneux found himself praying that God would give them a little luck and enable him to use its light for an attack.

'Skipper!' The voice was the radar operator's. 'Contact!'

As the alarm went, Molyneux' mug went flying and he was just about to reply when the voice of one of the waist gunners came. 'Skipper! I see him! Christ, I see the bastard!'

Taking his direction from the waist gunner, Molyneux picked up the submarine. It was on the surface and he could just make it out, following the convoy. Swinging the heavy aeroplane away from the moon's path, still keeping his eye on the submarine, he straightened out again, facing the moon. He could see the submarine now against the shimmering light, a perfect silhouette as if painted with black ink on stark white paper, the whole boat clear, even the periscope and the gun platforms carrying the double-barrelled 20mm cannon.

'I'm going to use the moon,' he said.

The sound of the idling engines filled the ears but everybody was quiet, listening for orders as the Catalina slid towards the path of the moon from the dark side. The intense boredom of all their past empty sorties was swept away and they were all prepared to press home the attack to the limit, regardless of what was thrown at them.

'No radio, operator,' Molyneux ordered. 'In case they're listening out. Make your sighting report after the first attack's been made.'

They had turned now, the moon beyond the submarine making it sharp and clear on the surface of the water. Molyneux held the lumbering Catalina steady, dropping down to within forty feet, the moonlight so bright he could see the rivets holding the Plexiglass round the flight deck.

'Now!' he said, and the depth charges dropped away as they swooped overhead.

The roar of the air being sucked into the submarine through the open hatch was loud enough to drown an aircraft's motors and, as the alarm went, the control room was filled with the sound of boots on the ladder as men tumbled down inside.

'Take her down!'

Within seconds, it seemed, they heard the murderous crashes of the depth charges and the boat was shaken violently. A terrifying thunderclap smashed against Lorenz' eardrums, driving the breath from his lungs and all sensible thought from his brain so that all that was left was a simple instinct to survive.

'She's rising!' The first lieutenant's voice rose to a scream. 'Bring her down! Bring her down!'

As the men at the controls laboured over their wheels, the submarine shot upwards, the bow rising so violently they had to grab for handholds to prevent themselves sliding towards the stern. Then she steadied and settled but, as she did so, the lights went out.

In the thick impenetrable darkness, standing in the doorway of the wardroom, terrified by what had happened, Lorenz felt himself barged out of the way as someone rushed past, then the emergency lights came on and he could see the looks of shock and alarm on the faces around him. All the electrical installations including the lights on the control panel seemed to be in pieces on the floor plates and the moving boots were crunching glass. The reports began to come in steadily, to be repeated to Schutze by the officer on the intercom.

'Batteries control panel smashed! Hydrophones gone! Radio equipment smashed! Hang on, hang on – say again! What's that? Compressors wrenched loose from their straps!'

Schutze had control of the boat now and was taking her down but, just when Lorenz was beginning to imagine they were safe, the telephone went again.

'Engine room reports water entering through a loose valve in the drain pumps, sir!'

Schutze frowned. Trying to control his impatience, he waited for further reports. They had been hard hit, he knew, and it would be touch and go. Lifting his eyes, he saw Lorenz standing at the entrance to the wardroom and for a moment wondered if the repeated attacks had anything to do with him. But no! No one would wish himself one of the most appalling deaths a man could think up. Schutze had been aboard a submarine which had been sunk by collision in the Baltic during training, and the horror of being trapped below was still with him. Even as the boat had sunk beneath his feet, he had heard the despairing screams of the drowning men behind him. The memory was still in his mind when another series of crashes indicated that their attacker was not yet done with them. There was a tinkle of falling glass and someone cried out.

The telephone went. 'Engine room, sir! Clutch between the diesels and the motors is jammed! High pressure lines have been ruptured!'

For a moment there was a tense silence then a voice came unsteadily. 'Depth gauges not working, sir. Steering gear and compass wrecked.'

U-1022 was little more than a hulk. Already the air was foul and Schutze recognised the smell of chlorine that told him sea water had got at the batteries.

'Take her up,' he said. 'We're going to have to fight it out on the surface.'

As he banked the Catalina to keep the spot where the submarine had disappeared up-moon, Molyneux could see quite clearly the swirl of water where it had disappeared and the foamy rings where the depth charges had burst.

'This bastard's not a certainty yet,' he said. 'Let him have it as soon as he appears.'

He banked the machine again, still down-moon, then the starboard gunner yelled, and as Molyneux' head turned, he saw the conning tower of the submarine emerge, dripping water that sparkled in the moonlight. Immediately figures appeared, scrambling for the batteries of 20mm guns forward and aft of the conning tower. A machine gun crashed out and Molyneux saw tracer going into the group. The submarine's after gun started firing but stopped again immediately. Then the forward gun started and a line of what looked like red golf balls soared up towards them. They came slowly at first, then very fast, but they seemed to take an incredibly long time to arrive and as they grew bigger Molyneux felt they were going straight through the Catalina. There was a crash as they were hit, and a tangle of bright pipes with oozing oil and a hole in the side of the aircraft you could put your hand through, but by this time they were overhead again and the last depth charges went down.

The blast as half a ton of Torpex went off in a tremendous 'whump' lifted four huge columns of water in a mighty curtain that hid the sky and whipped the men round the gun platform overboard like dolls. One of them managed to cling to the gun with enough strength to crack his ribs as the water cascaded down and surged across him, but the guns had stopped. The submarine seemed to lift then it slammed back into the hole where the sea had been blown away beneath it, sending vast gouts of water out on either side.

'God!' The navigator's voice came on the intercom, strained and awed by what they'd done. 'We've blown her clean out of the water.'

There was fire below now, then someone yelled that the last salvo had wrenched one of the diesels off its mounting. Lorenz was watching Schutze, his eyes wide and shocked. Schutze was still calm, trying to make his decisions quickly and without panic, but Lorenz could see the despair on his face. He had realized that fighting it out wasn't going to work and, with the air fractionally improved by their brief appearance on the surface, was hoping he might manage to save the boat.

'We'll have to take her down again,' he said, but they had just commenced their dive when there was a yell that the forward hatch had been blown open and, with the foredeck dipped below the surface, a torrent of sea water was pouring in.

'Avast diving,' Schutze yelled. 'Seal the forward compartment! Take her up! We'll have to abandon! Everybody on deck!'

As the boat lifted, her bow weighted by the water she had taken on board, her stern appeared first, emerging at a steep angle. Men were huddling at the bottom of the ladder and Lorenz moved quickly among them. Schutze gave him a cold look.

The depths were being called then the cry came, 'Up!' Immediately the men on the ladder flung open the hatchway and began to scramble out but, almost at once, Lorenz heard bullets clattering against the conning tower. Someone above him on the ladder cried out and there was a shout of alarm.

'Get him out! Get him out! He's jamming the hatch!'

Above him a man had been hit and his body was preventing the rest escaping. A man who had managed to scramble through the hatch was trying to scream instructions but then, as Lorenz's heart rose to his throat, choking him with his fear, he felt the boat stand on its nose. A man falling from above him almost swept him away. The screaming was growing louder now and Lorenz was having to use all his strength to cling to the ladder. His ears were full of the terror-stricken cries of men facing death, then a solid wet wall hit him, wrenching his fingers free and flinging him down. He fell into the control room but it was swilling with water and tilted to an impossible angle so that he slid across the floor to collide with the bulkhead. Trying to struggle upright, his mouth opened to scream and promptly filled with sea water, and the last thing he was aware of was the emergency lights in the control tower becoming obscured and blurred by the roaring green flood.

Eight submarines were sunk and only a single ship was lost. The *Maréchal Grouchy* bolted north for Conakry but was caught by the navy and taken under escort back to Freetown. It raised a lot of diplomatic fuss because she was supposed to be a neutral, but examination of her papers and her radio logs proved her to be anything but, and Vichy hastily dropped the matter. The vast convoy was supplied and watered and went on to the Cape and from there up to the Middle East. The new Sherman tanks, the new anti-tank guns and the new Priest self-propelled cannon helped defeat Rommel at Alamein and the rest is well known.

From then on in North Africa it was all victory and the French West African colonies followed the lead of the Equatorial and occupied North African territories and declared for De Gaulle. It was also, in a way, the beginning of the defeat of the U-boats. There were one or two more big battles in the Atlantic, then the tide turned, and in May 1943, with forty-one U-boats destroyed in a month, Dönitz withdrew them.

Many of the unimportant men who had done the hard work at Jum in the last few desperate days when the thing had hung in the balance never really learned what had been happening because, before it had been over forty-eight hours, a far more important event occurred. A telephone message was received at headquarters that sent Trixie Tristram running to the perfumed bower he shared with his friend.

'The ship's in, dear! We're leaving in the morning!'

This time it was true. Mail also appeared and someone said a new projector had arrived for the cinema, too, and they were going to have another go at *Blood and Sand*. But all the time-expired men were too busy handing out old unwanted clothes to the dhobi boys to be interested, the lineshooters occupied in packing up shields and spears made especially up-country to sell to British servicemen anxious to show their families what a savage place they'd been in.

The following morning, choked at the thought that they were actually going home and suddenly not sure they wanted to, they headed down the ramshackle jetty for the last time and scrambled aboard the pinnace, feeling they'd done their little bit for the war effort and suffered their share of discomfort, and expecting at least a little attention when they reached home. They weren't to know that when they arrived and tried to talk about it, men from such far-flung outposts as Grimsby and Felixstowe and Blyth and Aberdeen would sneer at them and sing 'Sand In My Shoes'.

Near the marine section slip, a gang of African technicians and a couple of white engineers were pushing a steam engine into place.

'What's that for?'

'Pile driver,' they were told. 'There's a big move on to open this place up. New jetty. New offices and crew room.'

'Makes sense,' Feverel observed dryly. 'Now we're going home they're going to make the bloody place fit to live in.'

The mooring party had been taken over by a sergeant – no less! – who had sought out Feverel the night before and informed him that he intended to put things straight. He hadn't even been in uniform when Feverel had left England and Feverel hoped he'd be able to cope – especially with the four-inch nails.

As they climbed aboard the pinnace and the seaplane tenders which were to take them down-river to where their ship – that blessed transport that was to take them home! – waited for them, Ginger had already forgotten Lizzie Morgan and his promise of marriage, and was trying to remember the name of the sailor's wife at Gosport he'd shacked up with before coming overseas. She wasn't a bad-looking bint and he wondered how she'd look in the leopard-skin gloves, handbag and hat he'd made. Not bad, he decided, and he didn't think Lizzie would miss him. Not much, anyway.

As he reached the deck, Corporal Fox asked the white-skinned man in unworn khaki – another sergeant! What was the place coming to? – who now had the pinnace, for permission to handle the wheel for the last time, and two hours later they were alongside the transport.

She was the most wonderful thing they had ever seen in their lives. Her name was *Largs Bay* and she turned out to be an ancient vessel from the last war with an enormous gun on her stern and stinking of rotten potatoes. As they scrambled up the side with their kit and their souvenirs, Nobby Clark was careful to make sure the bottom didn't fall out of his splendid leather-covered cardboard suitcase. The line he'd tied round it held it splendidly and it was the end that fell out; in a fury, he flung it into the sea after its contents. Safely on board, Corporal Feverel immediately scrounged a tablet of sea-water soap from one of the crew and headed for a bathroom. Sneaking into the officers' area, he found an unoccupied first-class cabin and took the hot bath he'd been dreaming of for nearly three years. But they were still in Freetown harbour and he had reckoned without the heat outside. His temperature hit the roof and he had to stand under a cold shower for half an hour to stop himself sweating. It didn't matter much, though. He was going home, and he was only sorry Kneller wasn't with them.

Kneeling alongside him near the Bic with the bewildered Ginger, Feverel had looked for injuries. Kneller's face was blackened so that his eyes looked spectral, and there were pale channels on his cheeks where tears had rolled down, but he was quite conscious and even appeared to be unhurt, despite the dazed look of pain on his features.

'You all right?' Feverel asked.

As his hand had touched his shoulder, Kneller had stirred and looked up. There was an expression of agony on his face as he shook his head and patted his ears. 'I can't hear you,' he said.

Watched by the woman, Feverel had put his mouth close. 'I said, are you all right?'

Kneller had stared at him, watching his mouth opening and shutting, then a look of anguish had crossed his face again and he had crouched down with his head in his hands, moaning with the pain of shattered eardrums, and Feverel had heard his voice coming, muffled, through his fingers.

'I can't hear,' he was wailing. 'I can't hear a bloody thing! I've gone stone deaf!'

The ship left without him because he was in the hospital on Tower Hill, dazed, bewildered, and deaf as a post.

Medals were handed out for North Africa, but West Africa, as usual, went unnoticed. Perhaps too many people had been involved. Perhaps they'd given too many for the desert and had none to spare. Perhaps, even, someone had decided medals would go to their heads, especially on top of a new jetty and new buildings and a new projector that had finally triumphantly worked its way through *Blood and Sand*. Perhaps the battle, despite the fact that they'd won it, had been too much a typical West African lash-up, and they were now entering on a new phase with everything done properly and didn't want to be reminded of the old days, of dud projectors and four-inch nails.

Whatever the reason, no one at Jum got a gong and, of course, Kneller never got his chance to sing, while Ettore Mori-Moncrieff never learned why he didn't pursue the magnificent chance he'd offered him. There wasn't much of a conflict going on at Jum but people could still get hurt.

As the man said, it was a bloody funny place to hold a war.

JOHN HARRIS

CHINA SEAS

In this action-packed adventure, Willie Sarth becomes a survivor. Forced to fight pirates on the East China Seas, wrestle for his life on the South China Seas and cross the Sea of Japan ravaged by typhus, Sarth is determined to come out alive. Dealing with human tragedy, war and revolution, Harris presents a novel which packs an awesome punch.

LIVE FREE OR DIE!

Charles Walter Scully, cut off from his unit and running on empty, is trapped. It's 1944 and, though the Allied invasion of France has finally begun, for Scully the war isn't going well. That is, until he meets a French boy trying to get home to Paris and so what begins is an incredible hair-raising journey into the heart of the French liberation and one of the most monumental events of the war. Harris portrays wartime France in a vividly overwhelming panorama of scenes intended to enthral and entertain the reader.

JOHN HARRIS

THE OLD TRADE OF KILLING

Set against the backdrop of the Western Desert and scene of the Eighth Army battles, Harris presents an exciting adventure where the men who fought together in the Second World War return twenty years later in search of treasure. But twenty years may change a man. Young ideals have been replaced by greed. Comradeship has vanished along with innocence. And treachery and murder make for a breathtaking read.

THE SEA SHALL NOT HAVE THEM

This is John Harris' classic war novel of espionage in the most extreme of situations. An essential flight from France leaves the crew of RAF *Hudson* missing, and somewhere in the North Sea four men cling to a dinghy, praying for rescue before exposure kills them or the enemy finds them. One man is critically injured; another (a rocket expert) is carrying a briefcase stuffed with vital secrets. As time begins to run out each man yearns to evade capture. This story charts the daring and courage of these men, and the men who rescued them in a breathtaking mission with the most awesome of consequences.

JOHN HARRIS

TAKE OR DESTROY!

Lieutenant-Colonel George Hockold must destroy Rommel's vast fuel reserves stored at the port of Qaba if the Eighth Army is to succeed in the Alamein offensive. Time is desperately running out, resources are scant and the commando unit Hockold must lead is a ragtag band of misfits scraped from the dregs of the British Army. They must attack Qaba. The orders...take or destroy.

'One of the finest war novels of the year'
– *Evening News*

THE UNFORGIVING WIND

Charting the disastrous expedition of Commander Adams who dies suddenly, this novel follows the misfortunes of his men across the Arctic. Whatever can go wrong does go wrong as transport, instruments, health and sanity begin to fail. The team seem irretrievably lost in the dark Arctic winter, frightened and half-starving even when they find a base. Only one man can rescue them, the truculent Tom Fife who must respond to the faint radio signals coming from the Arctic shores. A powerful and disturbing novel, this story aims to take your breath away.

TITLES BY JOHN HARRIS AVAILABLE DIRECT
FROM HOUSE OF STRATUS

Quantity		£	$(US)	$(CAN)	€
	ARMY OF SHADOWS	6.99	11.50	15.99	11.50
	CHINA SEAS	6.99	11.50	15.99	11.50
	THE CLAWS OF MERCY	6.99	11.50	15.99	11.50
	CORPORAL COTTON'S LITTLE WAR	6.99	11.50	15.99	11.50
	THE CROSS OF LAZZARO	6.99	11.50	15.99	11.50
	FLAWED BANNER	6.99	11.50	15.99	11.50
	THE FOX FROM HIS LAIR	6.99	11.50	15.99	11.50
	GETAWAY	6.99	11.50	15.99	11.50
	HARKAWAY'S SIXTH COLUMN	6.99	11.50	15.99	11.50
	LIVE FREE OR DIE!	6.99	11.50	15.99	11.50
	THE LONELY VOYAGE	6.99	11.50	15.99	11.50
	THE MERCENARIES	6.99	11.50	15.99	11.50
	NORTH STRIKE	6.99	11.50	15.99	11.50
	THE OLD TRADE OF KILLING	6.99	11.50	15.99	11.50
	PICTURE OF DEFEAT	6.99	11.50	15.99	11.50

ALL HOUSE OF STRATUS BOOKS ARE AVAILABLE FROM GOOD BOOKSHOPS
OR DIRECT FROM THE PUBLISHER:

Internet: www.houseofstratus.com including author interviews, reviews, features.

Email: **sales@houseofstratus.com** please quote author, title and credit card details.

TITLES BY JOHN HARRIS AVAILABLE DIRECT
FROM HOUSE OF STRATUS

Quantity		£	$(US)	$(CAN)	€
	QUICK BOAT MEN	6.99	11.50	15.99	11.50
	RIDE OUT THE STORM	6.99	11.50	15.99	11.50
	RIGHT OF REPLY	6.99	11.50	15.99	11.50
	THE ROAD TO THE COAST	6.99	11.50	15.99	11.50
	THE SEA SHALL NOT HAVE THEM	6.99	11.50	15.99	11.50
	THE SLEEPING MOUNTAIN	6.99	11.50	15.99	11.50
	SO FAR FROM GOD	6.99	11.50	15.99	11.50
	THE SPRING OF MALICE	6.99	11.50	15.99	11.50
	SUNSET AT SHEBA	6.99	11.50	15.99	11.50
	SWORDPOINT	6.99	11.50	15.99	11.50
	TAKE OR DESTROY!	6.99	11.50	15.99	11.50
	THE THIRTY DAYS' WAR	6.99	11.50	15.99	11.50
	THE UNFORGIVING WIND	6.99	11.50	15.99	11.50
	UP FOR GRABS	6.99	11.50	15.99	11.50
	VARDY	6.99	11.50	15.99	11.50
	SMILING WILLIE AND THE TIGER	6.99	11.50	15.99	11.50

ALL HOUSE OF STRATUS BOOKS ARE AVAILABLE FROM GOOD BOOKSHOPS
OR DIRECT FROM THE PUBLISHER:

Hotline: UK ONLY: **0800 169 1780**, please quote author, title and credit card details.
INTERNATIONAL: **+44 (0) 20 7494 6400**, please quote author, title, and credit card details.

Send to: House of Stratus Sales Department
24c Old Burlington Street
London
W1X 1RL
UK

Please allow for postage costs charged per order plus an amount per book as set out in the tables below:

	£(Sterling)	$(US)	$(CAN)	€(Euros)
Cost per order				
UK	2.00	3.00	4.50	3.30
Europe	3.00	4.50	6.75	5.00
North America	3.00	4.50	6.75	5.00
Rest of World	3.00	4.50	6.75	5.00
Additional cost per book				
UK	0.50	0.75	1.15	0.85
Europe	1.00	1.50	2.30	1.70
North America	2.00	3.00	4.60	3.40
Rest of World	2.50	3.75	5.75	4.25

PLEASE SEND CHEQUE, POSTAL ORDER (STERLING ONLY), EUROCHEQUE, OR INTERNATIONAL MONEY ORDER (PLEASE CIRCLE METHOD OF PAYMENT YOU WISH TO USE)
MAKE PAYABLE TO: STRATUS HOLDINGS plc

Cost of book(s): —————————— Example: 3 x books at £6.99 each: £20.97

Cost of order: —————————— Example: £2.00 (Delivery to UK address)

Additional cost per book: ———— Example: 3 x £0.50: £1.50

Order total including postage: ——— Example: £24.47

Please tick currency you wish to use and add total amount of order:

☐ £ (Sterling)   ☐ $ (US)   ☐ $ (CAN)   ☐ € (EUROS)

VISA, MASTERCARD, SWITCH, AMEX, SOLO, JCB:

☐☐☐☐☐☐☐☐☐☐☐☐☐☐☐☐☐☐☐

Issue number (Switch only):

☐☐☐

Start Date: **Expiry Date:**

☐☐/☐☐   ☐☐/☐☐

Signature: ————————————

NAME: ————————————————————————

ADDRESS: ————————————————————————

————————————————————————

POSTCODE: ——————

Please allow 28 days for delivery.

Prices subject to change without notice.
Please tick box if you do not wish to receive any additional information. ☐

House of Stratus publishes many other titles in this genre; please check our website (**www.houseofstratus.com**) for more details.